Chapter 1

He looked just as Kate remembered him, standing on the outside of the small gathering in front of the church. Jacob Cade had never mixed well. He might have his share of adoring women, thanks to his sizable fortune, but he seemed to treat everyone with the same impartial contempt. He was quietly standing there, his dark gaze glancing toward the road where his niece was due to arrive any minute. And despite his indifference to the crowd, he drew women's eyes. He was darkly tanned and rugged, his powerful legs outlined by the superb fit of his trousers, his broad shoulders straining against the fabric of his suit coat. His hands were lean and dark, and there were no rings on them. Jacob wasn't a sentimental man. He was an old-fashioned reactionary in everything from dress to attitudes, and he made no apologies for it. He didn't have to. He had enough money to make up his own rules as he went along.

"Lord of all he surveys," Kate muttered, glaring.

"Isn't he entitled?" Tom, her brother, laughed softly. "He's got enough fluttering female hearts in his pocket. Including yours…"

"Hush!" she bit off, nibbling on her lower lip.

"He doesn't know," he mused, glancing down at her. They were both tall, dark-haired and green-eyed. Although Tom, at twenty-eight, was four years her senior, they might well have been twins for the resemblance of their facial features. The same even, etched features highlighted both high-cheekboned faces, the faint remnants of a Sioux great-grandfather.

"I hate him," Kate said firmly, pushing a strand of hair back into the elegant French knot she'd twisted her long, straight hair into that morning.

"Sure you do."

"I do," she insisted. And at that moment, she really did. Jacob's sudden, violent dislike for her, which stemmed from an incident when Kate was eighteen, had put a severe strain on her friendship with Margo. It was odd, too, because Jacob had been good to the family when Kate was younger.

Kate and Tom had been adopted by their paternal grandmother after the death of their father. God alone knew where their mother was. She'd deserted them years before, and Kate had never stopped blaming her. The children had been badly scarred by the way their father had brought them up. Not even Grandmother Walker had known what they'd been through, because she hadn't been the kind of person who invited confidences. But she'd taken them into her home in Blairsville, South Dakota, just minutes from Pierre, the capital. Margo Cade had lived with her uncle Jacob Cade and his father, Hank, on Warlance since the unexpected death of her parents

DIANA PALMER

A prolific author of more than one hundred books, Diana Palmer got her start as a newspaper reporter. A multiple *New York Times* and *USA TODAY* bestselling author and one of the top ten romance writers in America, she has a gift for telling the most sensual tales with charm and humor. Diana lives with her family in Cornelia, Georgia.

KATHIE DeNOSKY

lives in her native southern Illinois on the land her family settled in 1839. She writes highly sensual stories with a generous amount of humor. Her books have appeared on the *USA TODAY* bestseller list and received numerous awards, including two National Reader's Choice Awards. Kathie enjoys going to rodeos, traveling to research settings for her books and listening to country music. Readers may contact her by emailing kathie@kathiedenosky.com. They can also visit her website, www.kathiedenosky.com, or find her on Facebook.

BESTSELLING AUTHOR COLLECTION

New York Times Bestselling Author

DIANA PALMER

Betrayed by Love

HARLEQUIN®

entertain, enrich, inspire™

Recycling programs for this product may not exist in your area.

ISBN-13: 978-0-373-18059-2

BETRAYED BY LOVE
Copyright © 2012 by Harlequin Books S.A.

The publisher acknowledges the copyright holders of the individual works as follows:

BETRAYED BY LOVE
Copyright © 1987 by Diana Palmer

THE ROUGH AND READY RANCHER
Copyright © 2011 by Kathie DeNosky

CONTENTS

Dear Reader,

It's been a very long time since I wrote *Betrayed by Love*, a story about a newspaper reporter from South Dakota named Kate Walker, who works for a daily paper in Chicago and is carrying a huge torch for rancher Jacob Cade.

While I was writing this book, I really wanted to push Jacob over a cliff by chapter three, and by chapter five I wanted to run a bus over him. But he redeems himself big time when Kate gets shot in the course of her news gathering. Kate and Jacob show up for a cameo later in Tom Walker's story in the anthology *A Long, Tall Texan Summer,* along with their son, Hunter.

I wrote *Betrayed by Love* in 1986 (it was published in Silhouette Desire in 1987), and this was only a few years after I gave up reporting full-time and came home to write books and raise our own son, Blayne. At the time I wrote the book, Blayne was six years old. Now, Blayne and Christina are raising my beautiful little granddaughter, Selena Marie, who is three years old. I never realized how quickly those days would end. The old saying that time flies as you get older is so true.

But back to the book—I had a wonderful time writing it, during a very sweet time in my own life. I hope you enjoy revisiting these early characters as much as I have.

As always, thank you, my wonderful reader family, for your kindness, your tolerance and your loyalty down all the long years. Thank you, thank you, for all that you do for me, just by being the kind people that you are.

Much love, many hugs, from Diana Palmer (who is still your biggest fan).

BETRAYED BY LOVE

New York Times Bestselling Author

Diana Palmer

years before. When Kate and Tom Walker had come to Blairsville to live with their Grandmother Walker, the girls had become friends. They'd spent time at each other's houses since early high school. Now Margo was marrying, and although Kate had declined the honor of being a participant in the wedding, she couldn't get out of attending. Not even to spite Jacob Cade.

As if he sensed her presence, his lofty head turned, shaded by a very expensive cream-colored Stetson. He was immaculate in a deep gray vested suit, elegance personified in spite of the fact that Kate had seen him work cattle and knew the strength in that long, lean body.

His square jaw lifted and he smiled in her direction, but it wasn't a kind expression of greeting. He was declaring war without saying a single word.

Kate felt her neck tingle and she clutched the small white and jade bag that matched her pale green suit. She lifted her own chin, daring him. She'd spent her adult life doing that. It was like a defense mechanism, a programmed response that kept her from throwing herself at him. If she fought him, he couldn't get close enough to do her very vulnerable heart much damage.

She seemed to have loved him forever, all her life. Her dreams were full of him, her mind haunted with memories. Jacob, smiling at her from horseback as she learned to ride with Margo as tutor. Jacob, sitting quietly in the porch swing while she and Margo danced with their young suitors at summer parties on the ranch. Jacob. All her young dreams had been wrapped up in one strong, very virile man. And then, like summer lightning, Jacob had become her enemy.

Something had been growing between them from the time she turned eighteen. It had been in his eyes, a vague smoldering interest that frightened her even as it intrigued her. While she'd been growing up, he'd been an indulgent older-brother figure who'd included her in Margo's parties and outings as naturally as if she'd been part of the family. She'd never confided in him about her upbringing, of course. Kate had told no one, not even Margo, the truth about those anguished days. But Jacob had been kind to her. When Grandmother Walker had a stroke, it was Jacob who sat up all night with Kate in case she needed him. When Tom got in trouble at school for fighting, Jacob went to the principal and talked him out of expelling Kate's hotheaded brother. Jacob had always been there, like an anchor, holding everyone steady in the raging current of life. And Kate had grown to love him, attracted by his strength and kindness and the single-minded determination that seemed to cling to him like the spicy after-shave he wore. And then their relationship had all gone sour in the space of a single night, and her friend Jacob had suddenly become her worst enemy.

Kate and a boy she was dating had been invited to a pool party at Margo's house in July six years ago. After an hour of swimming, during which Kate had hardly been able to take her eyes off Jacob's incredibly sensuous body in white trunks, she'd gone to the bathhouse to change. Kate had just stripped off her bathing suit when she saw a rattlesnake coiled on the sunlit strip of concrete by the wall. With a phobia for snakes that dated from childhood, her mind had gone into turmoil. In her hysteria, she'd forgotten that she was undressed. She'd screamed and Gerald, her date, had come running. The snake had crawled away through a hole. She was shaking and sobbing and Gerald, helpless to do anything else, was just holding her. And Jacob had walked in and seen them like that—seen Kate's nude body being held close against Gerald's tall form that was clad only in brief trunks.

Maybe he'd have listened to her explanation another time, but Kate had grown angry at her reaction to Jacob's hard, fit body, as well as his blatant attention to Barbara Dugan, a beautiful and blond neighbor. And she'd gone to Gerald in the pool and had kissed him in a totally adult way, an action that Jacob had seen. He could hardly be blamed, Kate realized, for thinking so badly of her. She was shocked at her own behavior, but she was confused at the force of her attraction to Jacob and her inability to do anything about it.

She thought she'd never forget the way Jacob had looked at her, his black eyes filled with contempt, his face devoid of any expression while Gerald, unnerved by Jacob's unexpected fury, stumbled over an explanation that sounded too dispirited to be convincing.

Every word of it was true, but Jacob hadn't listened to them. It was almost as if he'd wanted to believe only the evidence of his own eyes. That had been the last time she'd been welcome at Warlance. Despite Margo's pleading and threats, Jacob had stood firm. He didn't want his niece associating with a woman like Kate, he'd said. He'd thrown Gerald off the property on the spot, sending him away without a word.

Before Kate had joined Gerald in the car, she and Jacob had a grandfather of a brawl, one so hot that even old Hank Cade hadn't mixed in it. He'd moved out of earshot, watching his son raise hell while Margo tried desperately to referee.

"You won't listen, will you?" Margo had said, defending Kate. "It was innocent! There was a snake in the bathhouse!"

"Sure," he replied, his voice colder than Kate had ever heard it, his hard glare silencing Margo immediately.

Kate had clenched her hands by her sides, blazing

with bad temper and hurt pride. "Go ahead, then, believe I'm that kind of woman, even when you know I'm not!"

"I thought you were a little saint," he replied curtly, his gaze chilling her, "until tonight when your halo slipped and I saw you grow up."

She didn't understand the way he'd phrased it. Not that, or the unreasonable contempt in his tone. "Jacob, I'm not like that! And I don't lie—I've never lied to you!"

"I watched my mother go that route," he said in a haunted tone. "One man after another and denying the whole time that she'd ever cheated on my father. One day, she ran off with her latest lover and never came back. I've never forgotten what a hell she made of my father's life. I raised my niece to have a conscience and a sense of morality. I'm not having Margo exposed to women like you. Get off my place and keep off."

Margo had gritted her teeth, but her eyes had been eloquent as they apologized to Kate silently. Jacob in this mood was dangerous. And Kate understood.

"You won't listen," Kate said quietly. "I'm sorry, because I'd never willingly lie about anything. There's so much you don't know, Jacob," she'd added, her smile wistful and bitter. "Not that it would matter, I guess. You don't think people should stoop to being human. You want perfection in every way."

"Your grandmother would be ashamed of you," he said roughly. "She didn't raise you to be a loose woman. She never should have let you go to work for that damned newspaper."

Kate had gotten a summer job with the local weekly paper, and Jacob had been against it from the start, unlike Grandmother Walker, who thought women should do what they pleased in business.

Her job had been just something else he disapproved

of. Lately she had seemed to get on his nerves, to antagonize him for no obvious reason. This was the last straw, though. Kate knew that he'd never forget or forgive what he thought she'd done in that bathhouse. He'd stripped her of her pride and self-confidence—and without even raising his voice. That was Jacob. Always controlled. He never really lost his temper; he used it.

"I like reporting," she replied. "In fact, I plan to make a career of it. And now I'll be pleased to decontaminate your ranch by leaving it. I'm only sorry the snake didn't bite me, because then at least you'd believe me. Goodbye, Margo. I'm sorry your uncle won't let us be friends anymore."

"You can make book on it," he replied, his dark eyes glaring at her.

He'd given Kate an appraisal that spoke volumes before he turned and walked away without a single word.

That had been six years ago. In the time that followed, Kate had gone to journalism school for a couple of years and wound up working for a Chicago daily newspaper. She hadn't known anyone in Chicago, but Tom had a friend there, and the friend had pulled a string or two. Kate liked the big city. It was the one place she might be able to forget Jacob.

Jacob had relented just a little afterward. Kate was still unwelcome at Warlance, of course, but he'd stopped short of forbidding Margo to talk or write to her. Once Margo had even invited her to the ranch for a weekend, apparently with Jacob's blessing, but Kate had refused. She was still hurt from Jacob's unreasonable treatment. She hadn't even wanted to come to the wedding. But since it was being held in Blairsville, not on the ranch, she felt fairly safe. And Tom was with her. Dear Tom. She hated her own cowardice, but she clung to him.

"You're a reporter," Tom was saying, breaking into her silent reveries. "You've won awards. You're almost twenty-five years old. Don't let him intimidate you. It will only make him worse. You can't buckle under with people like Jacob. You ought to know that by now."

"Knowing it and using it are two different things. And I do hate him," she muttered, glaring at Jacob as he turned to speak to a nearby couple. "He's so lordly. He knows everything."

"He doesn't know you're still a maiden, I'd bet," Tom chuckled, "or he'd never have accused you of messing around in the bathhouse with that poor nervous little boy."

Her face flamed. "I'll never forgive him for that."

"He doesn't know what kind of upbringing we had," Tom reminded her. "He never knew our folks, remember. We were living with Grandmother Walker by the time you met Margo and became friends with her."

She smiled softly. "Granny was a character. Even Jacob Cade didn't run over her. You remember, he tried to make her forbid me to go on that overnight camping trip with Margo just a few months before he told me to stay off the ranch forever. Granny informed him that I was eighteen and could go where I pleased." She frowned. "I never did understand why he was so against it. We had a great time. There were college boys along, too, and chaperons... It was very well behaved."

"It should have been, since he went along as a chaperon," Tom mused.

"That was the only bad thing about the whole experience," she muttered.

"Liar. I'll bet you spent hours sitting and watching him," he whispered.

Her eyes fell. Of course she had. One way or another,

she'd spent her entire adult life mooning over the only man in the world who hated her. She wondered sometimes if she hadn't deliberately worked toward a career in reporting just as an excuse to leave Blairsville and get away from him. Chicago was as far away as she could manage. Now that Grandmother Walker was dead and Tom was working for an ad agency in New York, there was no reason to stay in South Dakota. But there was every reason to escape; she had to keep away from Jacob. Kate had never fancied growing old with her heart in shreds from his day-to-day indifference. Living in Blairsville, she'd have seen him frequently, and heard about him even more often. That would have been too painful to contemplate.

Her attention was caught by a flash of red as Margo's little sports car drew up at the curb, driven by her fiancé, David. He hopped out, resplendent in his white tuxedo with a red carnation in the lapel and a red cummerbund. He was fair, tall and very attractive.

"About time," Tom chided as the bridegroom paused beside them. "Where's Margo?"

"Arriving momentarily with her grandfather. I hope," David added with a tiny shudder. "Have you seen Hank drive?" he groaned.

"Yes," Tom replied with a sigh. "He's almost, but not quite, as bad as Jacob."

David laughed, and Kate hated herself for hanging so eagerly on to any tidbit of gossip about the man she loved.

"Jacob wrecked three cars before he got through college," Tom mused. "Our grandmother wouldn't let Kate go to Warlance unless Margo drove."

"I expected to see you both at the house," David began.

Kate was searching for an excuse when a shadow fell

over her, and her heart ran wild. It was like radar; she always felt Jacob before she saw him.

"So there you are," Jacob said, joining the group. He didn't even look at Kate. "Hello, Tom. Good to see you." He extended his hand and shook the younger man's firmly. There was only about four years between the two men—Jacob was thirty-two—but Jacob seemed a generation older in his attitudes. "Where's Margo?" he asked.

"On the way, with your father at the wheel, I'm afraid." David sighed. "Well, it's not my fault," he added defensively when Jacob glared at him. "We couldn't fit that expensive wedding gown you bought her into the car without taking it off first." He grinned wickedly. "I was all for that, of course, but Margo seemed to feel that it would shock the congregation."

Jacob wasn't amused, but Tom had to bite his lip. So did Kate, despite the tense undercurrents.

"My father is half-blind with cataracts he won't have removed," Jacob said coldly. "He's got no business driving at all."

"Hurry, let's rush and phone the state police," David offered. "What a great opportunity to have his license pulled."

Tom couldn't help it. He laughed. "Sorry, but I have this mental picture of the entire wedding party bailing the old fellow out of jail—"

Kate clung closer to Tom's sleeve. "There they are," she murmured, nodding toward the road, where a big Lincoln with Hank behind the wheel was just nudging against the curb and stopping.

"See?" David laughed as Margo got out of the car, escorted by a tall, silver-haired man who was an older version of Jacob but without his fiery temper and cold, domineering manner. "No broken bones, no ripped fenders, everything intact. Hmm, she does look a bit pale."

"Probably the stark terror of realizing she's marrying a crazy person," Kate offered, grinning at David.

"I'm not crazy." David defended himself with mock solemnity. "Just because I once, only once, went with Margo to a male strip joint—"

"A what?" Jacob demanded fiercely.

David actually flushed. "Uh-oh." He moved away. "Excuse me, have to rush. Getting married today, you see." He vanished.

"A what!" Jacob glared at Tom.

"It's a place where men take off their clothing while women wolf whistle," Kate offered, adding fuel to the fire. "Very educational." Well, she'd heard that they were, anyway. Kate herself wouldn't be caught dead in such a place, but Jacob might as well think she would, if it needled him.

Jacob's dark eyes were frankly insulting. "I can't imagine that you'd need any educating."

"How sweet of you to say so," Kate said with a demure smile.

The taller man didn't bother to reply. "See you inside," he told Tom, and walked off.

"Whew," her brother sighed as they started toward the rest of the congregation who were entering the church. "Talk about heat!"

"He hates me," she sighed. It had been a good act, but only an act. Inside, she was bleeding to death and no one could even see.

"I wonder if Jacob really knows what he feels for you, Kate," Tom remarked quietly.

But she didn't answer him. She walked up the steps and into the church, thinking as she went how very fortunate Margo was.

Chapter 2

The wedding was so beautiful that Kate cried. Sitting quietly near the pulpit, listening to the words that would bind David and Margo together, she felt a sense of loss for herself. She'd never hear those words, never know the overwhelming joy of pledging her life to a man who would love her back with equal passion.

Involuntarily, her eyes turned toward Jacob where he towered over David at the altar. He took such occasions seriously, and this one must have touched him, because he and his father had been responsible for Margo since her tenth birthday. As if he sensed her watching him, he glanced over his shoulder, his dark eyes catching hers. She didn't wait to read the expression in them; she quickly dropped her gaze to her lap. Such encounters with Jacob always left her feeling inadequate.

At last it was over, and the wedding guests gathered outside to pelt the lucky couple with dainty little sachets of rice. Margo reappeared shortly in a neat white linen traveling suit. David was at her side, his tuxedo exchanged for a sports coat and casual shirt and slacks. The newlyweds looked young and wildly excited, hardly able to keep their eyes from each other.

"Be happy, darling," Kate murmured, hugging Margo warmly before she climbed into the red sports car beside her new husband.

"I will. I really will." Margo glanced over Kate's shoulder. "Uncle Jacob looks as if he'd like to bite somebody."

"Probably me." David chuckled as Margo got in beside him. "I told him about our jaunt to the male strip joint."

"How could you?" Margo wailed. "He'll kill us!"

"He'll have to catch us first." David put the small car in gear with a wicked grin. "Goodbye, Kate. Goodbye, new Uncle Jacob!"

And they were gone before Jacob could say a single word.

Kate couldn't resist baiting him. It was a way of life. She glanced up at his strong, hard face with a small laugh. "Were you going to have a brief word with Margo about what to expect on her wedding night, Uncle Jacob?" she murmured discreetly, although they were away from the other wedding guests.

He glared down at her. "You might have done that yourself. I doubt if my experience would match yours."

"You might be surprised," she said.

He bent his tall head to light a cigarette, but his dark eyes never left hers. "Margo invited you to come down for a few days before the wedding to visit with her. You refused. Why?"

"Because of you," she said without hesitation. "You threw me off Warlance over six years ago and told me to never come back."

His broad shoulders shrugged, and muscles rippled like rapids in a river. He was overpowering this close— vividly male, abrasively masculine.

He stared down the long, straight road. "A few days after that pool party, one of the gardeners killed a rattlesnake in the bathhouse," he remarked quietly.

"Nice of you to apologize when you found out," Kate replied, almost shaking with suppressed rage. He could have admitted that six years ago, but he'd kept it to himself.

He looked down at her, and his eyes were cold. "There was a snake. But you were still naked in that boy's arms."

"I was scared to death, too," she returned. "I hardly knew what I was doing." She dropped her eyes to his tie. It was nice. Navy blue with red diamonds. "Never mind, Jacob. Think what you like. You always do, regardless of the evidence."

"Why did you go to Chicago to work?" he asked abruptly, his dark eyes glittering down at her through a wisp of cigarette smoke. "Why not Pierre?"

The question shocked her. It wasn't like him to seek her out deliberately and start talking. He never had before, at least.

She stared up at him helplessly, every single thought gone out of her head except how handsome he was. Darkly tanned, even-featured, he would have caught more sophisticated eyes than Kate's. She swallowed.

"Chicago is big," she said inanely, still staring up at him with wide, soft green eyes.

"So it is," he agreed quietly. As they stood together without a word for long, static seconds, he searched her face, probing softly, and she felt her knees giving way.

"The...wedding... It was nice," she choked out finally.

Her heart was trying to burst under the intensity of his long stare.

"Very nice," he agreed, his voice deeper than she remembered it.

"They're going to Jamaica," she added breathlessly.

"I know. Dad and I gave them the trip for a wedding present."

"They'll enjoy it, I'm sure." This was ridiculous, she told herself. She was a reporter, a whiz with words, even her city editor said so. Why was she stammering like a grammar school kid?

He was still looking in her eyes as if he couldn't get enough of just gazing at her. This is insane, she thought. Jacob was her worst enemy.

"You've changed," he said finally. "You're more mature. More poised. What do you do at that newspaper you work for?"

"Politics," she said without thinking.

"Do you like it?"

"It's very exciting," she confessed. "Especially the elections. You get involved, even though you try to report impartially. I think I jinx the candidates, though," she added with a sheepish smile. "Mine always seem to lose."

He didn't return the smile. He lifted his cigarette to his mouth again while Tom shifted restlessly in the background. It was unusual for Jacob and Kate to talk without looking for weapons.

Jacob dropped his cigarette and ground it out under his expensive boot. His dark eyes searched hers. "I suppose you and Tom will go back tonight?"

She nodded. "We have to. I've got an interview first thing in the morning."

His cleft chin lifted and he narrowed his eyes, searching hers. "That boy, Kate…"

"I never lied to you, Jacob," she whispered.

The change in his face was faintly alarming, explosive. The muscles in his jaw tautened, his eyes went black. "I can't remember a woman ever saying my name the way you do," he said half under his breath.

She had to fight from flinging herself into his arms and begging for his mouth. She looked at it now with aching hunger, followed its chiseled perfection with eyes gone misty from all the years of hopeless longing. Would it never end, this longing for him? He'd never touched her, never kissed her, in all the years she'd known him. She dreamed about it, about how it would feel. But it would never happen.

"I have to go," she said miserably.

His chest expanded slowly, as if he was taking a deliberate breath. "Yes," he said finally. "So do I. I've got to catch a train to New York for meetings about some cattle futures."

He was taking the train because he didn't trust airplanes, she recalled with a faint smile. He never flew unless it was a matter of life and death.

He did look every inch a businessman, all right. Her eyes adored him one last time. Now that Margo was married, she might never see him again. The thought was vaguely terrifying. That fright seeped into her expression, puzzling the tall man beside her.

"What is it?" he asked, his deep voice almost gentle.

"Nothing." She clutched her purse closer. "Well… I have to go."

"You said that."

She shrugged and smiled faintly. "Yes."

He didn't reply and she turned slowly toward Tom, her heart sinking.

"I get to Chicago from time to time," he said unexpectedly.

She turned, nervous and breathless. "Do you?"

His chin lifted again and his eyes lingered on her face speculatively. "I might take you out to dinner one night."

She tried not to let her enthusiasm show, but she failed miserably. "Oh, I'd like that," she whispered.

"So would I." He let his eyes run slowly down the length of her body, admiring it with sensuous candor. "You've been off-limits for a long time, Kate," he mused, catching her gaze suddenly. "But Margo's out of the picture now; there are no more barriers."

She didn't understand. "What?"

He laughed softly, but it wasn't humorous. "We'll talk about that sometime. Are you in the phone book?"

"Yes," she replied. "My first initial and my last name are listed. I'm in the Carrington Apartments."

"I'll find you." He turned away to glance at Tom, who was still hovering. "Can I give you a lift to the airport?"

Tom joined them, smiling. "Thanks, but we've got a rental car."

"Those do come in handy. I've got a train to catch. Nice to see you again, Tom." He extended his big, lean hand and shook Tom's. Then he glanced back at Kate with a peculiar smile. "I'll see you."

She nodded. "Have a nice trip."

"I usually do." He turned and strode off, while Kate watched him with her heart in her eyes.

"If he sees the way you're looking at him, the game's up," Tom teased, holding her by the arm to propel her to the Ford he'd rented. "Come down out of the clouds, girl. We've got to make tracks if we're going to catch our plane on time."

"Yes, of course."

"What were you talking about?" he probed.

"He comes to Chicago on business sometimes," she murmured, glancing out the window and catching sight of Jacob as he passed them in his big Lincoln. She sighed. "Oh, Tom. He wants to take me out to dinner."

"Horrors," Tom exclaimed, pulling out into the street. "Watch out."

She frowned. "Why?"

"For God's sake, Kate. Margo's married and you've just gone on the endangered-species list. Or hasn't it occurred to you that he's wanted you for years?"

Her heart skipped. "Me?"

"Of course, you," he grumbled. "Jacob looks at you as if you were a juicy steak with his name branded on it. He always has. My God, if it hadn't been for the fact that you and Margo were best friends, he'd have seduced you years ago."

"It isn't like that—"

"The devil it isn't," he persisted. "Listen, honey, I'm a man. I know how men think. Now that Margo's out of the picture, Jacob feels free to pursue you, and I do mean pursue. He's never believed you about that Gerald boy; he never will. As far as he's concerned, you're a city sophisticate, not a shy little country maiden. So watch it. I've heard stories about that man all my adult life, and I believe them. He's a mature, sophisticated man with a line of women an arm long, and he doesn't drag his feet. Did you really think that he was celibate all this time?" he added as he caught a glimpse of her shocked face.

"Margo said he never brought anybody home." Her voice faltered.

"Of course not—he wouldn't flaunt his conquests around Margo! Or don't you remember what a peculiarly old-fashioned man he is when it comes to women and liberation?"

"I remember all too well," she sighed, leaning back against the seat as she recalled his reaction that long-ago afternoon to the sight of her in a man's arms.

"Then keep it all in mind. He isn't in the market for a wife, honey," Tom added softly. "I know how you feel about him. But don't let your emotions blind you to the truth. What he wants is to satisfy a temporary hunger. When he marries, if he marries, it will most likely be Barbara Dugan, whose father owns the Double D Ranch adjoining his. It will be a nice merger and double his holdings, and Barbara isn't half bad to look at."

"Yes, I suppose you're right, Tom." She felt sick all over. How was she going to manage to say no to Jacob when the time came and he asked her out? She loved him so desperately that even a few minutes of his company would last her starving heart for years. She looked at her brother helplessly. "Maybe he cares about me, a little."

"Maybe he does," he said. "But don't you ever forget his mother and how he feels about the whole female sex because of her. He'll never marry a woman he's slept with."

She flushed despite herself and turned her eyes back to the road. "His mother ran around with everyone, from what Margo said. And poor old Hank just sat and did nothing."

"She was a wild woman, Grandmother said. Nothing like Hank, who was easygoing and pleasant and not very ambitious. She got tired of having nothing and went after the rainbow." He sat deeper in the seat as they approached the city. "I guess she found it eventually. She married that Texas oil magnate and lived happily until she died. But Jacob hated her for what she did to him and his father and brother, and he hated the humiliation of having to live down her reputation."

"He hasn't had a good impression of women," Kate said quietly.

"Keep that in mind. He won't let his emotions get in his way."

"I'll keep it in mind," she promised.

He started to say something else. But he just smiled and reached over to pat her hand where it lay on her purse. "How about some lunch before we catch the plane? What would you like?"

"Something adventurous," she said, quickly following his lead. "How about squid?"

"Yech! How about something civilized?"

She sighed. "Steak and potatoes, I guess?"

"Civilized," he emphasized. "Like a McDonald's hamburger!"

"Now, that's civilized." She laughed. "Drive on!"

Tom kept her mind occupied with wild tales about his advertising job in New York, and about some of his more eccentric clients—like the soap magnate who liked to listen to Tom's presentations while taking bubble baths with a background of Mozart pieces, or the chewing gum heiress who brought her purebred collies to each meeting, to make sure her beloved pets approved of the ad campaigns.

Her brother was the only living relative she had now, and she tended to lean on him the slightest bit. She felt guilty at her own rebellious feelings when he criticized Jacob. Perhaps it was a fair warning, although she didn't like facing that possibility. She preferred to think that Jacob had only just noticed her and wanted a new beginning for the two of them. So that was what she was going to think, whether or not her older brother approved.

She waved him off to New York soon after they landed in Chicago, and caught a cab back to her apartment. The sense of loneliness that washed over her was nothing new. She felt alone every time she walked away from Jacob. She wanted him, so badly. Would it be very wrong to have an affair?

Her father's harsh recriminations came back on cue. That kind of woman, he'd raged, his daughter wasn't going to become. He was going to make sure of it. And he'd harped on permissiveness, on the ills of modern society, on the terror of unwanted children, until he'd poisoned Kate's young mind. When she and Tom were in high school and went to live with Grandmother Walker, there was no free will left. Kate often wondered what her life would have been like if only her mother hadn't left. Her mother had been like Jacob's, according to her father. Her father had often sworn that Kate wasn't really his child, anyway, but she and Tom looked so much alike that Kate tried not to think too hard about it. That part of her life was over, anyway. Looking back would only bring more nightmares.

As she got into bed, drowsy with weariness, she wondered if Tom had been right, and Jacob really had wanted her for years. She flushed with the memory of that long, speaking look he'd drawn over her body. Yes, he did seem to want her now. And she wanted him, wanted the union, the total belonging of being in his arms with nothing between them.

She turned into her pillow, burning with new desires. If only Jacob had believed her about that misunderstanding... But on the other hand, mightn't knowing the truth turn him off completely? If Tom was right, and Jacob preferred sophisticated women, wouldn't he be likely to walk away from Kate if he knew she was a virgin?

On that troubling thought, she closed her eyes and slept.

Chapter 3

The brief vacation from work seemed vaguely unreal to Kate once she was back at her desk at the Chicago daily newspaper where she worked. And, as usual, everything was in a virtual frenzy of confusion.

Dan Harvey, the city editor, was the only man functioning at full capacity. There was an unwritten law somewhere that city editors didn't fall victim to insanity. Kate often wondered if that was because they caused it.

Harvey presided over the newsroom, and he managed story assignments as if it were delicate choreography. In the hierarchy of the newsroom, there was a state news editor who dealt with breaking stories outside the city and worked with the few stringers, or correspondents, the paper maintained outside the city proper. There was a feature editor, a wire services editor, a society editor, just to name a few, with all of them—Harvey included—under the watchful eye of the managing editor, Morgan Winthrop. Winthrop was a veteran reporter himself, who'd worked his way up the ranks to his present position. Next to the editor in chief, James Harris, and the publisher, Winthrop was top man in the paper's power structure.

At the moment, Kate was under Harvey's gimlet eye while she finished the last, grueling paragraph in a rapidly unfolding political story about a local alderman who'd skyrocketed to fame by spending a week in a local neighborhood besieged by crime.

It was just hard to think with a tall, bald man standing over her, glancing pointedly at his watch and tapping his foot. She hoped he'd get bunions, but he probably caused those, too.

"Okay." She breathed a sigh of relief and showed him the screen on the terminal.

"Scroll it," he instructed, and began to read the monitor from his vantage point above her left shoulder as she started the scrolling command. Since the word processor screen would only show a portion of the whole story, this command was used to move each line up so that another appeared at the bottom until the end. Harvey pursed his lips, mumbled something, nodded, mumbled something else.

"Okay, do it," he said tersely and left her sitting there without a tiny word of praise.

"Thanks, Kate, you did a great job," she told herself as she entered the story into the memory of the computer. "You're a terrific reporter, we love you here, we'd never let you go even if it meant giving you a ten-thousand-dollar raise."

"Kate's getting a ten-thousand-dollar raise," Dorie Blake yelled across the bustling city room to Harvey. "Can I have one, too?"

"Society editors don't get raises," he returned with

dry humor, and didn't even look over his shoulder. "You get paid off by attending weddings."

"What?" Dorie shot back.

"Wedding cake. Punch. Hors d'oeuvres. You get fed as a fringe benefit."

Dorie stuck out her tongue.

"Juvenile, juvenile," Harvey murmured, and went into his office and closed the door.

"Tell Mr. Winthrop that Harvey goosed you behind the copy machine," Bud Schuman suggested on his way to the water fountain, his head as bald as Harvey's, his posture slightly stooped, his glasses taped at one ear.

Dorie glared at him. "Bud, they took out the Linotype machine ten years ago. And our managing editor doesn't listen to sob stories. He's too busy trying to make sure the paper shows a profit."

"Did they take out the copy machine?" he asked vaguely. "No wonder I don't have anyplace to leave my files…"

"Honest to God, one day he'll lose his car just by not noticing where he parked it." The older woman shook her red head.

"He's still the best police reporter we have," Kate reminded her. "Twenty-five years at it. Why, he took me to lunch one day and told me about a white-slavery racket that the police broke up here. They were actually selling girls—"

"I should be lucky enough to be sold to Sylvester Stallone or Arnold Schwarzenegger," Dorie sighed, smiling dreamily.

"With your luck, they'd sell you to a restaurant, where you'd spend your twilight years washing plates that had contained barbecued ribs," Bud murmured as he walked back past them.

"Sadist!" Dorie wailed.

"I've got three committee meetings, and then I have a news conference downtown." Kate shook her head, searching for her camera. "Alderman James is at it again." She grinned. "He's just finished his week in the combat zone and is going to tell us all how to solve the problem. With any luck, I'll get the story and have it phoned in to rewrite in time to eat supper at a respectable hour."

"Do you think he's really got answers, or is he just doing some politicking under the watchful eye of the press?" Dorie asked.

Kate pursed her lips. "I think he cares. He dragged me out of a meeting at city hall and enlisted me to help a black family in that ward when their checks ran out. You remember, I did a story on them—it was a simple computer error, but they were in desperate straits and sick..."

"I remember, all right." Dorie smiled at her. "You're the only person I know who could walk down back alleys at night in that neighborhood without being bothered. The residents would kill anybody who touched you."

"That's why I love reporting," Kate said quietly. "We can do a lot of harm, or we can do a lot of good." She winked. "I'd rather help feed the hungry than grandstand for a reputation. See you." She slung the shoulder strap of the camera over her shoulder, hitched up her little laptop computer in its plastic carrying case, and started off. She could use the computer for the committee meetings and even the alderman's breaking story. She had a modem at home, so when she fed the notes into it, she could just patch them into the newspaper from the comfort of her living room. It certainly did beat having to find a phone and pant bare facts to someone on the rewrite desk.

Unfortunately for Kate, the little computer broke down at the last committee meeting, just before she was to cover the alderman's speech. She cursed modern science until she ran out of breath as she crawled through rush-hour traffic toward city hall. There was no time to go by the paper and get a spare computer; she'd just have to take notes by hand. Great, she muttered, remembering that she didn't have a spare scrap of paper in her purse or one stubby pencil!

She found some old bank envelopes under the car seat while she was stuck in traffic and folded them, stuffing them into the jacket of her safari pantsuit. It was chic but comfortable, and set off her nice tan. With it, she was wearing sneakers that helped her move quickly on crowded streets. She'd learned a long time ago that reporting was easier on the feet when they had a little cushioning underneath.

As she drove her small Volkswagen down back streets to city hall, she wondered if Jacob had been in town and had tried to get her but failed, since she'd been working late. She'd been so excited about that remark he'd made that she'd been crazy enough to invest in a telephone answering machine, but she knew many people would hang up rather than leave a message. She spent her free time sitting next to the telephone, staring out the window at the street below. And when she wasn't doing that, she haunted her mailbox for letters with a South Dakota postmark.

It was insane, she kept telling herself. He'd only been teasing. He hadn't really meant it. That reasoning might have convinced her except that Jacob never teased.

He had to mean it. And all her brother's well-intentioned arguments and warnings would go right out the window if Jacob ever knocked on her door. She'd follow him into burning coals if he asked her to, walk over a carpet of snakes… anything, because the hunger for him had grown to such monumental proportions over the long, empty years. She loved him. Anything he wanted, he could have.

She was curious about his feelings. Tom had said that Jacob didn't know what he felt for Kate. But Jacob wanted her, all right. Her innocence didn't keep her from seeing the desire in his dark eyes. It was what would happen if she made love with him that puzzled her. Would he be flattered when he knew she was a virgin? Would he even know it? They said only doctors could really tell. But he was a very experienced man—would he know?

She parked in the municipal parking lot, glancing ruefully at all the dents on the fenders of her small orange VW Beetle. They were visible in the light from the street lamps.

"Poor little thing," she said sympathetically, glaring at the big cars that surrounded it. "Don't worry, someday I'll save up enough to get your fenders smoothed out."

Someday. Maybe when she was ninety... Reporting, while an exciting job, was hardly the best-paid profession in the world. It exerted maximum wear and tear on nerves, emotions and body, and salary never compensated for the inevitable overtime. It was a twenty-four-hour-a-day job, and nowhere near as glamorous as television seemed to make it.

What was glamorous, she wondered as she made her way up to the alderman's offices, about covering a story on an addition to the city's sewer system? One of the meetings she'd just come from had dealt with that fascinating subject.

Alderman Barkley H. James was talking to people as reporters crowded in. People from print and broadcast media had begun setting up, most of them wearing the bland, faintly bored look that seemed to hallmark the

profession. It wasn't really boredom, it was repetition.
Most of these reporters were veterans, and they'd seen
and heard it all. They were hard, because they had to be.
That didn't mean they were devoid of emotion—just that
they'd learned to pretend they didn't have it.

She slid into a seat beside Roger Dean, a reporter on a
local weekly. Roger was nearer forty than thirty, a daily
reporter who'd "retired" to a weekly. "Here we are again,"
she murmured as she checked the lighting in the office
and made corrections to the settings on her 35-mm camera. "I saw you yesterday at the solid-waste-management
meeting, didn't I?"

"It was a foul job, but somebody had to do it," Roger
said with theatrical fervor. He glanced at her from his
superior height. "Why do they always send you to those
meetings?"

"When it comes to issues like sanitary-disposal sites,
everybody else hides in the bathroom until Harvey picks
a victim."

He shuddered. "I once covered a sanitary-landfill-site
public meeting. People had guns. Knives. They yelled."

"I have survived two of those," she said with a smug
grin. "At the first, there was a knock-down-drag-out
fight. At the second, one man tried to throw another one
out a window. I was jostled and shoved, and I still think
someone pinched me in a very unpleasant way."

The alderman interrupted the conversation as he began
to speak. He told of mass unemployment, of poverty beyond anyone's expectations. He told of living conditions
that were intolerable, children playing in buildings that
should have been torn down years before. Slums, he told
his audience, were out of place in the twentieth century.
The mayor had started the ball rolling with his excellent
program of revitalization, Alderman James said. Follow-

ing the mayor's example, he vowed to continue the program in this crime-stricken neighborhood.

He'd interested a group of businessmen in funding a mass renovation of the neighborhood, citing figures that showed a drop in crime corresponding directly to the upgrading of slums. He threw statistics at them rapid-fire, and outlined the plan.

When he was through, there was the usual sprint by reporters to call in stories to the rewrite desk on newspapers or to anchor people at radio and television stations. This was the culmination of a story they'd all been following closely for the past week, and that made the alderman's disclosures good copy.

Kate was almost knocked down in the stampede. She managed to find a quiet corner to phone the office and give them the gist of the speech so that they'd have time to get it set up for the next edition.

She collapsed back against the wall when she was through, watching Roger come toward her slowly as if he hadn't a care in the world.

"I thought you had a computer," he said.

She glared at him. "I did. It broke. I hate machines, not to mention you weekly reporters," she muttered. "No wild dash to file your story, no gallop back to your desk to do sidebars..."

"Ah, the calm and quiet life," he agreed with a grin. "Actually, they say weekly reporting kills more people than daily reporting. *You* don't have to write up your copy then proof it again and do corrections and make up ads and answer the phone and do jobwork in the print shop behind the office and sell office supplies and take subscriptions—"

"Stop!"

He shrugged. "Just letting you know how lucky you

are." He put his pen back into his shirt pocket. "Well, I'm off. Nice to see you again, Kate."

"Same here."

He glanced at her with a faint smile. "I could find time to work you in if you'd like to have dinner with me."

She was tempted. She almost said yes. He wasn't anybody's idea of Prince Charming, but she liked him and it would have been nice to talk over the frustrations of her job. "Come on, I'll buy you pizza."

She loved that. But when she thought about the unwashed dishes and unvacuumed floors and untidy bed at her apartment, her chores were too much to walk away from.

"Thanks, but I've got a mess at home that I've got to get cleaned up. Rain check?" she asked and smiled at him.

"I'd start rain for a smile like that," he said with a chuckle. "Okay. See you, pretty girl."

He winked and walked off. She stared after him, wondering how anyone in her right mind could turn down a free meal. She made her way out of the building, her thoughts full of the broken computer and of how much information from the meeting would be lost for the follow-up story she had to turn in tomorrow. Well, fortunately, she could always call and talk to the committee members. She knew them and they wouldn't mind going over the figures for her. People in political circles were some of the nicest she'd ever known.

She drove back to her apartment thinking about the new lease on life that crime-ridden neighborhood was going to get. The story she'd done for the alderman had concerned a black family of six who'd been removed from the welfare rolls without a single explanation. The father had lost his job due to layoffs, the wife had had to have a mastectomy, there were four children, all barely school age.

The father had tried to call and ask why the checks weren't coming, but the social workers had been pressed for time. Someone had put him on hold, and then he'd gone through a negative-sounding woman who'd informed him that the government didn't make mistakes; if he'd been dropped from the rolls, there was a good reason. So when Kate went to do the story, the first thing she did was to call the social agency to ask about the situation. A sympathetic social worker did some checking and dug into the case, refusing to accept the superficial information she was given. Minutes later, she called Kate back to report that a computer foul-up was responsible. The family had been confused with another family that had been found guilty of welfare violations. The error had been corrected, and now the small family was getting the temporary help it needed. That, and a lot more, because Kate's story had aroused public interest. Several prominent families had made quick contributions, and the family had been spared a grueling ordeal. But the story had haunted Kate. Society was creating more problems than it was solving. The world, Kate philosophized, was just getting too big and impersonal.

She parked her car in the basement of her apartment building and checked to make sure her can of Mace was within reach. It gave Kate a feeling of security when she had to go out at night. She lived in an apartment building that had a security system, but all the same, crime was everywhere.

It had been a long day. She wanted nothing more than to lie down after a hot bath and just read herself into a stupor. Even with all the difficulties, though, she had a feeling of accomplishment, of contributing something.

God bless politicians who cared, and Chicago seemed to be blessed with a lot of them. She wondered if the other reporters who'd been following the story were as pleased as she was.

The elevator was sluggish, as usual. She hit the panel and finally it began the slow upward crawl to the fourth floor. She got off, ambling slowly to her door. She felt ancient.

The phone was ringing, and she listened numbly until she realized that she'd forgotten to turn the answering machine on. She unlocked the door and grabbed the receiver on the fourth ring.

"Hello?" she said, her voice breathless and curt. "If that's you, Dan Harvey, try the rest room. That's where everybody runs to hide when you need a story covered—"

"It isn't Harvey," came the reply in a deep, familiar voice.

Her heart slammed wildly at her rib cage. "Jacob?"

She could almost hear him smiling. "I've been ringing for the past hour. I thought you got off at five."

Her breath was sticking in her throat. She slid onto an armchair by the phone and tried to stop herself from shaking. It had been two weeks since Margo's wedding, but it felt like years. "I do," she heard herself saying. "I had to cover a story at city hall and the traffic was terrible."

"Have dinner with me," he said in a tone she'd never heard him use. "I realize it's short notice, but I didn't expect to be in town overnight."

She could have died when she remembered almost accepting Roger's offer of a meal. If she had… It didn't bear thinking about!

"It's going on six-thirty," she said, glancing at her digital clock.

"Can you be ready in thirty minutes?"

"Do birds fly?" she croaked. "Of course I can!"

He chuckled. "I'll pick you up then."

"But, wait, you don't know where I live," she said frantically.

"I know," was all he said. And the line went dead.

She looked at the receiver blankly. Well, so much for being cool and poised and keeping her head, she thought ruefully. She might as well have taken an ad in her own paper, a display ad that read: I'm yours, Jacob!

It took her only ten minutes to shower and blow-dry her hair, but finding the right dress took fifteen. She went through everything in her closet, dismissing one outfit as too demure, another as too brassy, and still another as dull and disgustingly old. The only thing left was a silky black dress with no sleeves and a deeply slit bodice that laced up. It was midknee, just a cocktail dress, but she liked its sophistication. She wore the garment with black velvet pumps and a glittering rhinestone necklace. And even if she did say so herself, she looked sharp. She left her hair long, letting it fall naturally around her shoulders like black satin, and she didn't wear much makeup. Jacob didn't like cosmetics.

He was prompt. The buzzer rang at precisely seven o'clock, and with trembling hands she pushed the button that would unlock the front door of the apartment building.

Minutes later, he was at the door. She opened it, shaking all over, while she tried to pretend that she was poised. And there he was, resplendent in a black dinner jacket and trousers, with a pleated white shirt and elegant black tie, the polish on his shoes glossy enough to reflect the carpet.

"Nice," he murmured, taking in the black dress. "I'm glad you didn't want a fast-food hamburger."

She flushed. It sounded as though he had expected her tastes not to be simple. "I…"

"Get your purse and let's go," he said tersely. "I've booked a table for seven-thirty."

She didn't argue. She felt on the sofa for her purse, locked the door behind her and followed him into the elevator.

"You didn't say what to wear," she faltered, stopping short of admitting that she'd dressed to the teeth just to please him, not because she expected to go anywhere fancy.

He leaned against the rail inside the elevator and stared down at her with easy sophistication. He looked like a predator tonight, and she realized with a start that she'd never been alone with him before. It was an entirely new kind of relationship, being a woman in his eyes. Everything was different suddenly, and her heart was beating like thunder.

"You're nervous around me," he said finally. "Why?"

Her slender shoulders rose and fell. "I always have been," she said quietly. "You're very intimidating."

"You're not a child anymore," he replied, his dark eyes narrowing in that bronzed face. "For tonight, you're my date, not Margo's best friend. I don't expect to have to quote etiquette or tie a bib on you."

He was being frankly insulting now, and she felt her pride reassert itself. "If you'd rather go alone…?"

He glared at her. "I might wish I had, if you don't stop this shrinking-violet act. If I'd wanted a shy little virgin, I'd have found one."

But she was! She almost told him so, too, and then she realized that it might ruin her whole evening. For years she'd wanted to be with him, to have one magical night to live on. And here she was about to send it up in smoke.

She managed a smile for him, hoping it was coquettish enough. "Sorry," she said. "It's been a long day."

He accepted her excuse after a cursory appraisal. They got off the elevator and he took her arm to lead her to his car. He'd rented a Mercedes, silvery and elegant.

"It's like yours," she said slowly as he helped her into the car. The Cade family had two cars—a black Lincoln and a silver Mercedes—as well as other ranch vehicles.

"It *is* mine," he corrected her. "You know I hate airplanes. I drove here."

"It must have taken all day," she faltered.

He got in beside her. "Two days," he said. "But that was because I stopped in Wisconsin. I had some business with a dairy farmer there."

Knowing how Jacob drove, she was surprised that he'd made it to Chicago alive. She peeked at him. "No speeding tickets?"

His eyebrows arched. "I beg your pardon?" he asked coolly.

She stared at the purse in her lap. "How many cars was it you wrecked during college?"

"I am not a bad driver," he replied arrogantly. He moved out into the traffic, barely missing a passing car. The driver sat down on his horn and Jacob glared at him. "Idiots," he muttered. "Nobody in this city can drive worth beans. I've had five close calls tonight already, just like that one."

Kate was trying not to double over laughing. It wouldn't do, it really wouldn't.

"And it wasn't three cars," he added. "It was two."

She glanced up to find a frankly amused gleam in his

dark eyes. She smiled at him in spite of herself, marveling at the way the motion drew his eyes briefly to her lips.

"Who did you think I was when you answered the phone?" he asked carelessly.

"My city editor," she told him. "I get stuck with all the terrible assignments because the other reporters hide out when he wants a victim."

"You mentioned you were out covering a story," he recalled, pausing at a traffic light. He drew a cigarette from the pack in the glove compartment and lit it lazily. "What was it?"

She told him, outlining the alderman's plan for the neighborhood and the mayor's successful program of revitalization in problem areas of the city. "Cities seem pretty impersonal, and then something like this happens. It makes me feel better about urban areas," she said with a smile. "I like Chicago."

He glanced at her curiously, but he didn't say anything.

Her eyes sought his dark face, noticing how handsome he looked as the colorful city lights played over his features. "You've never asked me out before. In fact," she said softly, "I used to think that you hated me."

He pulled the car into a vacant space in front of a plush downtown restaurant, cut the engine and turned to look at her, his dark eyes steady and faintly glimmering. "Hate and desire are different sides of the same coin," he said quietly. "I couldn't very well seduce my niece's best friend."

Her heart went wild. "I…didn't realize," she faltered.

"I made damned sure you didn't realize," he said softly, watching her intently. "I've tried to protect Margo. That's why I never brought women home. You were a tough proposition, anyway—the first woman I ever wanted who was completely off-limits."

He said *wanted*, not *loved*. She had to remember to make the distinction as Tom had warned. Careful, girl, she told herself, don't let him get under your skin.

The trouble was, he was already there, very deep. She loved him too much.

"But now Margo's married," he said softly, reaching out to stroke a long strand of black hair in a way that made her body ache. "And I don't have to hide it anymore. You're almost twenty-five. You're a responsible, independent woman and you live in the city. I don't have to handle you with kid gloves, do I, Kate?"

She didn't mind how he handled her. That was the whole problem. Part of her wanted to clear up his misconceptions, to tell him about her childhood, about her very strict upbringing. But another part of her was afraid that if she told him the truth he'd hightail it back to South Dakota and never come near her again. And so she bit her tongue to keep from denying what he'd said.

He finished his cigarette leisurely, leaning forward to stub it out. The movement brought him so close to Kate that she could see the thickness of his black eyelashes, the tiny wrinkles at the corners of his eyes. She could smell the expensive cologne he wore and the fainter tang of the soap and shampoo he used.

He turned before he leaned back, catching her eyes. It was the closest she'd ever been to him. Her heart felt as if it were going to burst when he put one lean hand at her cheek and began to slowly, sensuously rub his thumb over her soft lips.

"You don't wear layers of makeup," he said softly. "I like that. And you dress like a lady." His gaze went down to the laces of her bodice, lingering there before moving up again to meet her eyes. "Are you wearing anything under that witchy dress?"

It was too intimate a question. She averted her face, trying not to look like the gauche innocent she was. "Why don't you feed me?"

He laughed softly. "All right. We'll do it your way."

Do what? She didn't even ask; it was safer not to know the answer.

The restaurant was crowded, but they had a nice table on the upper level of an interior that featured exquisite crystal chandeliers and an atmosphere of affluence that made Kate feel frumpy even in the expensive dress she was wearing. She'd had to save money for weeks to afford it; most of the other women who were sitting around this restaurant looked as if they could lay down cash for a Mercedes.

"Don't look so intimidated," Jacob mused as they were seated. "They're just people."

She laughed nervously. "If you knew how I grew up…" she began.

"I do. I've seen your grandmother Walker's house," he replied easily. "It was an old Victorian, but still elegant in its way."

"I grew up," she repeated, "in Nebraska. On a farm. My father was—" she almost said "a lay minister," but she changed it to "—poor. My mother left when Tom and I were just babies. Dad kept us until his death." Of a brain tumor, she could have added, one that made him crazy. She shuddered a little at the painful memories. After all these years, she still had a very real fear of male domination. She could hear her father shouting, feel the whip of the belt across her bare legs whenever she triggered his explosive, unpredictable temper.

"I grew up rich," Jacob replied. "We inherited money from my great-grandfather. He made a fortune back in the late 1880s, when a blizzard drove out half the cattlemen in the West. The old devil had a knack for predicting bad weather. He managed to get his cattle east before that devastating snowfall. He made a fortune."

"Money seems to bring its own responsibilities," she remarked, studying his hard, lined face and cool, dark eyes. "You never seem to have any time to yourself."

A corner of his mouth tugged up. "Don't I?"

She looked down at the white linen tablecloth. Piped music was playing around them, very romantic, while white-coated waiters tended to the crowded tables. "Not during the day, at least," she said, qualifying her words. "When Margo and I were girls, you were always being hounded by somebody."

He was watching her, his gaze purely possessive. "It goes with any kind of business, Kate. I'd hate a life of leisure."

He probably would. He didn't keep his body that fit and muscular by sitting behind a desk.

"I guess I would, too," she mused. Her slender fingers touched the heavy silver knife of her place setting. "Sometimes my job gets unpleasant, but there are compensations."

"I suppose there would be. You work with a lot of men, don't you?" he asked.

There was an unflattering double meaning in his words. She looked directly into his searching eyes, trying not to be affected by the increase in her pulse from his magnetism. "Yes," she said. "I work with a lot of men. Not just at the office, but in politics, rescue work, police work—and in all those places, I'm just one of the boys."

His gaze dropped to her bodice. "So I see."

"I don't work in suggestive clothing," she fired back. "I don't make eyes at married men, and if you're going to start making veiled remarks about what you saw in the bathhouse six years ago, I'm leaving this minute!"

"Sit down."

His tone was like ice, his eyes frankly intimidating. The cold note in his voice made her feel sick inside. She sat down, shaking a little with reaction.

"I know what it looked like to you," she said half under her breath, coloring as she realized the interest she'd raised in other diners, who glanced at the dark man and the pretty woman obviously having a lover's quarrel. "But it wasn't what you thought."

"What I saw was obvious," he returned. "Gerald was damned lucky. If it had been my niece, even if she'd invited it, I'd have broken him like a toothpick."

That was in character. He fought like a tiger for his own. But not for Kate. He thought that she was little more than a tramp and that she didn't need any protection. It surprised Kate sometimes that he was so willing to believe the worst about her, when everything pointed to the contrary. He'd known her for years and he'd been so kind to her. And then, in one afternoon, he'd done an about-face in his attitude toward her. She'd never understood why.

"Lucky Margo, having you to spoil her," she said, with a wealth of pain in the words. She stared at her lap. "Tom and I never had that problem."

"Your grandmother wasn't poor," he argued.

She clenched her teeth. "I didn't mean money." It was love she and Tom had lacked. Grandmother Walker, not a demonstrative person, had never made any concessions in her way of life for them. She'd demanded that they grow up without frills or the handicap of spoiling.

He paused while the waiter brought menus. Kate studied hers with no enthusiasm at all. He'd killed her appetite stone dead.

"What do you want?" he asked carelessly.

She glanced up at him with a speaking look, and he actually laughed.

"Talk about looks that could kill," he murmured. "Were you wishing I was on the menu?"

"I hate you," she said, and meant it. "The biggest mistake I've made in years was to agree to come out with you at all. No, I don't want anything on the menu. I'd like to leave. You stay and enjoy your meal, and I'll get a cab—"

"That isn't all you'll get if you don't sit down, Kate," he replied quietly. "I hate scenes."

"I've never made one in my life until tonight," she said shortly. Her green eyes were huge in her ashen face as she stared across the table at him. How could he treat her this way when she loved him to distraction?

He stared at her with a mingling of emotions, the strongest of which was desire. She was, he thought, the most delicious tidbit he'd ever seen. He'd spent years chiding himself for his unbridled passion for her. Now the barriers were down, and he couldn't seem to handle the confusion she aroused in him. God, she was lovely! All his secret dreams of perfection, hauntingly sweet and seductive. He wondered how many other men had wanted her, had been with her, and the strength of his jealousy disturbed him. It didn't matter, he told himself, he had to have her. Just once, he told himself. Just once, to know that soft, sweet body in passion. Then the fever would be gone. He'd be free of her spell.

She couldn't know that he'd suddenly seen her as a woman when she'd kissed that boy so hungrily. It had gotten worse when he'd confronted them in the bathhouse, and the desire he'd felt for her had almost knocked him to his knees.

He hadn't even meant to take her out tonight. But the lure of her was irresistible. He couldn't stop. And it wasn't bad that she was experienced; he was even glad, in a way, because he had too many scruples about seducing innocents. If he made love to a virgin, he'd feel an obligation to marry her. It wasn't a modern outlook, but then he wasn't a modern man. He was country bred and raised, for all his money.

She looked sad, he thought, studying her. His own emotions confused and irritated him. He wanted her until she was a living obsession in his mind. He ached all over already, and he hadn't even touched her. His dark eyes narrowed, studying her. She was lovely, all right. A walking, breathing temptation. Yes, it was just as well that she wasn't innocent. If he didn't believe her to be sophisticated, he'd never be able to seduce her.

He leaned back in his chair and let his eyes wander over her bodice, where bare skin peeked through the lacing. "Look at me."

She stared back at him with trembling lips, almost shaking with fury. He'd ruined it. All her beautiful dreams had crumbled. Her voice choked when she spoke. "I shouldn't have come with you. Roger Dean offered me a nice pizza. I should have settled for that."

His chin lifted. "Roger who?"

"Roger Dean," she shot back, gratified that he looked irritated. "He's a reporter for one of the other papers. A handsome and very nice man," she added. "And he likes me just the way I am."

So she did have other men. That touched something vulnerable inside him and hurt it. Unsmiling, he stared at her. "Did you turn down a date with him to come out with me?" he asked, as if he expected she did things like that often.

"I turned him down before you called," she shot back. "Sorry to shatter your black image of me."

He sighed deeply and paused long enough to give the waiter an order for steak and a baked potato.

"What do you want?" he asked Kate politely.

"I'll have a shrimp cocktail and coffee," she murmured.

"You need more than that," Jacob said.

"That's all I want, thank you." She gave the waiter the menu with a wan smile, and Jacob noticed how worn she looked, how tired. He knew suddenly that it was a sense of excitement gone sour.

"I've spoiled the night for you, haven't I?" he asked with sharp perception.

Her lips curved into a rueful smile. "I broke speed records getting ready," she said. "Went through every dress I had in my wardrobe to find something nice enough to wear for you. I suppose I was a little excited, being asked out by you after all these years, when I thought I was more of a pest and irritation than someone you…wanted to date." Her eyes glanced off the expression of frank surprise in his. "I should have remembered how you feel about me. It's my own fault. Nobody held a gun on me."

His heart did odd things inside his chest at that confession. He hadn't thought she might want to be with him. At times he'd wondered if she might feel a little of the physical attraction for him that he felt for her. But Kate was mysterious. She was close-lipped and very private, in spite of her modern outlook.

"Maybe we could bury the hatchet for once," he murmured, feeling this way for the first time in his life. The self-confidence he'd always had with women was lacking tonight. He felt something new with Kate, and everything in him was fighting it. She confused him, disturbed him. She had to be sophisticated, but why did she sound so damned honest? She'd sworn once that she'd never lied to him, and he'd had to fight not to believe her. He couldn't believe her, because if he did... He stared at her, feeling something tingle inside him as her face colored. He couldn't prevent a warm, quiet smile.

His smile could open doors. She stared at him with wonder. He'd never smiled at her like that. She returned his smile with interest. "Perhaps we could," she said, her voice husky.

He reached across the table and found her hand, lifting it in his to study it. No rings of any kind. A slender, graceful hand with neatly rounded fingernails, no trace of polish on them. He frowned a little. Touching her made his breath come quickly.

Kate's breath caught as he rubbed his thumb slowly over her palm, whipping up sweet storms of emotion. He looked up into her eyes, holding them, searching them, in a silence that whirled away the other diners and the whole world.

His fingers gripped hers with sudden passion, his face hardened, his breathing stopped in his throat. "Kate," he whispered roughly, and his fingers began to work their way between hers in an act as intimate as kissing. He had sensitive hands, very lean, darkly tanned and strong from hours of working cattle, fixing equipment, doing all the things that ranch work required even of the boss.

Her hand trembled as his eyes held hers in a contact that was as arousing as the slow, exquisite tracing of his fingers between hers. She felt her breath quickening, her body reacting to the newness of it all.

"Years," Jacob whispered roughly, his dark eyes blazing into hers as his body caught fire with the electric contact. "I've waited years for tonight, Kate."

Did he mean…could he mean…? She swallowed down a burst of excited confessions and bit her tongue. She had to take it slowly—she couldn't blurt out undying love and ruin everything. She looked at their joined hands, hers so pale in his dark, strong one. She'd waited years, too, and tonight was the reality after the golden dream. But was his dream the same as hers? Had they been waiting for the same reason?

Chapter 4

The waiter brought food and broke the spell. Kate went through the motions of eating, but her mind was on the wondrous emotions she was feeling with Jacob. He was content now to discuss general subjects, nothing intimate. But underneath it all, she suspected that he was still as disturbed physically as she was. His eyes were much darker than usual, and he hardly took them off her.

He finished his steak and leaned back to look at her. "Want dessert?" he asked gently.

She was excited by that note in his voice. It was tender, and openly warm. "No," she said. "I don't really like sweets."

He chuckled. "Neither do I, although I'm partial to an apple cake. Janet, our housekeeper, bakes one occasionally when my father asks nicely."

"Your father is a nice man," she said quietly.

"Nice. That about sums it up. No one, ever, could accuse me of being...nice," he added with a cool look.

"We can't all be fiery and hard," she reminded him.

"If I hadn't been, we'd have lost Warlance twelve years ago," he said shortly. "There is such a thing as common sense. My father was spending capital faster than the ranch was making it. Ranching has seen hard times in past years. Every year, more ranchers go bust."

"You never will," she muttered.

"I'm not superhuman," he replied surprisingly, "and I've made some bad mistakes. But a soft attitude gets you nowhere in business. My father should have been an inventor. He'd rather putter around in his workshop than talk cattle futures."

She searched his face. "Your mother wasn't a dreamer, was she?" she asked softly, daringly.

His dark eyes seemed to blaze up for an instant. He stared at Kate. "I hated her," he said half under his breath. "From the day I was old enough to understand what she was doing to my father, I hated her. She was nothing but a tramp, with an eye out to opportunity. She sent for me once, after she married that Texan, and I went. It was almost amusing, watching her try to explain."

"You didn't even listen, did you?" she asked sadly.

His eyes grew cold. "You can't imagine what my childhood was like."

Yes, she could understand, she thought. With his black pride, it must have been pure hell. "You went away to school eventually, didn't you?"

"Dad got tired of being called into the principal's office twice a week," he replied. "I was in scraps constantly."

She searched his hard face. "My father said that my mother was like that." She spoke hesitantly, her voice soft and unsteady. He looked up, curious. "I never knew her, you see. And my father was very sick and his mind came and went. But he seemed to always be afraid that I was going to be like her."

He had to bite his tongue almost through to keep the sarcastic words from pouring out. Wasn't she like that? He frowned at her bitter expression, amazed at his own lack of sensitivity. What was it about Kate that made him doubt every word she said? Why was it so impossible for him to trust her?

"I made sure that Margo knew right from wrong," he commented. "I didn't browbeat her, but I got my point across. So did my father." He didn't want to hear about Kate's childhood, or know any more about her than he already did. He didn't know why, either. What he felt for her was only desire, surely. And every time he looked at her, that got worse.

"Are you ready to go?" he asked.

"Yes. Of course."

She watched him pay the check, feeling numb. She'd bored him, and now he was going to take her home and go back to South Dakota. It might be months before she saw him again. Or she might never see him again. He didn't seem to like her any better now than he had before. His attitude was even colder, in a way.

He took her arm and led her out into the silky night, into the sounds of traffic and the bright lights. "I'd never get used to living in the city," he remarked as he helped her into the Mercedes and then moved to the driver's side. "I like wide spaces too much," he told her as he got in the car.

"I couldn't sleep for a long time when I first moved here," she said with a soft smile. "The sirens and horns kept me awake. It's a far cry from howling dogs and low-ing cattle."

"Yes."

She watched his face as he started the car and pulled away from the restaurant. Well, why deny herself that pleasure, she asked bitterly, when he'd be gone in a few minutes and it would be the first and last time she'd be alone with him.

He stopped at a traffic light and turned his head just a fraction of an inch to look at her. His dark eyes searched hers.

"You're staring," he said bluntly.

"I know," she replied, her voice soft and full of dreams.

He reached out and caught her hand, bringing it to his hard thigh. He held it there as he drove, letting her feel the ripple of muscle as he eased up and down on the ac-celerator, his fingers linked into hers, caressing.

By the time they reached her apartment house, his nerves were stripped and raw. He cut off the engine and turned to her, releasing her hand slowly. She was still watching his face, shadowed under the streetlight, and his heart was beating wildly with a kind of hunger that challenged every ounce of control he had.

Kate felt her pride falling away. She loved him so much. What comfort was pride when, after he left, she'd be alone for the rest of her life?

"Oh, Jacob, kiss me," she whispered, pleaded, her shy hands touching his, faintly tremulous. "Just once—!"

The words drove him crazy. He reached for her, his body on fire. He turned her face up to his, feeling fiercely male, possessive. His breath came harshly as he looked down into her hungry eyes.

"Open your mouth and put it against mine, Kathryn," he whispered huskily, drawing her face up to his.

The words thrilled as much as those hard, warm hands on her cheeks. It had been the secret longing of her life. To kiss him…

Her eyes closed on stinging tears as she obeyed him. For years she'd dreamed of this, ached for it, prayed for it. It was happening. She could feel the hard, smoky warmth of his lips as she fitted hers slowly to them, trembling a little with the sudden freedom of being allowed to love him, to express all she felt physically.

"Jacob," she breathed brokenly, sliding her hands against his shirtfront, inside the jacket which he'd unbuttoned when they'd climbed into the car. She could feel hard muscle and something springy, like hair, under the soft fabric. She moved closer, pushing upward against his mouth in aching hunger.

He eased her head against his shoulder as he slowly increased the pressure of his mouth, opening her lips fully to the sudden moist penetration of his tongue. Even in that, he was delicate, teasing before he took possession, guiding her into an intimacy that was overwhelming in its sweet pleasure.

Her fingers were still stroking over his breastbone, and she felt his hand move over them, shifting them, while he flicked the buttons open.

He put her hand into the small opening he'd made, spreading the palm over thick hair and moving it sensuously back and forth to show her the motion he liked.

The hunger grew suddenly, like a flash flood on the desert. One minute he was delicately teasing, the next, he was crushing her back against the seat and his mouth was fiercely demanding. Kate gave without reservation, in heaven at the tempestuous ardor that outmatched even her dreams. She began to moan softly, unaware of the sudden, unbearable desire that was coiling in the body of the man above her.

He drew back, his breathing faintly unsteady, his heart like a drum under her hand.

"We can't sit down here doing this all night," he whispered. His dark eyes searched her shadowed ones. "Do we go to your apartment or my hotel room? Or do I go home alone?"

It should have been the latter. She should have told him that she was a virgin, that he was asking something of her that he had no right to ask, especially considering his treatment of her. But maybe he wouldn't know. She'd been alone all her life. Wasn't she entitled to one bright memory in all that darkness? To one sweet hour in a man's arms, pretending that he loved her as much as she loved him? Surely, loving gave her that right.

"Don't...go home," she whispered.

He searched her eyes for a long moment, hiding the sweet triumph he felt at her capitulation while he tried not to wonder if she always gave in so easily to a man.

He released her and got out, opening her door for her. They went up to her apartment in a stoic silence. She felt uneasy, and the feeling got worse as she opened her apartment and let him inside.

She turned to tell him that she wasn't sure, to explain about her past. But he turned her, very slowly, expertly, so that her back was against the door. And he bent, his mouth breathing on hers, into hers, as his lips formed the very shape of her mouth and teased it.

In the soft, semidark silence of her apartment, with the outside sounds of sirens and horns fading into nothing, she felt his hands at her hips. And then his body was easing down completely on hers, pressing her back against the steely cold of the door. She felt the hardness of his body and knew instinctively what was happening to him. Her own body reacted to it in a way she'd never expected, by arching gently to press up against his hips, to encourage his ardor.

He trailed his fingers from her hip to her thigh and back up again, coaxing her to repeat the involuntary movement. And all the while, his mouth was growing more intimate with hers, tasting her in a new, tender way.

He shifted her just a little and she felt his hand at the laces that held her bodice together.

She trembled at the newness of what he was doing, a little shocked at the feel of his hands touching her there. Her eyes opened, big and curious. That amused him, because he was certain that he wasn't the first man to touch her. But she was hungry for him, and that was satisfying.

He had the last of the laces undone now, and he started to push the fabric away from her full, soft breasts, when her hand instinctively caught his wrist in a token protest.

"Don't pretend, Kate," he said softly. "I told you before, I don't want anything to do with a virgin."

That meant that he was going to walk out the door and never come back if she admitted that she was innocent. She bit her lip worriedly. Would he know when he had her in bed? Could men tell, especially experienced men? He'd be furious....

"What a look," he murmured, bending to her soft mouth. "Stop biting that lip," he whispered. "Bite mine instead."

He nibbled at her, arousing new and unexpected twinges of pleasure. She caught at his shirt when he began again to push the fabric away and she felt his fingers tracing around the edges of her breast.

"Relax," he breathed, feeling her tremble. "We've got all night. There's no hurry."

But there was, because she was frightened of having him find out the truth. She loved him. She wanted nothing more out of life than to give him a night that would haunt him all his life.

She wasn't experienced, but she was a great reader. She knew a lot about men that came from wildly romantic books, and now she drew on it.

Her hands went into his shirt, her nails drawing through that thick dark hair to the warm skin underneath. Her hips arched in a slow rhythm against his, brushing his thighs sensuously.

He shuddered, and the mouth over hers grew rough. His hand stopped its teasing and swallowed her breast whole, his palm rubbing against the hard nipple, his fingers contracting.

She felt him tremble faintly, and knew a wild fever of exultation. He was so aroused that he was losing control. She could feel it, taste it, in the sudden roughness of passion she'd aroused in him. He shifted, lowering his body, one knee finding its way between her thighs. He removed his hand from her breast and, still holding her mouth under his, stripped her to the waist. Then he was against her, his hard chest against her soft breasts, his hips against hers with a sudden intimacy that dragged a shattering cry from her throat.

She was on fire for him. His hands were on her skin now, touching her in ways she'd never dreamed a man would ever touch her. He managed to undress them both while they stood there, her mind in such a fever of tension and hunger that it was an actual relief to have his hard, warm body against hers with no barriers to the beauty of shared nudity.

His mouth was demanding, insistent, as he lifted her, finally, and carried her into the bedroom. He had barely taken time to whip off the coverlet when his body was over hers, his mouth burning on her skin as he explored every single inch of her.

By the time she felt him position her, she was trembling all over, her eyes blurred by a mist of shuddering need.

"Jacob," she moaned, tears in her eyes as she looked up into a face dark with passion, eyes so black they were almost frightening.

"Don't talk," he whispered. He pinned her down, his hands locking with hers, his hips shifting over her prone body.

"Be...careful," she managed through lips that felt parched.

"I won't hurt you," he breathed. "Just relax."

By the time she realized what he was saying, he was already becoming part of her body. She watched his face, awed by what she saw and felt. Her hips tautened, but he brushed a gentle hand over her thighs, soothing her, his eyes burning into hers.

She shuddered. It wasn't just discomfort, it was pain. He bent then and put his mouth on hers, biting into it with shuddering hunger as his body began to move jerkily.

She pushed at his chest, but it was too late. He thought her moans were pleasure; he thought her sudden, sharp, shifting movements meant she was reaching a pinnacle. Her reaction pushed him over the edge for the first time in his life. He drove for his own fulfillment, losing himself in a frenzy of passion that exploded in a fire storm of ecstasy. He cried out with the anguished force of it, his body racked by coiling muscles.

It was all he could do to protect her. He barely made it at all, gasping for just enough air to breathe, his nostrils full of the exquisite scent of her, his body resting on her silky softness, so exhausted with pleasure that he could have died and not minded.

A long time later, he became aware of broken sobs. He lifted his dark, damp head and looked down into her pale face, her eyes filled with tears.

"I hurt you?" he whispered belatedly.

She pushed at his chest. "Please…"

Her expression said it all. He rolled away, scowling. That wasn't the look of a woman who'd been loved. "Wait," he called as she started blindly toward the bathroom. "For God's sake, come back here and let me make it up to you—"

"Make it…up to me?" she whispered. "I'd rather die than let you do that again! Oh, God, how horrible!"

She ran into the bathroom and locked the door, feeling sick to her soul at what she'd let him do. It had been painful at first, and then he'd succeeded in making her feel things she wanted to forget. Great throbbing surges of pleasure that had made her feel wanton, that had made her want to bite and claw and rake him with her nails. And just as that pleasure had begun, he was already through with her. The frustration had her wild, sick with anguish. So that was sex. A woman was teased with fulfillment while a man drowned in it. It was horrible, almost to reach the sky, only to plummet down in unsatisfied anguish. And he wanted her to go through that again, just so that he could enjoy himself? She was too frustrated to begin to think straight, to understand any of it. She burst into tears.

The man dressing coldly in the next room was feeling some frustrations of his own. His lovemaking had been called a few different things over the years, but horrible was a new one. His own loss of control was what hurt the most, that he'd been that vulnerable and that she knew it.

He hadn't pleased her, but he hadn't realized just how far gone he was. If she'd been willing, he could have made it up to her. But the expression on her face, in her eyes, had been damning. He'd disappointed her. He'd…disgusted her. He zipped his trousers and shouldered furiously into his shirt. He wanted to throw things. For God's sake, didn't she realize she'd worked him into that frenzy? Why push him out of control and then complain when she didn't reach fulfillment? What had gone wrong?

He finished dressing and the more he thought about what she'd said, the madder he got. Horrible, was it? Well, she needn't worry, she'd never have to suffer him again in that respect. He combed his hair, glaring at his own reflection in the mirror, feeling more unsettled than he could ever remember.

Coming from the bathroom were muffled sounds that made his sense of frustration and confusion even worse.

"Open this door, or so help me, I'll break it down," he said in a voice that dared her to disobey.

She wrapped a bath sheet around her aching body and opened the door a fraction. She couldn't meet his eyes, so she only looked as high as his taut jaw.

"For services rendered," he said with a cold smile, and tucked a hundred-dollar bill in the bath sheet. "Maybe that will make up for your lack of enjoyment."

And he turned and stormed out the door, leaving her in tears of mingled disappointment and cold fury.

It didn't occur to her, because she knew nothing about men in intimate situations, that his own frustration and guilt and wounded male vanity, coupled with an unprecedented loss of control, had caused him to make that final insulting gesture. She took it at face value. All those years of loving him, wanting him, and this was how it had ended. He'd only wanted her body. He hadn't even known that she was innocent. He'd used her and then walked out without a kind word.

She bathed the scent of him from her body and pulled on a granny gown that covered her from head to toe. She stripped the bed, threw the sheets into the washing machine and went to sleep on her sofa. As she cried herself to sleep, she wondered if she'd ever be able to look at that bed again, much less sleep on it.

The next morning, what she'd done hit her right between the eyes the instant she woke up. She was a fallen woman. At least, that's what her father would have called her. It was probably what Jacob thought, too.

She got up and got dressed for work, her mind and body aching, haunted by guilt and bitterness about her own weakness. Now she was going to have to sweat it out, because despite what she imagined was his attempt to take precautions, there was still a chance that she could become pregnant.

Oddly enough, the thought of having Jacob's child, despite what he'd done to her, wasn't at all disturbing. It would be nice to have something small and sweet to protect and cuddle. It would be nice to have someone of her own. Then reality surfaced, and she could imagine herself trying to keep such an event secret from her own brother, Margo—and Jacob. If she realized the possibilities, he must, too. Despite his anger, he'd keep up with her through Tom. If she got pregnant, he'd know. And the world would end. She had no intention of being forced to marry him because of a baby. She'd run away to Africa with the Peace Corps. She'd sign on as a gunrunner. She'd… It was eight o'clock in the morning, for God's sake. She'd be late!

She got to the office just in time to be sent out on assignment to a fire. It was a small one, thank God, and no injuries occurred. But she liked the oblivion of being caught up in the dark excitement. And when she got back to the office, she went and asked the managing editor if there wasn't a slot open on the police beat.

"Sure," Morgan Winthrop told her. "But do you think you'd like that kind of thing, Kate? It's a pretty gory job."

"Let me try," she pleaded.

"Okay," he said after a minute. "It's yours."

She could have kissed him. Now she'd have something to occupy her mind, something to keep her on her toes and away from memories that would destroy her. Eventually she might have to cope with the devastation Jacob had wrought on her emotions, but not just yet.

Tom called her a week later, but she didn't tell him anything about her disastrous date with Jacob or her new assignment. He was working on a big new account at the ad agency and would be out of town for a week or so. But he was going to stop by to spend a couple of days with her on the way back, if she didn't mind. Of course not, she assured him, grateful that it wouldn't be right away. She was going to need a little time to cope with her fall from grace.

It was hectic, getting into the routine of the new job. She worked with Bud Schuman, the police reporter who'd often regaled her with tales of old Chicago. He seemed to be at least sixty years old, but she never dared ask his age. He might be ninety.

He kept a police radio with a few forbidden crystals in it that picked up channels he shouldn't have had access to.

"Now, now, it's not exactly dishonest," he told her. "It's psychic. At least, that's what I tell the police when they want to know how I found out something. That's another thing, sweet, never ask them if there's anything going on. Ask them if a particular thing is going on and if they've made an arrest. You can always check the police blotter if you have to."

It was an experience, she found, working with the veteran reporter. He seemed to know everyone at the local police precinct, as well as the civil defense people, the ambulance services personnel, the firemen and rescue workers and even most of the secretaries. He taught her little loopholes in information gathering that she'd never have suspected and ways of digging out facts that were nothing short of mystifying.

As Morgan Winthrop had warned her, it could be a gory job. There were murders and suicides and traffic fatalities. There were on-the-job accidents and people incinerated in fires. There were drowning victims and abused children and the occasional shoot-out. At times, the job was even a bit dangerous. But it gave Kate very little time to think, and that made it acceptable.

The only bad times were at night, when she was alone in her apartment. She'd accepted a date with Roger Dean just to get out and away from the ghost that haunted her, but it had been a minor disaster. She and Roger had nothing in common except reporting, and although they had enough stories to tear apart and comment on, their personal views of life were poles apart. Kate found herself thinking of Jacob when she was with Roger. It wasn't really fair to compare other men with Jacob, anyway. He was one of a kind.

She wondered if Jacob ever thought about the night he'd spent with her, or wondered afterward about her reaction to it. It must have wounded his pride to think that she'd found him "horrible," especially when she hadn't explained what she meant. But what he'd done to her was even worse. She'd kept that hundred-dollar bill as a reminder, so that she wouldn't ever again forget what kind of man he was. She should have listened to Tom's warning. He'd known from the beginning what Jacob was up to, and she hadn't. She'd thrown away all her ideals for that one magic "night to live on." And it had been a nightmare of discomfort, embarrassment and guilt. Even now, she flushed every time she thought about it. She'd even gone so far as to trade the bed for a new one, just to rid herself of the memory.

If only she could keep Jacob out of her mind. She knew him now in every way there was. How he made love. What he looked like in passion. Every inch of that magnificent body without the civilizing veneer of clothing. Her eyes closed. It had started to be so beautiful, and then her own fear of his realizing that she was a virgin had driven her to arouse him beyond his control. She wondered if that loss of control was normal. She knew so little about men. Perhaps any of them could go crazy in a woman's arms, but she hadn't expected Jacob to be so vulnerable.

The one thing she had to be thankful for was that she wasn't pregnant. She'd known only a week later that she had nothing to worry about on that score. But the guilt continued.

On the evening that Tom arrived, she'd just covered a grisly murder that had terrorist connections. An underground radical group had apparently murdered a Middle Eastern family in town and Kate wondered if she'd ever forget what she'd seen in their home. It was that kind of story that made her new job less than perfect. It was one thing to see crimes solved, but quite another to see the graphic results of them.

"You look whacked, Sis," Tom remarked over the small meal she'd prepared for them. "Hard day?"

"Harder than I can tell you," she sighed. "I've got a new beat. I think it's beating me," she added humorously.

"What are you doing now?"

"Police beat," she said in between bites. "We had a massacre today."

Tom put his fork down. "That's no job for you," he said. He searched her face. "What's happened? Something's gone wrong, hasn't it?"

She wanted to tell him, to confide in him as she had when they were children. But this was too personal, too intimate, to share even with a brother.

She dropped her green eyes to the table, ruffling her hair. She'd had it all cut off the day after her date with Jacob, another vain attempt to kill the memories. It was very short, and it gave her a sophisticated look. She was more mature now, and her eyes had a haunted look that added to it.

"I'm all right," she said.

"Are you in trouble?" he asked bluntly.

She bit her lower lip. "No."

"I didn't mean that kind of trouble," he said with an amused smile. "You're not the liberated kind. You'd never sleep with a man without marriage."

Boy, was he in for a shock. She studied her fingernails. "Well, Tom, actually—"

The sudden jangling of the phone made her jump. She got up and went to answer it, her heart running away. Every time it rang, she expected it to be Jacob, God knew why. It never was, of course. It never would be.

She lifted it. "Hello?"

"It's Bud," her coworker said abruptly. "I've just fallen down the steps and twisted my damned ankle. I can't walk. The police have cornered that bunch that killed the family." He gave her the address, which she scribbled down on a piece of paper. "Got your camera? Harvey may send a photographer, but there was nobody on the place when I left. Get going, girl, you may get an exclusive! I was tipped off!"

"You bet!" she told him. "I'm on my way."

She hung up, her eyes unnaturally bright as she searched for her camera and checked to see that the batteries were fresh and everything worked. "I've got to run out for a few minutes," she told Tom, who was watching her curiously. "The police have nabbed the gang that killed that family I told you about. I'll be back as soon as I can."

"I don't like this," Tom said curtly. "And there's something I have to tell you. I didn't just happen along by accident. Jacob asked me to come."

She gaped at him, her face going white, her eyes huge. "Jacob?" she whispered.

He frowned. "What the hell's going on?" he demanded. "He wasn't even coherent. Well, he was, but he kept saying something about making a decision and that he wanted to talk to you, but he knew you wouldn't open the door to him if I didn't come."

She stared wildly around. "Jacob—coming here?" she asked in a choking tone.

"Yes. Tonight. That's what I was leading up to—" he began again.

"I have to go." Her hands trembled. She clutched the camera and grabbed up her purse. "I'll be back when I can."

"Can't someone else do this for you?" he asked helplessly.

"No. Goodbye, Tom." She glanced at him from the door, her face ashen, and then she was gone, a blur of jeans and jacket.

It wasn't fifteen minutes later that Jacob arrived. Tom let him into the apartment, his eyes haunted, his face drawn. Jacob didn't look much better.

"She isn't here," Tom told the older man. "There's some kind of police bust going on. She's down there with a camera getting the story."

Jacob glared at Tom. "She was doing politics, wasn't she? What in hell is she doing covering police news?"

Tom watched him closely from his armchair. "That's what I wanted to know. She wouldn't tell me."

Jacob went to the window, restless and oddly hesitant. He opened the curtain and stared out, his tan suit straining against hard muscle. "No, I guess she wouldn't," he said.

"It's none of my business," Tom began, watching the taller man. "But there's something you need to know about Kate. I don't think you'd be cold-blooded enough to seduce her, but there are things you have to understand, just in case the thought crosses your mind. So I'm going to tell you about it. Our father was a lay minister."

The broad back stiffened. The face Tom couldn't see had gone a pasty white. "Was he?"

"He had a brain tumor. Our mother left when we were young, because she had the misfortune to fall in love with another man. There was no affair. She divorced our father before she remarried, but he got custody because of his religious affiliation. The court didn't know, you see, that he was crazier than a bedbug."

Jacob had turned and he stared at Tom without speaking.

Tom got up, stuck his hands in his pockets and paced. "He drummed morality into us until Kate and I were terrified of sex. He made it into something incredibly bad. His mind was going, of course. He loved our mother and she'd betrayed him. All that worked toward making him worse. In the end, Kate smiled at a boy at a supermarket, and our father beat her right there in public with a belt. It took three men to stop him, and he went into convulsions. He died right there."

Jacob sat down heavily in a chair, his eyes wild.

Tom stood over him. "Kate should have told you. I had to, in case you've got some half-baked idea of seducing her. She's so much in love with you that she just might give in. But afterward… She's carrying so many scars from childhood, I don't know what she might do."

"In…love with me?" Jacob was ash white.

"Don't tell me you didn't know?" Tom shook his head. "Honest to God, Jacob, everybody knows. There's never been a man in Kate's life except you. She's got pictures of you that she begged from Margo hidden all over the apartment. I'll bet money there's one even here—aha." He opened the drawer in a small table by Jacob and produced a dog-eared photograph of Jacob on a horse, one that Margo had taken years ago.

Jacob put his head in his hands. He felt sick to his soul. "She's a virgin, isn't she," he said dully, stating it, not even asking.

"She and I both are," Tom said without embarrassment. "Those kinds of scars are hard to get rid of. I expect I'll marry someday, regardless. But it will take one hell of a woman to accept me the way I am. It'll take one hell of a man to accept Kate."

Jacob wanted to jump out the window. He couldn't remember a time in his life when he ever felt suicidal, but he felt that way now. He remembered Kate's odd reluctance to be touched, and then her reaction to him, her final words. Of course he'd hurt her, and he'd made it worse…that hundred-dollar bill.

He stood up, his face like rice paper, his eyes blazing. "Oh, my God," he breathed. He looked at Tom. "My God, why didn't you tell me?"

Tom frowned slightly. "You seemed to dislike her..." he began.

"Dislike her." Jacob's voice was haunted, his eyes as dead as winter leaves. "I'd have walked over fire to get to her. But I couldn't let her see how I felt. A man can't give a woman that kind of hold on him, Tom!"

Tom stared at him blankly. It was all such a puzzle. Kate's distraught attitude, Jacob's shock at learning the truth. What was going on?

The buzz for the front door downstairs was as loud as a bomb in the silence of the apartment. No one could get into the apartment building unless the person in the apartment they wanted to visit pushed a button to open the outside door. Tom and Jacob exchanged glances. "Maybe she forgot her key," Tom said. He pressed the button. "Yes?"

"Police," came the terse reply. "Is there a Tom Walker here?"

Tom glanced at Jacob, his face a study in fear. "Yes. I'm Tom Walker. Come on up." He pressed the button.

Jacob didn't know how he was going to live with what he'd learned tonight. And if something had happened to Kate, before he had time to try and make it up to her...

Tom opened the door on the first knock. A tall, uniformed man stood there. The expression on his face spoke volumes.

"It's my sister, Kate, isn't it?" Tom asked with terror in his voice.

The man nodded. "There was a shoot-out when the terrorists made a break for it. One of the men had an

Uzi automatic. Kate was behind a sign. The bullets penetrated. We had her taken to the hospital."

"She's still alive?" Jacob asked from behind Tom, his
voice odd.

"She was when the ambulance left," the policeman
continued. He searched Tom's white face. "I'm sorry. I
think it was a gut wound."

Tom stared at him blankly, but Jacob didn't. His hands
were clenched at his side and he exchanged a look with
the policeman that was all too knowing.

"I'll drive you to the hospital," Jacob said quietly.

"Yes…if you would." Tom turned to thank the policeman.

"I've only known young Kate for two years," the griz-
zled veteran said. "But she's quite a girl. If you tell her
something in confidence, she'll keep it to herself. Not a
lot of people in any profession can do that—especially
reporters. I'm sorry. I liked her."

He nodded and left them to follow.

"Why put it like that?" Tom growled as Jacob locked
the door behind them, his heart like lead in a body that
had gone numb with shock. "Why use the past tense?"

"You don't know what a gut wound means," Jacob
said dully. "I do."

Tom looked at him and seemed to go even paler. "No,"
he whispered. "Oh, no."

"Maybe he was mistaken," Jacob said. His hopes lifted
faintly at the thought. "Let's go and see."

"If you know how to pray, we might try that," Tom
murmured.

Try it? Jacob hadn't stopped since the ordeal began.
He led the younger man down to the elevator, think-

ing blindly that if Kate died, he didn't want to go on living. The thought was as shocking as what had happened to her.

Chapter 5

Kate was just going into surgery by the time Tom and Jacob got to the hospital. Tom thought privately that they might have done better to take a cab. Jacob's driving was none too confidence inspiring even on good days, and the older man had almost wrecked the car twice getting there. Nothing showed on that impassive face, but Jacob's eyes were terrible to look into. For a man who had vowed never to let any woman get a hold on him, Jacob looked for all the world as if Kate had a good grip.

Tom went to the emergency desk to ask for news while Jacob sat numbly on a vinyl-covered sofa. The waiting room was filled full with ragged-looking young men, and a few babies crying miserably while their mothers shifted them and looked resigned and worn. Jacob glanced at one of the babies, a chubby little one with a smile on its face, and found himself smiling tenderly at it. He'd always thought that one day he'd have a child, but he'd never been able to commit himself to marry anyone. And then it occurred to him that he might have made Kate pregnant.

He'd tried to protect her, but it was a halfhearted measure at best. It suddenly occurred to him that if he had given her a baby, he might have cost two lives with his misguided desire. He got up abruptly and stared toward Tom.

The younger man was talking to a man in green cotton pants and shirt. The older man looked grave and shrugged when Tom asked a somber question. He patted Tom on the shoulder, smiled reassuringly and walked away.

"Well?" Jacob asked quickly, his eyes dark and haunted.

"That was the surgeon," Tom mumbled. He leaned against the cold wall and stared ahead at the opposite wall. His eyes were wet. "They're going to do an emergency exploratory to see how much damage the bullet did. We won't know anything for about an hour."

"How is she?" Jacob's dark eyes narrowed with worry.

"In pain," Tom replied tersely. "It hit a rib and punctured her lung. The lung collapsed."

"Poor little thing," Jacob said, closing his eyes.

"I feel sick all over," Tom said blankly. "Jacob, she's all I've got."

Jacob stared at him. "What about the man who did it?"

"Two of the terrorists were killed, the rest are in custody. It could have been any one of them. Nobody knows." He folded his arms across his chest and sighed restlessly. "I still don't understand how it happened. Kate's never been interested in doing police news. She hates that sort of thing, but apparently she requested the job."

Jacob turned away, his face expressionless. He knew why she'd taken the job, all right. Kate had been looking, consciously or subconsciously, for a way out, an escape from the guilt she surely must have felt. Her sense of anguish had been compounded by his own callous treatment of her. That hundred-dollar bill was going to haunt him for the rest of his life, whether she lived or died. He'd never felt so sick or frightened, and there was absolutely nothing he could do.

A balding older man with a cane hobbled toward them, pale and anxious. He went right past Tom and Jacob to the information clerk. "Kate Walker," he began breathlessly, "how is she? Do they know anything yet?"

Tom and Jacob glanced at him. "That must be the reporter whose place she took," Tom began. "He hurt his ankle—"

Jacob's eyes flashed black murder. With an economy of motion he went for the older man.

"Jacob, no!" Tom burst out. He dived toward the taller man, yelling for assistance. Two other men from the waiting room helped, and it took all three of them.

The reporter stared at Jacob, aghast, his face going even paler. "Let him loose, boys," he said quietly. "God knows I deserve it. I never should have called her to go in my place."

Jacob shrugged off the other men, but he stood quietly, breathing heavily.

The man hobbled closer. "You must be her brother," he said to Jacob. "I'm Bud Schuman. Kate works with me. I'm so damned sorry—"

"I'm her brother," Tom interrupted, moving forward with a faint smile and a wary glance at Jacob. "And Kate wouldn't blame you, Mr. Schuman. You're a hero of hers. She talks about you all the time."

"I hope she'll talk about me again, even if she cusses a blue streak the whole time," Bud said miserably. "I'm just so sorry. I never think about the risk, you see. I've done this most of my life. And Kate, forgive me, is just one of the boys at the office. We never think of her as a woman. That's why Winthrop gave her the police beat."

Even as he spoke, Morgan Winthrop came storming through the emergency room door. He needed a shave and he looked as if he'd been dragged out of bed.

"Why the hell didn't you call Joey Bradshaw?" Winthrop demanded. "He was sitting home watching reruns of *My Three Sons*, and he carries a piece. At least he could have shot back! So help me God, I ought to slug you, Schuman!"

"Wait your turn," Bud Schuman mused miserably. "There's already a line forming." He indicated a still-smoldering Jacob and a quiet, anguished Tom.

Winthrop glanced at them. "Family, I gather? What can I say?" He jammed his big hands in his raincoat pockets. "Do they know any more now than they did five minutes ago?"

Tom shook his head.

"Sergeant Kovic told me she'd been hit in the abdomen," Winthrop continued gravely.

"Rib cage," Tom countered. "They're taking her into surgery now to see how much damage there is. The bullet passed through a sign, but it came from an automatic Uzi—an illegal weapon with apparently strong velocity. We don't know how bad it is, but the least she's got is a collapsed lung."

Winthrop grimaced. "Poor kid. She's a hell of a reporter, you know. Does features, politics, even the police beat with a flair. Cops like her, too. They'll tell her things that Schuman here can't pry out of them with a fork."

"That's a fact," Bud said. "They like her because she never lies to them. She does exactly what she says she will. Kate never lies."

Jacob turned away. He'd known Kate for eleven years, and strangers knew her better than he did. It was a sobering, painful fact.

"Who is he?" Schuman asked Tom when Jacob was out of earshot. "My God, I thought my number was up before you slowed him down."

"Jacob Cade," Tom replied. "He's a neighbor of ours back home."

"Thought I recognized him," Bud murmured. He smiled sheepishly. "Kate keeps a photo of him in her desk."

"Kate keeps photos of him everywhere." Tom sighed. He stared at the taller man. "I never expected it to hit him this hard. I thought he hated her."

"Hate and love are first cousins," Winthrop said philosophically. He studied the rigid back of the pacing man. "I know how he feels. I've been there." He lifted his shoulders heavily. "How about some coffee? It looks like a long night."

For another hour, Jacob paced while Winthrop and Tom and Bud Schuman sat and reminisced about Kate. And then, all at once, the waiting was over.

They gathered around the surgeon quickly.

"She'll make it," the surgeon told Tom, smiling. "The bullet broke a rib and went through the lower lobe of her lung, where it tore some tissue—we had to remove that lower lobe, but she'll never miss it. We put in a drainage tube to reinflate the lung and drain it and we're giving her blood. Amazing." He shook his head. "Two inches lower and it would have been fatal. Two inches to the outside, and it would have missed her altogether. But she's a pretty fortunate young lady, just the same."

Tom sighed. "Can I see her?"

"She wouldn't know you were there," the surgeon replied. "She'll be in intensive care for tonight, and if she does all right, we'll move her into a private room tomorrow. You can come back in the morning and see her." He clasped the younger man's arm. "Go home and sleep, if you can. I imagine it's been a bad time for you."

"It has. Thanks for all you've done," Tom said with a weary smile. "And I'll go home, but I won't sleep."

The surgeon smiled and walked away.

"Thank God," Bud Schuman sighed. "My God, when they said she'd been hit in the stomach, I thought she was done for. Obviously, she doubled up when the bullet hit..." His mumbled remark was interrupted by an accidental shove from his boss, who saw the horror in Tom's young eyes. Shoptalk wasn't for outsiders. Newsmen got an education in forensic medicine along with a good basic knowledge of clinical details from working with police and coroners.

"Say good-night, Schuman, and let's go. I'll even drive you." Winthrop shook hands with Tom. "I'll keep in touch. Try to get some rest. Call me if I can help."

"Thanks," Tom said.

Winthrop and Schuman left, and Jacob moved to the waiting area, half-empty now.

"Let's go," Tom said. "I've left the phone number with the desk. They'll call if there's any change."

Jacob turned, his eyes dark and full of pain. "I did that to her," he said numbly.

"Listen, you can't love to order," Tom said with blissful ignorance of what had really happened between Kate and the man standing near him. "Life isn't that simple. Kate will get over you, and she'll be fine. She just needs a little time."

"I hope she has it," Jacob said quietly. "Oh, God, I hope she does."

"I'll make us an omelet," Tom offered as they left the hospital. "Good thing I can cook, or we'd starve by morning."

Back in the apartment, Jacob paced some more. Restlessly, he glanced around the room, learning new things about Kate all the time. He saw what she liked to read, that she did handcrafts, that she loved gardening, that she fed birds outside her window on the small ledge. He learned about the people she'd helped and the affection her neighbors had for her by the bits and pieces of her life scattered around the apartment. And there was no resemblance at all between this woman and the shadowy figure of her he'd built up in his mind.

"Stop worrying, will you?" Tom asked after they'd eaten and he'd watched Jacob push food around on his plate. "Nothing is going to change what happened. We need some sleep. I'll take the guest room and you can sleep in Kate's bed."

"No," Jacob said shortly. He turned away, lowering his voice. "No. I'll stay in the guest room."

"All right," Tom said, trying to figure out the older man's odd reaction. "No problem. I'll set the alarm in time to have breakfast before we leave for the hospital."

"Yes." Jacob walked out of the room, grateful that Tom couldn't read the expression in his eyes. Sleep in Kate's bed, with those memories all around… Hell couldn't have been more unwelcome. He hadn't noticed that she'd replaced the bed.

But he didn't sleep. By five o'clock in the morning, he couldn't stand it any longer. He dressed, scribbled a note for Tom and left the apartment.

The nurse in the intensive care unit was a crusty old veteran named Gates, but Jacob got to her. Despite the fact that it wasn't visiting hours, she allowed him ten minutes, without really knowing why. It was something in those dark, tortured eyes. This was a man who wanted absolution, and that young woman he'd come to see wasn't responding as well as Nurse Gates would have liked. Sometimes there was a healing power in a caring voice—the philosophy wasn't based on medical evidence, but it was often true. So she broke a lifelong rule and let him into the small cubicle.

Jacob had only been in a hospital twice—once when his mother had died, and once to visit Kate's grandmother just before she died. But those visits had been nothing like what he was now facing. Kate was hooked to a dozen tubes and wires, and machines made humming, throbbing, whispering noises around her pale, quiet body.

She was stretched out under crisp white sheets in a regulation hospital gown, her hair short now and unwashed, her face pinched and white, her eyes closed, long lashes against pale skin. He looked down at the soft mouth he'd kissed so hungrily, at the body his had possessed, at the slender hands that had clung to him, adored him. He drew in a shuddering breath. Kate.

He drew up the single chair in the cubicle and tossed his gray Stetson onto the floor with careless indifference. He took Kate's free hand—the one that wasn't attached to tubes and wires—in his, and turned it over to look at it. It was cool, and the nails were short, smooth and devoid of color. It was long-fingered, strong for a woman's hand, graceful.

"What a hell of a place for Kate Walker to be," he said, his deep voice quiet and soothing in the mechanical orchestra around him as he spoke to her, just as if she could hear him. "You don't even like mechanical things, do you, Kate? Bird feeders on the window and plants all over the apartment, gardening books on the shelves. No, this isn't your kind of place at all. You need sunlight and open land and room to plant things."

He shifted in the chair, twining her hand slowly into his, studying the way her fingers looked against his, their pale length so natural looking in his firm grasp. "I never knew you at all, did I?" he murmured. "I heard your co-workers talking about you and until then, I don't guess I really thought of you as a person. As a woman, sure. I've wanted you for a long time, Kate. A long, long time. Ever since I saw you kissing Gerald what's-his-name in my swimming pool and found you nude in his arms in the bathhouse, I've been obsessed with you. And once Margo was out of the picture, I figured you were fair game. I could satisfy the hunger I've always felt and you'd stop haunting me."

His face hardened. "But it didn't work out that way. I said some hard things, and you don't even know why I was so cruel that night. It was because I sensed the truth about you. Oh, yes, damn it, I knew deep down that you were innocent, but I was so hungry for you that I wouldn't listen to my conscience. And now it's killing me, Kate."

He cupped her hand in both of his and lifted his eyes to her still figure in the bed. "You see, I didn't know that you loved me," he said, his voice slow and tender and deep with wonder. "My God, nobody ever loved me!" he bit off. "Not like that. There were pictures of me all over the apartment…." He paused, staring blankly at her hand. Somewhere inside, pain was racking him. "Then I knew just how badly I'd hurt you all these years. Accusations, indifference, sarcasm… And you took it all, like a lady. You loved me, and I hurt you in every way there was. That's the hardest thing of all to live with."

His fingers curled hungrily around hers. "Tom doesn't even know why I feel guilty. He doesn't know why you asked for the police beat, but I do. Anything dangerous, isn't that how it goes, Kate? I've tried that route myself these past three weeks. I almost wrecked the car twice, I've ridden murderous stallions, I've started fights. It hasn't been any easier for me than it's been for you. The guilt is killing me. And now this. If you die, how will I go on living? And what if you're carrying my child?" he added quietly, voicing the fear that had driven him here before dawn. "Oh, Kate, I'm…alone. I never minded before. But now…"

He drew her palm to his lips, cherishing it with his mouth, his dark head bent, the hunger in him like a living, breathing thing, and no longer only physical. "Don't die, Kate." His voice broke abruptly, and he paused until he could control it. His fingers tensed and he felt sick and apprehensive. "I don't think I can live in a world that doesn't have you in it somewhere, even if you hate me for the rest of your life."

There was a faint movement in the hand he was holding. He lifted his dark head and looked. Yes. Her fingers had tried to close around his. He stood up slowly, his eyes on her pale, quiet face. She was breathing strongly now, with a steady rhythm. And as he watched, she stirred. Her eyes opened, but they didn't see him. She groaned.

Before he could call Nurse Gates, she was in the room. She patted him on the shoulder. "Good man," she said. "That was just what she needed, to know that someone wanted her to live. Go and have breakfast. She'll be fine now. I've been a nurse for twenty-five years, and believe me, I know a patient on the mend when I see one. This one will go home."

Jacob tried to speak, but he couldn't quite manage the words. He couldn't remember ever being so choked with emotion. Instead, he bent and brushed a kiss against the leathery old cheek and winked.

She smiled up at him, eighteen again for a space of seconds, then turned back to her patient, and Jacob went out of the unit and down the hall to phone Tom.

Kate was out of the intensive care unit by early the next day. But only Tom was allowed in to see her. He didn't have the heart to tell Jacob that Kate had almost had hysterics at just the mention of the older man's name. Letting him into her room had been out of the question.

But at the end of the second day, Jacob asked about it. And Tom took a deep breath and told him the truth.

Jacob hadn't really expected her to remember what he'd said to her in the intensive care unit. In a way, it was a relief, because he'd been vulnerable with her, and that irked him. He'd let his guard down. But never again. So she didn't want him to visit. Well, they'd see.

He sat back down in the waiting room, picking up a copy of *Field and Stream* to thumb through.

"Jacob, you did understand what I said?" Tom asked hesitantly.

"I understood. But she'll see me sooner or later, if I have to sit here until hell freezes over." He smiled vaguely in Tom's direction and kept reading.

"Why do you want to?"

Jacob didn't look up. "I don't know."

"Terrific answer," Tom mumbled as he walked away.

Jacob looked after him with dark, troubled eyes. How could he have confided to Tom that he had to know if Kate was pregnant? With a heavy sigh, he stared blankly down at the magazine. And maybe it was more than that. He wanted to see her moving, see her eyes open, even if they were filled with hatred. He wanted to see for himself that she was all right before he left town. He'd have to go back soon. Work was piling up. But right now, Kate was what mattered the most.

When Tom went back into the room, she was propped up in bed, still a little drowsy from the medication, favoring the left side of her rib cage, which was bandaged. They'd made a small incision about six-inches long beside the bullet hole for the exploratory surgery. It was held together by staples, of all things, and it was sore, like her broken rib. There hadn't been anything they could do about her rib, but they would put her in a rib belt when the drainage tube came out in three or four days, and that would hold it in place until it healed.

"He won't go home," Tom said from the doorway, smiling. "He says he'll sit there until hell freezes over or until you decide to talk to him, whichever comes first."

Kate stared at her hands on the sheet, trying to ignore the wild beating of her heart. Jacob's stubbornness was unexpected. But why should he want to see her? She thought of the hundred-dollar bill and was surprised at how much the memory hurt, despite all that had happened in the meantime.

"He may have a long wait," she said drowsily. "I don't want to talk to him."

Tom took the chair beside her bed and sat down. She did look like hell, he thought. She was pale and drawn, and her dark hair had no luster at all. Her lips were faintly cracked with dryness and her eyes were deep-shadowed with pain and fatigue. But, then, Jacob didn't look much better himself. He frowned.

"Kate, what's going on?" he asked gently.

Her thin eyebrows shot up. "What do you mean?"

"Something happened between you and Jacob. He's been like a wild man since you got shot. Bud Schuman came into the waiting room and it took three of us to keep Jacob from killing him."

Surprise after surprise, she thought numbly. She stared at her brother with wide, curious eyes. "Jacob did?"

"He sat with you in the intensive care unit, too," he added quietly. "I don't know what he said, but apparently they think whatever it was helped get you back on the right track."

She shifted, grimacing. "I don't remember."

"I guess not. You were pretty much out of it about then. Thank God for modern medicine and the sign that slowed the bullet down a little before it hit you."

"It wasn't Bud's fault," she said.

"You're the only person with that particular point of view," he assured her. "Winthrop threatened to fire him, and he wasn't too pleased with himself, either."

"Did someone get the story?"

"You were the story," he replied. "Front page and a banner headline."

"I told you I'd get the front page one day," she smiled wanly.

"What a heck of a way to go about it," he said with a grin. He leaned forward, holding her hand. "Jacob hurt you somehow, is that it?"

She forced herself to meet his eyes and smile. "We had a horrible argument," she said, then added, "which I don't want to discuss."

"Oh." He shrugged. "Well, you don't have to worry about having him make sarcastic remarks about your morals anymore, at least. I set him straight. I told him everything."

She went two shades paler and her heart stopped beating. "What did he say?" she asked in a whisper.

"He didn't say anything, actually." He studied her face.

"He went as white as you just did and the one glimpse I got of his eyes was enough." He paused for a minute. "Yes, I know, Kate, we agreed that we'd never tell anyone. But Jacob isn't anyone. And you love him."

Her eyes widened, darkened. "Oh, Tom, you didn't tell him that, did you?" she asked, and her whole expression was pleading.

She'd been through enough already, he thought, and Jacob wouldn't mention it. Why make it worse? "Would I tell him something like that?" he said, evading the question.

"I hope you wouldn't," she replied. "I don't have a lot of pride left."

"He'll sit there for a week if he has to, you know," Tom said after a minute.

She stared at him without speaking. He didn't know why Jacob wanted to see her, but she did. And because she did, she gave in, fighting the nervousness and apprehension she felt at having to see Jacob again.

"All right," she said. "Let him come in. But only for five minutes."

He smiled. "Be right back."

Kate sat and watched the door, her eyes unnaturally wide, her face even whiter and more strained than it had been. And minutes later, the door opened slowly and she bit her lip to keep from crying. Jacob had hurt her terribly, and not just physically. Over and over again, she'd heard his bitter words, felt the cold rustle of that hundred-dollar bill he'd put in the towel against her breasts. It was all she could do not to break down at just the sight of him.

Chapter 6

It was impossible to look into those dark eyes. After one quick glance at his rigid features, she averted her gaze to his boots. Gray boots, highly polished, crafted with expensive hand-tooled leather, they matched the hat dangling idly from his lean hand. A Stetson, too; she recognized the distinct JBS-initialed silver pin and feather hatband decoration of the true Stetson. Jacob never wore any other kind of hat.

"How are you?" he asked as he approached the bed.

Her heart pounded wildly, her breath caught in her dry throat. "They say I'll be fine in about six weeks or so."

"That isn't what I asked."

He was much too close. She could smell the particularly spicy brand of after-shave he wore, and a faint leathery scent on top of it. He was wearing a dark blue suit, and she hated noticing how it flattered his dark complexion.

"I hurt," she said curtly.

"Yes, I know, Kate."

Surely that note in his voice wasn't tenderness. But she had to look and see, and the minute she lifted her eyes, his dark ones trapped them.

"You're still pale, but at least you're conscious this time," he murmured.

"What do you want, Jacob?" she asked tersely.

"To see for myself that you're healing properly." His dark eyes dropped to the sheet her slender hands were clutching. "You came close to the edge."

"I'll be all right. You can stop feeling guilty. I'm tough."

He smiled faintly. "You've had to be, haven't you?" he asked, and his eyes held new knowledge of her.

"Tom shouldn't have told you," she returned. She felt shaky inside, having him know about the past. "I've never even talked to Margo about it."

"You do realize that if I'd known, I'd never have made any snap judgments about you, despite the circumstances?" he asked gently.

"You enjoy thinking the worst of me."

He shrugged. "I guess it seemed that way to you." He twirled the hat in his fingers and stared at her for a long moment.

"I'm not pregnant," she told him bluntly, flushing a little as she guessed correctly the question he was about to ask. "That should make you very happy."

He pulled up the chair beside the bed and sat down in it slowly. He crossed his legs and rested the hat on one knee. His hand automatically reached for a cigarette and just as quickly withdrew without it. Her lung hadn't completely inflated. The tube, which was still draining fluid out of the lung they'd operated on, wouldn't come out until the X rays showed that the lung was fully inflated again, or so the surgeon had told him and Tom.

"Babies shouldn't be made that way," he said finally, leaning back to watch her reaction. "Not out of a man's blind passion and selfish motives. I know you hate my guts, Kate, and I don't blame you. The way I treated you that night was unforgivable. If it helps, I'll never get over handing you that hundred-dollar bill. I haven't slept an entire night since."

She lowered her eyes to the high polish of his boots and felt her body tremble with reaction as the memory came washing over her. Jacob, touching her, kissing her, his body rigid with passion...

"I don't want to remember," she whispered fiercely.

He knew why, too, and just barely escaped a heated reply. But God knew, she was entitled to a little retribution. He'd hurt her terribly that night. He dropped his hat on the floor and leaned forward. "Come home with me, Kathryn."

Her body stiffened convulsively under the sheet. "What?"

"You can't stay by yourself in Chicago. Tom's got to go back to work in a few days. You won't have anybody to take care of you."

"I can take care of myself," she said tightly. "Thank you just the same."

He got up, towering over her, his eyes deeply troubled as he reached down and took her hand in his, refusing to let go even when she tried to withdraw it.

"Don't fight me," he said tautly. "I'm all too aware that I helped put you here. At least let me try to make up for it in the only way I can."

Her face felt hot. She stared at his white shirt, hating

her own embarrassment and shame. Her eyes closed. "Go away, Jacob."

"A bullet might be kinder than sending me away."

She frowned and opened her eyes to stare up at him. He didn't look as if he were kidding. His face showed nothing of what he felt, but his eyes were haunted.

"I have to do something, Kate," he said quietly. "I know you hate me, but—"

"Oh, no," she said. Her eyes ran over his dark face like hands. "No, it isn't…hatred." She lowered her gaze to the strong hand holding hers. "It isn't even completely your fault. I could have stopped you if I'd told you the truth. I knew that. But there had been too many years of antagonism. I was too embarrassed to talk to you about my hang-ups, and afterward…" The color blazed in her face. "I wanted to die," she whispered, and the tears stung her eyes suddenly. "I'm so ashamed."

"Kate." There was an anguished tone in his voice. He brought her hand to his mouth and kissed the palm hotly, hungrily. "Honey, don't. Please don't."

She turned her face into the pillow and the tears flooded down her cheeks. He bent over her, his free hand gently smoothing her hair, his lips touching her forehead, her eyebrows, her closed eyes. She smelled him, could almost taste him. No, she thought, he felt only pity and guilt for her, and she didn't want those emotions from him.

"No," she pleaded. Her eyes opened, wide and dark green, frightened eyes that had a hunted look. "Jacob, I don't want—"

He put a long finger across her pale lips. His eyes searched hers much too intensely. "Kate, I've never tried to be gentle," he said hesitantly, as if he were finding the words with difficulty. "I'm not even sure I know how. Don't push me away before I get started."

"I don't want pity," she whispered tearfully.

"Neither do I," he whispered back. He traced her lips with his finger, fascinated by the way they pursed at the light movement. "Do you like that?" he asked absently.

She had to hold on to her pride. She had to remember how horrible he'd been to her. His finger tracing her lips was making it difficult to think.

"Yes, you do like it, don't you?" he breathed. He bent his dark head and watched her eyes close helplessly as his lips brushed with aching tenderness over hers. His nose brushed against her cheek as he nuzzled her face with his.

"Jacob," she protested, but it was more moan than objection.

He brought her hand to his hard cheek and pressed it there, palm down, savoring its soft coolness. "I want my hundred-dollar bill back."

It was the last thing, the very last thing, she'd expected him to say. Her eyes flew open, astonished.

"You heard me." He nibbled her thumb sensually, his dark eyes watching her. "And I take back every damned insulting remark I've ever made. Would you like to know why I insulted you like that with money, Kate?"

"I…because I ran from you, I guess," she faltered.

He shook his head. "You hurt my pride," he said quietly. "I didn't want to believe you were innocent. I hurt you, but I didn't realize it. I was convinced that you were experienced and that I hadn't measured up to your other men."

Her lips parted helplessly. "I…didn't realize," she whispered. "Did you, really?"

Incredible, the way it felt to talk to her like this. His blood felt as if it contained bubbles. He'd never admitted such a thing before. But honesty with Kate was easier than he'd expected. She didn't snap or use sarcasm or make wild accusations.

He actually smiled, and his smile was genuine. "I did, really."

Her eyes fell to his chest. She wanted to explain to him why she'd said what she did, what she'd been feeling. But she was painfully shy with him now, and the memory alone was enough to embarrass her.

He brushed her hair away from her forehead. "Do you know, I've never come closer to an apology in my life."

She smiled faintly. "I never expected one."

"I'm a hard case, Kate. I'll break before I bend an inch. That's the truth. I can't change."

As his lips touched her forehead, she felt a sense of amazement. This couldn't be Jacob. Perhaps she was dreaming. Or in a coma. Or dead.

Her eyes lifted to his, soft with tenderness, and he caught his breath. Yes, she loved him, all right. Apparently love endured anything, if that aching sweetness in her eyes was anything to go by. With his fingers, he touched her mouth, fascinated by it, by that radiance that chased away all the shadows, all the pain. She loved him.

He frowned, because he still wasn't sure that he wanted to be loved. But she was different from his usual kind of woman; a new experience. He'd grown jaded, cynical about women. They only wanted his money or a good time. But here was Kate, whom he'd known half her life, and suddenly sex was something profound and he didn't want anyone else.

"You look stunned," she remarked curiously. "Are you all right?"

He shifted, standing up straight, although his hand retained possession of hers. "I don't know."

"What is it?"

He scowled down at her, searching her face, her eyes. He'd been less wary while she was unconscious, when he was faced with the possibility of losing her forever. Now, with the obstacles out of the way, the old fears were back. Kate wasn't the kind of woman a man played around with. If he started anything with her now, he'd have to finish it. That meant marriage and kids—responsibilities he'd always thought of in the distant future, not the present. Kate loved him. But did he want that?

She didn't understand the sudden shift in his attitude. He'd gone away without moving a muscle. And then it dawned on her: He was afraid she'd die and he'd have her on his conscience. Now he was feeling relief and guilt and a little shame, and he was already regretting his impulsive offer. Jacob didn't want anything permanent; he'd made that clear the night he seduced her.

She felt an overwhelming sadness. He didn't want anything from her except to be forgiven for what he'd said and done. That was all. She might love him, but he had nothing to give her. She stared up at him quietly. Well, at least he didn't know how she felt. That was the only consolation she had. And she wouldn't let him know, either.

"It's all right," she said unexpectedly, and forced a smile. "You don't have to worry about me anymore. I'll be fine. I think I'll go to New York with Tom. I can stay in his apartment while I'm getting back on my feet."

She said it too quickly. He saw immediately what she was trying to do. It hurt him that she cared enough to put his comfort above her own, even when she needed him so desperately. She didn't want to go to New York, but she didn't feel welcome at Warlance.

"You're reading me wrong, Kate," he said quietly. "I'm not thinking of ways to back out of the invitation."

She flushed. "You seemed uncomfortable about it," she replied.

"I'm uncomfortable about a lot of things lately." He looked and sounded tired. Dead tired. There were dark circles under his eyes and he looked as worn as he felt. All that waiting. Tom hadn't been alone; Jacob had been with him every step of the way.

"You need sleep," she said abruptly.

"Do I?" He stuck his hands in his pockets and stood beside the bed, looking down at her pale, quiet face. "You need it more."

"I don't sleep well," she confessed. "I keep hearing the bullets."

"All the more reason to get out of the city for a while. You can't work for several weeks. You'd probably go crazy in your apartment." He pursed his lips. "Come with me. I'll build you a greenhouse."

Her face went two shades of pink and she stared at him wildly. "What?" she breathed, overcome that he should hit accidentally on the one big dream of her life lately.

"You garden, don't you?" he mused. "You have dozens of books on horticulture. I'll make sure you have a place to practice your hobby while you're recuperating."

It was like a dream coming true. She wanted to be with him, even though she knew it was only guilt that motivated him. To be near him, just to be allowed to sit and look at him, was all of heaven. That, and a greenhouse, too. She had to be dreaming.

"That would be a lot of trouble," she began, trying to be sensible.

"Not particularly," he replied. "I've got the space, and there are a few experiments I'd like to try with new strains of forage grasses."

"Well…"

"You're running out of excuses," he observed.

She sighed, folding her hands. "I'd like to go," she confessed. "But I'll just be in the way, and Janet has enough to do. And Barbara won't like it," she added, avoiding his eyes.

He hadn't seen Barbara Dugan in so long that she was little more than a memory. He blinked. "What does Barbara have to do with it?" he asked curiously.

"Everybody says you'll marry her eventually. Her land adjoins Warlance."

"My God, Kate, so does Billy Kramer's, but I'll be damned if I'd want to marry him for it."

His dry sense of humor was something she'd forgotten during the long antagonism of the years. She was the one person he'd never joked with in recent memory.

"I just don't want to foul up your life," she said doggedly, ignoring the humor.

"As if it isn't pretty fouled up now," he murmured, watching her closely. "You won't cramp my style, Kate, or get in my way. I'll take care of you until you can take care of yourself again."

She was weakening. Her big, soft eyes searched his, vulnerable and frightened.

He moved closer to the bed, his protective instincts aroused and bubbling over. "I won't hurt you again," he said quietly. "I swear to God I won't."

Her eyes fell. "All right," she sighed. "I'll go with you, if you're sure—"

"I'm sure."

She lay back again and closed her eyes with a weary sigh, wincing as the movement caused her pain. "Shot's worn off." She grimaced.

"I'll tell the desk on my way out," he replied. "I've got

a few details to take care of." He brushed his hand lightly over her hair. "Can I bring you anything?"

"No, thank you," she said.

"Then I'll see you later."

He paused at the door to look back. She was in pain again, and in a good deal of it from her rigid posture. He went past Tom, motioning the younger man to follow, and explained at the desk what was wrong. The nurse smiled and immediately went to take care of Kate.

"What did she say?" Tom asked him.

"I talked her into going home with me," Jacob said. "She'll do better in the country, and you can't watch her and work at the same time."

"I'm not arguing," Tom mused. "I'm just wondering how you managed to convince her. She said the two of you had had a royal falling out."

"We did. But maybe we understand each other a little better than we did."

Tom lifted his eyebrows. "You didn't tell her what I told you?"

Jacob shook his head. "I didn't think revelations would be good for her state of mind. And you'd better believe I won't take advantage of how she feels while she's with me."

"I never thought you would," Tom said honestly. "You aren't the type to play around with virgins."

It was a good thing that Tom didn't know the whole truth, Jacob thought with bitter humor. "I want to go and speak to her boss about a leave of absence. She'll be upset if her job's gone when she comes back."

So much for Tom's hope that Jacob might be feeling something deeper for Kate. As he feared, the other man felt only guilt and pity. Jacob was already making plans for her return to Chicago. How Kate would hate knowing that. Tom smiled forcibly. "That might be a good idea."

"I'll be back afterwhile."

Jacob turned and left Tom in the waiting room. He didn't know why, but he needed to get away, to think.

He walked for over an hour, his mind blank, seeing the city without really noticing anything about it. He turned finally and went down the block where the newspaper office that Kate worked for was located.

Morgan Winthrop was sitting at his massive desk, giving somebody hell over the telephone when Jacob walked in. As soon as Winthrop saw the other man, he cut the conversation short and hung up.

"How's Kate?" he said without conventional greetings.

"She's sitting up today, for short stretches, at least," Jacob told him. "I'm taking her home with me to recuperate. I want to pay her salary while she's out and let her think the paper's doing it."

"And I thought I was a blunt man," Winthrop mused.

"It saves time to come to the point." He studied the older man. "She's too proud to let me pay her bills, so it's the last resort."

"Okay. I'll set it up with the payroll department and we'll settle it between ourselves." He named a figure that Kate drew each week.

"Hell," Jacob muttered, "I spend more than that on fertilizer and salt blocks!"

"People don't work at reporting to get rich."

"So I see. All right, I'll send a check over in the morning. And not a word to Kate."

Morgan Winthrop was darker and broader than Jacob, and his eyes had a faintly haunted look. "Maybe I'm talking out of turn, but do you know how Kate feels about you?"

Jacob's face hardened. He almost didn't answer at all. "Yes," he said finally. "But she doesn't know that I do."

"My wife and I had a major misunderstanding two years ago," Morgan Winthrop said quietly. "She went away to Paris to recover from the argument we had and I let her. The day she was due to leave for home, the taxi-cab that was taking her to the airport was involved in a wreck and she was killed instantly. Don't ever assume that you have all the time in the world to clear things up."

"Yes. I learned that three nights ago," Jacob said. "How did you know?"

"Kate keeps a photo of you in her desk."

Jacob's eyes narrowed as he studied the older man. After a minute, he slowly pulled out his wallet, opened a section of it with plastic inserts and showed something to Winthrop.

The older man only nodded. "Take care of her."

"I always did," Jacob replied. He put up the wallet. "Not a word about the paycheck."

Morgan Winthrop smiled. "What paycheck?"

Bud Schuman was at his desk when Jacob started out. He deliberately dropped a pencil and bent over to find it.

Jacob didn't even glance in his direction. But when he got out the door, he was chuckling softly to himself. The old reporter was a character, and if Jacob had been just a little more forgiving, he might have spoken to him. But he couldn't forget that Schuman might have cost Kate her life with that tip.

He stopped by Kate's apartment long enough to have dinner, and then he went back to the hospital. He found a stranger sitting by Kate's bed holding her hand.

It took all his willpower not to lift the man by the collar and drop him out the window.

"Well, well, you must be Kate's brother. I've heard a

lot about you," the tall, heavyset blond man said pleasantly, rising to shake hands. "I'm Roger Dean. I work for a nearby weekly newspaper, and I've been trying to seduce Kate for years without success."

Kate turned beet red and wished she felt well enough to get under the bed. Jacob had turned an odd shade of dusky red and his black eyes were flashing danger signals.

"That isn't Tom," Kate said quickly. "Roger, this is Jacob Cade. His niece and I are best friends."

"Sorry about the mistake. Nice to meet you, anyway," Roger grinned pleasantly. "Just like Kate to jump in front of a bullet. I've warned her for years about following the police around…."

"Kate's coming home with me to South Dakota," Jacob said, his voice pleasant enough. But his stance was threatening, and his eyes were saying a lot more. He looked purely possessive—dangerously possessive as he moved to Kate's side and deliberately blocked Roger's attempt to take her hand.

Roger wasn't thick. He knew immediately what was going on. He smiled at Kate.

"Glad to see you're better, kid. Now don't go roping steers and such, okay? And I'll see you again before you leave."

"All right," Kate said softly. "Thanks for coming, Roger."

"I wouldn't have missed it. I always wanted to be part of a gun battle. Oh, well, maybe I'll get caught in a tornado or something one day. See you, pretty girl. Nice to have met you, Mr.…Cade? So long."

Jacob watched him go with an expression Kate couldn't quite classify. He frightened her a little.

"Damned prissy lunatic," he muttered under his breath. "Is he unbalanced?"

"He was only kidding, Jacob. I went out with him once or twice."

He turned on his heel, his gaze possessive. "Never again," he said, without apology for the command in his tone.

She stopped breathing. At least it felt like that. Her green eyes searched his dark ones with wary curiosity. "You don't own me, Jacob," she began hesitantly.

"Under the circumstances, I have every right in the world to feel possessive about you," he replied. "I don't want another man's hands on you, ever."

She flushed crimson.

"Yes, I know," he continued, unabashed, "you don't want mine on you, either. I don't blame you. But one day, I may even change your mind about that. Now, let me tell you what I've arranged with Winthrop about your leave of absence."

He sat down and told her the fiction without jeopardizing the fact, and she was too bemused by his attitude toward Roger to question any of it. By the time her mind was clear, Tom was there and the conversation became general. The men were still talking when she finally slept, just as visiting hours ended.

Chapter 7

To get them back to South Dakota, Jacob had wanted to charter a private plane, a large twin-engine one with plenty of room for Kate to relax in without being cramped or crowded. But the doctor had said that because of her lung injury, she wouldn't be able to fly for at least two months.

"But you hate flying," she blurted out when he mentioned it in the hospital.

He shrugged. "I could have managed. But the doctor said you couldn't fly."

"It's only a rib...."

"And part of your lung," he continued for her, his gaze sharp and challenging. "So I've chartered a bus. A big one. Dad is going to pick us up in Pierre with the Lincoln and I'll send someone to Chicago to pick up the Mercedes."

"You're going to a lot of trouble."

He lifted his chin, studying her downcast face. "A little pampering isn't going to hurt you."

"Getting used to it from you is ironic, though," she said.

He hesitated uncharacteristically and studied his clasped hands. "Old enemies, is that how it goes? But we weren't always, Kate," he reminded her. "There was a time when we were friends."

She smiled, remembering. "You were kind to me, then."

"You were the only friend Margo had," he said. "You still are. It's made things rough, in more ways than you realize."

"Yes. You didn't feel free to seduce me as long as she was around. You had to set a good example for her, didn't you?" The minute the words were out, she regretted them.

"You make it sound cold-blooded," he said with surprising patience. He sounded almost kind, and when she looked up, his eyes were indulgent. "Kate, I wanted you. But even then, if you'd said no, I'd have backed off. You see, I hadn't counted on just how little self-control I was going to have when things heated up. I lost my head when I began to kiss you in the car."

She hadn't thought Jacob ever lost control, although she remembered how rapidly he'd lost it that night. She'd pushed him beyond his limits. Perhaps he was still angry about it. She remembered the way they'd kissed, too, and the aching sweetness of his mouth on hers. It seemed like such a long time ago.

"I suppose that happens from time to time," she said noncommittally.

"It doesn't happen to me."

She looked up into half-amused, half-irritated dark eyes. "Oh."

His brows drew down just a little as he studied her. "Didn't anyone ever tell you that men get unmanageable pretty fast when a woman responds without restraint."

Her eyes searched his, frankly fascinated with the tenderness in them. "No. I read a lot of books, though...."

"Someday you and I are going to have to have a little talk about birds and bees," he murmured dryly.

"That really won't be necessary. I don't have any inclination to build nests or make honey."

He nodded. "That's understandable. But eventually you're going to learn that women get as much pleasure from sex as men do."

"They do not!" she shot back, remembering the hollow, incomplete feeling, the anguished frustration she'd felt that night.

"Not the first time, certainly," he said easily. "Not when the man takes it all and gives nothing back. That's another first, in case you're interested. I'm not a selfish man."

This conversation was getting out of hand. It was too soon for such an intimate talk with him. She toyed with the sheet. "When are they going to let me out of here? Has Tom checked?"

He pursed his lips. "Evasive maneuvers, I see," he mused. "All right, I'll let you get away with it this time. Your doctor says you can go next Friday morning, if you're still doing this well by then. That will make it about the tenth day and, according to your doctor, that's considered a pretty short stay for this kind of injury."

"I'm so tired of bed," she said with a sigh.

"Don't expect to climb trees the minute you're discharged," he countered. "You won't be exercising very much until that broken rib heals and that will take about five more weeks."

"What medical school did you graduate from?" she murmured with a faint smile.

"I got in a fight once and had two ribs caved in with a two-by-four," he said. "I remember how it hurt to even dance with girls, much less do anything more strenuous."

There were so many questions she wanted to ask, but it wouldn't do to put them into words. He wouldn't like it. He felt sorry for her, guilty for seducing her. That was all he felt—he wanted no part of her emotional hunger. She had to keep that in mind before she made a fool of herself.

"No comment?" he asked.

She shrugged, grimacing. "I don't have any right to be curious about your private life, Jacob," she said quietly.

"No right or no interest?" he asked, his voice deep and soft.

Her eyes found the floor and stayed there, hiding from him. "Wouldn't you like some coffee?"

"I guess so," he sighed. He got to his feet, gazing at her intently. "Can I bring you anything?"

She shook her head. What she wanted, nobody could bring her.

Unexpectedly, he reached down and touched her hair gently, feeling a sudden protective stirring deep inside himself. "I know it's a lot to ask, but will you try to stop looking back? There's nothing either of us can do to change what happened."

"I know that," she said, her voice subdued. "I don't blame you, Jacob."

"Don't you?" He sounded bitter, and when she looked at him, his expression was hard and mocking.

"My father was…was a fanatic," she said softly. "You can't imagine what it was like."

"Oh, but I can," he said. His dark eyes searched hers.

"If I'd had any inkling of your upbringing, I'd never have touched you."

"Don't you think I knew that?" she asked, vulnerability in her tone as she watched him.

His hand smoothed the dull sheen of her short hair. "Did you want me so badly, little one?" he asked tenderly.

Her lower lip trembled and tears threatened. "I wanted…" She bit her lip, hard. Love, she could have added. Just a little love, a little respite from the loneliness and longing of years. She closed her eyes. "It doesn't matter now. I'm very tired."

She was closing up like a flower at night, shutting him out. He could imagine what she was about to admit, but she didn't want him to know how she really felt. His lean fingers brushed her pale cheek.

"Get some sleep. I'll come back when Tom does."

"He was going to pack some things for me."

"He already has. Your case is sitting beside your front door."

Her eyes opened, the expression in them was very vulnerable. "Jacob, I could still go with him…."

"He can't look after you and work. I can."

"You shouldn't have to. I'm not your responsibility."

He almost smiled at her dogged expression. "Kate," he said softly, "hasn't it occurred to you yet that I might want you to be?"

"No, it hasn't, and no, you don't," she returned. "You feel guilty and sorry for me. You needn't pretend it's anything else, and I don't want to go home with you on sufferance—oh!"

Before she could finish the tirade, his mouth had moved softly over hers, touching her lips with aching tenderness. She smelled his spicy aftershave, tasted the faint tobacco tartness of his breath. It was all she could do to keep from responding.

"I don't have time for guilt and pity," he whispered against her moist lips. "I'm a busy man with autumn coming on. But I'll make sure you have enough on your mind to keep you from brooding while you heal. Now stop hunting for excuses and go to sleep. We've got a long trip ahead of us."

Her fingers curled beside her head with impotent anguish. He was sorry for her; she knew he was. He'd regret this generous impulse, and he had no idea what his remorse would do to her. His kindness was a double-edged sword, taunting her with the shadow of an emotion he'd never feel for her.

His hand smoothed over her fist, his own fingers untangling hers in a slow, sensuous caress while he held her wide eyes.

"I know you don't trust me," he murmured. "Your emotions are like these fingers, Kathryn, tied in knots to protect them from me. There's no need for that anymore, but I'm going to have to prove it to you. So just take your time, honey, and we'll go from here. No more looking behind us." He eased her fist open and brought the palm to his warm mouth. "Sleep tight."

She watched him go with troubled eyes. Life was getting more complicated by the minute.

Tom went with them to the ranch, just to see Kate settled, and she thought secretly that Jacob was glad of the company. He was impatient. He didn't like riding any more than he liked flying, and it was an all-day trip from Chicago to Pierre with infrequent stops to eat and rest. Jacob passed the time by talking to Tom while Kate curled up in a long row of seats she had all to herself, with the armrests lifted out of the way.

She'd insisted on getting into the bus on her own, but she was sore and weak by the time they reached the bus station in sprawling Pierre. Jacob lifted her easily, tenderly, and carried her to his waiting Lincoln, with his father behind the wheel.

"Hi, Kate," Hank Cade grinned, his silvery hair blowing in the breeze. "Hello, Tom. How was the trip, son?" he asked Jacob.

"Just great," Jacob said through his teeth as he eased Kate into the backseat so that she could stretch out.

"He hates planes," Hank told Tom who was climbing in beside Kate. "But he hates riding in buses just as much."

"Most sane people hate flying," Jacob replied. He opened the driver's door. "Move over," he told his father.

Hank glared at him indignantly. "I can drive," he retorted.

"Then do it, but not in my car," Jacob replied. "I'm not stupid enough to ride with you."

"I'm a better driver than you are! At least I never wrecked more than one car!"

"Those accidents weren't my fault," Jacob said imperturbably, sliding into the car with enough force to move his father to one side. "I was hit all three times."

"Because you pulled out in front of people, tailgated and ran stop signs!" Hank accused.

"I'm a good driver," Jacob muttered. He started the car and shot off away from the airport, narrowly missing a car that had just turned into the parking lot. "Damned fool," he muttered at the stunned, innocent driver. "Should have watched where he was going."

Kate was trying not to laugh. She looked at Tom and almost burst with suppressed amusement.

"He was a damned fool, all right," Hank agreed, "for getting onto a highway when you were driving a car!"

"Calm down," Jacob mused. "Remember your blood pressure."

"Why should I when it doesn't ever remember me."

"Why didn't Janet drive you out here?"

"Our housekeeper knew she'd have to ride back with you, so she very sensibly stayed behind to fix lunch," Hank replied.

Jacob glared at him. "I drive better than you do."

"So could I, if I could see!"

"Have your damned cataracts taken care of."

"No fancy doctor's cutting on my eyes!"

Kate exchanged an amused glance with Tom. These fights between father and son were familiar territory. The exchange brought back gentle memories of another time, when Jacob had been an easygoing, caring friend instead of the sarcastic stranger of more recent years. The passengers in the backseat kept quiet and listened all the way to Warlance, while Jacob and Hank went back and forth about everything from the state of local politics to the condition of the cattle on the ranch.

Minutes later, they wound up the long dirt road that led to Warlance. Like most of this part of South Dakota, the country was rolling plains with trees in only occasional patterns around the far-flung houses. The state was sixteenth in the nation in land area, but forty-fifth in population. It had what Jacob had always called "elbow room," and in a big way. Warlance's nearest neighbor, the Dugan ranch, was over ten miles away.

The big white two-story house that Hank Cade's grandfather had built was set in a frame of oak trees, while cattle grazed in the moderate warmth of a north-western fall along tributaries of the Missouri River, which divided South Dakota right down the middle. To the northeast was Pierre, the state capital. To the south-west were the Badlands. To the far west were the Black Hills. To the north was the Cheyenne River Indian Reservation. All around, there was history. To Kate, the wide-open country with its smooth hills and isolated buttes was a treat to the eye. Chicago had given her a bad case of claustrophobia at first— She was used to clear horizons and a satisfying lack of trees to clutter up the view. And nothing in the city, despite its beauty, had made up for the lack of open land and sunshine and air as fresh as the winter snow.

"I'd forgotten how large Warlance was," Tom remarked as they wound up the drive. Big Hereford bulls grazed on one side of the dirt road, heifers and calves on the other.

"It seems to get bigger all the time when Jay isn't around," Hank had the grace to admit. He grimaced. "It's one crisis after another. And I've been saving the worst until last, son. Chuck Gray quit yesterday."

Jacob glared at his father. "Why?"

"He said to tell you he'd rounded up one damned bull too many," he replied. "You might remember that fall is the season we round up the bulls," he told those in the back seat. "Somebody always gets stepped on or gored or kicked. This year it was Chuck. He went to work for a ranch over in Montana."

"Damn it," Jacob cursed as he pulled up at the steps. "He was the best wrangler I ever had."

"You should have let him wrangle horses instead of telling him to help round up bulls, then, son, like I told you," Hank said smugly. "If you'd have listened to me—"

"I did listen to you, damn it. You're the geezer who told me to let him help round up bulls!"

Hank shrugged. "Well, then, why did you listen to me?"

Jacob snapped off the engine with a vicious switch of his fingers and glared at his father. "Why in hell don't you go off sailing to Tahiti like you always swear you're going to?"

"Now, son, if I did that, who'd look out for you?"

Kate started to laugh. "I'm sorry," she apologized, trying to stifle her mouth when Jacob glared toward her. "I was just thinking about...something."

"Sure. I'll bet," Jacob got out of the car and lifted her out, ignoring her protests, as Tom and Hank paused to get the luggage from the trunk.

"Janet! Open the front door!" Jacob called, his voice carrying all the way to the corral, where two cowboys looked their way.

"You could break glasses with that voice!" the old, heavyset woman in a green housedress and pink bedroom slippers grumbled as she ambled out the door and held it open. "Afternoon, Kate. It's good to see you. I'm not making any comments about him, though. I was just getting used to peace and quiet, and here he comes back. I bet he's gotten Mr. Hank in a fever and is already planning ways to turn my beef roast into bile at the supper table."

"You're fired," Jacob said through his teeth.

"Well, I won't go, so there," Janet shot back. "You shut your mouth and stop throwing orders at me, young man. I used to put diapers on you when you were five feet shorter than you are now!"

"For God's sake, stop reminding me," he retorted, carrying Kate inside the dark hall. "Don't we have a light in this hall, or are you on another conservation binge?"

"Waste not, want not," Janet replied smugly, "and don't trip with Miss Kate."

He muttered something that Janet couldn't hear and Kate flushed.

He walked off down the hall to one of the guest rooms on the ground floor, just two doors down from his own room. At least, Kate imagined it was still his room. It had the same heavy antique furniture that he'd been using when Kate had visited Margo so many years before.

"We hardly use the upstairs anymore," he commented as he put her down on a spotless powder-blue coverlet under a canopied bed. "It's cold as hell in winter and too hard for Janet to go up and down when she has to clean it. We try to save her legs when we can, despite the fact that we ought to stand her up against the fence and shoot her."

"You'd miss her," Kate chided.

He leaned over her, his hands beside her head, his dark eyes piercing. "Maybe. How's the rib?"

"Just a little sore," she said softly. He was so good to look at. Involuntarily, her eyes ran over his hard face, tracing every line of it.

He saw the helpless pleasure in her expression and found himself smiling gently at her obvious delight in looking at him. He hadn't realized how exciting it could be to know that Kate loved him.

He bent a little and threatened her mouth with the minty warmth of his own, watching her eyes dilate and half close, watching her lips part for him. Yes, she wanted his mouth. He nuzzled her nose with his, hearing her breathing change in the stillness of the room. His own was quickening. It aroused him to feel her immediate response.

Because it did, he drew back, frowning a little. He had to keep things in perspective. Kate was here to heal, and he was providing for her out of guilt. Wasn't he? He blinked at his own confused reactions.

"Rest for a bit," he said, rising. "We'll have something to eat directly. I've got to sit down with my father and see what's happened while I've been away. Tom can keep you company."

"Of course. I don't need to be entertained, you know," she added with a faint smile.

"You don't need to be left alone to brood, either," he replied. He let his eyes wander down the length of her body, which was elegant in a pale gray pantsuit with a green ruffled blouse. She was pretty when she dressed up, and her body tormented him with memories. He remembered it in the first tentative seconds of passion, remembered it twisting softly under him, her moans quickly arousing him to that unexpected loss of control. His body tautened with the memory of a fulfillment so staggering, it still haunted him.

"Do you still like mystery novels?" she asked unexpectedly.

His eyebrows shot up. "Of course."

"I do, too. Do you have some new ones I could read while I'm here?"

"I've got dozens that I've acquired since your last visit," he replied. "You're welcome to borrow them."

"Thanks."

"Janet says one of your men wants to see you," Tom interrupted, smiling at Jacob as he brought in Kate's suitcase. "Something about some barbed wire that didn't come."

"Great," Jacob muttered. "I leave for a few days and the whole damned spread falls apart."

He went out, still muttering, and Tom exchanged wry grins with Kate. "Just like old times, isn't it?" he asked. "Jacob's more like his old self since Margo's wedding."

Kate didn't comment. "Sit down and talk to me," she said instead. "We haven't really had a chance to visit since you came over from New York." She settled back against the pillows with a weary sigh. "Tell me about your job."

He did, and went on to keep her in stitches with tales about his boss. His stories passed the time, and he kept on talking until Kate dozed off. He watched her, his green eyes worried. Kate had been odd lately—ever since Margo's wedding. He felt that her present state had something to do with Jacob, and that what happened had been more than a simple argument. But even though he loved her, he knew that she wouldn't welcome his interference. With a sigh, he got up and covered her with a quilt. Poor Kate, he thought. Her life had gone from bad to worse lately. And being around Jacob, considering her passion for him, was going to be more torment for her. He wondered why in the world she'd agreed to come here. He wished he and Jacob were friendly enough that he could ask. There were so many mysteries between his sister and Jacob. He hoped she wasn't going to let herself in for any more heartache than she'd already had.

Chapter 8

Tom stayed two days, just long enough to see Kate settled; then he had to go back to work. At first she was lonely, but Janet made time to talk to her. Somehow Jacob was always early or late for meals, so that Kate had them with Hank and Janet. She didn't know if that was by accident or design on Jacob's part. He'd been acting strangely ever since her arrival, as if he were deeply regretting his impulse to bring her to the ranch to recuperate. Feeling a sense of tension, Kate made a point of staying out of his way. She knew he didn't have much free time, anyway, since it was fall. He and his men were busy getting the cattle to winter pasture, selling calves, moving out culls, moving in replacement heifers, checking for disease, tagging, doing all the hundred-and-one things that raising cattle required from season to season.

Her doctor in Chicago had made Jacob promise to have his own physician examine Kate forty-eight hours after they arrived in South Dakota, just to make sure no damage had been done. Jacob kept his word, and Dr. Wright checked Kate to make sure her broken rib was mending properly. She was still a little sore, but nothing like the way she had been those first few days. They'd removed the staples just before she left the hospital, and the rib belt, oddly enough, didn't hurt the stitches or the small incision where the drainage tube had been in her side. She was told to come back on the fourth week after surgery to have more X rays done, and if they were all right, she could dispense with the rib belt. At least, she thought ruefully, it no longer hurt to cough or sneeze or laugh, so she had to be getting better.

Hank had ridden into Blairsville with them to see the doctor, so there hadn't been any opportunity for Kate and Jacob to talk. Perhaps Jacob had wanted that, because he seemed reluctant to spend any time with her.

Of course, Kate hadn't expected to see much of Jacob, and she didn't complain about his absences. But at the end of her first week on the ranch, he came into her room unexpectedly as she was halfheartedly watching a television comedy special from the easy chair by the window.

He was wearing denims and a blue-checked western shirt, and his boots were still dusty from working. He smiled at the picture she made in her pale blue caftan, curled up in the pink chair with her feet bare.

"Are you watching that?" he asked, nodding toward the screen.

"Sort of," she said and smiled. "I'm okay. You don't have to entertain me. I don't want to get in the way."

She always put his comfort first, he thought with faint irritation. She wouldn't intrude on his privacy for anything, not even to ask about those books she wanted to read. Since she'd been at Warlance, she'd kept very much to herself, not bothering anyone. He felt a bit uncomfortable around her, and he'd made sure they weren't alone for any length of time. She didn't seem to mind his absence, and ironically, he found that frankly annoying. He'd been working hard; he hadn't had a spare minute to entertain her. But he felt guilty all the same, and her sacrificial attitude caught him on the raw. Any other woman would have demanded attention, been petulant and insistent and haughty about it.

"Don't you ever get tired of sainthood?" he asked unexpectedly, because he was tired and worn and impatient with her lack of spirit. "My God, all you need is a halo!"

The attack surprised her. She hadn't expected him to take off the gloves until she was well, but perhaps her very presence in the house angered him. His conscience was obviously bothering him since he found out the truth about her past, and having to see her every day was only adding to his sense of guilt.

She looked up at him quietly. "I should never have come," she said then. "You haven't changed one bit. You're about as thrilled to have me here as you'd be with a toad in the house." She got to her feet slowly, because she was weak and her side was still a little sore, but she faced him squarely. "I hate to even ask it, but will you please get me a ticket on the next bus out of here? Failing that, I'll call Tom."

The situation was getting out of hand too quickly. He hadn't realized she'd take him at face value, but he should have remembered her obsession with not imposing.

"I'm tired," he said shortly. "I'm short-tempered and ill and I want to bite somebody. You were handy."

She stared at him unblinking, startled by the blunt admission.

"When I want you to leave, I'll say so," he snapped.

His eyes darkened at the sight of her in that witchy blue caftan. He didn't think she was wearing anything under it, and that disturbed him even more.

"Excuse me, I thought you were asking me to leave," she said in a subdued tone.

He moved forward with a rough sigh and took her gently by the arms, easing her back down in her chair. He knelt in front of her and looked into her wounded eyes.

"Either you've forgotten, or you don't know," he began softly, "but I'm not an easy man to get along with. I have a black temper and I'm not shy about using it. If you don't learn to stand up to me, you're going to have one hell of a time trying to stay here."

"I don't want to fight," she said miserably. "I'm weak as a kitten, I miss my job and my brother, and I've got too much time to think."

He hadn't considered that. Her admission took the starch out of him all at once. "You've been keeping to yourself ever since Tom left," he reminded her. "I didn't know if you were shy, or just preferred your own company." He touched the arm of her chair idly. "Kate, I like being by myself. It's a hard habit to break. If you want to talk, I'll listen. If you want to be with me, all you have to do is say so."

Her eyes closed on a wave of embarrassment. "I don't need company, thank you," she said proudly. "Except that I'll have to ask you to get someone to drive me to the doctor next Friday for those X rays." And he could make what he liked of that; she wasn't going to beg him to spend any time with her.

"Talk about pride," he mused, watching her. "I thought I had a monopoly on it. You'd damned well rather crawl there than ask me to take you, wouldn't you?"

Her eyes opened, glaring. "You know I would," she

whispered, and at the moment, she meant it. She felt an almost primitive dislike of him and the hold he had over her emotions.

It was going to be more difficult than he'd thought. She was as proud as he was, and she wasn't about to let down her guard. Not after what he'd done to her. It was going to be like pulling teeth just to get her to talk to him. Love was one thing. Trust was something else again. She might worship him from afar, but he was just beginning to understand that she was trying her best to shut him out, to keep him at arm's length.

"Why don't you come and keep me company while I do the book work?" he asked unexpectedly.

She stared at the screen. "I'd rather watch this. But thank you anyway."

He moved around her and switched the television off.

"Jacob!"

He ignored her protest. He bent and lifted her gently in his arms, careful not to jar her, and carried her out of the room and down the hall to his study. She was thinner than he remembered, and frankly delicate. He didn't want to know how much she weighed now. The wound and his treatment of her had taken their toll.

"You're as tight-lipped as I am, and about half as proud. You won't give an inch, and neither will I. You're not going to hole up in that room and shut me out. I didn't bring you here to watch you hibernate."

She felt his strength as he put her down on his burgundy leather sofa. She couldn't imagine that she'd really heard him say that, and her eyes mirrored her surprise.

"I thought you liked being alone," she said absently.

"So did I." He stood up and looked at her. Her hair was growing. Janet had helped her wash it, and it was clean and soft and shining.

"I need a robe…."

"Why?" he asked quietly. "Hank's playing poker with one of his friends, and Janet's gone home for the night. We're by ourselves. There's no one to see you except me."

Her face colored delicately. He cocked an eyebrow.

"You aren't shy?" he asked. "You don't have anything I haven't already seen."

The color grew worse. She averted her shamed eyes from him to the waxed floor with its Indian rugs.

"I'm sorry," he said tightly. "That was the last thing I should have said to you."

The apology helped, but she couldn't raise her eyes. He was bringing back too many painful memories.

He eased down on the sofa beside her, his dark eyes on her head. "I've never been so wrong about one human being in all my life," he said. "I wish you could have talked to me about it."

Her arms felt chilled. She folded them, staring at the rug. "It was too painful to talk about," she said. "My father was unbalanced. We knew it, but we were so little, Jacob. There was nothing we could do, no one we could turn to. By the time he died, we were…horribly scarred, mentally."

"And physically?" he probed, his jaw clenching as he remembered what Tom had told him about the circumstances of her father's death.

She dug her nails into her arm. "And physically," she said through her teeth. "Didn't you see the scars that day at the pool house?"

"I didn't see anything but red," he replied. "My God, I could have killed that boy!"

She looked up, shivers of pure pleasure going through her at the fiery darkness of his eyes. "He was only trying to help. You know how afraid I was of snakes. And I'd already made you suspicious by the way I kissed him." She lowered her eyes to the opening of his shirt, where thick black hair was visible against tanned skin. "You were playing tag with that Dugan woman...."

And Kate had been jealous. His heart raced with the knowledge. It explained a lot of things. He wanted to question her, to bring her feelings out into the open. But that wouldn't do. He didn't want her to know that he was aware of her feelings.

"She was playing tag with me," he replied casually. "I like Barbara. I always did." He pushed back a lock of her hair that had fallen over one eye. "She's engaged, did I tell you? To the Hardy man she always fancied."

Her heart skipped. "Is she?"

"Yes, she is. So if you'd planned on marrying me off to her, you're out of luck. I guess I'll just stay a bachelor."

"Then who'll inherit Warlance?"

He studied her blushing cheeks, drinking in the scent of roses that clung to her slender body. "Good question. I've only thought about children in recent years. I'm thirty-two. Eventually I'll have to marry, if I want an heir."

"I don't imagine you'll have any trouble finding a candidate," she said, avoiding his stare. Certainly not, she thought bitterly. The line would form at the gates and Jacob would be wined and dined and hunted like a fox.

"Won't I?" He leaned back, one arm behind her, his lean body elegant in its relaxed position. "I'm rich, Kate."

"So?" she replied, glancing at him.

"How will I know I'm not getting a gold digger?"

"Give it all away," she whispered conspiratorially.

He smiled faintly. "I'm not that desperate."

"Then you'll never know." Her gaze traveled over him,

and she forced herself to look away before her eyes betrayed her.

She didn't know that they already had. Jacob's chest swelled with the knowledge that she wanted him. Her soft eyes had been shyly covetous, running down his body like hands. She could arouse him just by looking at him that way. He pursed his lips, wondering if she was even aware of the effect she had on him.

"When did you know you weren't pregnant?" he asked unexpectedly.

She went hot all over, and mumbled, "The next week."

His dark eyes searched her averted features. "I sweated it out, too," he said. "I knew you wouldn't talk to me, or want to see me. I called Tom and fed him some wild story about wanting to talk to both of you, just so he'd come down from New York and run interference for me. I had to know if there was going to be a child."

She gritted her teeth. "Well, there isn't, so you needn't worry."

"I'm not sure that I was worried," he mused quietly, touching her caftan where a fold of it rested on the sofa. "I wanted to know, that's all."

"I wouldn't have told you," she said.

He knew that, now. She'd have protected him even in that kind of circumstance. His dark gaze lifted and caught her wide green eyes. "Oh, but I'd have found out, Kate. Just the possibility of it would have kept me ten steps behind you until I knew one way or the other."

"And if...?" she probed hesitantly.

"You know me well enough that you don't even have to ask," he replied.

She lowered her eyes to his jeans, where the fabric lovingly traced the powerful muscles of his thighs. "You'd have married me."

"A man will do most anything when there's a child involved, if he has any sense of honor at all," he reminded her. He didn't add that the thought of having a child with Kate didn't bother him one bit. In fact, he'd felt vague disappointment when he'd learned that she wasn't pregnant. That had puzzled him. He couldn't equate that disappointment with desire. And it was only desire that he felt. Wasn't it?

"Well, it's a good thing it turned out this way," she said wearily, leaning her head back with her eyes closed. "I don't want to participate in any shotgun weddings. I'm not even sure I want children at all."

"Why?" he asked, shocked.

"They make people do crazy things," she said, remembering her father's cruelty.

"You can't judge all parents by yours," he began.

"Why not? You judge all women by your mother," she replied, turning her head to study him.

He started to speak and then closed his mouth, brooding for several seconds. "I do, don't I, Kate," he agreed after a little while.

"That must have been hard on you."

"Do you remember your mother?" he asked, evading her question.

She shook her head, and her eyes hardened. "Just bits and pieces. Mostly what my father said about her. She was a tramp. She ran off with another man and deserted Tom and me." Her lower lip trembled. "He beat me…!"

"Oh, God," he breathed, finding the thought unbearable. Frowning with something like pain, he reached for her, bringing her with exquisite tenderness across his lap to cradle her against him. "Oh, God, honey…!"

The comforting was sweet and heady, and she cried into the slow, pulsating warmth of his throat, clinging with her good arm because she couldn't lift the other without pain.

"I hated my mother," she wept. "I still do. How could she leave us? How could she?"

He smoothed her hair, nuzzling it with his hard cheek. "I don't understand parents any better than you do," he said quietly. "My mother ran off and left us without a word, and Hank never tried to find her or bring her back. I asked him why once, and he said that you can't make people stay with you if they don't want to. It sounded like a cop-out at the time, but the older I get, the better I understand it. In a way, he was saving us all more heartache."

"You never forgave her, did you?"

His hand stilled on her hair. "She was on her deathbed," he said softly. "And after all the pain, she was still my mother. Yes, Kate. I forgave her. And that's something I've never even told Hank."

She moved her face softly against his throat, feeling proud that he was willing to share something so personal with her. "I don't think I could have been that generous," she whispered. "I'll never forgive mine."

"Do you know where she is?" he asked.

She shook her head. "I've never had the money to try and trace her. I don't think I would even if I could. Tom and I suffered so horribly because of her. At least Hank was good to you."

"That he was, the old devil. We fight, but I'd die for him, you know."

She smiled. "I know."

It was nice, holding her in the silence of the room, hearing the wind outside beginning to cool the air. She fit against him so perfectly, and he remembered vividly how it felt to hold her with no fabric between them. Her breasts were pushing against his chest, and she was wearing only the light caftan over them. He could feel her nipples, taut with arousal, stabbing into the hard muscles of his chest, and his hand contracted in her hair.

She felt his sudden movement with faint curiosity, and drew her head back to look into his dark eyes.

"What is it?" she whispered.

He started to tell her what it was, but he wondered if she even realized that her breasts were telling him intimate secrets about her innermost desires. He sighed heavily and eased her back onto the sofa before he got to his feet and moved away. "Nothing, honey," he said. "I've got to get on my books. What would you like to read?"

"One of those new mysteries," she suggested, curious about his sudden withdrawal. Did he find her distasteful now?

He pulled down one of the big hardcover books and handed it to her. "Want me to tell you who the murderer is?" he asked with a faint grin.

"You do, and I'll throw something at you."

"Not with your left arm, you won't." He frowned as she moved and he saw the smoothness under that caftan. "Kate, are you wearing the rib belt?"

"The doctor said I didn't have to at night," she reminded him.

"I didn't jar you when I carried you in here?"

That seemed to concern him, and it made her feel vulnerable and very feminine. "No. I'm fine."

He nodded and went to sit behind his desk with a pencil and several pages of figures spread out in front of him. Kate tried to read, but it was so exciting just to sit and watch Jacob as he worked. His hair was very thick, almost black, and it gleamed in the overhead light. His hands were lean and dark and strong, very long-fingered, and his wrists had a faint covering of dark hair on their backs. His arms were long and muscular, straining against the soft fabric of his shirt. The shirt itself was unbuttoned at the throat, and the exciting glimpses she got of hair-covered tanned flesh were wildly arousing. His chin was strong, very stubborn. She smiled, letting her eyes run up from it to his firm, sensuous mouth with its thin upper lip and slightly fuller lower one, a mouth chiseled like that of a Greek statue. His nose had a crook in it; he used to be in fights all the time in his youth. And his eyes...

She flushed, because his eyes were staring right back at her, faintly amused by her uninhibited scrutiny.

"Enjoying yourself, Kate?" he asked humorously, and then could have bitten his tongue off at the flaring embarrassment on her face.

"I'm sorry. I didn't mean to stare at you." She looked doggedly down at the book without seeing a single word in it.

Jacob drew in a slow breath, hating his own blatant mockery. He hadn't meant to make fun of her feelings for him. It was just the way she looked at him. It had a strange, disturbing effect on his body. Everything about her did, lately. He'd worked himself into a stupor for no other reason than to slow down the feverish hunger she aroused, to fight the fire. She didn't know how often he lay awake reliving that night they'd spent together. She'd given him a kind of fulfillment he'd never had with anyone else, a shuddering completion that could knock the breath out of him just in memory.

He started to speak, but she seemed involved in the novel. He turned his attention back to his books, forcing himself not to look at her again. That caftan was the most seductive garment he'd ever seen her in. She probably thought it was concealing and proper attire. Actually, she could only have aroused him more by going stark naked.

It was hard for Kate to concentrate after that mocking remark of his. She felt self-conscious, afraid even to look up at him. Her old self would have been more than able to stand up to him, but she was weak and tired and there had been more nightmares than she wanted to admit. She could close her eyes and hear the sound of the bullets, feel the sudden, horrible impact of the bullet that had hit her, feel the unbearable pain that never seemed to end.

She closed her eyes with a faint shudder. Reporting had been a dream job before this happened. Now she was afraid. Afraid of what she might be expected to do. She realized that the accident was a freak-one of those things that happened one time out of several thousand, but her nerve was shattered. She was only just realizing that she couldn't go back to police reporting. That meant that if there wasn't another slot open at the paper—and they didn't have a large turnover—she might not have a job to go back to. Her check came regularly, once a week, and that was nice of Mr. Winthrop. The paper had insurance that would pay her hospital bill. But she was going to have to have a job, and what if there wasn't one available?

"What's wrong?" Jacob asked quietly.

She hadn't realized that he was watching the drift of expressions across her face. She forced a smile. "Nothing. I was just figuring out who the murderer is."

"Sure. With the book upside down."

She glanced down. Sure enough it was. She righted it, fumbling a little because she'd been caught.

He put down his pencil with a sigh and came around the desk. "Kate, you can't spend your life looking back."

She wouldn't meet his eyes. "I realize that."

"In no time at all, this will all be a bad dream."

She set the book aside and slowly got to her feet. "I'd like to go back and lie down. I think I can sleep now. Thanks for the company."

He stopped her before she got three feet, his hands strong and gentle on her arms. She could feel his warm breath in her hair.

"Talk to me."

She stiffened under his hands. "I'm all right. I don't need to confess anything, thanks."

He sighed heavily. Nothing was working out as he'd expected. She was every bit as zealous about privacy as he was. "I'm not used to other people, either. I talk to no one, least of all Hank, about things that bother me. I keep everything in." His fingers pressed her arms slightly, caressing. "This is as hard for me as it is for you. If you keep pulling back, we'll never be able to communicate with each other."

"I'm afraid of you," she said quietly.

"I'm not blind. I realize that. You've got every reason to feel that way, after what's happened. You let your guard down with me, and I betrayed you. That's going to take a lot of forgetting." He drew her slowly back until she was pressed against his warm chest, and his cheek nuzzled her clean, soft hair, making her heartbeat run wild. "I told you in the hospital that I've never tried to be gentle. It was the truth. Even with women, in intimacy…" His hands smoothed down her bare arms under the caftan. "I can't sleep at night anymore, remembering how I hurt you," he said under his breath. "I've avoided you ever since we got here, because I can't bear being reminded…"

She turned, curious. "Jacob, you didn't shoot me," she said.

"I pushed you in front of the gun," he replied, his

eyes narrow and dark and haunted. "You were looking for a way out."

She turned beet red under that knowing stare. Her eyes fell to his chest, to its strong, quick rise and fall. "Police reporting can be dangerous in a city the size of Chicago," she said finally. "I thought it would help me to stop thinking about…what happened. I wasn't consciously trying to commit suicide."

"You don't know how I've blamed myself."

"You didn't know." She lifted soft, tender eyes to his. "I wanted you," she whispered shyly.

"I wanted you, too," he said quietly. He touched her hair, brushing it back, his dark eyes curiously soft in the silence of the room. "God help me, Kate, I still do."

Her heart ran wild. Just to hear him admit it in that deep, slow voice was enough to increase her pulse rate. She watched his face come closer, his eyes fall to her soft mouth. Her breath caught; being close to him was exquisitely sweet.

He saw the expression on her face and it aroused him unbearably to know how much pleasure she felt when he came close. His heart felt like a drum inside him as he brushed his hard mouth across her soft one.

"Kate," he groaned when he felt her immediate response. He drew her gently against him and his mouth opened.

She let him kiss her, drowning in the sweetness of being near him, being wanted by him. If this was all he could ever give her, it would be almost enough.

She moaned softly at the gentle penetration of his tongue inside the sweet darkness of her mouth, at the achingly tender caress of his fingers just under her arms as they moved with delicate precision toward her breasts.

Without any sense of self-preservation, she drew back
to give him total access to her body.

"This is so sweet with you," he whispered huskily
against her mouth as his thumbs found just the outer
edges of her breasts and began to trace the swell. His
mouth nuzzled hers, and he felt like flying, his powerful body vibrating with a totally new kind of pleasure.

Kate couldn't speak at all. His hands were arousing
her to a fever of passion. She wanted him to touch her.
She looked up at him, adoring him with her eyes as his
mouth taunted hers.

He smiled tenderly at her open hunger. It amazed
him that she could still welcome him after the way he'd
treated her. Love, he thought dazedly, must be a powerful thing, to forgive so much. He wanted to give her
pleasure, whether he felt it or not. He wanted to adore
her with his hands, his mouth, to know the sweetness of
her body in satiation.

She tried to lift her arms around his neck and grimaced when the left one wouldn't move up without pain.

"Don't do that," he whispered, smoothing the aching
muscles under her left arm. "You're not well enough to
use that arm, even to hold me with it."

She was burning for him, aching. "Jacob," she
breathed adoringly.

He brushed his mouth over her closed eyes. "I'll hold
you," he whispered back, "but not too close. I don't want
to hurt that rib."

One lean arm slid behind her, gently supporting her,
and he looked down at the caftan as he slowly drew his
thumb onto her breast and saw the peak clearly outlined
under the silky fabric.

Kate could hardly breathe. That light, teasing touch
was madly exciting. She rested her cheek against his

broad shoulder, watching the play of emotion on his dark face as he touched her.

"I never gave a damn about this kind of love play before," he whispered. "My God, it's exciting."

She touched the lean fingers that were caressing her, fascinated by the pleasure they gave, her own hand trembling on them. "Yes."

His dark eyes lifted to search hers, sharing a new kind of intimacy with her. "Still afraid of me?" he whispered.

"Not…like this," she said shyly.

The tips of his fingers drew across the taut nipple and her breath caught. He watched her eyes, swelling with pride at the way she was reacting to such very light lovemaking. "Do you like it?"

Her body was trembling. "Yes."

As her coworkers had said, she was painfully honest, even when it must have bruised her pride. "I like it, too," he breathed. "I haven't touched a woman, in any way, since that night with you."

She found it difficult to talk at all. "Haven't…you?"

"I dream about you," he whispered, easing his mouth down against hers. "Night after lonely night, I dream about what you gave me…."

The words dissolved into an aching groan as he kissed her, and even that was different. There was tenderness in him now, along with an almost tangible desire.

She accepted his mouth as gently as she accepted the hand that slowly, surely, covered her breast. She made a soft sound under his mouth at the tiny consummation after the agony of longing his fingers had caused. Her own hand held his there, caressed it softly, savored the deep, aching pleasure of his touch on her body.

"Making love to you…gives me such pleasure," he whispered against her lips. His mouth opened, brushing lazily, softly over her own, deeply arousing. His knees felt weak, his body felt lighter than air, as if he could fly. His free hand slid into her thick hair, savoring its silkiness while his other hand grew gently insistent, his fingers tracing the hard peak, feeling her own fingers touching, coaxing.

"Jacob," she moaned. She caught his hand in hers, and he stopped, letting her lift it away.

"All right," he whispered. "I'll stop."

"No." Shyly, she drew his hand back to her body.

His body went rigid. He looked at her with an explosive kind of protectiveness surging inside him.

"No, sweetheart," he whispered tenderly. "No, not now."

She blushed, averting her face. She'd offered herself to him, and he'd rejected her just like he had before…

He tilted her chin up and made her look at him. "I want you," he said softly. "Right now there's nothing in the world I want more than to lie you down on that sofa and strip you and draw you under my body in passion." He shuddered at his own description, then drew himself up short. "But you've got a busted rib, little Kate, and for all that tenderness we just shared, I don't feel like being a gentle lover right now." He bent, crushing his mouth roughly against hers. "I feel like that, Kate," he breathed as his teeth nipped softly at her full lower lip. "I want to throw you down and ravish you…!"

Her breath caught. She clutched at his hard arms; the hunger for him was so strong.

"Yes, you want that, too, don't you?" he asked huskily, watching her face. "Even after last time…."

"I came so close last time," she whispered, shaking. "So close, and I could almost touch the sun, and then it was over."

He seemed to stop breathing. He'd thought that she hated sex because of what he'd done to her; she'd even said that it was horrible… Of course, if she'd thought so, she wouldn't be letting him touch her now.

He framed her face in his hands. "Say that again," he whispered.

She felt shy and embarrassed all at once. "You heard me," she faltered.

"I hope I did," he breathed fervently, probing her eyes. "My God, you can't imagine how it hurt my pride when you said it was 'horrible….'"

Her lips fell open. She hadn't even considered his point of view. Her face colored, but she didn't lower her eyes. "Oh, Jacob, no…I didn't mean…I felt empty. All that hunger, and I felt that there should have been something more, and there wasn't. It was kind of like a sneeze that backs up…" She smiled self-consciously and then she did lower her eyes. "I wanted to explain, but it was so difficult. I didn't understand what was happening to me."

"Oh, my God," he whispered. He drew her against him, protective, his hands holding her head, cradling it to his chest. He closed his eyes. "So that was it." He nuzzled his face against her soft hair. "I should have known, but when I realized how innocent you were, I wasn't surprised that it might have seemed horrible. A man in the throes of passion isn't the best kind of partner for a virgin."

"You wouldn't have been that way if I hadn't pushed you," she admitted. "I'd read all those things I did in a big, sexy novel, and when the heroine did it, the hero was rather reserved and slow…"

He actually laughed. "No wonder they call it fiction," he mused.

"I didn't want you to stop," she whispered. "I knew if

you thought I was a virgin, you'd go away and I'd never see you again."

"You'd have seen me again, all right. Or didn't you realize that I was just as attracted to you as you were to me?"

"Not at the time," she replied. She sighed, content to stand forever in his gentle embrace.

"Are you all right?" he asked.

"I'm happy."

He realized with a start that he was, too. Happiness wasn't something he normally contemplated. He enjoyed life well enough; he liked his work. But happiness… He looked down at the dark head so trusting against his broad chest and felt flooded with contentment. She made him feel protective and tender and ablaze with passion. An odd mixture to be aroused by a little virgin.

That amused him, and he chuckled softly. "I'm tired," he said. He kissed her hair. "And you should be, even if you aren't. I'm going to carry you back to bed, and then I'm going to turn in, too. The book work can wait. It's been a damned long day."

She felt vague disappointment. It had been so sweet to stand in his embrace. "You don't have to carry me…." she began.

He lifted her gently, smiling at her. "Yes, I do. I like carrying you. It makes me feel manly and strong and macho and all those other descriptive words that men aren't supposed to feel in our enlightened society."

He started off down the hall and she laughed gently, sighing. "I like being carried," she admitted. "It makes me feel feminine and protected and vulnerable and all those other descriptive words that women aren't supposed to feel when they're liberated."

"I guess you and I are throwbacks to another age, Kate."

"I expect so." She closed her eyes, savoring the strength of his arms, the masculine scent of him as he carried her down the long hall into her room, and laid her on the bed.

He bent over her, his hair slightly mussed, his shirt open at the throat, his body powerful in that arched position, his dark eyes glittering down at her. "Lucky girl," he murmured wickedly, "to have a broken rib at such a convenient time."

She smiled up at him. As protective as he'd suddenly become, she didn't think it likely that he'd take advantage of her. "Thank you for bringing me back here," she murmured. "I hope you sleep well."

He bent and brushed his mouth over her forehead carelessly. "If you wake up frightened, come find me. I'll take you in with me for the rest of the night."

"Oh, you couldn't…!"

"No one would know, Kate," he said quietly. "Hank sleeps until eight, and Janet doesn't do the bedrooms until noon. I'd make sure you were in your own bed before I got ready to leave. And nothing would happen, despite the way I've teased you tonight," he added firmly. "I've made one big mistake with you. I'm not going to compound it by adding another seduction to the list."

And how was she supposed to interpret that, she wondered as he turned out the light, smiled at her, wished her good-night and shut the door.

She closed her eyes with a sigh and found that she was, after all, pretty sleepy. But somewhere in the middle of the night, machine guns started firing all around her and she screamed, sitting straight up in the darkness with terror choking her.

Chapter 9

The door opened seconds later, and the light went on. Jacob was beside her in an instant. Apparently he'd been to bed, because he was wearing navy-blue pajama bottoms and nothing else. His broad chest was sensuously bare, as she'd rarely seen it, rippling with darkly tanned muscle and thick hair that ran in a wedge down past his pajama trousers.

"Nightmare?" he asked gently, studying her pale, tear-stained face.

"Yes. The gun…" She put her face in her hands. "Oh, Jacob, will they never stop?"

"One day, I expect. Come on."

He moved the covers aside and lifted her gently against his broad, hair-matted chest. She curled close, loving the spicy smell of his body, delighting in the feel of the thick hair under her cheek and her free hand.

"Don't do too much of that," he murmured with black

humor as he turned out her light and closed the door on his way back to his own room with her.

"Hmm?" she asked drowsily.

"Stroking my chest with that little hand," he whispered at her ear. "It arouses me."

"Oh." She stilled her fingers with a small laugh at her own ignorance. "Sorry."

"Yes. So am I." He carried her into his dark room and kicked the door shut behind them. "Hold on. Every time I get up in the night, the bed moves from where I left it."

She smiled at the admission, and sighed gently when he put her down on the sheets, which were still warm from his body. A second later he slid into the bed beside her.

"Come here," he murmured, drawing her head against his shoulder. "Just lie still and don't play with my chest, and everything will be fine."

"I've never slept with anyone before," she confessed drowsily.

"You slept with me," he reminded her.

"We didn't sleep."

He sighed heavily. "No, we didn't." He brushed his lips against her forehead. "Is it getting easier, that blight on your spotless conscience?" he asked gently.

"A little."

"Would it get easier," he asked, his voice deepening, "if we married?"

She wasn't sure she'd heard him at all. She stiffened a little in the darkness, aware of his warmth and strength and quick breathing beside her.

"Think about it, Kate," he said. "You might get used to the idea."

"I won't let you marry me out of guilt, Jacob," she said finally. "Marriage seems to be hard enough even when people love each other. And we don't," she added, forcing herself to tell the lie.

He knew it was a lie, of course. He smiled in the darkness, and touched her face. "Suppose I told you that I loved you," he asked, thinking how comfortable the words felt, even though he didn't quite mean them.

"Suppose you told me that Warlance was in Tibet," she said. She closed her eyes, wishing with all her heart that he could say those exquisite words and mean them.

"Aren't you tired of living alone?" he asked, changing tactics. "We could live together—like friends, if that's how you want it."

It would solve all her problems and create more at the same time. She didn't know how she could live with him and face the day-to-day anguish of hiding her true feelings while she got used to his indifference.

"No, Jacob," she said. "It wouldn't work. But thank you."

That caught him on the raw. He was trying to do the right thing, to ease her conscience, to take care of her, to make up for what he'd done. And she was throwing the offer back at him.

"Listen, honey, there are plenty of women who'd give their eyeteeth to marry me, even just for my money," he said curtly.

"So marry one of them," she replied, forcing her tone to be light and careless.

"Most women don't want a platonic marriage."

"Other women wouldn't, I expect," she faltered.

"I don't want other women," he said coldly, and then felt himself go rigid with the knowledge that it was the truth. He didn't want to look at anyone except Kate, much less go to bed with anyone else. "If I can't have you, I'll go without."

In the darkness, her own heartbeat sounded very loud. She stared at the dark ceiling. "I don't understand."

"Neither do I. Maybe I've got a guilty conscience. I don't go around seducing virgins. I hurt you, and remembering it hurts me. Maybe I've got a hang-up."

"You'll get over it."

"Will you?" he asked. He rolled over, looking down at her in the faint glow from the outside security lights. "Will you forget that night, as long as you live?"

"Well, no, but..."

"Will you ever want another man to make love to you?" he persisted.

"No." It sounded blunt, but it was the way she felt. "No, I couldn't let any other man touch me. Only you... that way."

His body burned with pride. Even though he'd hurt her, she hadn't stopped wanting him. She loved his touch, and he knew it, and it made him feel like a giant.

"Only me." He brushed his mouth over her closed eyes, and his hand smoothed down over her caftan, quickening her breathing as he touched her breasts and found their tips already hard and welcoming. "Someday, I'll take you right up to the sun in my arms, Kate."

"Ja...cob," she bit off.

He found the buttons under her arm, and unfastened them, enough to allow the slow, gentle intrusion of his hand onto bare flesh.

"Oh, God, you're soft, Kate," he breathed, sliding his fingers tenderly over her bare breasts. "Soft and exquisitely silky. Baby, you're so sweet to touch."

She moaned helplessly as her body turned to flame. Her good arm lifted. She found the buttons on the shoulder and fumbled them open and pulled the fabric completely aside.

"Yes," he whispered, feeling her hunger reflected in his own body. "Yes, I want it, too."

He moved her into the thin strip of light that filtered in through the window. "I want to see this sweet body," he said huskily. "I want to get drunk on the sight of you."

Her body trembled as she saw his eyes, felt his hands blatantly caressing her. His gaze went to her body, and she saw him smile at the wild reaction he coaxed from her as he teased the tips of her breasts.

"Lie still," he whispered, bending. "I don't want to hurt you. No, honey, don't start arching up toward my mouth. I'll give you what you want without any coaxing."

He kissed the swollen softness with tender lips, sliding his hands under her to support her, lift her. He heard her sharp, gasping little moans, and had to fight not to deepen the drugging intimacy. But he knew how delicate she still was. He couldn't have her, not yet. But he could make love to her in this exquisitely tender way. He could have those sweet little cries she'd never given to another man; he could touch her as no other hands ever had, or would.

It made him drunk with pleasure. In his passion, he nipped her, and she caught his head and made a frightened sound.

He lifted his chin to look at her, smiling down. "Men get carried away, remember?" he whispered. "You're silky and sweet under my mouth, and when I think about how virginal you are, I feel savagely male."

"You...bit me."

"Not hard enough to hurt," he whispered. "I never would. It's a kind of love play. A way of expressing passion."

"Oh." She stared at him, her eyes soft with love, wide with curiosity.

"Your upbringing scarred your emotions, I know. But will you try to remember that what we're doing together is part of life? That men and women were created to join, to become one in physical union?"

"Yes, but...but not in lust," she whispered.

He frowned faintly, his hands stilling. "Kate, do you think that all I feel for you is lust?"

She lowered her eyes to his broad, hair-matted chest, watching the ripple of muscle as he shifted over her. "Isn't it?"

He didn't know how to answer her. He was just realizing that what he felt wasn't physical alone. He wanted to please her. His own satisfaction didn't seem so important these days. He touched her face, loving the very structure of it, the softness of her skin. "No. I don't think it ever was. If I hadn't gone over the edge that night in your apartment, I'd have made sure you never wanted to forget what we did. I had these exquisite fantasies about loving you half to death."

Her heart jumped. How sweet that sounded. She looked up at him, her eyes so soft that he got lost in them. "I'm sorry about what I said to you..."

He brushed his mouth over hers. "Not half as sorry as I am about that damned hundred-dollar bill."

"I understand now."

"I could have lost you," he said under his breath. "The doctor said if that bullet had gone two inches lower, you'd have died."

"But it didn't, and I didn't," she reminded him. Her hands lifted to his chest, trembling a little at the delicious feel of all that muscle and its furry covering. "What did you say to me when you came into the intensive-care unit?"

"Things."

She moved her hands softly, and he tensed. "What kind of things?"

He nuzzled her face with his. "Very personal ones, that I wouldn't repeat cold sober or in broad daylight. I'm rather glad that you don't remember hearing them."

Now she really was curious. What could he have told her that he didn't want her to know? He was such a private person, so alone. But then, so was she.

"I think you pulled me back," she confessed. She looked at his chest, watched it ripple as she caressed it. "I didn't care about living."

"That's what bothered me. You were close to the edge, and I'd given you every reason in the world to look for a way over."

His breath caught as her hands moved again. He wavered between the need to let her caress him and the stupidity of not stopping her before things got any hotter than they already were.

"Kate...I really think that we'd better stop now."

She looked at the rigidity of his chest and understood. With a deep sigh, she moved her hands to his arms instead. "What a pity, when I was just getting the hang of it," she murmured dryly, although her heart was going mad.

"I feel the same way. But you can't handle passionate lovemaking until that rib heals."

She blushed. "No, I don't suppose so."

"It would be passionate, too," he breathed, slowly fastening the caftan over her breasts. "I'm shaking like a teenage boy right now."

She wondered if he'd ever admitted to that with any other woman. She almost asked, but she was too jealous of him to want the answer. She watched his dark face while he finished closing the buttons on her shoulder.

"Jacob, tell me what just happened wasn't out of guilt."

"Guilt?" He stared down at her for a long minute until, with a rigid smile, he moved onto his side and reached for her, pulling her gently against the length of him, his hands pressing her hips slowly against the unmistakable contours of his body. "Does this feel like guilt? Or are you still innocent enough to think a man can fake desire?"

Her legs felt trembly. She caught his hands, but he wouldn't release her. "I don't know a lot about it," she said.

"This," he emphasized, shifting her against him gently, "is a hell of a nuisance. I'm not usually stupid enough to encourage it unless I'm in a position to satisfy it. It's damned uncomfortable."

She was flaming by now. "Oh."

He released her and rolled over onto his back, arching a little as the ache increased before it finally began to subside. He forced himself to breathe normally, to relax.

"In the old days, about the time you decided to drive me crazy with Gerald what's-his-name, I could hear your voice on the phone and have that happen," he said quietly. "Of course, it's diminished a little over the years."

He sounded dry, and she sat up, staring down at him. Yes, he was smiling, just faintly.

"Now do you begin to understand what happened that night?" he asked, his voice deep and gentle. "I've wanted you for so many years that I dreamed about you all the time, and then there you were, wanting me back, and we were in bed together. A loaded gun wouldn't have stopped me."

"You wouldn't come near me, all those years," she said.

"I knew what would happen if I did," he replied. He

drew her back down again, her head using his shoulder as a pillow. "There was Margo, and you were friends. I didn't want to have to explain to my niece why she couldn't play around with boys when I was playing around with her best friend."

"You wouldn't have played around with me after the first time," she reminded him.

He smiled, touching her hair gently. "That's true enough. It still makes me feel incredibly male, knowing that I was the first. I'm only sorry that I didn't give you the pleasure I felt."

She stared at the steady rise and fall of his chest. "Will we ever make love again?" she whispered, blurting it out.

"If you marry me, we will," he replied after a minute. "Otherwise, I don't think my conscience, or yours, will let us."

She had to fight tears. "That kind of marriage wouldn't work."

"Let it lie, for now. We'll plug along for a while and see how it goes." He brushed his lips across her forehead. "Sleep well."

"Are you all right now?" she asked softly.

He chuckled. "I'm all right." He drew the covers over them with a long sigh. "Curl up against me and we'll try to sleep."

He turned on his side and drew her back into the curve of his body, and she caught her breath at the delicious sensations it produced.

"Just try not to move around too much," he whispered into her ear.

She laughed, because she could feel why. It was magic, this closeness that had come so unexpectedly, this intimacy that was warm and sweet and tender. She sighed, linking her fingers into the hand that curved across her arm. He felt warm and strong at her back, and she knew there wouldn't be any more nightmares. Not this night. She closed her eyes, wishing that it could last forever.

But she awoke the next morning in her own bed, and at first it seemed that the night before had been a sweet dream. She sat up, and with the movement, she caught the spicy scent of Jacob's cologne still clinging to her. And beside her, on the next pillow, was a white rose, like the few roses still blooming on the bush outside the back door.

She picked it up and inhaled its dew-kissed fragrance, smiling softly to herself. No. It hadn't been a dream after all.

She put on her rib belt and got dressed, feeling young and extraordinarily happy. Jacob had asked her to marry him.

That didn't mean that he loved her, of course. But it had to be a start of some kind, if he'd been thinking about it.

In jeans, a loose green knit blouse, and boots, she went slowly down the hall and into the dining room. Hank was gone, but Jacob was still there, pushing eggs around on his plate absently.

He looked up when she walked in, and his eyes kindled as he smiled at her.

"Finally," he murmured. "I wondered how much longer I could push these damned cold eggs around on my plate without making Janet suspicious."

"Were you waiting for me?" she asked, returning the smile.

"What do you think?" he slid back his chair and stood up, holding out his hand. She took it and was drawn gently into his hard arms and kissed with warm, rough affection.

"Good morning," she whispered under his lips.

"Good morning yourself. Did you find the rose?"

She smiled. "Yes. Thank you."

He kissed her eyelids. "I wish your rib was healed, Kate, because I want you a hell of a lot closer than this."

"Me, too," she breathed. She could feel his heart beating against her breasts. "Did you sleep?"

"Eventually," he mused, drawing back. "I lay and looked at you for a long, long time before I finally did. We're going to have to get married, Kate."

She looked down at his chest. She wanted to say yes. She wanted him. But a tiny part of her knew that it would be disastrous. He might be feeling new things with her, but that didn't necessarily mean he loved her. He admitted himself that a great deal of what he felt was physical. That would wear off, when he was totally satisfied, and what would they have left?

"I can't marry you."

"Why?"

He sounded indignant. She met his dark eyes. "Jacob, desire isn't enough. Without love…"

"You love me, though, Kate," he said quietly, watching her face. "You always have."

She seemed to stop breathing. She searched his eyes. Was he guessing…?

"Tom told me everything, just before they took you to the hospital," he said. "I even saw the photos of me…"

Her reaction was unexpected. She tore away from him, wild-eyed, oblivious of the shock in his face and the pain in her rib.

"Well, my God, it's all right," he said shortly, because her actions surprised him. "There's nothing to be embarrassed about."

But there was. Kate was dying inside. She felt as if her

soul had been stripped naked in front of an audience. She went alternately red and white, and then the tears started.

It was just too much to have Jacob know everything. What he felt had been pity; now she was sure of it. Pity and guilt, because she loved him and he'd hurt her. Now he was trying to make up for that hurt, and she'd believed that he was just beginning to feel something for her. What a fool she'd been!

He started toward her, and she jerked back.

"No," she whispered tearfully. "No, don't you ever touch me again. I don't want your pity, Jacob!"

She turned and ran down the hall into her room, closing the door and locking it behind her. She didn't even hear him knock, or try the doorknob, and after a minute he called her name.

She ignored him, falling onto the bed in tears. She didn't know what she was going to do, but she couldn't stay at Warlance. Outside, thunder rattled the house and lightning struck toward the ground as the storm brought wind and pelting rain. Kate closed her eyes, grateful for the noise that drowned out Jacob's voice. She pulled the pillow over her head to make sure she couldn't understand. He sounded coaxing, then demanding and, finally, furiously angry. The sound of his boots stalking off down the hall was loud enough to penetrate through the pillow. With a sob, she buried her face and cried until her chest was sore again.

Chapter 10

Kate spent the rest of the morning in her room, not leaving it until she was certain that Jacob had gone out. Then she sat in the living room, trying to decide what to do. It was raining outside, and she thought about the cowboys out in the chilly, wet weather. She thought about Jacob, and felt her heart go cold.

Why had he admitted that Tom had told him? Was it because she'd refused to marry him, and he'd been irritated when she didn't jump at the chance? Did he think that she was so selfish that she'd marry him just because she wanted it, without any thought for what it would be like for him? Being tied to a woman he didn't love would make him miserable for the rest of his life. Loving sometimes required sacrifices, but apparently he didn't know that.

One thing was certain; she had to get away from here. She couldn't bear the embarrassment of being around

Jacob and knowing that she had no secrets from him. Her eyes closed as she relived the sweetness of the night before. The memory turned bitter when she realized that pity had motivated him. He knew that she loved him. That slow, tender loving had been because he thought it would please her, just another way of making restitution for the hurt he'd dealt her in Chicago. Maybe he wanted her, too, but she knew it hadn't been out of love, and that was what hurt the most.

The tears came again, pouring down her cheeks. She had to go back to Chicago. But if she did, what was she going to do? She knew she couldn't work for another week or so at least, and even then, doing police news was going to be impossible. She was drawing her paycheck, but that would run out when her recuperation period was over. She had pitiful little savings. So what was she to do? She didn't feel right about imposing on Tom, although she knew he'd come for her if she called him.

She was still worrying about the future when Hank came in, tossing off his yellow slicker, muttering under his breath. He glanced at Kate and grinned sheepishly.

"Sorry, I got carried away. My son," he said, nodding toward the front door, "is out there in his shirt-sleeves, getting drenched, and the temperature is dropping. So naturally I asked him did he want a raincoat. He said some words I won't repeat and stomped off mumbling something about hoping he catches his death." He frowned. "Did the two of you get into another argument or something, Katie?"

He was the only person who ever called her by that nickname. She shifted restlessly on the sofa. "Well... kind of."

"Kind of?"

She grimaced. "Jacob asked me to marry him and

I said no." She noted the shock on his face. "Well, he doesn't love me, Hank," she said. "It wouldn't be right."

He whistled. "I never thought I'd live to see the day he'd propose to any woman. Now the miracle has happened, and you have to go all righteous and say no. Are you crazy?" he asked. "My gosh, girl, I'm sixty years old. If he doesn't get a move on, I'll never have grandkids. And you're a nice girl. We all know and like you—he couldn't do better if he looked for years." He sat down across from her. "See here, Kate, you need to think about this."

"I have thought about it." She blushed, lowering her eyes. "I love him, and he knew all the time—Tom told him. Jacob blurted it out this morning when I said I wouldn't marry him, and I'm so hurt…!"

She was crying and Hank felt awkward. He patted her hand gently. "Now, now," he said, grimacing. "Now, now."

"I want to leave," she whispered. "But I've got nowhere to go."

"He'd just come after you if you left," he said reasonably. "Jay don't give up when he sets his mind to something, you know. That is, if he don't kill himself working out in the pouring rain."

"Doctors say that you don't catch cold even in the rain unless you've been exposed to a virus or something," she said, more to reassure herself than to convince him.

"Yeah, but there's a virus going through the bunkhouse, one of those chest things with bronchitis. I sure hope he doesn't get it."

So did Kate, but she didn't know what to do. She couldn't even face Jacob right now, much less go out and start trying to tell him what to do.

"You might get one of the men to hit him over the head

and drag him back here," she suggested as she dabbed at the tears on her face.

"There's a thought. Are you okay now?"

She forced a smile. "I'm okay."

"Don't make such heavy weather of it. Everything will work out." He smiled. "Now go get some lunch and I'll go out and try to save Jay from himself."

"All right. You're a nice man, Hank."

"Why, sure I am," he agreed. "And you're a nice girl. Too bad we can't include Jay, but he ain't nice."

"Once in a while…" she protested.

"Maybe. Go on, now."

She got up and went off to find Janet. But if she expected Hank to get anywhere with his stubborn offspring, she was disappointed. Night came, and Jacob was still out. By the time she went reluctantly to bed, he hadn't put a foot in the door.

The next morning, he was still at the table when she came down after a sleepless night. Her heart jumped. She'd expected him to be gone already.

She tried to find words, but couldn't. Having him know everything in her heart made her feel vulnerable and nervous.

It was too late to run. She pulled out a chair and sat down, glancing quickly at Jacob.

He was pale, and when he asked her to pass the bacon, his voice sounded hoarse.

"All that rain," she said hesitantly. "You've caught cold."

"Maybe I'll die," he shot back, glaring at her. "I hope if I do that I lie on your conscience like lead, Kate."

She flushed and pulled her eyes to the coffee she was pouring into her cup. "I didn't ask you to try and drown yourself."

"You won't marry me," he said coldly.

"You know why, too."

"I wish I could understand why women are so damned secretive about their feelings," he muttered. He put his fork down and glared at her. "What difference does it make if I know that you care about me? The world hasn't stopped turning, has it? The sky hasn't fallen on your head!"

"It's embarrassing!" she shot back.

"Why?"

She looked at him and away, stirring too much cream into her coffee while she tried to deal with the intimacy of the conversation. "I feel vulnerable."

"Maybe I do, too, Kate."

She laughed bitterly. "How could you? You don't care about me."

There was a long pause, and she looked up to find him watching her with eyes that looked strange, unusually dark. "I'm still in the learning stages about that," he confessed, his voice husky. He cleared his throat, and coughed. "Damned cold rain. I feel like hell."

"Why don't you go back to bed?" she ventured.

"Loving me doesn't give you the right to mother me," he replied curtly, and glared at her shocked expression. "I don't want to go to bed, thank you. I've got cattle to look after."

"You can't look after them if you die," she replied. Talking about her feelings was beginning to feel natural—at least with him it was.

"I won't die." He sipped his coffee, made a face at the eggs and bacon and stood up. "I can't eat. I'm going out."

But when he started to move, he swayed. Kate jumped up without thinking and got under his arm. His body felt hot, and when she reached up to feel his forehead, it was blazing.

"Jacob, you've got a fever. A high one," she announced.

"I do feel a bit woozy. Here, now, honey, don't put that rib at risk. I can lean against the wall."

"Just lean on me. I won't let you hurt my rib," she protested. "Let's get you to bed."

"I haven't got time for this, Kate," he grumbled. But he went with her, feeling sick and hollow—and oddly elated because Kate loved him. It had hurt more than he wanted to admit, having her run from him because he'd blurted that out about her feelings. His feverish eyes looked down on her dark head. She was one in a million. And she was going to marry him, one way or the other. He wasn't letting her get away.

"Now, lie down while I get these off," she said when they were beside his bed. She watched him lie down, and reached for his boot.

"No, you don't," he replied, glaring at her. "You aren't supposed to do any lifting, or pulling, and boots don't come off without some work. Get Hank."

She sighed. He was right. "Okay. Where is he?"

"Probably at the barn. The vet was coming to check some new stock for us." Stretched catty-cornered over the coverlet, his hat off, his feet hanging off the mattress, he closed his eyes. He looked sick.

"I'll get him. You stay put."

He opened one eye. "Worried about me?" he asked, and grinned wickedly.

She glared. "It would serve you right if I ignored you."

He closed the eye again. "No, it wouldn't. It feels good, being loved," he said in a slow, tender voice, and he smiled.

She flushed, and tried to find the right words to reply. He was confusing her.

He opened his eyes to study her reaction, and the smile was still there, even more tender than before. "Put on a raincoat before you go out," he reminded her. "I don't want you to catch cold."

A warm glow grew inside her. She smiled back at him, fascinated by his unexpected tenderness. Then she quickly went out, a little afraid of his new attitude.

Hank came at once, and when he saw Jacob, he immediately phoned the doctor, who said to bring the patient in. Kate got him into a raincoat and they stuffed him into the cab of the pickup and drove him into Blairsville.

It was a bad case of bronchitis, with a viral infection aggravating it. The doctor gave Jacob an injection and prescriptions for antibiotics and a cough syrup. They picked up the prescriptions on the way home. Then Hank got him undressed and into bed, Janet made him chicken soup and Kate sat with him while Hank went out to work.

He slept most of the day. Kate watched him with loving eyes, enjoying the unique experience of being allowed to look at him without having to worry about being seen. Even pale and feverish, he delighted her hungry eyes.

She left him only long enough to eat a quick dinner and then went back to his bedside with a cup of coffee to keep her warm. By night, he was stirring.

"I feel worse now than I did when I got up," he murmured.

"Darkness before dawn," she said cheerfully.

He smiled at her. "I guess. You should be in bed."

"I'll go in a little while."

"If you're going to stay, how about reading me something?"

"What would you like to hear? One of those murder mysteries?"

"I'd rather hear market news. There's a recent cattlemen's association magazine on my dresser."

"Okay."

She got it and read him an article about new marketing techniques and a report on forage grasses.

"That reminds me," he murmured, "I've got the boys building a greenhouse for you. It should be finished in a day or so. Then we'll get you some pots and potting soil and some plant stock from the nursery in Pierre."

"You don't need to worry with that," she said, pleased that he'd remembered his promise, and sad that she wouldn't get to use the greenhouse. "I'll be able to leave in another week, you know," she added quietly.

He opened his eyes and looked at her, without any subterfuge or camouflage. "I want you where I am."

She flushed. "I have a job…."

"Quit it," he said.

The color grew worse. "Jacob, I—"

"I can support you. I've got a damned empire out here, except at tax time. We can live on beef for a while, even if the money gives out. You can grow things in the greenhouse and we'll have vegetables year-round."

He didn't sound as if he were joking. "You don't want to marry," she reminded him. "You've always said you didn't."

"I've said a lot of stupid things, Kate. Haven't you noticed?" He moved onto his side so that he could see her. "Listen, don't you want kids?"

"Well, yes," she admitted, her eyes lingering with hopeless longing on his dark face.

"My kids?" he persisted gently, smiling.

She averted her eyes. "I'll kill my brother," she said through her teeth.

"He's in New York, and I'll protect him. I told you, I like being loved. Nobody ever loved me before, except family."

Memories flashed through her mind. A deep, slow voice, faintly unsteady, whispering that. Her eyes widened, holding his. "You said that…you told me that when I was in the intensive care unit. You said, 'Don't die on me…'"

The smile faded, and he held her eyes relentlessly. "Yes. And I told you that I didn't think I wanted to live without you. Would you like to hear me say it again?"

"You were just overwrought," she said.

"I still am. I want you." He reached out and caught her hand gently in his. "Don't turn away like that. Wanting isn't some unforgivable sin. It's part of that emotion you don't want me to know you feel for me." He smiled at her softly. "Kate, you like planting things and watching them grow. Well, I guess God does, too. He arranged things so that a man and a woman do the planting, and the baby is the little seed that grows. Life is a miracle, Kate."

She searched his dark eyes quietly. "I was punished every time I smiled at a boy," she whispered. "All Tom and I heard was how sinful sex was."

"Your father was a sick man, honey," he said gently. "He was sick, and maybe he had more responsibility than he could handle."

"If my mother hadn't left us—"

He drew her hand to his mouth. "My mother left me, too," he reminded her. "It wasn't my fault when she left, any more than you were to blame for your mother's desertion. Maybe she had a reason. You were very young when she left. It's hard for a child to understand adult reasoning."

"I used to cry for her at night," she told him. "I missed her so much."

"Maybe she missed you and Tom, too." His eyes narrowed. He'd just had an idea, but he wasn't going to share it with Kate just yet. Not until he worked out the details.

Kate didn't answer. She looked at the lean, strong hand holding hers, and involuntarily her fingers stroked over the back of it.

"I wish I felt better," he murmured, watching her. "I want to make love to you."

She felt heat tingle through her. For an old-fashioned reactionary, he had a sexy way of talking to her. She felt naive with him.

"So shy," he mused, turning her hand over so that he could lock his warm fingers into hers. "And I've hurt you without even realizing how much, all these long years we've been apart. I wish I could take back every painful thing I've ever said to you."

"You said what you felt at the time. There's no need for any regrets," she replied quietly.

"Think so? Get my wallet off the dresser, honey."

Frowning, she found the battered black cowhide wallet and handed it to him. He struggled into a sitting position, knocking the covers off his broad, hair-matted chest, and opened the wallet. He thumbed through the plastic inserts to the one he'd shown Morgan Winthrop at the newspaper office. He turned it, and showed it to Kate.

She stared at the picture, dumbfounded. It wasn't something he'd just stuck in there to impress her. From the faded, wrinkled condition of it, and the age she was when it had been taken, he'd been carrying the photograph around for a lot of years. It was of her, at one of

Margo's parties, in a Mexican skirt and peasant blouse, with her long hair settled around her bare shoulders and her mouth smiling at the photographer. There was a brilliance in that smile that puzzled her, until she remembered that Jacob had taken the picture for Margo, who'd been in it with her. He'd cut it to fit his wallet, removing Margo's image in the process.

"I never knew why you looked so beautiful until Tom told me the truth," he said, watching her rapt expression. "And then I realized that the light in your eyes in that picture was for me. I've carried it everywhere with me, for years. Having it with me made me feel at home wherever I happened to be." He reached out and took the wallet back from her, glancing warmly at the picture before he closed the wallet and gave it to her to put on the dresser.

"You wanted to be a reporter, you see," he said, studying her face when she sat down again. "You wanted the city. I wasn't about to put myself in the position of losing out to a career. So I scotched down what I was starting to feel for you, and I found a reason to hate you. That kept you from looking deeper."

She felt her breath stop in her throat. He'd been starting to feel something for her. He hadn't known how she felt, but he was sure she wanted a career instead of marriage. What an irony.

"I...went to Chicago so I wouldn't wear my heart out on you," she confessed. "We all thought you'd marry Barbara someday because she was rich like you, and beautiful and sophisticated."

"Bull," he said curtly. "She was a decorator piece, great for standing in ballrooms and taking to expensive restaurants. I had in mind a woman who'd like being pregnant by me and spending her life looking at cattle and dust and hay."

Her lips parted. "Oh."

"The family ranch, like the family farm, is becoming a thing of the past, Kate, and do you know why? It's because people on farms aren't having a lot of kids anymore. It's unfashionable. They have a son or two, and the son hates the country, so he leaves. Dad grows old and sells the farm." He pursed his lips, letting his dark eyes travel slowly over Kate's tall, slender body. "We could make a lot of babies together."

She gasped. And he laughed, wickedly, seductively, watching her like a hawk.

"Little cowboys," he said softly. "Little cowgirls. I could even learn to change diapers and give bottles, unless you wanted to nurse the babies." His dark eyes went to her breasts and he felt himself going rigid with sweet memories. "Oh, God, Kate, I'd love to watch you nurse them," he whispered fervently.

She was shaking by now. She loved him so desperately. And he wanted children; children would bind them. But even as she wanted it, would have died for it, she realized that their marriage would be only a travesty, with all the love on her side. Someday, inevitably, Jacob would fall in love with someone else and he'd leave her. Nothing would alter that. Her love alone wasn't enough to build a future on.

"No." She forced the word out without looking directly at him. "I'm sorry. I can't." She turned back toward the door.

"You love me, damn it!" he said, exasperated.

"Love on one side isn't enough," she said miserably. "It wouldn't be enough for you, eventually. Someday you'll realize that it was just desire shadowed with pity, Jacob." She opened the door, hiding the tears she couldn't let him see. "Good night."

When she closed the door behind her, he was cursing steadily, watching her go with a kind of impotence he'd never felt. Damn women, damn female logic, damn it all! If he'd felt halfway well, and if she'd been completely healed, he'd have argued away all her protests. But as things stood, he couldn't do anything. He lay back on the pillows with a weary sigh and closed his eyes.

He could have told Kate he loved her, he supposed. The words didn't even feel uncomfortable. But she was certain that his conscience was responsible for how he felt, and that wasn't true. And desire wasn't the only emotion he felt. A man didn't carry a woman's photo around with him for years out of desire alone. But he wasn't quite ready to deal with that much emotion. Not yet. Only, if he didn't do something fast, Kate was going to walk right out of his life. And he couldn't deal with that at all.

He slept on those troubled thoughts, and woke up with a fresh idea. Perhaps he should change tactics.

Kate was at the breakfast table, her face pale, her eyes a little puffy, as if she'd cried all night. He sighed, looking at her eyes. Incredible, that stubborn streak in her. She was still protecting him from himself. Or trying to.

"Want to see your greenhouse today?" Jacob asked, grinning at his father as he took his place at the head of the table and dragged the bacon platter closer. He was still a little hoarse and weak, but he wasn't about to let those minor irritations get him down. He was well on the way to normal.

"Greenhouse?" Kate echoed with her coffee cup halfway to her lips. She brightened immediately. "You mean they're through with it?"

"Haven't you missed the hammering for the past day?" Jacob teased gently. "Yes, they're through. And just in time, because the first snow isn't far away now. I've had them add an emergency generator and a heating system, so that you won't have to worry about power failures. If you get busy, you'll have strawberries in December."

"Strawberries in December." She sighed. But then she looked at him and her face fell as she realized that in December she wouldn't be here anymore. She'd been noble and turned him down. She'd be back in Chicago looking for work, and pretty soon. Her month was almost up.

"What's that sad look for?" he asked.

"I'll be gone," she said. "In December, I mean."

"No, you won't," he said good-humoredly. "We're getting married."

"We are not!" she tossed back, setting her lips into a thin line. "We went over all that last night, Jacob."

"You did, but I didn't." He added eggs to his plate and a biscuit thick with apple butter. "Pour me some coffee, will you, honey?"

"That's the way, son. Just ignore whatever Kate says and marry her anyway," Hank agreed. "Well, Kate," he coaxed when she glared at him, "you have to understand how desperate Janet and I are to marry him off. He's been in a better humor altogether since you've been on the place. We wouldn't want him to revert to type, would we?"

"I don't care what he reverts to. I can't marry him," Kate said doggedly.

"He's rich," Hank coaxed. "Handsome. He'd spoil you rotten. You'd have lots of kids and I'd get to babysit them...."

"Like hell you would," Jacob shot back. "I'm not having you teach my sons how to shoot pool and play blackjack and drink whiskey!"

"Well, it never hurt you none, Jay," Hank said reasonably.

"He let you drink whiskey when you were a little boy?" Kate asked Jacob with wide, curious eyes.

"Of course he did," he muttered. "He let us do anything we wanted. That way we didn't use his whiskey bottles for targets and put burrs in his sheets at night."

"You little monster," Kate accused.

"I had my good points," Jacob replied, finishing his breakfast.

"Did you?" Hank said, puzzled.

"I love you, too," Jacob muttered at him.

"I'm glad, but it's Kate you ought to be practicing on. Why don't you take her to see that greenhouse?" Hank suggested with raised brows and a grin.

"I did have that in mind. I don't need any heavy-handed pushes, thanks."

"Suit yourself, son," Hank said innocently, and bent over his eggs.

Jacob swallowed the rest of his coffee and, noticing that Kate, too, had finished her breakfast, drew her chair out for her and led her down the hall toward the back door.

"Going to show Kate the greenhouse, are you?" Janet asked with a grin, looking from one to the other approvingly. "Nice day for it."

Jacob said something under his breath and herded Kate out the back door.

"Janet is one of a kind." Kate laughed, looking up at him.

"Thank God," he said without a pause.

She shook her head. "It's like an armed camp around here. Do you and Janet and your father fight all the time?"

"Only during daylight." He linked her fingers into his and smiled down at her. It was a sunny, warm day, unseasonably so, and he was in his shirtsleeves. She was wearing jeans, as he was, and a blue print shirt much like the one that covered his broad chest and muscular arms.

"We match," she said without thinking.

"Indeed we do." His hand tightened. "We'll find we have a lot in common. We both love the land, we're dyed-in-the-wool conservationists and, if I remember, you even like animals."

"It isn't enough. Please don't harass me, Jacob," she asked quietly. "It's not fair."

"You want to marry me."

"More than anything," she agreed, her voice husky and soft. "Except your happiness."

"Stubborn woman," he sighed.

"I guess I am. And I haven't even told you how grateful I am that you let me come here to get back on my feet."

"Don't be absurd," he bit off as they reached the huge greenhouse. "I don't want gratitude."

"Jacob, this is awfully big," she said dubiously.

"I told you I had a few experiments of my own in mind." He opened the door for her and she walked inside, aghast at the amount of space she was going to have. The aisles were covered with pine shavings, and there were tables the length of the building. Hoses were connected everywhere, seed starters were sitting in boxes along the walls. Kate just shook her head, awed.

"I never expected anything like this. Oh, Jacob, it's… heavenly!"

He smiled. "I'm glad you like it."

"Like it!" She turned impulsively and hugged him. "You're wonderful!"

He *felt* wonderful with her soft body pressed against him and her face bright and radiant. His hands went to her shoulders to hold her lightly, and his breath caught. It was like flying. His head spun when she touched him.

"You're welcome," he said at her temple.

His faint reticence got through to her and she started to draw away, embarrassed. But when she looked up and saw the indecision in his face, she stood still.

"You've never touched me voluntarily before," he said quietly.

She smiled hesitantly. "I don't suppose I have," she confessed. "You always seemed to have an invisible Keep Away sign around your neck."

"And now I haven't?" he persisted.

"Well...it's less noticeable," she mused.

"Then since it is," he murmured, bending, "why don't you kiss me?"

Her breath caught. That tender note in his deep, drawling voice was new, too. She closed her eyes as his mouth came close enough to capture her own, and then she held on and put her heart into it.

Seconds later, he was the one who drew back, all too quickly.

"We'd better look at some seed catalogs," he said through his teeth, and the eyes that looked down at her were dark with hunger. "Before all my good resolutions go up in smoke."

"Yes." Since she'd refused to marry him, she supposed he didn't feel entitled to make love to her anymore. That was vaguely disappointing, but she had to face reality. This was how it was going to be from now on.

But if she expected him to get better humored as the days went by, she was doomed to disappointment. His temper became shorter and his irritation grew as he drew away from any physical contact at all.

Chapter 11

Kate spent most of her free time puttering in the greenhouse while Jacob tried to work himself to death. Things were relatively peaceful for three days. And then, on the fourth morning, Jacob sat down at the breakfast table in a black study.

He glared at her as she paused in the doorway in her pale yellow slacks and blouse. "I don't give a damn if you don't want to marry me," he said out of the blue. "Go back to Chicago and get shot at, for all I care."

"Thanks, I will," she returned, sitting in the chair Hank had pulled out for her. "I'm glad to see you're feeling like your old irritable self, Jacob."

"These eggs have curdled, for sure," Janet grumbled as she put them down roughly in front of Jacob. "I've never in my life seen a man in such a bad temper. Kate, I wish you'd marry him and put him out of his misery."

"Me, too," Hank sighed, glancing at her. "Janet and I would never forget you for making the sacrifice."

"I don't want to marry her anymore," Jacob muttered, hacking at his bacon. "This bacon is too hard!"

"Then why don't you go out and cut yourself a piece of beef off one of your cows and eat that?" Janet snapped back.

"And the eggs taste like leather."

"I knew you'd curdle them," the housekeeper returned. She put her hands on her hips and scowled at him. "And I'll bet the coffee's too weak and the biscuits are too crumbly to suit you, too!"

"As a matter of fact, yes," Jacob said.

"Then you can get breakfast in Blairsville in the morning," Janet replied, "because you won't get any here!"

"I'll fire you!" he shot at her.

"Go ahead. I couldn't get a worse boss in hell!"

Jacob put down his fork, glared at everyone and stormed out of the room.

"Thank God, now we can eat in peace," Hank said with a sigh. He smiled at Kate, who was a little paler than normal. "Still holding out, are you?"

"He doesn't love me," she said doggedly. "I won't tie him down. He thinks it's what he wants, but someday he may fall in love."

Hank didn't say a word. But he was smiling as he bent over his eggs.

It was the day that Kate was due to go in for her one-month checkup. She was sure Hank would be deputized to take her, or one of the men, but it was Jacob who waited for her in the Lincoln at the front steps.

He looked out of sorts, as he had for days. He glared, as he had for days. But he opened the door for her, and was as coolly polite as a host could be.

"I guess you'll be headed back to Chicago in no time once you've got the all clear from the doctor," he said as they went lazily down the highway.

"I guess so," she responded without much pleasure. She didn't relish the thought of picking up where she'd left off. The memories were too fresh.

"Don't expect another proposal from me," he continued shortly, "because you aren't getting one."

"I didn't expect to." She stared out at the rolling landscape. The horizon seemed to be years away, and there was such a feeling of spaciousness, of freedom here in South Dakota. She wondered how she'd lived without it. But she shouldn't get too used to it; she was leaving soon. She might as well get used to not seeing Jacob, too, because in no time her precious few weeks with him would be a sweet memory. She felt empty already, and she hadn't even left.

He stopped suddenly in the middle of the deserted highway, and turned to her. "Is it because I've made sex into some kind of nightmare for you?" he asked abruptly, ignoring her flush. "Is that it? Are you afraid to trust your body to me again because I hurt you so badly?"

She felt on fire. "Jacob, I don't want to talk about it, please!"

"Just tell me the truth."

She closed her eyes. "You didn't hurt me that badly," she said through clenched teeth. "It's not because I'm afraid of you."

"So you keep saying." He sighed roughly and eased down on the accelerator. His expression didn't waver as he turned onto the road that led to Blairsville, and he didn't speak again.

The doctor checked her over, pronounced her fit enough to return to work and smiled as she left his office. Jacob paid the bill, against her protests, and led her back to the Lincoln.

"I'm well," she said. "I can go back to work, officially."

"Well, hooray," he muttered as he put her in, got in beside her and started the car.

"You can stop feeling guilty now," she said under her breath, sitting rigidly in her seat. "I don't hold anything that happened against you, all right?"

He wasn't listening. The day was unseasonably warm, and he turned off onto a dirt road that led deep into the woods, to a secluded little glade where a stream bubbled across the road and the wind blew through a small stand of trees.

"Why are we stopping here?" she asked uneasily.

He turned to her, his dark eyes blazing. "Because I'm sick to death of having you try to save me from myself. Why in hell do you think I want to marry you out of guilt and pity? I'm not stupid enough to try and build a long-term relationship on that kind of emotional quicksand!"

She tried to speak, and stammered, "Then, why?"

"I like being with you," he said curtly. "God knows why, you drive me nuts most of the time. I like doing things with you, I even like being alone with you." He searched her face slowly. "I'd even like to have kids with you. Despite the bad beginning we had, we've grown pretty close since you've been at Warlance, Kate. Close enough to gamble on marriage. At least, I think so."

She could hardly think at all. He was knocking down her arguments one by one. "I want to marry you," she whispered brokenly. "I want it more than anything on earth, Jacob. But it's such a risk, don't you see?"

"All I see," he whispered back, "is a body I ache for in the darkness, a mind that matches mine thought for thought and a woman I'd kill for."

Holding her eyes with his, he slid the seat back and unfastened first his seat belt, then hers. He moved closer without saying a word, but the expression in his dark eyes was speaking as he bent to her mouth.

It was the slowest, softest kiss they'd ever shared. She felt his arms enclosing her, his fingers easing into her hair to hold her head where he wanted it as he began to deepen the kiss.

She made one token protest that turned into a soft moan, and then she yielded to his tenderness. Birds called back and forth, the bubbling stream made itself heard even through the closed windows. The wind blew softly. But Kate was feeling his hands touching her, turning her, gently discovering her. She was hearing Jacob's rough breath against her soft mouth, and feeling his heartbeat against her breasts.

He turned her, moving her so that she was lying on the seat. Vaguely she heard him opening a door to make more room. The bubbling sound increased, like her heartbeat. She looked up at him—breathless, curious, searching.

She started to speak, but he smiled and shook his head. He bent again to her warm lips and began to nibble at them.

His hands eased her blouse out of his way, so that he had access to her lacy bra. That, too, was easily disposed of. His mouth was on that soft skin, nibbling, tasting, covering first one taut breast and then the other in a silence that grew hot with expectation.

It was a lesson in arousal. She'd never realized how many nerves she had in her body, or how sensitive they were to a man's hands and mouth. He smoothed his lips over her skin like hands, and she didn't feel her slacks and briefs slide down her legs, because his mouth was like a narcotic. She couldn't get enough of it.

His shirt was gone and she was touching him in all the ways she'd wanted to. He guided her hands down his sides, and she discovered somewhere along the way that his jeans were loose and pushed away as well.

His forearms were taking most of his weight when he moved against her and her eyes opened, misty and soft and inquiring.

"It's broad daylight," she whispered, gasping as she realized where they were, with both doors open in the middle of a field.

"So it is," he mused softly, moving even closer. "Broad daylight, and no secrets between us. And I want you to the point of madness. I want you to see how much, feel how much." He bent to her mouth, cherishing it with aching tenderness, and his heart beat roughly over her taut breasts.

"Jacob, we mustn't…" she whispered, but she moaned as well, because her body was throbbing with arousal.

"I want you for my wife, Kathryn," he breathed against her ardent mouth. "I want you to be the mother of my children. I'm not asking you to give yourself a second time without a commitment. I'm asking you for the rest of your life. And I'm going to show you what beauty there can be in intimacy when two people share it unselfishly."

She could feel how hungry he was. His body was keeping no secrets from her. She searched his dark eyes. "It isn't…just desire?"

He smiled gently. "If that was all it was, any woman would do," he said quietly.

"And any woman won't?" she persisted breathlessly.

His mouth brushed her eyes, her nose. "I don't want anybody except you, Kate. There isn't going to be another woman, ever."

"Oh, Jacob, you might fall in love…." she moaned.

"Yes," he said against her parted lips, "I might at that. Lie still, sweet, and let me love you. Let me show you how it should have been that first time."

She didn't answer him. She didn't have to. Her long, slender legs moved, just enough to admit the vibrant masculinity of his body.

"This time," he whispered into her mouth as he began to bite at it sensuously, "you and I are going to fly into the sun together."

"Someone might come here...." she protested with her last logical thought.

"No." He moved, ever so gently, and his eyes held hers as she felt the first tender probing of his body. He saw her gasp, felt her hands grasp his arms. "Relax for me," he whispered. "I promise, it isn't going to hurt at all. Join with me, Kate. Let your body be one with mine."

She bit her lower lip. She was thinking of all the reasons why she shouldn't.

He knew that. His hand moved down, and she gasped at the sudden throbbing wave of passion that trembled over her skin. "Don't think," he whispered. "Just lie back and let me do it all. Let me give you pleasure. Let me teach you."

She was trembling. He moved, careful not to jar her too much, and she felt him as she had that night. Only now it wasn't hurting. Her eyes grew wide with every slow, adept movement of his hips, and he watched her the whole time, adjusting his motions to the needs of her soft body under him. He whispered things—sweet, shocking things—and his hands guided her with unbearable patience, until she was as wild for him as he was for her.

She bit back a sharp moan and he smiled through his own hunger, because he knew what that meant—that sound, and the sudden twisting of her body and the dilation of her eyes. Yes, she was feeling it now. He moved more deeply, more fiercely, and she closed her eyes and began to make noises that incited him.

His hair-matted chest rubbed with sweet abrasion against her bare breasts as he increased the rhythm, and the sounds outside were drowned by the sounds inside.

She was whispering things to him now, secret things, and he laughed and bit her shoulder, her mouth, her throat as the spiraling tension caught them both up in a whirl-wind of warm pleasure.

Her eyes opened as the coil began to tighten suddenly. His face was damp with sweat and his jaw was clenched and he was breathing fiercely above her. She matched his movements, reached up to him and, as her fingers touched his face, it all exploded.

Magic. Madness. The sun, blazing colors, roaring surf, a feverish crashing together that brought with it the first rapture of her life. The first anguished burst of ecstasy. The first fulfillment.

She came back very slowly to the sounds of the trees and the wind and the birds. She was shaking, and so was he. His heartbeat was heavy over her breasts, his body had a fine tremor.

She began to kiss his throat, his chin, his hard mouth, and he returned the caress with satisfying ferocity.

"Sweet," he whispered roughly, his eyes blazing into hers. "Pleasure beyond bearing. I thought I might die trying to hold you to me."

"Yes." She touched his mouth with wonder, searched his eyes. Her breath caught. "Jacob...you didn't..." She swallowed. "There could be a child."

He smiled lazily. "Yes." He kissed her closed eyelids, her nose, her mouth. "I'm sleepy."

"So am I." She brushed back his thick, dark hair. "What are we going to do?"

"Get married, of course," he murmured. "And I'm not asking you, Kate. You'll damned well have to do it without a proposal, because I'm not giving you a chance to turn me down again."

He was offering heaven, especially after what they'd just shared. Her worried eyes searched his. "You might fall in love someday," she whispered for the second time.

He kissed her eyes shut. "What did we just share, if it wasn't love?" he whispered.

Her eyelids came open again, and she was staring at him.

He hadn't meant to say that. It had just popped out. But as he looked down at her lovely face, he could believe that he'd meant it. Sex had never been like this before. He brushed back her hair. "No heavy thoughts right now," he whispered. "Kiss me."

She did, warmly, softly, and then he moved reluctantly away and helped her dress with exquisite tenderness. In between soft kisses, he gathered up his own disheveled clothing and got it in order again.

He sat back, smoking a cigarette, while she stared at him from the shelter of his arm.

"I didn't hurt your rib?" he asked belatedly, searching her face.

She shook her head. "I wouldn't have noticed even if you did."

He hugged her close. "Thank God. And have we removed a few scars in the process?" he asked gently, searching her eyes. "Have I made up for that night?"

She flushed. "Yes."

"From now on, it gets better every time. Next week

we're getting married, and have I got a wedding present
for you, young Kate," he added with a secretive smile.

"What is it?" she asked.

"Wait and see," he mused, and kissed her again, tasting
nectar on her mouth. He sighed. "Now, no more second
thoughts. Nobody's forcing me to the altar. All right?"

She searched his face, loving him too much to refuse
again. All her noble principles had gone up in smoke in
his arms. He was addictive. She couldn't give him up.

"All right, Jacob," she breathed.

He smiled after a minute, and pulled her closer.

The wedding ceremony was performed at Warlance,
and Margo and David attended, surprised and delighted
to find two old enemies exchanging rings.

Jacob beamed at his lovely bride in her acres of white
satin and lace, and amid baskets of flowers they exchanged their vows, with Hank and Janet and Margo
and David and Tom and a scattering of neighbors in at-
tendance, including a strange city-looking woman in a
blue hat sitting all alone.

The rings in place, the vows spoken solemnly, Jacob
removed her veil and kissed her gently. The ceremony
had been so beautiful that she cried. If he'd loved her, it
would have been heaven itself. But, she told herself, she
couldn't ask for the moon.

"Imagine, you and Uncle Jacob getting married,"
Margo whispered during a brief pause in Kate's bedroom. "I thought you hated each other."

"So did we," Kate grinned, changing into a pink dress
for the small reception. There wasn't time for a honey-
moon, but it didn't matter. Jacob had promised her Paris
in the spring.

"Did you notice that elderly woman in the audience—

the one with the blue hat? I thought she was Ben Hamlin's sister, but nobody seems to know her."

Kate pursed her lips. She'd noticed the woman, all right. There had been something vaguely familiar about her. Perhaps she was an old neighbor who'd moved away, or some acquaintance of the family.

"Speak of the devil," Margo murmured wickedly when they opened the door and saw the heavyset woman in the blue hat coming toward the bedroom. She had on just a touch of makeup, and she was rather attractive even for her age. She was nervous, too, twisting a handkerchief out of shape in her slender hands.

"Kathryn?"

Kate blinked. So the woman did know her. "Yes?"

"Excuse me, I'll go find David," Margo said and left the room.

The woman in the hat searched eyes as green as her own. "You don't know me, do you?" she asked hesitantly and her eyes brimmed with tears. "How could I expect you to? He stole you away from me when you were just a baby…."

Kate's eyes widened. She stared at the older version of herself. No wonder the woman had seemed so familiar. All the long years of hatred and bitterness and anguish came back and boiled over.

"You deserted us," Kate accused furiously. "You left us, and he beat me, he beat Tom!"

The older woman stared at her helplessly with tears stinging down her cheeks. She tried to speak, failed, tried again. "He stole you, Kathryn. Took you away and hid you, and I had nothing. No money, no place to live… I'd sneaked away to get a lawyer, so I could divorce him and get custody of you and Tom. There was a man, a sweet, gentle man, who wanted you both and would have been so good to us after that…that creature your father be-came—" She sobbed and caught her breath. "I had it all worked out, and then he found out, and before I could get back out to the farm, he was gone." She pressed the handkerchief against her eyes. "He was gone with both my babies, and I didn't even have the price of a bus ticket to try and find you."

Kate heard the words with a sense of unreality. She stared at her mother blankly. This wasn't how her poor, tormented father had related the past.

"He…stole us?"

"Stole you, my sweet," the older woman said huskily. She stared at her daughter with eyes full of pride and love and pain. "I waited tables in a bar for two years to save enough money to start looking, but by then it was too late."

"And the man, the one you were going to marry?" Kate prodded.

"I turned him away," came the unexpected reply. "I had a horrible feeling about what you and Tom were going through, Kathryn. How could I be so callous as to build my happiness on your pain?"

Kate took a slow breath, vaguely aware of Jacob watching from the other room. She searched her mother's eyes. "You've been alone all this time?"

"All this time," her mother replied softly. "I'd already exhausted all the government agencies, and I'd long ago forgotten that your father's mother lived in South Dakota. He'd hardly ever mentioned her. And then, your new husband came into the restaurant where I work and told me that you and Tom were alive and that he'd bring me to see you." The tears started again through a smile. "I haven't stopped crying for days. I don't care if you hate me; it's enough just to be able to look at you."

"Oh, Mama, don't—"

Kate went into the older woman's arms as if there hadn't been a single day between the past and the present. She rocked her, comforted her, and felt the pain slowly dissolving as she realized what it must have been like all the long years. At least she'd had Tom. Their mother had had no one, only a terrible fear for her children and loneliness.

Tom was beside Jacob now, grinning, and when Kate saw him, she realized that the two of them must have been plotting this together. When Tom joined them, their mother drew him close, too.

"My boy," she wept. "My baby boy. When I first saw you, I could hardly believe so much time had passed. And now I've found you, and Kate, and it's like a dream. Like another dream, and I'm so afraid I'll wake up, as I usually do, and find you gone."

"We won't be gone, Mama." Tom laughed. "Neither will you. Kate and I will shuttle you back and forth between South Dakota and New York for a while before we let you go home."

"Of course we will," Kate agreed, pulling back to borrow her mother's handkerchief and dry her red eyes.

"I'd love that," their mother said, beaming. "I really would. And then I think I may say yes to the man who's been proposing for the past twenty-two years—"

Kate gasped. "He's still waiting for you, after all these years?"

"Love doesn't wear out, Katie," her mother said with a wise, world-weary smile. "Not if it's real. Yes. He's still waiting. And so was I, until I found my babies."

"Some babies." Tom grinned at his sister.

"Speaking of which," Jacob mused, joining them to slide a possessive arm around Kate's shoulders, "I hope you like grandchildren. Kate and I have a large family in mind."

"I'd love that." Mrs. Walker sighed, glancing from one to the other. "And right now, I'd like to wash my face. I must look a mess."

"You look just like your children to me," Jacob replied, "but help yourself."

"Yes, and then hurry back. We've got so much to talk about," Kate said gently.

"I'll do that." Mrs. Walker touched Kate's hair, and Tom's cheek, and went off into the bedroom, sniffling a little.

"Oh, Jacob," Kate sighed, studying her new husband. "How long did you plan this?"

"A couple of weeks. Tom helped." He smiled. "We thought you might want to see what having a mother was like."

"I'm so glad," she said warmly, and hugged Tom. "Isn't she nice?"

"Our mother would have to be," Tom chided. "Now, excuse me while I grab some punch. My throat's apt to get dry from talking so much when we start this new family reunion."

"Are you happy?" Jacob asked quietly, studying Kate. "It was a hell of a gamble, but it seems to have come off without a hitch."

"For all those years, I blamed her when she was as miserable as we were." She sighed, staring up at him. "How could I have been so blind?"

"Aren't we all blind, from time to time?" he asked. He touched her hair softly, loving its silky feel. She was beautiful in her neat dress, and he looked as if he could die just looking at her. She was his now, and all the barriers seemed to come down at once. He drew her to one side of the hall, away from prying eyes, and held her there.

"I was blind about you, wasn't I, Kate? I never had any idea how much you cared about me until I saw all those photos you kept of me...." He took a steadying breath and his jaw tautened. "My God," he breathed, his hands hurting her a little where they held her upper arms, "you'll never know what I went through those first twenty-four hours after you were shot. My world went black. If anything had happened to you, I don't know how in hell I'd have stayed alive."

She wasn't sure that she was hearing him. Her eyes stared blankly at his hard face, hanging on every word.

"You felt responsible," she whispered. "There was no need to feel that way."

"I...loved you," he whispered, biting off the words with a kind of pain he couldn't hold back any longer. His gaze fell to her bodice, so that she wouldn't see his eyes. "For a long time. But I'd seen what love did to men, giving women a hold. My own mother tormented Hank half to death because he loved her. I wasn't going to let that happen to me. So I convinced myself it was only desire, and once I had you, it would fade away."

He laughed bitterly, lifting tormented eyes to hers. "But it didn't get better, Kate. I went home and got drunk and stayed drunk, and still I could hear you crying." He shifted restlessly, his eyes hungry on her rapt face. "And then I was going to go back and have it out, but you got shot. Then Tom told me everything." His eyes closed. "And the light went out of the world."

She touched his face tentatively, hesitantly, her fingers trembling. "Oh, Jacob!"

His eyes opened, blazing with possession. "I love you," he whispered roughly. "I always have. So you see,

Kate, there's not really much danger of my falling in love with anyone else."

She didn't try to answer. She reached up and put her mouth softly against his hard one. He lifted her against him and held her. He kissed her and she responded with all the lonely hunger of all the long years. His arms were bruising, and she welcomed their involuntary fierceness, because she understood the passion they were betraying. She felt it, too, burned with it, ached with it, and her mouth demanded as much as his own. She moaned suddenly, her legs beginning to tremble, and he pulled back.

His hard face was taut with passion. "I want you," he whispered roughly. "I want you the way it was that day in the front seat of my car, so tender and slow that I thought I'd die of the pleasure. I want to make love with you and know that you love me as much as I love you."

She touched her mouth to his chin, his neck, trembling with shared emotion. "I want that, too," she breathed. "I never dreamed it would happen, that you'd be able to care for me, ever."

His hands smoothed her dark hair, ruffling it. "Not even when I showed you your picture in my wallet?" he murmured against her throat.

"That was the only hope I had," she whispered. "That, and the way you practically threw Roger Dean out of my room in the hospital."

He lifted his hand, his eyes fierce. "I wanted to throw him out the window," he returned. "You were mine. I didn't want any other man near you."

"There never will be." She sighed. She leaned back against his encircling arms. "I like children," she said.

He smiled. "So do I."

She smiled slowly. "Well?"

"Don't tempt me," he muttered, bending to kiss her hungrily. "Wedding guests never go home," he groaned.

"You're the one who insisted on inviting so many," she whispered against his lips.

"Damn my own stupidity," he murmured.

"We can have punch and cake—"

"I don't want punch and cake. I want acres of bed and you in the middle of it, even if all we do is hold each other…."

"Now cut that out, you two," Tom called. His mother was holding his arm as he confronted Jacob and Kate with a mischievous grin. "You've got your whole lives to do that, but only a few precious hours to spend with your family before I spirit Mom off to New York with me."

"I guess you're right," Jacob said, damping down the fires. He smiled warmly at Kate. "We have the rest of our lives together."

Kate pushed back her disheveled hair, never more beautiful, with her green eyes sparkling and her face bright with love and laughter. "What a beautiful thought," she whispered to Jacob.

He took her hand and brought it to his lips. "Isn't it, though?" he said with a grin. And as he led her along the hall behind Tom and Mrs. Walker, Kate felt as if she were walking on dreams the whole way.

* * * * *

Dear Reader,

When I sit down to read a book, my first choice has—and probably always will be—a cowboy story. Whether he's from Wyoming, Texas or one of the other western states, there's just something about a man in jeans, a chambray shirt, boots and a wide-brimmed cowboy hat that sets my pulse to racing. That's why when I first started writing, I knew exactly the kind of stories I wanted to tell and the heroes that would bring them to life.

In one of my first books for Harlequin Desire, *The Rough and Ready Rancher,* Flint McCray is one such hero. Strong-willed, honorable to a fault and sexy as sin, he needs nothing more than his son, his ranch and an expert trainer for his stallion. But when horse trainer Jenna "J.J." Adams invades the sanctity of his all-male domain, she not only establishes that she's quite skilled at training his horse, she seems more than capable of taming Flint's heart as well.

I hope you enjoy *The Rough and Ready Rancher* as you read how Jenna sets out to prove to Flint that she's the cowgirl he needs riding at his side for the rest of his life.

Happy trails!

Kathie DeNosky

THE ROUGH AND READY RANCHER

USA TODAY Bestselling Author

Kathie DeNosky

To Kathie Brush, who was there when the dream began.
To Bonnie and Huntley for encouraging the dream.
And to Tina Colombo and Joan Marlow Golan
for making the dream come true.

And to Wes Bennett, Braden Rathert and
Forrest the Intern Boy. Thanks for the laughter,
the encouragement and playing the music
that inspires me to write.

Chapter 1

Flint McCray stopped thumbing through the papers on his desk to glare at his ranch foreman. "If Adams doesn't show up within the next hour, he's out of a job."

"Simmer down, Flint." Brad Henson lowered his lanky frame into a soft, leather armchair. "Cal Reynolds assured me J. J. Adams is the best horse trainer he's ever seen step into a round pen. You know if the guy has Cal's stamp of approval, he should be worth the wait."

Flint considered Brad's words. Reynolds was one of the most respected quarter horse ranchers in the state of Texas. His word should set Flint's mind at ease, but gut instinct told him something didn't ring true about the whole situation. "If Adams is so good, why haven't I heard of him before now?"

"Let's face it, since you got custody of Ryan you've had more important things on your mind than finding a trainer for that son of a sidewinder you insist on calling a horse."

Pride and a sense of awe filled Flint at the mention of his son. "Now that I have Ryan, Black Satin's training should be all I have to worry about for a while."

His expression grave, Brad shook his head. "I don't think so. We got hit again last night."

"The herd up on Widow's Ridge?" At Brad's tight nod, Flint slammed his ink pen on the desk. "How many this time?"

"Near as I can figure about fifteen head." Brad hesitated, then squarely met Flint's furious gaze. "You haven't heard the worst. Rocket became one hell of an expensive steer overnight."

"On Widow's Ridge?"

Brad nodded. "He had help getting there, too. Either that or he's learned to open and close locked gates."

"Damn!"

"Looks to me like somebody's trying to even a score, Flint."

"Castrating a twenty-five-thousand dollar bull? No question about it." Flint leaned back from his desk to rub the bridge of his nose with thumb and forefinger. "But I'll be damned if I can figure out who it would be or why."

"Flint, you'd better get down to the barn," Jed Summers shouted, rushing into the room. "Some kid's shinnied the fence and is standin' smack-dab in the middle of Satin's corral."

Flint grabbed the wide brim of his black Resistol, jammed it on his head and bolted from the chair. With both men hot on his heels, he covered the distance to the horse barns on the far side of the ranch compound where several of his men had gathered in horrified fascination. For Flint time stood deathly still, and the air became smothering as the stallion bore down on the slender form inside the corral. Dust swirled where the stallion churned up dirt with his hooves, the beast's intent clear. But to Flint's amazement, the boy showed no sign of fear and sidestepped the charge at the last possible moment.

Black Satin's blue-black coat gleaming, Flint watched the horse paw the ground and shake his head, preparing to make another pass. Flint felt a moment of hope when the unconcerned youth began a litany of unintelligible words the stallion seemed to consider, appeared to understand. But a muttered curse from one of the men broke the spell, and the horse reared on powerful hind legs, his hooves slashing the air as he screamed his rage.

Besides having a death wish, Flint couldn't imagine what the kid was up to, but he'd seen enough. "Brad, ease around and open the gate," he ordered, his voice a low monotone. "Jim, you and Tom get your ropes ready. If Satin doesn't go for the pasture when that gate opens, I want a loop on him from each side." Readying himself, he placed a booted foot on the bottom rail of the fence. "Hold him in a cross-tie long enough for me to get that damned kid out of there."

When the horse failed to take the freedom the opened gate offered, Flint vaulted the fence and hit the ground running. His arms closed around the slight body at the same moment two ropes settled over the stallion's neck. Tossing the youth over his shoulder, he hauled the kid from the corral.

"What the hell were you doing in there?" he demanded, setting the boy on his feet.

"My job."

Flint started to berate the kid for pulling such a dangerous stunt, but his voice lodged somewhere between his vocal chords and open mouth when the brim of the lowered hat rose and twinkling, gray eyes locked with his startled gaze. Her unquestionably female lips forming a smile, the woman removed the battered Stetson, and a thick cascade of dark-blond hair fell to her shoulders.

"I'm J. J. Adams," she said, extending her hand.

Flint felt as if a mule had kicked him right between the eyes. Ignoring the gesture, he allowed his gaze to slide the length of her. The curves disguised by her loose denim jacket suddenly became quite apparent. Firm, round breasts rose and fell with her labored breathing, and her jeans, worn white in certain tantalizing areas, were filled out to perfection.

He shook his head, and his gaze traveled back to her face. Lightly tanned, her cheeks glowed with a naturally rosy blush, making them appear to have been kissed by the sun. The effect was one makeup couldn't achieve—no matter how expensive.

Her soft features and small-boned frame only confirmed what Flint's brain tried to deny: she was a woman all right, and a damned good-looking one.

Jenna clamped her lips tight against a startled gasp at the man's rugged features. He for darned sure wasn't the type to suffer from the lack of female attention. He had a tiny, white scar at the corner of his right eye and a day-old growth of beard shadowed his lean cheeks. A muscle ticked along his firm jaw, but the dark-brown hair hanging low on his forehead seemed to soften his otherwise unhappy demeanor.

She swallowed hard. She would bet her best pair of dress boots that if he ever smiled he could charm a prudish old maid right out of her garters.

His wide, muscular shoulders, narrow hips and long, sinewy legs attested to the fact he kept himself in excellent physical condition. An amused grin played at her lips. When he'd hauled her out of the corral, he'd moved with the effortless power of a racehorse, and she had no doubt about the identity of the "Thoroughbred" glaring down at her. His authoritative presence, arrogant stance and dark scowl could only mean one thing. This was none other than Flint McCray, the lord and master of the Rocking M Ranch—her new employer. And at the moment he looked mad enough to spit nails.

Jenna's smile widened. Time for the showdown. "I'm your new horse trainer. Sorry I'm late, but Daisy broke down just this side of San Antonio, and the mechanic had a hard time finding a universal joint for a truck of her considerable years."

He shook his head. "I don't know what kind of scam you're running here, lady, but I'm not buying it."

When one of the men coughed in an obvious effort to stifle a bout of laughter, her new boss took hold of her elbow and started for the house. "The show's over, boys. Get back to work. I want that herd up on Widow's Ridge moved back down here by headquarters. Brad, *you* come with me."

Several minutes later they walked into McCray's study. It resembled any number of others she'd had the "privilege" to enter over the past few years. Leather and wood dominated the masculine domain and, without looking, she knew the shelves behind the desk housed books on the cattle industry, horse ranching and animal husbandry. Her gaze drifted to the opposite side of the room where, like most Texas ranches, a leather map of the property with the ranch brand burned into one corner graced the wall above the fireplace.

Nothing out of the ordinary, she decided, frowning in thought. On the mantel, beside the antique clock, sat a glass dome; the diamond necklace inside twinkled from the shaft of late-afternoon sun streaming through the window.

She sat in the empty chair beside the ranch foreman and tried to shrug it off. McCray's life was none of her concern, and his choice of decorations of little or no importance. If he wanted to park a pile of cow patties on his fireplace, it was his business. But still, she found the delicate jewelry out of place in the otherwise masculine room.

Flint hung his hat on the hook beside the door, then lowered himself into the chair behind his desk. He eyed the woman seated across from him. He was having a devil of a time coming to grips with what had happened when he'd escorted her to the house. On contact, a jolt of electricity as powerful as if he'd grabbed hold of a 220-volt wire had run the length of his arm and exploded in his gut. If he had that kind of reaction just touching her elbow through the layers of her clothing, he wondered, what would happen if his hands roamed the silkiness of her soft skin?

He mentally cursed himself as nine kinds of a fool. The woman was running a scam and, distracted by her looks, he'd almost swallowed the bait.

"Before your face freezes in that awful frown, let me explain," she said. "I use my initials for business purposes. My full name is Jenna Jo Adams."

Her serene attitude grated on his nerves. "I'm sure you'll understand I'd like to see some form of identification."

Her smile accommodating, she took her driver's license from the breast pocket of her jacket and handed it to him.

Examining her ID, Flint shook his head and gave it back. "You couldn't possibly be Adams. He's one of the top trainers in the business. That takes more years of skill than you are old."

Her smile faded. "I've been working with horses most of my twenty-six years. And I'm good." She shook her head. "No. I'm not just good. I'm *damned* good." Raising one perfect brow, she added, "But age isn't the issue here, is it?"

"No." Flint had to give her credit. She had her share of pluck. But he didn't need a gutsy female with an inflated opinion of herself around. He glanced at the glass dome on the mantel. He'd had enough of that type of woman to last him a lifetime. No, he needed a horse trainer. "I'd like to thank you for your time and trouble, but after careful consideration, I don't think you'd be suitable for the job."

Her expression calm, she smiled. "Why don't you just come out and say it, McCray? J. J. Adams isn't a man."

Glaring back at her, Flint said nothing.

"When I spoke with Mr. Henson a few months ago, my gender didn't seem to be a problem."

Flint turned his attention to Brad. "You knew my expert trainer was female?"

"No." Brad's face mirrored his astonishment. "When I talked to Cal, he transferred me to his administrative assistant and she—"

"Mr. Henson, you talked to *me,* and not once did I say I was Cal's admin assistant." Her eyes lit with amusement. "When Cal turned the phone over to me, I told you if there were no objections to the fee and requirements listed, you were to have Mr. McCray sign the contract and mail it back in care of the Lazy R." Turning to Flint, she smiled. "Which you did."

Flint picked up his copy of the document. "I signed this under the assumption I'd be dealing with a seasoned trainer. You couldn't possibly have the experience it'll take to turn a stallion like Black Satin into a reining horse champion, not to mention the strength to control him."

"I'm not up to dancing this afternoon, McCray, so let's stop two-stepping around what you're really trying to say. You don't want me training your horse—not for lack of experience or strength which, by the way, I have more than enough of. You're having a problem with the fact that I'm a woman."

Flint felt his control of the situation slip another notch. "You misrepresented yourself," he said, waving the contract at her. "I won't deal with anyone who uses deception to get a job."

"I believe if you'll take another look, you'll find I haven't deceived you in any way. My fee and what you may expect from my services have been spelled out in great detail."

"Do part of your *services* include getting yourself killed?" Flint pointed his finger at her. "That stunt you pulled out there was one of the most harebrained I've ever seen."

"I'll admit my methods are unorthodox, but let me assure you—they work." She shrugged. "Satin and I were getting along just fine, until you and your men got him excited."

Jenna could tell her composure grated on the man's nerves. Every point he brought up, she'd been able to shoot down with amazing ease. He was mad as a hornet and itching for a fight, but she refused to take the bait. Flint McCray would just have to get used to the fact that the best man for this job was a woman. Besides, she couldn't afford to start canceling contracts if she ever intended to reach her goal. And she was close. Very close.

"I don't want you training my horse," McCray said tightly. "Satin is out of championship bloodlines and should have a great future. But after meeting you, I find you could be detrimental to my goals."

Anger, swift and hot, raced through Jenna. If there was one thing she knew, it was how to turn a high-spirited animal into a top show horse. After all, she'd been a trainer for six years and around horses all her life. "Last year I had a second-place winner at the National Reining Horse Association Futurity, two that took first in similar competitions, and three of this year's top contenders are horses I've trained."

"You were highly recommended by Cal, Miss Adams. But—"

"But nothing." She stood, braced her hands on his desk, then leaned forward. "If you had a valid reason for wanting to cancel the contract, I'd be the first one to rip it up. But you don't. The fact that I'm a woman outside of a round pen or an arena is immaterial. When I step inside, I'm generic. I'm neither man nor woman. I'm a horse trainer. And *that* is all you should be concerned with."

He rose from his chair to take a similar position on the opposite side of the desk, bringing them nose to nose. "I'm canceling the contract, Miss Adams."

"The name's Jenna, and you can't. It's ironclad, unless both parties agree on its nullification. And believe me, before I relent, chickens will start giving milk." Walking to the door, she turned to smile at her enraged employer. "Check with your lawyer, *boss*. I think you'll find I've covered all the bases. Either I get paid for training your horse, or I get paid for doing nothing. Period. It's your choice. But let me remind you, my waiting list has the majority of your competition on it. The only reason I agreed to train your horse exclusively and put you ahead of my other clients was as a personal favor to Cal. Otherwise, a year from now, you'd still be sitting here with an untrained stallion."

She closed the door behind her with a quiet click, but only managed to walk a few feet before she stopped to lean against the wall. Her whole body trembled, and her knees had turned to jelly.

She'd learned long ago to deal with a certain amount of animosity from some of the more narrow-minded horsemen. But when McCray attacked her abilities and experience, he'd crossed the line. If he'd explained from the beginning that he would rather not deal with her, or that he felt uncomfortable with the situation, she'd have considered letting him out of the contract. But there was no way she'd back down now. She had a point to prove.

Jenna smiled to herself. This would be a first for her. Along with training a horse for championship competition, she'd been presented with the golden opportunity of teaching a prized jackass a lesson or two in the bargain.

Her grin turned to a giggle when an enraged curse, then the sound of a receiver slammed onto its cradle, came from Flint's office. Apparently his attorney had just given him the good news. J. J. Adams *would* train his horse and, short of paying her for nothing, there wasn't a thing he could do about it.

Smiling, Jenna pushed away from the wall. It was time to get her things from Daisy and find a place in the bunkhouse.

Flint rubbed his forehead in an attempt to ease the mounting tension. "Hilliard said he remembered the contract as being one of the clearest he'd ever seen. No gray areas or hidden loopholes. Either she does the job, or I pay through the nose to get out of it. Then I'd still have to find another trainer."

"I should have checked around and found someone else," Brad said, his expression dismal. "Cal didn't say anything about J. J. Adams being a woman."

"I'm not blaming you or Cal." Flint glared at the closed door. "Miss Adams has obviously practiced this little deception before with her initials and gotten quite good at it. She had ample opportunity to identify herself when you discussed the contract. Besides, *I* should have had the name investigated before signing on the dotted line." He leaned back, his gaze zeroing in on the glass dome on the mantel. "It might not be a bad idea to have her checked out, anyway."

Brad rose to leave. "Do what you think is best. Since one of her requirements is a room in the bunkhouse, I guess I'd better get her settled in before supper."

"No. She's the only single woman under the age of sixty within a thirty-mile radius, and I won't have her causing trouble among the men." Flint followed Brad down the hall. "She can have one of the rooms upstairs."

"I'll tell her."

Flint shook his head. "From now on, leave Jenna Adams to me. Let's see how she likes dealing with someone who's immune to the distraction of a pretty face."

Leaving the house, Brad shrugged. "You're the boss."

Continuing down the hall to the kitchen, Flint called, "Whiskers, I need you to get one of the guest rooms ready."

In an exaggerated flurry of activity, the old man stirred the contents of a large pot on the stove, then turned his attention to a ball of dough on the counter. "Ain't I got enough to do without you comin' up with more?"

"You sound a little hassled. Has Ryan been keeping you busy?" Flint asked, running his finger along the top of a chocolate frosted cake.

Whiskers picked up a wooden spoon to slap the back of Flint's hand. "Stay outta that cake. It's for supper." He shook the spoon at Flint. "Ridin' herd on that kid of yours is like tryin' to keep a young buck out of a honky-tonk come Saturday night. It just cain't be done."

Grinning, Flint put a large amount of icing into his mouth. "You'll have to take a nap before we eat."

"Now, boy, you know I don't never do more than rest my eyes a mite durin' the day."

Flint bit back his laughter. Whiskers's snoring, while he "rested his eyes," could stampede a herd of cattle.

"Where's Ryan?" Flint asked, looking around for his son.

"Outside rustlin' up a peck of trouble, I reckon." Whiskers again stirred the boiling concoction in the pot. "I heard an awful ruckus comin' from the office a while back. What got your nose outta joint?"

The chocolate flavor in Flint's mouth suddenly tasted like mud. "The woman who's going to train Satin."

"Woman?" Whiskers turned to stare, openmouthed. "Was that the little gal I saw cross the yard and head for the bunkhouse?"

"Yes."

"Have you gone loco? That ain't no place for a lady."

"I never intended for her to stay with the men." Flint scowled as Whiskers headed for the stairs. "That's why I told you to get one of the guest rooms ready."

"Don't just stand there bumpin' your gums. Git out there and help that gal in with her things," Whiskers called over his shoulder. Trudging up the steps, he continued to mutter. "Mule-headed sidewinder ain't got the manners of a day-old jackass."

Disgruntled by the whole situation, Flint searched for Jenna and found her in front of the bunkhouse. He stood by and watched her pull a scarred suitcase from the seat of an ancient, rusted-out pickup truck. As much as he would like to, he couldn't ignore years of training in Texas etiquette and stepped forward to take it from her. "You'll be staying up at the main house."

"That's not necessary, McCray. I'll be comfortable in—"

"Your comfort doesn't concern me," Flint interrupted. He slammed the truck's door. "I have a ranch to run, and I don't intend to stand back and watch you turn my men into cowpunching Casanovas. You're here for the sole purpose of training Black Satin, not to fill up your Saturday nights with romantic encounters. You'd do well to remember that."

"Now, hold it right there, cowboy." She poked his chest with her finger, the contact making him feel scorched. "I have no intention of socializing with your men, but if I did, it wouldn't be any concern of yours. What I do on my own time is *my* business." She wrestled the suitcase from him. "And don't slam Daisy's door. You'll knock off the rust holding her together."

She started for the house, but spun around to glare at him. "I don't know what your problem is, but your attitude toward me sucks saddle soap. As long as I do my job, you have no reason to complain. And you'd do well to remember *that*."

Flint watched her march toward the house. It shouldn't matter to him what she did so long as his horse got trained. But the sight of her well-shaped backside and long, slender legs made his mouth go dry. Those legs of hers went all the way up to—

Disgusted with himself, Flint shook his head. Just how could he expect his men to turn a blind eye to something like that, when he couldn't? He, more than any other man, should be immune to Jenna Adams and her considerable charms, after the way she'd duped him into hiring her.

But he'd be the first to admit she was one hell of a sight in a fit of temper. Her sparkling gray eyes promised a passion that would consume a man when he loved her. And the husky quality of her voice had whispered over his senses like a piece of soft velvet. His body tightened. How would *his* name sound when she cried out as he pleasured her?

Flint took hold of the reins to his runaway imagination. Whiskers must have put locoweed in that damned chocolate icing, he decided, starting off in search of his son. He wanted to get better acquainted with Jenna Adams about as much as he wanted to get up close and personal with a rattlesnake. She would train his horse, then be on her way.

And that's just the way he wanted it.

Chapter 2

Jenna placed the last of her clothes in the dresser, then turned to survey her room. Southwestern print curtains framed the tall, old-fashioned windows and matched the coverlet on the natural pine bed. On the wall above the headboard, a large dream catcher adorned with rawhide thongs and hawk feathers assured sweet dreams for the bed's sleeping occupant. On the polished bedside table beneath lamps made from Native American pots, two Kachina dolls in the images of the eagle and buffalo stood watch.

She smiled. It wasn't a feminine room by any means, but the bright colors against the off-white walls made it seem warm and friendly. "Just the opposite of its owner," she muttered, heading for the stairs.

She followed a tantalizing aroma, stopping just inside the spacious kitchen to inhale deeply. "Something smells wonderful."

Whiskers turned to give her a toothless grin. "Hope you like son of a bit—" His weathered cheeks reddened above his snow white beard. "—gun stew."

Laughing, Jenna patted his arm. "I've had it before and no matter what you call it, I'm sure yours is delicious."

He took a tray of sourdough biscuits from the oven. "Your room okay? It's been a while since we've had us a lady round here, and it might not be as purty as what you're used to."

Jenna swallowed hard. How long had it been since anyone cared if she liked her room, or if she even had one?

"Everything's fine," she said around the lump in her throat. "Thank you."

"Whiskers, look what I found." A small boy of about four flung open the screen door and ran into the kitchen.

When the child spotted Jenna, he stopped so fast he almost dropped the box he held. "Who are you?"

"Ryan McCray, mind your manners," Whiskers scolded. "You didn't even give this here little gal so much as a howdy-do."

"Sorry," Ryan said, his smile friendly. "Howdy-do. Who are you?"

Jenna laughed when Whiskers sighed his exasperation. "I'm Jenna Adams."

"Wanna see what I found, Jenna?" He held out his treasure for her inspection. "It's a kitty."

Afraid to move, Jenna and Whiskers froze.

"What's the matter?" The puzzled child looked from one adult to the other. "He's kinda smelly, but you can pet him."

"That's a dad-gummed polecat," Whiskers exclaimed.

As if in slow motion, Ryan set the box on the floor and the three of them watched the half-grown skunk climb out. Jet-black with twin stripes of white running the length of its back, it waddled around the kitchen sniffing its new surroundings.

"Don't nobody move," Whiskers commanded, his voice reduced to a hoarse whisper. When the animal ambled toward the door, he reached for the broom in the corner, eased forward and used the handle to push open the screen. "Get Ryan outta here while I take care of this varmint."

"I want my kitty," Ryan protested loudly.

Afraid the child would upset the animal, Jenna placed her hand over Ryan's mouth and backed them from the kitchen. But she'd only gone a few feet when she encountered an immovable object planted in the middle of the hall.

Flint tensed, every nerve in his body alert to the soft warmth of the female bottom resting against his thighs. His hands came up to hold her there. He told himself he was only trying to steady her, to keep her from falling. But turning to glance over her shoulder, her body shifted to brush the most vulnerable part of his anatomy and the jolt of awareness coursing through him felt as if he'd walked into an electric fence.

He gritted his teeth and tried to ignore the urgent signals pulsing through his body. He had to focus on the way she'd maneuvered herself and Ryan from the occupied part of the house. A mixture of anger and suspicion overtook him. Had she been trying to kidnap his son?

"What in blazes are you doing?" Flint demanded, his voice echoing through the unnaturally quiet house.

An acrid smell suddenly permeated the air, followed by a vehement curse from Whiskers.

"Skunk," she said, covering her nose.

Flint brushed past Jenna and Ryan to enter the kitchen.

He coughed several times, then pinched his nose shut and scowled at Whiskers. "How did it get in here?"

"You're gonna have to sit down and teach that young whelp of yours which critters to leave be," Whiskers said angrily. "He thought the dad-burned thing was a cat." He limped over to turn off the simmering stew, a colorful string of curses accenting his steps. "Now we ain't got no supper, and we'll be takin' meals outside on the picnic table for a month of Sundays. And it's all your fault. If you hadn't started your bellerin', I'd a had it outta here before it had a chance to spray its stink."

"Daddy, I want my kitty back," Ryan wailed from the hall.

"When was the last time you took a bath, Whiskers?" Brad asked, stopping just inside the back door. The other ranch hands piled up behind him.

Tom Davison fanned the air with his hat. "Whew-ee! This place smells like a cross between Jed's feet and a damned old billy goat."

"Whiskers, did you finally die and somebody just forgot to tell you?" Jim Kent choked out.

"Outside," Flint gasped, bolting for the door. He stood in the yard taking cleansing gulps of air. When Whiskers came to stand next to him, Flint moved upwind. "Do you mind?"

"Consarnit all. It weren't my fault that kid got hold of a polecat." Whiskers pointed to Ryan when he and Jenna joined the group. "I cain't figure out how he kept from gettin' bit when he picked it up. Those things can have the hydrophoby, you know."

Worried, Flint knelt down in front of his son and searched for any signs of an open wound. "Did it bite or scratch you, Ryan?" he asked, his voice sharpened by his concern.

Ryan's chin quivered and he shook his head. "No. What's hydo...hydotrophy?"

"Hydrophobia. It's another name for rabies," Flint explained gently. He gave Ryan a reassuring hug. "It's a dangerous disease some wild animals carry. That's why I don't want you trying to catch any more of them. Understand?"

Ryan nodded, the matter forgotten. The wind shifted, and he wrinkled his nose. "You stink, Whiskers."

Clearly exasperated, the old man opened and closed his mouth several times in search of epithets suitable for ladies and young ears. "Well, you don't smell like no rose, yourself, boy."

When his stomach rumbled, Jed asked, "What are we gonna do about supper?"

His complexion a sickly green, Jim swallowed so hard his Adam's apple bobbed up and down several times. "How can you think about your gut now? I'll be off my feed for a week."

"I can't help it," Jed complained, his stomach growling again. "I'm hungry enough to eat that danged skunk."

Whiskers folded his arms across his chest. "Well, I ain't goin' back in there till the place airs a mite."

Jed pointed to Jenna. "What's she doin'?"

Flint turned in time to see Jenna take a deep breath and head back toward the kitchen door. Several minutes later, tears streaming down her face, she deposited an armload of luncheon meats, condiments and two loaves of bread on the picnic table at the side of the house. She coughed several times, but to his amazement she didn't stop. She headed right back inside.

When she returned to add a six-pack of beer, several cans of soda and a bottle of tomato juice to the pile on the table, Whiskers elbowed Flint. "Don't that beat all you ever seen?"

She wiped her eyes with her shirtsleeve and slumped down in the dappled shade of an oak tree. He and his men stared in awe.

Tipping his hat, Jed broke the silence. "Thanks, ma'am."

"Whiskers, you…and Ryan need…to wash off…with the tomato juice." She coughed several times, then leaned back against the trunk of the tree. "It should take care of the smell on your skin, but you'll probably have to burn your clothes."

Admiring her in any way was the last thing Flint wanted, but when he washed Ryan with the juice, he had to give her credit. She'd braved the pungent odor when the rest of them wouldn't.

After helping Ryan into the clothes Whiskers had retrieved from the clothesline, Flint walked over to hand her a sandwich and can of soda. "Here. You've earned this."

She took the soft drink, but refused the food. "Thanks, but I don't have much of an appetite right now."

Flint squatted down beside her, plucked a blade of grass and began to twirl it between his fingers. After what she'd just done for Ryan and his men, she deserved some sort of appreciation. But the words wanted to stick in his throat.

Damn. Eating crow wasn't something he had to do often and it didn't come easy. "I…appreciate what you've done." He cleared his throat. "And earlier—in the hall— I guess I might have been a little harsh. But I'm sure you can understand, since my ex-wife died and I gained custody of him, I'm very protective of my son."

Jenna gave Flint a suspicious look. He did seem to

be trying to establish a truce, although it wasn't exactly a gracious one. "Don't worry about it," she said. "I've always been that way with my brother, Cooper, even though he's older."

Flint looked thoughtful. "Cooper Adams is your brother?"

Not surprised he recognized the name, she nodded.

"He's one of the best bull riders I've ever seen. I watched him score a ninety-four at the rodeo in Mesquite and a ninety in Amarillo. Didn't he make the National Finals a few years back?"

Jenna nodded. "Year before last he took second place in bull riding and fourth in the all-around competition."

Ryan's eyes grew round and he plopped down between them. "Wow! He must be real brave."

Remembering another bull rider and the two thousand pounds of enraged beef that had ended his life, a shudder ran the length of her spine. She stared off into the distance. Forever etched in her memory, the image would haunt her until the day she died.

"Bulls can be very dangerous," she finally managed.

"Daddy won't let me go down to the bull pens." Ryan glared at his father. "I'm not allowed to go around any of the animals without a grown-up."

"Maybe he's afraid you'll get hurt," Jenna offered, grateful for the distraction.

"Not my daddy. He's not afraid of nothin'." When he gazed up at Flint, Ryan's expression instantly changed to admiration.

Jenna smiled at the pride in the little boy's voice. She remembered thinking much the same about her own father. She reached out to ruffle Ryan's hair. "I'm sure he isn't."

Flint watched with a trace of envy. How would it feel to have her run her hands through his hair?

Try as he might, Flint couldn't erase the memory of how she'd felt when she backed into him in the hall. He glanced down at his callused hands. Her curves had filled them to perfection, and they itched to hold her again.

"I wanna be a bull rider when I grow up," Ryan said, jumping to his feet, his face animated.

Snapped back to reality, Flint smiled and caught his son in midhop to swing Ryan up onto his knee. "Last week you wanted to be a Jedi knight. The week before that you were going to play a guitar and change your name to Garth."

"I can still do all that stuff, too. But I wanna be a bull rider and go to all the rodeos."

"I'll clean the kitchen while the men finish eating," Jenna said suddenly, rising to her feet.

Flint shook his head. "No. We'll—"

"Are any of you willing to volunteer for Purge Patrol?" she asked the men gathered around the picnic table. Gazes darted off to the distant horizon and boots shuffled, but the men remained silent. She turned to walk toward the house. "I rest my case."

What kind of game was she playing now? Flint stared after her. If she thought being helpful would pardon the way she'd tricked him with that contract, she was in for a big surprise.

He gave himself a mental pat on the back for a lesson well learned. Now that he knew how she operated, there wasn't any kind of scheme she could think up that he couldn't deal with.

Jenna stepped out onto the front porch to watch the golden glory of the setting sun fade into indigo darkness.

Like a comfortable quilt, a wondrous tranquility began to settle across the land, and pinpoints of light dotted the vast heavens above. The chirp of crickets soon introduced a chorus, and bass-throated bullfrogs down by the creek joined in. Somewhere in the distance, spotlighted by a full moon, the mournful solo of a lone coyote completed the lullaby, transforming the evening into a hymn of praise by nature's wild creatures.

Despite the warm temperature, Jenna wrapped her arms around herself to ward off a chill. This time of night always reminded her of her solitude.

It wasn't supposed to have turned out this way, she thought sadly. Life should be shared.

"Nice night, isn't it?"

Startled, she spun around to find Flint leaning against one of the support posts in a shadowed corner of the porch. "I didn't know anyone was out here."

"Sorry. I didn't mean to frighten you."

Embarrassed that he'd witnessed her pensive mood, she dropped her arms to her sides and turned back to watch the last glimmer of light slip below the horizon.

Several minutes stretched between them before Flint spoke again. "The smell has cleared out of the kitchen. Thanks."

Jenna shrugged. "The skunk didn't bless us with a full dose, and what he did spray missed the porous surfaces. Nothing the tomato juice and ammonia couldn't take care of."

"That's all it took?"

She smiled. "A large amount of elbow grease and a can of air freshener helped."

"How did you know what to do?"

"Just something I picked up along the way." She walked over to the swing and sat down. "When you've

traveled as much as I have, you learn things without remembering how or when."

"I've been meaning to ask you about that," he said, his
voice containing a hint of suspicion. "Usually the horse
goes to the trainer, not the other way around."

Jenna started the swing into motion. Let him think
what he wanted. But instead of ignoring him as she intended, she found herself trying to explain. "I find a horse
is more relaxed in a familiar environment, and it's much
easier to gain his trust. Once I've done that, I can teach
him just about anything."

Flint pushed away from the post and walked over to
sit on the porch rail in front of her. "So, you've been traveling around like this a long time?"

"All my life."

"Wildcatter's daughter?"

She shook her head. "Daddy followed the rodeo circuit." She stared out into the darkness. "Home has always
been a camper on the back of a pickup truck."

A frown creased Flint's brow. "Now, hold it. You had
to have stayed somewhere long enough to get your education."

"Momma taught us for a while." Jenna swallowed
hard. She didn't want to remember certain events of her
childhood. It was too painful. "Later, Cooper and I kept
up with our studies by correspondence until we'd earned
the equivalent of our high school diplomas."

The night suddenly closed in and, disturbed by unpleasant memories, she rose from the swing. "I'd better
get some sleep. I'd like to start Satin's training first thing
in the morning."

"Is there anything special you'll need?"

"No. He's already wearing a halter, so I assume he's
trained to lead?"

Flint nodded.

She opened the screen door, but turned back, only to collide with his broad chest. His large, callused hands caught her shoulders to steady her, and Jenna's stomach did a wobbly cartwheel at the sight of his handsome features so close to her own. He stared down at her for several long moments. She watched his firm lips part, heard his harsh intake of breath. When he gathered her more fully against him, her pulse pounded in her ears at the intense desire in the depths of his slumberous, brown eyes, and the scent of his clean, masculine skin.

She brought her hands up to push herself free. But the feel of his rock-hard chest made her knees go weak, and she found herself clinging to his solid strength for support. How could a man she didn't even know cause her to go into total meltdown? More important, why was she allowing it to happen?

Somewhere in the back of Jenna's mind an inner voice cautioned that she was flirting with disaster. But when Flint's lips came down on hers to brand her with his kiss, the warning faded into oblivion.

His hands roamed from her shoulders to tangle in her thick hair, and every cell in her body tingled to life. His thumbs slid along the column of her throat, and a molten surge of need gathered at the core of her. She tried to press her thighs together against the sweet pain of mounting desire, but the heat of Flint's muscular leg, lodged between hers, had the intense sensations threatening to consume her. She tightened her legs around his in an effort to ease the burn and heard a groan rumble deep in his chest. Cupping her behind he pressed her higher along the rough denim covering his thigh.

The slamming of a door somewhere inside the house

jolted Jenna back to reality, and she pushed against him. "Please—"

Releasing her, she watched Flint jam his hands into the front pockets of his jeans and walk over to lean against the newel post. His back to her, he took a deep breath. "Was there anything else you needed, Jenna?"

His sudden withdrawal and dispassionate tone helped to douse the last traces of her desire. "No."

Bewildered by her body's betrayal, and furious with herself, she allowed anger to take charge. She tried to wipe away the feel of his kiss with the back of her hand. "And I certainly didn't need *that*."

"You didn't turn it down."

"I didn't ask for it, either."

Flint turned to face her, his smile meaningful. "Come on now, darlin'. We're both too old to play games. Why else would you force yourself into my arms?"

Outraged, Jenna saw red. "I turned to ask you to keep your men away from the corral tomorrow while I work with Satin. Nothing more." She jerked the screen door open. "Let's get something else straight while we're at it. *You* grabbed *me*. And if you weren't so full of yourself, you'd admit it, McCray."

The sting of Jenna's words hit like a physical blow as Flint silently watched the door bang shut behind her. He had reached for her, but only to steady her, to keep her from falling. What he couldn't figure out was why he'd allowed it to go beyond that. Maybe it had been the way she'd looked up at him with those big gray eyes—eyes that promised not only ecstasy and fulfillment, but mirrored a loneliness as deep as his own.

He cursed a blue streak. Whatever the reason, when he felt her soft, pliable body beneath his hands he'd displayed all the finesse of a steam roller.

Flint stepped off the porch and headed for the east pasture to check on the herd. He had to forget the feel of Jenna pressed against him, the taste of her lips clinging to his.

He shook his head. Why he'd allowed her to get under his skin remained a mystery. But one thing was certain. No matter what her eyes promised or how tempting the moment became, he wouldn't let it happen again. He'd learned long ago that beyond the green of his money, he was nothing more than a dust covered cowboy with very little to offer a woman. It was a lesson he'd learned the hard way. And he kept the diamond necklace he'd bought for his ex-wife in a glass dome in his office to make sure it was one he wouldn't forget.

He'd just been too long without a woman's softness, that's all, he reasoned. Every man needed physical release from time to time. And he was overdue. Way overdue.

Jenna lay awake long after she left Flint. She'd had time to reflect on the incident, and her anger had cooled toward him, but not with herself. He might have initiated the encounter, but she could have called a halt to it at any time.

So why hadn't she?

She stared at the ceiling, listening to Flint climb the stairs and go into his room. What was there about the man that made her so spineless? Had he been as effected by their kiss as she'd been?

She'd been kissed many times before and never felt the way she had tonight. But the moment he'd taken her into his arms, her common sense had flown away like a big, green bird.

Not even Dan's kisses had brought her to such a fevered state. And she'd loved him.

A mix of guilt and sadness suffused her when she thought of the young man she'd promised to marry. By now they should have been getting ready to celebrate their sixth anniversary. But life had taught her that plans change and guarantees for happiness weren't handed out for the asking. Dan had died that day on the dirt floor of the rodeo arena, and she'd had to learn to get on with her life.

Jenna impatiently wiped a tear from the corner of her eye, turned to her side and forced herself to relax. She'd wasted enough time feeling sorry for herself. She had a new horse to work with tomorrow, and she needed rest to meet the challenge. Besides, trying to figure out her reaction to Flint McCray was like trying to solve a crossword puzzle with no clues.

Drifting toward the peacefulness of sleep, the sound of shots being fired brought her to instant awareness. Rolling to the side of the bed, she landed on the polished hardwood floor with a jarring thump. Her hand hit the nightstand, and something sharp pierced her palm, but after a startled cry, she ignored the pain and began inching her way toward the door.

Maybe she should reexamine her position on insisting Flint honor their contract, she thought, her heart pounding hard against her ribs. If she was going to have to dodge rifle slugs, she'd be more than glad to go.

When the door crashed open, Jenna barely had time to cover her head with her hands before a large body landed on top of her.

Chapter 3

"What in God's name are you doing on the floor?" Flint roared.

He levered himself to a sitting position. The light of the moon, shining through the part in the curtains, illuminated Jenna's still form and the thin line of blood trickling down the side of her face. His heart stalled right then and there. He couldn't tell the extent of her injuries, but clasping her shoulders, he hauled her up into his arms.

"I'm...warning you...McCray—" she took a deep breath "—if this keeps up, I'm going to demand hazardous-duty pay in addition to my regular fee."

"Did you see or hear someone?" he asked, cradling her to his bare chest.

"No."

Her warm breath against his skin sent a shiver snaking down his spine and a fire burning at his gut. Damned if she didn't feel made to fit his arms. He cleared his throat to get words past the cotton clogging his throat. "Then why did you scream?"

"I have a tendency to do that when people shoot at me."

"Shoot at you? You mean, you thought…" Relieved, he couldn't help it. He laughed out loud. "That was Whiskers's truck backfiring." Remembering the blood, he sobered instantly and tightened his embrace. "Where are you hurt?"

"My hand. I hit it on something when I rolled out of bed."

Flint had a hard time concentrating on what she said. Her small, scantily clad body felt wonderful, and the intensity of his reaction stunned him. He was overwhelmingly, completely, undeniably aroused. And it had almost been instantaneous.

He shook his head and tried to ignore his mounting desire. He had to have just set some kind of record. A man of thirty-three wasn't over-the-hill by any means, but he for damn sure wasn't a randy teenager with nothing but seething hormones racing through his veins. Over the years he should have gained at least a modicum of restraint.

Distracted by his changing body, it took him a minute to realize Jenna was pushing against him. He got to his feet and pulled her up with him. "Let's see about your hand."

Pulling her out into the hall, he turned on the overhead light and gulped back a groan when his eyes adjusted to the brightness. Here he stood, harder than the Rock of Gibraltar, gazing down at the half-naked woman responsible for his almost painful state. Now how was a man supposed to ignore a situation like that? It would take a saint or a blind man to overlook the possibilities. And Flint was neither.

He cursed under his breath and tried to ignore the outline of her nipples pushing at the thin fabric of her T-shirt. He normally considered T-shirts shapeless and unappealing. But this one draped her to perfection and made him want to run his hands under the hem, to expose every inch of her to his hungry eyes.

That wouldn't take much, he decided. The damned thing barely covered her panties and exposed enough delectable skin to send his blood pressure up fifty points.

Sounding like the pop-off valve on a pressure cooker, he expelled the breath he hadn't realized he'd been holding. The phrase, Calf Ropers Like It Tied Up, printed across the front of the garment had his imagination running wild and his body right along with it.

"Wait here," he said, his voice more harsh than he intended. He forced himself to move toward his room. It wasn't her fault his imagination already had them all but experiencing the throes of passion. But her eyes had perused his body like a lover's caress, and heaven help him he'd loved every minute of it.

Jenna watched Flint walk down the hall to his room. When he turned on the light, it had taken all of her strength to keep from staring at his perfectly sculpted chest and washboard stomach. A thin coat of dark-brown hair covered muscles made hard by years of physical labor, and from his tan she would bet he often removed his shirt while he worked.

She swallowed hard when she remembered the narrow, dark line arrowing down below his navel to draw attention to the open snap at the waistband of his well-worn jeans. Jeans that hung low on lean hips and emphasized the fact that he was all male and thoroughly aroused.

She was only seconds away from having to fan herself when he walked back into the hall, jamming the tail of his shirt into the waistband of his jeans.

"Put this on," he ordered, shoving a robe into her hands.

The fabric caught on a large splinter protruding from her palm, causing her to wince.

"Sorry," he muttered. "Let's go see to your hand."

"What about Ryan?" she asked, belting the robe.

Flint took her by the elbow to usher her toward the stairs. "His room is on the other side of the house. I was checking on him when you screamed. He's so active during the day, by bedtime he could sleep through an all-out war."

When they entered the office, Jenna sat in the chair across from Flint's desk and held her hand out for his inspection. "It's just a splinter. No big deal."

He whistled low. "It looks like a log." Retrieving the first aid kit from his desk, Flint took her hand in his. He examined the wound, his large hand dwarfing hers. She knew she shouldn't, but she liked the contrast.

"Have you had a tetanus shot recently?" he asked, his attention on her hand.

"I make sure I keep all my immunizations current." His hands engulfed hers as he worked to remove the splinter and she wondered how they would feel caressing her—

"Ouch!" Her erotic thoughts shattered when he continued to probe for any traces of wood he might have missed. "What are you trying to do, McCray? Drill for oil?"

He poured hydrogen peroxide over the area, applied an antiseptic ointment, then wrapped her hand in gauze.

"I think I got it all, but it'll probably be sore for the next few days."

Jenna glanced up when he continued to hold her hand. Their gazes locked and the charge of excitement coursing between them took her breath. When he took an antiseptic pad and sponged the blood from her cheek, she wondered if she'd ever breathe again. Shaken by the feel of his hand caressing hers, the gentleness he displayed wiping her face, she jerked her hand from his.

"Why do I get the idea you wouldn't have been surprised if someone had fired shots at us?" she asked, cursing her breathless tone.

Jenna settled back into the armchair to focus her attention on Flint. She wasn't going anywhere until she had an explanation. Besides, at the moment, she seriously doubted her legs would support her.

"You might as well tell me what's going on. I have a right to know."

"It's none of your business."

She jerked her thumb toward the door. "What happened upstairs just made it my business. You weren't altogether sure I hadn't seen someone. If I'm going to have to be looking over my shoulder, I'd like to know why. It's something I don't take lightly." She gave him a pointed look. "And I don't think you do, either."

Flint slumped into the chair behind his desk and ran a weary hand over his face. If their positions were reversed, he'd be pounding on the desk, demanding an explanation.

But her calm demeanor unsettled him, and suspicion began to cloud his mind. Could Jenna already be familiar with the situation? Was she somehow involved in stealing his cattle? Why hadn't she been hysterical when she thought someone was shooting at her? Nicole would have been. Hell, his ex-wife went off the deep end when she broke a fingernail.

"We've had some trouble with rustlers," he stated, watching for her reaction.

"Spreads the size of the Rocking M will always be targets of cattle thieves," she said. "But rustlers usually steer clear of a ranch headquarters. Besides, stealing cattle is one thing. Prowling around an occupied house is an entirely different matter. And that's exactly what you thought had happened."

"It's just been the past couple of days that things have started getting ugly." He searched for any indication she might be aware of the situation. When he found none, he continued, "Last night they castrated a twenty-five-thousand-dollar bull."

She sat forward, her eyes wide. "Why wasn't an animal that valuable closer to the house?"

"He was. Somehow he managed to get through two locked gates and across a six-hundred-acre pasture."

"He had help," she said flatly. "Have any other ranchers had similar problems?"

He shook his head. "Not yet."

"This is more than just a case of cattle rustling," she stated. "It sounds like someone is trying to seek revenge."

"But I'll be damned if I can figure out who it is or why they're doing it," he agreed. He wasn't used to talking with a woman about his ranching problems. Nicole had never cared what went on as long as the money kept rolling in.

"Have you checked with the state brand inspectors?" she asked. "They should be able to tell you who brought the cattle into the stockyards. Maybe you could catch them that way."

Flint propped his elbows on the arms of his chair and

steepled his hands in front of him. She certainly knew enough about the workings of the cattle industry to implicate her, but then so did most people used to being around livestock. And her shock at the mutilation of the bull seemed genuine.

Jenna Adams was either a damned good actress or innocent of any involvement. One way or the other, he'd know for sure when the investigator finished running a check on her background.

"Of course I've notified the authorities," he answered. "But the only cattle with the Rocking M brand that have gone through any of the yards are the ones I've sent."

She arched a brow. "Then where are they? They didn't just vanish into thin air."

"The sheriff found some hides bearing our brand in a remote area about seventy-five miles from here," Flint answered. "From all indications, the rustlers are butchering the cattle in the back of a refrigerated trailer. By the time they reach the packing house, the beef is dressed out."

"No hides. No evidence," she said, nodding. "But what about the USDA? Why haven't they caught the uninspected beef?"

He shrugged. "Who knows? It could be an inspector on the take or a packing house with a counterfeit stamp."

He left his chair. "Either way, it doesn't make much difference. After the events of last night, I'd say they're getting impatient. It's just a matter of time now before they screw up." His voice grew cold, his smile deadly. "And when they do, I'll be there to nail the bastards."

As she rose to her feet, a shiver ran the length of Jenna's spine. She wouldn't want to be in the rustlers' boots when he caught up with them. One look into those intense brown eyes told her Flint McCray could be a very dangerous adversary.

She felt Flint's gaze boring a hole into her back as she climbed the stairs and entered her room. In his eyes, she knew no one was above suspicion. Not even her.

But that didn't matter. He could think whatever he liked. But if she'd known he had this kind of problem on his hands, she might not have been so insistent that he honor their contract.

She shook her head and immediately dismissed the thought. Running from trouble was a coward's way out.

And no one had ever been able to call Jenna Adams a coward.

"I tell ya, Jed, I thought I had that truck fixed or I'd a never loaned it to you last night," Whiskers said, wiping the counter. "If Flint hadn't said it scared Jenna into hurtin' herself when it backfired, I'd a sworn you made it up."

"Believe me," Jenna said, entering the kitchen. "It happened."

"Mornin', Miss Adams." Jed pointed to her bandaged hand. "After what happened last night, I'll bet you're just about ready to cut your losses and run."

She shook her head and sat down to a delicious-looking plate of biscuits and gravy. "It'll take more than a splinter to keep me from training a potential champion."

"Flint said you got hurt," Whiskers said, worriedly. "Maybe you'd better not try to work with Satin this mornin'."

Touched by his concern, Jenna smiled and held out her bandaged hand for his inspection. "I'll be fine. I've worked with much worse injuries than this."

"I just don't like the idea of a little gal like you climbin' in the corral with that black devil," Whiskers stated, picking up Jed's plate to scrape the contents.

"Hey, I'm not finished," Jed complained.

Whiskers placed the plate in the sink. "Yes, you are."

Jed started to protest, but stopped when a gnarled finger pointed his direction.

"Somebody has to keep track of the vittles you poke down, 'cause it's for danged sure you don't know when to push away from the table." The old man propped his hands on his hips. "The rest of the men finished up fifteen minutes ago. Now, get your shiftless butt outta here so I can get my work done."

Jed jumped to his feet. "If you keep mean-mouthin' people, somebody's gonna tear your head off and shout down the hole."

"Then who'd feed your worthless carcass?" Whiskers asked.

"That's the only thing holdin' me back, old man." Jed grabbed his hat and walked through the door.

Shaken by the man's obvious anger, Jenna's appetite deserted her. "I'm not very hungry, Whiskers." She rose from the table. "But thanks, anyway."

"You cain't be done." When she nodded, he threw up his hands. "No wonder you're such a puny little thing."

"She has to be wiry and quick to work with horses like Satin," Flint said, walking into the room.

Jenna ducked her head to conceal her astonishment. That wasn't the argument he'd used yesterday when he tried to break their contract. He'd accused her of not having the strength to work with his horse, or any others, for that matter. What had changed his mind?

She decided to ignore the comment. All her concentration needed to be focused on Satin and his training. If she allowed her mind to wander while she worked with the stallion, she could confirm Flint's first observation.

And she'd rather run naked through a briar patch than let that happen.

She adjusted the shotgun chaps she'd put on before coming downstairs. "Speaking of Satin, I'd better get started."

Flint's mouth went dry when he noticed the way the leather hugged Jenna's slender thighs and framed her blue-jeans-clad buttocks. He shifted from one foot to the other and swallowed hard. It was all he could do to keep from reaching for her.

For the life of him, he couldn't forget what had taken place last night on the porch and in the hall. Her legs had felt incredible tangled with his when he'd kissed her. And the memory of her, half-naked, lying in his arms on the floor, had already driven him to a cold shower this morning.

Flint observed the way the open seat of the chaps emphasized the movement of her firm little bottom as she walked toward the back door. He thought his mouth might drop open.

"Dinner's at twelve," Whiskers called after her. His eyes dancing merrily, his toothless grin wide, he turned back to Flint. "Unless the big bad wolf gets ahold of her first."

It took every ounce of effort Flint could muster to keep from turning a deep crimson. He should have known Whiskers would notice his discomfort. The old man had the eyes of a hawk.

Whiskers laughed. "I'm glad to see you takin' an interest in that little filly. She's a danged sight more tolerable than the one you used to be hitched up to."

"I don't know what you're talking about," Flint lied. He removed his hat from the peg beside the door. "I have no interest in Miss Adams aside from her training Black Satin."

"Is that why you look like you're gonna make her your next meal?"

Flint turned to glare at his housekeeper. "Dammit, Whiskers. I don't—"

"Save it, boy. I've had the oven on this mornin' and there's already plenty of hot air in this kitchen." Whiskers moved to the table to stack plates. "If I was forty years younger, I'd lasso her myself. Mark my words, that little gal's a keeper if ever I seen one."

"I have no intention of keeping her or any other woman." Flint's scowl deepened. "If you'll remember, I gave it a try and it turned out to be a disaster."

Whiskers waved a spoon at Flint. "Any time you play with a wildcat, you're bound to get scratched. I told you about that woman before you ever got yourself hitched up to her. She's the very reason you're gun-shy now."

"I'm not gun-shy." Flint shook his head. "I just don't intend to make the same mistake twice. That's all."

"There ain't no way you could with Jenna."

"Just when did you become an expert on women?"

Whiskers put the dishes in the sink and poured them each a cup of coffee. Motioning for Flint to take a seat, he lowered himself into a chair on the opposite side of the big oak table. "You can tell a quarter horse from a Thoroughbred, cain't you?"

Flint knew he should let the matter drop, but instead of walking away, he sat down. "What do horses have to do with women?"

Whiskers grinned. "Jenna's like a quarter horse—"

Flint laughed. "I'm sure she'd be flattered by the comparison."

"Are you gonna shut your trap and listen?"

"Okay. Go ahead."

"Well, like I was sayin', she's pretty, but she's got a lot of heart, too. She don't let things make her skittish when there's a job to be done." Whiskers nodded. "Yessiree, when the chips are down, she'd be right there givin' all she had and wouldn't give up until she couldn't go no more—just like a quarter horse." The old man's voice took on a disgusted tone. "On the other hand, Nicole was a true Thoroughbred. A real beauty to look at, but flighty and temperamental as hell. Give her a cross-eyed stare and she couldn't even make it to the startin' gate, let alone run the race."

"But there's one thing you're forgetting," Flint reminded him.

Puzzled, Whiskers scratched his beard. "What?"

"I don't need a woman. I'm happy with my life. I have Ryan and the ranch—"

"Horse spit! You and Ryan rattle around this place like BBs in a boxcar. A house this size needs a whole passel of kids. And you need a little gal like Jenna to cozy up to so you can get 'em."

His cup halfway to his mouth, Flint stopped to glare at the old man. "Have you lost your mind, Whiskers? I just met the woman yesterday."

"And you've been in a hot fizz ever since," Whiskers shot back.

Flint gritted his teeth, then lied right through them. "I have not. As far as I'm concerned, Jenna Adams is an employee—the same as Brad or any of the others."

Whiskers shook his head and got to his feet to start the dishes. "I never thought I'd live to see the day I'd be callin' Flint McCray a liar."

Without a word, Flint placed his cup on the table, rose from his chair and left the house. He stopped in the middle of the ranch yard, his hands clenched into tight fists. He took a deep breath in order to calm himself.

But in all honesty, being called a liar wasn't what had Flint's anger close to the boiling point. It was the truth in Whiskers's words. The old man's observations had been right on the money. He had been tied in knots since Jenna's arrival. And Flint didn't like at all that it was so damned obvious.

Jenna shortened the *lunge* line until Satin became more manageable. She loped him in a tight circle around her for a few more minutes, then tied him to a post for grooming. She recognized the signs of an active mind and an overabundance of energy. But unlike some horses she'd trained, he wasn't rebellious and difficult.

He did have a tendency to become aggressive and try to charge when excited or frightened, but she knew it stemmed more from him being a stallion and pasture raised, than from a hatred of humans. Once he learned there was nothing to fear, she would train him to channel his spirited nature into a constructive pattern and turn him into a champion reining horse.

"Hi," she said when she noticed Flint standing at the fence. She'd wondered how long it would take him to check on the progress she was making with his prized stallion.

"How did it go this morning?" he asked after she'd turned the horse into the small pasture behind the corral.

"Pretty good." She coiled the rope she held. "He has a lot of potential."

"He seems to have settled well."

"High-energy horses usually do, if you can keep them from getting bored." She turned to watch the stallion gallop across the pasture. "That's why I prefer a varied program for horses like Satin. His temperament can't tolerate the monotony of constant drilling exercises."

"What do you have planned this afternoon?"

"Nothing." She let herself out of the enclosure. "He's had enough for now. Tomorrow I'll repeat what he's learned today and introduce a new activity or two." She shrugged. "The next day I may only work with him for a half hour or so."

Flint scowled. "Isn't that wasting time?"

"No." She started for the house. "It's a precaution."

He caught her by the arm. "Since my money is paying for this, would you care to elaborate?"

Jenna felt the tingling begin where his hand clasped her upper arm, then make a beeline to the pit of her belly. Why did he have to do that? Why couldn't he just leave her alone and let her do her job?

Her gaze locked with Flint's a moment before she pried his fingers, one by one, from her arm and turned to walk away.

"You didn't answer me. I want to know why you're wasting the afternoon."

She needed to escape his disturbing presence in order to regain her equilibrium. But Mr. Can't-Leave-Well-Enough-Alone wasn't about to cooperate.

She turned to face him, her voice terse. "Satin has a high mental energy as well as physical. That has to be taken into account when planning his training." When Flint's scowl deepened, she blew out an exasperated breath. "Wouldn't you say you're a person with a lot of drive?"

"Yes, but—"

"How would you like to have a job doing the same repetitive task day after day?"

"I'd quit."

"Exactly. You'd get frustrated with the lack of mental challenge." She pointed to the pasture. "Satin's like that. He needs to be kept guessing as to what we're going to do next. It keeps him interested and his attention on the task at hand."

His mouth twitched a moment before a roar of laughter rumbled up from his chest. "You mean to tell me you practice horse psychology, too?"

Jenna felt like punching him. "If I were you, I wouldn't think it was all that funny, McCray. From what I've seen, you and your men haven't done such a great job with him."

His grin disappeared. "What's that supposed to mean?"

Satisfied she had his attention, she smiled sweetly. "You called *me,* remember? Evidently you recognized he was beyond your limited realm of experience." She started for the house. "Leave his training to me and you'll have a champion. Interfere and you'll be stuck with the results."

Flint stood rooted to the spot. He watched Jenna march the distance to the back door, but he didn't dare move for fear of exploding. He'd been raised in the saddle, and she might just as well have called him a greenhorn.

He spun around and went to the pasture where the working horses were kept. He caught and saddled his favorite gelding, then loaded fencing supplies and a hammer into a set of saddlebags.

When he swung up into the saddle, Brad called, "Where are you going? It's dinnertime."

"To blazes with dinner," Flint growled.

He touched his spurs to the horse. He'd ride fence, check to see if he could find any sign of who might be causing all the trouble and hopefully forget he'd ever heard of Jenna Adams.

* * *

Dealing with Flint McCray was like trying to convey a message to a rock, Jenna thought as she climbed the stairs to her room. Shout at it, try to reason with it, even ignore it. The results were the same. Stubborn and immovable, the damn thing just sat there waiting to trip you up.

She closed the door behind her, then stripped out of her chaps and dusty clothing. Maybe a good sit-down, soak-until-you're-pruny bath would help her relax. She walked into the adjoining bathroom, turned the water taps on and eased herself into the big, claw-footed bathtub.

Since her arrival on the Rocking M, her emotions had been yanked around like a yo-yo, with Flint controlling the string. He'd accused her of deceiving him to get the job, scoffed at her training abilities, kissed her in a way she'd never been kissed before, then accused her of pushing herself at him. Now they'd come full circle. They were back to scorn and doubt.

Jenna reclined against the cool porcelain. Why did she find it so hard to resist Flint?

She closed her eyes and tried to remember the reason she'd come to the Rocking M, the job she had to do. But images of Flint kept flashing through her mind. His mouth descending on hers. His warm, firm flesh beneath her fingers. His body pinning her to the floor.

She sighed. The man could drive a saint to sin with his kiss and a pacifist to violence with his stubbornness.

Unfortunately, any way she looked at it, Flint was the most infuriating and, at the same time, seductive man she'd ever met.

Flint rode into the ranch yard well after dark. Bone tired, he slowly dismounted and led his horse into the barn. He'd searched every inch of Widow's Ridge for anything left by the rustlers that the sheriff might have missed, tightened strands of barbed wire and repaired the hinges on every gate he came to, whether they needed it or not. He'd worked off his anger, but hadn't found a clue as to the rustlers' identity or been able to tire himself enough to forget his new horse trainer and the way she made him feel. The woman had the unbelievable ability to make him furious enough to choke her, and hard as granite, all at the same time.

In retrospect, Flint had to admit he wasn't as angry with Jenna as with himself and his reaction to her. For some unfathomable reason, when she stood up to him and managed to hold her own in an argument, he found it incredibly sexy and arousing.

She met him as an equal, using the admirable weapons of logic and reason to get her point across. Things a man could identify with, understand.

And that was what threw him off balance. He wasn't used to those qualities in a woman. His ex-wife hadn't possessed them. Nicole had relied on tears and tantrums to get her way.

"Flint, we need to talk," Brad said, entering the barn.

Flint studied his foreman's tense expression. Whatever Brad had to say would be better faced over a drink. "Let me wash up first. I'll meet you in the study."

"I'll pour the Scotch," Brad said, walking from the barn.

Fifteen minutes later Flint sat behind his desk, his hand gripping a glass of amber liquid. "They got another twenty head last night?"

His face grim, Brad nodded. "I hate to say it, but it's my guess someone here at the ranch is involved."

Flint's mood darkened. "There's no other explanation. Whoever's doing this has to have somebody here feeding them information. I didn't decide to bring that herd up to the east pasture until late yesterday afternoon."

"What I can't figure is who it would be or why," Brad said. "All the boys have been with us for some time, and I haven't heard any complaints about the work or the pay. If one of them had an ax to grind, you can bet I'd have wind of it by now."

"Well, whatever the reason, it's crystal clear somebody's out to destroy the Rocking M," Flint said dispassionately. "And me in the bargain."

Chapter 4

A trickle of sweat slid down Jenna's spine, and she rotated her shoulders to dispel the odd sensation. When the rivulet slipped below the waistband of her jeans, she decided this was as close to hell as she ever cared to get.

A gentle breeze ruffled the leaves on the tall oak tree at the side of the house, but did little to diminish the oppressive, midafternoon heat. For more than a week temperatures had been soaring as a heat wave baked the panhandle with blast-furnace intensity, and she'd even had to change her working schedule with Satin to early morning in order to keep from overheating.

His round little cheeks flushed from the heat, Ryan asked, "Are you gonna play? It's your turn."

Jenna glanced at her cards. "Do you have any fours?"

"Go fish!"

She smiled at his triumphant giggles and reached to take a card from the pile between them. But movement in the distance caught her attention, and her smile faded. She had no idea who the rider was, but he should be shot for running a horse flat out in this kind of heat.

When the animal drew closer, Jenna's eyes widened and her breath lodged in her throat. The stirrups of the saddle slapped wildly against the horse's ribs, the seat ominously empty. The sight of a riderless horse usually indicated a cowboy in trouble and was a major source of anxiety in big-ranch country, especially in this kind of heat.

Jumping to her feet, Jenna threw her cards on the picnic table. "Go get your dad, Ryan." Knowing that many horses headed for the barn or corral after finding themselves without a rider, she ran toward the enclosure where the working stock were kept.

She was waiting when the gelding came to a shuddering stop in front of the closed gate, his chest lathered with sweat, foam dripping from around the bit in his mouth. Approaching slowly to avoid startling the agitated animal, she reached up and took hold of his bridle to keep him from shying away. She cringed when she noticed the reins, wrapped around the saddle horn. It was an undeniable indication the rider's departure from the saddle had been sudden and quite unexpected.

"What happened?" Flint called, his long strides closing the distance between them. "Where's Jim?"

"I'd say he's somewhere between here and wherever Brad assigned him to work," Jenna answered. Running a reassuring hand along the gelding's neck, she eased to the horse's heaving side to loosen the cinch. "Did Brad go over the schedule with you this morning?"

Flint nodded, his features grim. "Jim was supposed to check the grazing conditions up at Devil's Gorge."

"What's up, Flint?" Whiskers asked when he and Ryan reached the pair.

"Looks like Jim's gotten himself into a wreck," Flint said, heading for the barn. When he returned, he placed the saddle he carried on the top rail of the fence, then caught one of the horses in the corral. "I'll ride up there—"

Jenna started through the gate to catch one of the other horses. She couldn't bear the thought of staying at the ranch when she might be of some help to the friendly young cowboy. "I'm going with you."

Flint blocked her path. "No, you're not." He shook his head as he led the bay from the enclosure. "This isn't a pleasure trip, Jenna."

"Don't be a stubborn jackass, McCray." She jerked her thumb over her shoulder. "You've got a man down out there somewhere with God only knows what kind of injuries, and the sooner he's found, the better."

His eyes narrowed, he stopped his preparations to stare at her over the horse's back. "My main concern is finding Jim. Once I cross the dry wash up there, I'll be traveling over some of the roughest country this side of hell. It isn't even accessible by truck. I for damn sure don't need the added responsibility of watching out for you."

She raised her chin. "I can take care of myself. Besides, two riders can cover more ground than one."

"She's got herself a point," Whiskers agreed. "You're gonna have to bring Jim out on horseback. If he's busted a leg or something, you might need the extry help. Me and Ryan can meet you with the truck this side of the dry wash, in case he needs to see a doctor."

Flint didn't like his options one damned bit. Why did his only source of help have to come in the form of a petite, desirable blonde? His reaction to her made him as nervous as a long-tailed cat in a room full of rocking chairs. And after making a fool of himself several times in the first twenty-four hours of her arrival on the Rocking M, he'd made it a point to avoid her like the plague.

He'd kept himself busy during the days with hard, back-breaking work in order to ease the ache he'd had since that first day. But at night, when he lay alone in his bed, the physical exhaustion did little to erase the taste of her sweet lips, the feel of her softness pressed to his body.

Flint frowned as he checked his watch. Damn! He didn't have a choice. He couldn't wait for his men to get back from their assigned areas of the ranch to start a search. There wouldn't be enough daylight left, and Jim might be in need of immediate attention.

Cursing under his breath, Flint jerked the sorrel's reins from Jenna and handed them to Whiskers. "Cool down Jim's horse." He ignored the old man's knowing grin and turned back to Jenna. "I'm going up to the house for some medical supplies. If you're not ready to go by the time I get back, I'll leave without you."

Whiskers rolled his eyes. "You sure know how to sweet-talk a gal."

Flint ignored the comment and headed to the house. What he wanted to do with Jenna wouldn't require words, but it for damned sure would be sweet. Shaking his head, he entered the study, collected the first aid supplies and packed them into a set of saddle bags. He needed to keep his mind on what had to be done.

When he returned to the corral, he shoved a rifle into the boot on his saddle, then tied the saddlebags and an extra saddle blanket to the back. "I'm warning you right now," he said, a muscle along his jaw tightening. "If you can't keep up, you're on your own. I'll go on without you."

Jenna mounted the buckskin she'd saddled. "Don't worry. If I take a fall, you can always do the decent thing and put me out of my misery."

He sucked in a sharp breath and thought about the misery *he* was experiencing. Beads of sweat that had nothing to do with the afternoon heat popped out on his forehead and upper lip. One look at Jenna's slim legs wrapped around the buckskin had his jeans feeling way too small, and his throbbing body reminded him he was about as miserable as a man could get.

"Don't tempt me," he growled. Hoping his face revealed none of the battle raging within his taut body, he shoved his boot in the stirrup and gingerly swung up into the saddle.

Whiskers watched Flint and Jenna nudge their horses into a lope and head in the direction of Devil's Gorge. Disgusted, he shook his head as he looked down at Ryan. "When you get to be a young buck and wanna start courtin', remind me to be the one to teach you 'bout how to chitchat with a gal."

Flint focused on the heat waves shimmering in the distance as he and Jenna made their way toward Devil's Gorge. When a slight breeze whispered past, mesquite branches stirred and prairie grass swayed, but instead of relief, the flurry of hot air only made the heat more stifling.

His concern for Jim grew the farther they went. Flint had hoped to meet the man somewhere along the trail. Maybe a little red-faced at losing his seat and having his horse head for home, but nonetheless, moving on his own steam. But the closer they got to the gorge, the less likely that eventuality became.

Apparently, Flint's worst fears were going to be confirmed. Jim was most likely down and not moving at all.

A heavy cloak of guilt settled over Flint. He should be shot. He'd tried to insist Jenna stay behind, when in truth he could use all the help he could get in his search to find Jim.

But along with worrying about Jim, Flint had also been concerned with the torment his own nervous system suffered every time he got close to Jenna. That's why he'd exaggerated a little about the area being the roughest country this side of hell.

Okay, he admitted to himself, he'd exaggerated a lot. But the more time he spent with her, the more he wanted to spend. And that was something he wasn't exaggerating.

Jenna followed Flint as he crossed the wash and threaded his way through the outcropping of knife-edged rock. He hadn't spoken more than twice since they'd left the ranch, and that was just fine with her. For the past few days, Flint McCray had all the personality of a wooden fence post, and she'd just as soon try to communicate with one as to hold a conversation with him.

Oh, she hadn't expected him to fall all over himself with gratitude when she'd offered to help him search for Jim. But she hadn't thought he would act like a badger with a hangnail, either.

She wouldn't have persisted in coming along, but a downed cowboy in this kind of heat could dehydrate rapidly, and finding him as soon as possible could mean the difference between life and death. She'd come along for Jim's sake, not because she wanted to spend more time with Mr. Congeniality.

"How do you manage to get cattle in here, McCray?" she asked, guiding her horse around another boulder.

"We bring them in from the east. There's a narrow pass about four miles from here. This is a shortcut."

They rode in silence for several more minutes, before she pointed to the vultures tracing slow circles in the sky not far ahead. "That doesn't look good."

"Damn! I was afraid of this."

Nudging their horses into a lope, they approached the spot directly beneath the birds.

"There he is." Jenna winced at the sight of the still, crumpled body. Praying they weren't too late, she jumped from the buckskin and ran to the man's side. "Jim. Jim, wake up."

Flint knelt and placed his fingers against the young cowboy's neck.

"Is he—" She couldn't bring herself to voice her fear.

Flint shook his head. "His pulse is strong. But I'd say he's well on his way to dehydrating." Taking a canteen from his saddle, he wet Jim's bandanna. "Here, see if you can bring him around so we can get some water into him."

Jenna knelt so her body shielded the man's scorched face from the blazing sun. "Come on, Jim." She bathed his parched skin with the cloth. "You've got to wake up."

She watched Flint retrieve the saddlebags from his horse, then open Jim's shirt to run his hands along the cowboy's torso. "I'd say from that bruise on his side, he might have a couple of cracked ribs." His face grim, Flint nodded at the odd angle of Jim's lower leg. "And his leg's broken just below the knee."

When Flint used his pocket knife to cut Jim's jeans and peeled back the fabric, he muttered a succinct curse. The sight of the twisted leg caused Jenna to turn away and swallow against the bile rising in her throat.

"You going to be all right?" Flint asked.

"Yes."

She turned back to face him, and her expression told Flint she was relying on pure grit to do what had to be done. "Good, because the swelling around his boot is cutting off the circulation to his foot. I'm going to need you to hold his leg steady while I try to get it off. Think you can do it?"

Her face pale, Jenna's resolute gaze locked with his. "Yes."

The sparkle of determination in the clear, gray depths of her eyes, the squaring of her slender shoulders, convinced Flint that Jenna was a pressure player. She wouldn't turn tail and run, no matter how unpleasant the situation became. Even if she had to rely on sheer raw nerve, she'd see the job through to the end.

Unbidden, Whiskers's sage words whispered through his mind. *When the chips are down, she'd be right there givin' all she had and wouldn't give up until she couldn't go no more.*

On impulse, Flint reached out, placed his hand at the nape of her neck and pulled her forward for a quick, hard kiss. "Hang in there, darlin'. You're doing just fine."

His lips, pressed even briefly to hers, sent a shock-wave straight to the pit of his belly. He'd only meant it as a gesture of encouragement, but his body wanted to argue the point.

"Ready?" Flint asked, determined to ignore the tightening in his groin.

He watched Jenna clamp her lips together, then reach down to steady Jim's leg. He could tell this was hard for her, but she wouldn't give up. He admired that kind of grit.

Flint split the side seam on the boot's shaft. "Hold him tight, while I try to ease this off."

Regaining consciousness, Jim groaned. "Hurts...like hell."

"Just a little bit more, partner." To help distract the man from his obvious pain, Flint asked, "What happened?"

"Coming back from the gorge...I caught sight of a coyote dragging a calf hide." Jim's breath caught as Flint worked to free the swollen foot. When the pain eased a bit, Jim continued, "Like a damned fool, I dallied the reins around the saddle horn, pulled my rifle and gave chase. I never figured on running across a buzzy-tail, though. One whiff of that rattlesnake and old Red went berserk. He piled me in two jumps, then kicked me in the ribs for good measure."

Flint worked to free Jim's foot. "Did you get the coyote?"

"Hell, no!" Jim chuckled feebly. "That old prairie wolf turned around pretty as you please and watched the rodeo. Then I swear it sounded like he had a good laugh as he trotted off."

"He probably did. I imagine you and Red put on quite a show." The foot finally pulled free of the boot, and Flint blew out a relieved breath. He handed Jenna his canteen. "Here, try to get some water into him."

When she placed the canteen to Jim's cracked lips, he took a sip, then gazed up at her. "Damned nice to wake up lookin' into the face of an angel." Paling, his lopsided grin suddenly turned to a grimace.

"It's okay, Jim," Jenna said, her voice gentle. "We're here now. Everything will be all right."

Envy swept through Flint when she laid a comforting hand on Jim's cheek. The sound of her velvet voice saying another man's name, the sight of her hand caressing the young cowboy's jaw, had Flint wishing he were the one stretched out on the ground with his head resting in her lap.

He gritted his teeth against the irrational thought, rose to his feet and went to the bay's side to unfasten the extra saddle blanket. "Jenna, take off your belt." He walked back to place the blanket beside Jim's injured leg, then removed his own belt. "I'll need yours, too, Jim. Can you get it off?"

Jim struggled for a moment to sit up, but pain forced him to sink back against Jenna. "Give me a minute…to catch my breath…and I'll try again."

"I'll get it," she said, reaching for the buckle.

Flint watched her hands, so slender, so soft, hover above Jim's waist. How many times in the last few days had Flint caught himself reliving the feel of her hands touching *his* skin? Remembering the effect they had on *his* body? Now those same hands were tugging at another man's belt, mere inches from…

If Jenna unbuckled a man's belt, it damn well better be his.

Cursing, Flint brushed her hands aside, helped Jim to a sitting position and made short work of removing the leather strap. "Support his leg while I get this blanket under it," he commanded, ignoring the exasperated look she shot him.

He fashioned a makeshift splint out of the stiff pad, then secured it with the belts. When he finished the task, he looked up to see Jenna helping Jim remove his tattered shirt.

"What do you think you're doing?"

"Didn't you say he might have some cracked ribs?"

"Yes."

"Then don't you think it might be a good idea to tape them?"

Flint knew he was acting the fool and being completely irrational, but he couldn't seem to stop himself. To watch her help Jim out of his clothing, to see her gentle hands touch his bruised side, was more than Flint could take.

He bent to tape the man's ribs, then helped him stand on his good leg. "I don't like having to do this, but we don't have a choice, Jim. We're going to have to ride out of here. Think you can stay upright in the saddle?"

His lips white with pain, Jim sucked in a sharp breath and nodded. "I'll give it a damned good try."

"He can double up with me," Jenna offered, steadying the cowboy from the opposite side.

Flint shook his head. "He's going to need support, and you're not strong enough."

"I'm stronger than I look."

"Don't be ridiculous—"

"If you two don't mind," Jim interrupted, "I'd like to get to a doctor before this leg falls off."

"Jenna, bring the horses over here." Flint felt guilty as hell. Jim needed immediate medical attention, and all Flint wanted to do was argue with Jenna. Well, that wasn't all he wanted, but it did help to ease some of his pent-up tension. And for now, that would have to do.

After Jenna led the horses to his side, Flint tied the saddlebags to the buckskin's saddle, lifted Jim onto the bay, then swung up behind him. He steadied the younger man with his arms as Jim's body went limp.

"Hang on," Flint encouraged the now-unconscious man. "Whiskers is going to meet us at the wash."

A half hour later Flint guided his horse across the sandy bottom of the ravine, relieved to see Whiskers and Ryan waiting for them on the other side with one of the ranch trucks.

"I put some blankets and pilla's in the back so Jim could lay down," the old man said. "How long has he been out?"

"Since we left the gorge." Flint rode the bay up to the truck, then stepped down into its bed. Lifting the limp cowboy off the horse, he laid Jim on the blankets and elevated his leg with the pillows. "Besides a broken leg, he's got some bruised ribs and he's partially dehydrated."

"Daddy, is Jim gonna be all right?" Ryan asked, his small chin trembling.

Flint jumped down from the truck bed. Swinging Ryan up into his arms, he assured, "He'll be fine. We'll take him to the hospital in Amarillo, and they'll fix him up good as new."

"I don't like hospitals." Tears threatened to spill from Ryan's big brown eyes. "People go there and never come back."

Flint's chest tightened at the fear in his son's eyes. Since Nicole's death, the child had been terrified of hospitals. Hugging him close, Flint tried to absorb Ryan's fear. "Hospitals also make people well."

Jenna dismounted and walked over to them. "Ryan, would you like to ride back to the house with me while your dad and Whiskers take Jim into Amarillo? We could finish that game of Go Fish."

"Can I, Daddy?" Ryan asked, looking hopeful.

Flint's gaze met Jenna's. Her reassuring smile had him smiling right back. "Sure. If Jenna doesn't mind."

"I'd be more than glad to have the company." She took Ryan and set him on the bay. "Go on and take Jim to the hospital. We'll be waiting for you at the house."

Flint stared at her a moment longer before climbing into the back of the truck with the injured cowboy. He tried to fight his reaction to her words, the feelings they caused. But knowing she'd be there awaiting his return sent a warmth coursing all the way to his soul.

Jenna sat in the porch swing, her arms wrapped around the sleeping little boy in her lap. She'd always wanted children, and if things had worked out, she would have had a child about Ryan's age. A sandy-haired little boy or girl with laughing, green eyes just like his or her father's.

For the first time in six years Jenna allowed herself to freely remember the gentle young man she'd planned to marry. But no longer was the image of his face so vivid or the sound of his voice as clear as it had once been. The passage of time had healed the hurt of losing him, taken care of the pain. But it had also eased him into a comfortable part of the past.

A past she had learned to live with, but would never, as long as she lived, forget.

For a long time she'd waited for someone to awaken her. To tell her it had all been a terrible nightmare, that Dan wasn't gone. But it had happened, and all the waiting in the world wouldn't change it.

Now she waited again. Waited for word on Jim's condition. Waited for Flint.

In the distance twin beams of light split the darkness as a truck approached the house. Her pulse quickened as the ebony curtain of night closed in behind them. The wait was over. Flint was home.

After he parked the truck, he and Whiskers climbed the porch steps. "How's Jim?" she asked, careful not to wake Ryan.

"He's gonna be just fine," Whiskers said, patting her shoulder. He yawned and shook his head. "I'm gettin' too old for these shenanigans. I'll see you two in the mornin'."

The screen door banging shut behind Whiskers

brought Flint out of the daze he'd been in since the truck lights flashed across the porch and he'd spotted Jenna in the swing, his son cradled to her breast. Was there any sweeter sight to a bone-weary man than that of a woman and child holding a vigil for his return?

"How long has Ryan been asleep?"

"About an hour." She looked down at his son and smiled. "He wanted to wait up for you, but just couldn't stay awake. I promised I'd have you put him to bed."

Flint sat down beside her. "I'm sorry it took so long, but Jim had to have his leg pinned. Since he doesn't have family around here, Whiskers and I waited until he came out of surgery." He shrugged. "It just didn't seem right to leave him alone."

She nodded. "You did the right thing. It's awfully frightening to lie in a hospital bed and know there's not a soul around who cares what happens to you."

Flint gave her a sideways glance, but she stared straight ahead. There wasn't a doubt in his mind that she hadn't spoken from experience.

"What happened?"

"I came down with pneumonia after a case of flu and had to be hospitalized."

"What about your brother? Why wasn't he with you?"

She sighed. "As always, Cooper was off at some rodeo. I had no idea where he was or how to get in touch with him."

He knew it wasn't any of his business, but dammit Flint didn't like the thought of Jenna being sick and all alone. "Couldn't you have contacted your parents?"

She shook her head. "Daddy had an accident." She paused to take a deep breath. "He never fully recovered. He passed away a year later. That was long before my stay in the hospital."

"And your mother?" Flint could tell talking about her past had dragged up some very painful memories.

"Momma—" her voice cracked "—she was gone, too."

Flint put his arm around her and drew her to his side. When she started to pull away, he held her close. He told himself he was only offering comfort, lending her his strength. But the feel of her tucked against his side, the herbal smell of her recently washed hair, soon had him admitting that he'd been looking for an excuse to hold her again, just waiting for the time when he could take her in his arms.

"I guess we'd better get to bed," Jenna said, taking a shuddering breath.

Flint swallowed hard. "What?"

"It's late. We need to get some sleep." She handed Ryan over to him, then rose from the swing. "After I've finished with Satin tomorrow, I'll talk to Brad and find out where he needs me to work."

Confused, Flint stared up at her. "What are you talking about?"

"With Jim in the hospital, you're a man short." She shrugged. "I can't think of one good reason why I shouldn't help take up some of the slack."

"No."

"Don't be ridiculous," she said frowning. "You can use the help. And I don't mind at all."

The idea of her doing hard physical labor, didn't sit well. "I said no."

"And why not?" She propped her hands on her hips. "I'm perfectly capable of moving cattle, riding fence and checking water holes."

Flint came to his feet. "It's hot, dirty work."

She arched a brow. "And training horses isn't?"

He knew by the look on her face, that she thought she had him. But he wasn't going down without a fight.

"It's not part of your contract."

"Neither was cleaning up after a skunk. But that didn't seem to bother you."

Ryan squirmed at the sound of the raised voices, causing Flint to whisper, "We'll discuss this in the morning."

She threw up her hands as she brushed past him. "Fine!"

"We'll see how *fine* tomorrow morning," Flint muttered when the screen door slammed shut behind her.

The possibility that Jenna could suffer an injury similar to Jim's just about turned Flint wrong side out. There was no way he'd ever let that happen if it was within his power to prevent it.

Chapter 5

"Give it up, Jenna. It's not going to happen," Flint said as he glared at the woman seated across the desk from him. She had presented a convincing argument as to why he should allow her to help out with the ranch work, but he stood firm. He didn't want to take the chance of her getting hurt.

"Don't be pigheaded, McCray." She sat forward. "You need the help, and as long as I've got time between sessions with Satin, there's no reason for me to be idle."

"No."

She went on as if he hadn't spoken. "I could prowl the pastures, check the windmills and water holes, take a head count and report any sick or injured cattle."

"I said *no.* Working alone can be dangerous."

"I could team up with one of your men."

The thought of Jenna with any other man caused Flint's stomach to churn. "You don't know the area."

Her eyes flashed. "That's horse biscuits and you know it. I'd be working with someone who does, and besides, if you hired somebody else, they wouldn't know any more about the ranch than I do. Probably less. At least I've ridden the part between here and Devil's Gorge."

"You stay away from Devil's Gorge," he ordered.

She hurriedly rose to leave. "No problem."

Flint started to emphasize that he hadn't consented, but the phone rang, and as he answered it, Jenna made good her escape.

Two hours later Flint and Ryan rode across the southern quadrant of the ranch. Flint told himself they were just out for a pleasure ride. He'd promised to take his son horseback riding for the past two days and it was mere coincidence they'd headed south. The fact that Jenna was working with Tom Davison had nothing to do with the direction he'd chosen.

Get real, McCray. After talking with Brad, Flint hadn't been able to saddle the horses fast enough. Tom had a reputation with the ladies Don Juan would have been proud of. And, whether he liked it or not, it irritated Flint to think of Jenna alone with the good-looking cowboy.

"Look, Daddy." Ryan pointed to the herd of cattle ahead of them. "There's Jenna and Tom."

Flint's heart came up in his throat when he saw Jenna ride into the middle of the herd, separate a six-hundred-pound steer from the bunch, then move into position to rope the beast.

"Dammit all," he muttered.

Technically he hadn't even given her permission to ride the pasture, let alone consented to let her play cowgirl. But, too far away to stop her and unable to leave

Ryan alone with his horse, Flint had no choice but to watch the scene unfold.

Jenna's body moved in perfect time with the buckskin as they chased the steer across the pasture. When she swung the loop over her head, Flint held his breath. With any luck she'd miss. But a sick feeling settled over him as he watched the rope sail through the air to drop over the brute's head with picture-perfect accuracy. She immediately turned the horse so the steer was in position for Tom's heel shot and in no time at all, they had the animal stretched out on the ground between them.

Flint would have admired such expert roping if not for the fear twisting his gut. To hold an animal like that, Jenna had to have tied her rope to the saddle horn. If you didn't know what you were about, that could prove disastrous. The steer could have switched back and charged the horse, run under its belly, or hit the end of the rope so hard it jerked the horse down.

He watched them dismount, doctor the steer, then exchange a high-five before they wound up their ropes. By the time he and Ryan reached the pair, Flint could have chewed nails in two.

"You can head for me anytime, sweetheart," Tom said. Turning to face Flint, the cowboy smiled. "Did you see—"

"Jenna, take Ryan back to the house," Flint ordered. "You're done for the day."

"But I haven't finished—"

"I said you're done. Now get back to the house."

She hesitated a moment, then mounted her horse and rode up beside Ryan. "What's your problem, McCray?"

Flint's gaze never left his ranch hand. "I need to discuss something with Tom."

The man's eyes locked with Flint's. "Do what he says.

It seems the boss has some things he wants to get off his chest."

Once Jenna and Ryan had ridden out of earshot, Flint rested his arm on the saddle horn. "You've been doing ranch work long enough to know what can happen when you head a steer like that. And especially if the roper isn't experienced."

"Jenna told me she'd headed before," Tom said, his expression tight. "And the way she roped that steer—"

"Could have gotten her hurt or killed," Flint interrupted. "If you'd like to continue working on the Rocking M, I'd better not hear of you putting her in danger like that again." Flint knew he was being a class-A jerk and unreasonable, but he couldn't seem to stop himself. "And while we're on the subject, Miss Adams is off-limits. She's here to do a job, and I don't want her distracted."

Tom gave him a measuring look. "Is that the real reason, or are you staking a claim, boss?"

Before he could think twice, Flint nodded. "Consider the deed filed."

"Jenna, do you like dogs?" Ryan asked.

"Sure," she answered. "Why?"

"I want a puppy."

Flint stopped his horse beneath a cottonwood and listened to his son's excited voice. He smiled as he dismounted and ground-tied the bay. They were seated on the bank of a stream, and it was apparent Ryan had talked Jenna into taking him fishing after they returned to the house.

His mood light, Flint headed in the direction of the voices. He'd done a lot of thinking since leaving Tom in the south pasture, and he'd reached several conclusions.

He'd avoided Jenna, thinking it would cool his attraction to her. But if anything, it had only made matters worse.

His smile turned to a satisfied grin. He could tell she hadn't been unaffected by him, either. So why not take advantage of the time they had together?

Now all he had to do was convince Jenna.

"The other day you wanted a kitten," Flint said. He walked over to where Jenna and Ryan were fishing. "If you had a pet, who would take care of it?"

"I would!" Ryan threw his pole aside and jumped to his feet. "Can I have one?"

Flint chuckled as he hoisted his son into his arms. "I think we could handle a puppy a lot better than your choice of striped cats. But you have to promise to look after it."

"Oh, I will, Daddy. When can I get my puppy? Today?"

Flint winked at Jenna and set Ryan on his feet. "We could make a trip into Amarillo this afternoon, but what about your fishing trip?"

Jenna felt her heart drop to the pit of her stomach when Flint directed his devastating smile her way. She'd been right. Not only could he charm an old maid right out of her garters, the poor old soul would probably fall all over herself trying to take them off.

"Jenna, you don't want to fish anymore, do you?" Ryan asked, his expression hopeful.

Still shaken, it took a moment for her to realize what the child said. "No, I don't suppose I do."

She watched Flint reach down, but instead of picking up Ryan's fishing pole, his hand came to rest atop hers. Their eyes locked, and she felt warmed to the depths of her soul. When his large palm enclosed hers to pull her up beside him, her heart skipped a beat and her stomach did acrobatics.

Jenna hastily pulled her hand from Flint's, lost her balance and immediately experienced the strange sensation of flying. A split second later the cool water of the stream closed over her head and her seat bumped the mushy bottom of the creek bed. A large object splashed beside her and, struggling to stand in the waist-deep water, she parted the wet strands of hair hanging in her eyes to watch Flint's hat float by. She'd caused him to lose his balance, too.

Ryan giggled. "Jenna, watch out."

Before she could ask what he meant, strong arms closed around her legs and she again slipped beneath the surface. Thrashing, she regained her footing, and when Flint stood up beside her, she treated him to a faceful of water.

"Now you've done it," he said, his deep laughter sending a warmth racing through her body.

When he started toward her, his grin promising retaliation, Jenna headed for the bank. But the lazy current slowed her progress, and Flint caught her around the waist.

She strained against the hard band of his arm. "You really don't want to do this, McCray."

"Why not?"

"I don't like being dunked."

He chuckled and hauled her back to the middle of the creek. "I didn't like being pulled into the water or splashed, darlin'."

Laughing, she didn't sound nearly as convincing as she'd have liked. "I didn't mean to do that. Honest."

"And I don't mean to do this," he said, tossing her back into the water.

Jenna managed a gulp of air before she went under and, moving beneath the surface, managed to get behind him. Her well-placed push to the back of his knees achieved the desired result. Flint went under like a ton of bricks.

He resurfaced, reached out and pulled her to his solid frame. "Truce?"

"Tru-truce," she agreed, her voice a husky whisper. His proximity played havoc with her senses, and she was shocked to find she'd twined her arms around Flint's neck.

"Are you guys gonna get out of the water so we can get my puppy?" Ryan asked, clearly impatient with the two adults.

"Sure." Flint's eyes never wavered from hers. "I have an idea. Why don't you take the poles and head back to the house? We'll be right behind you."

When Ryan grabbed the poles and started across the field, Jenna watched a slow smile spread across Flint's face as he carried her to the bank. He had something on his mind all right, and it had absolutely nothing to do with getting his son a dog.

If she had any sense, she'd start running and not stop until she crossed the Oklahoma line. But when he set her on her feet, her traitorous body refused to budge from the spot.

She watched Flint retrieve his Resistol from a snag of branches a few feet downstream, then walk toward her. His wet clothing clung to his skin, defining every muscle, every part of his anatomy. She swallowed hard. The soft, wet denim cupped him like a lover's caress and emphasized the fact that he was all male and thoroughly aroused.

He stopped in front of her, and she tried to focus her

gaze on something—anything—above his belt. His hair was plastered to his forehead, and water dripped from his chin, but she didn't think she'd ever seen a man more devastatingly handsome. The look in his dark-brown eyes held her captive, and like a night creature caught in head-lights, she had no will to flee.

She moistened her lips. "We should go."

"No doubt about it," he agreed.

He reached out to caress her cheek and wipe a droplet from the corner of her mouth with the pad of his thumb. She shivered when he lowered his mouth to hers. Slowly, thoroughly, he caressed her lips before he sought and found entry inside.

When he molded her to him, fireworks ignited in her soul. The feel of her breasts crushed to his hard chest, the firmness of his arousal pressed to her lower belly, sent fiery tendrils of need wrapping around her. Shoving all thought aside, she let her feelings take control.

His hand roamed from her back to cup the sensitive flesh of her breast, the tip puckering at his touch. He teased with his thumb as his lips nibbled a path to the sensitive hollow at the base of her throat. She breathed deeply, absorbing the masculine scent of him in every cell of her body.

"We'd better leave," he murmured against her sensitive skin. "Ryan will be upset if he doesn't get his puppy today."

Jenna's sanity slowly returned, mesmerized by the sound of his husky baritone. She allowed him to lead her to the side of the big, bay gelding. Air seemed to be in short supply when she finally managed to ask, "Aren't we going to walk?"

"Nope." Flint effortlessly lifted her into the saddle.

"Do you have any idea what walking a quarter of a mile in wet underwear can do to a man?"

She grinned at his pained expression. "I suppose there would be a certain amount of…um, chafing."

"To the point of emasculation," he muttered. He swung up behind her and settled her atop his muscular thighs.

Her body heated at the feel of him touching every part of her backside and it truly surprised her that steam wasn't rising from their damp clothes. "I could walk," Jenna offered, her voice little more than a whisper.

"Not on your life, darlin'." Clamping an arm around her middle to draw her close, he nudged the horse into a slow walk. "What kind of gentleman would I be if you walked while I rode?"

His warm breath, so close to her ear, sent a tremor coursing through her. Jenna cursed her weakness, even as it thrilled her. "I don't know what you're up to, Mc-Cray, but—"

"I'm just giving you a ride back to the house, darlin'."

"—we don't even like each other."

"I like you fine. I just don't trust you." Flint nipped at the column of her neck. "But that doesn't mean we can't enjoy each other while you're here on the Rocking M."

Jenna bit her lip to keep from moaning, but when his words finally penetrated her addled brain, she stiffened. Throwing her leg over the saddle horn, she tried to wrestle herself from his grasp. "Turn me loose, you low-down, sorry excuse for a snake!"

Surprised by her sudden outburst, it was all Flint could do to keep them both in the saddle.

He reined in the horse. "Not until you calm down."

She stopped struggling to glare at him. "How do you expect me to calm down when you've just the same as said I'm dishonest. Put yourself in my shoes, McCray. How would you react?"

He looked over the top of her head and in the distance watched Ryan enter the house. He'd be inclined to deck whoever had the nerve to doubt *his* honesty. But he wasn't the one in question.

"You used your initials on our contract, knowing full well I'd think you were a man. That's the same as fraud, darlin'."

"Would you have hired me otherwise?"

"No."

"It's men like you who force me to use J.J., instead of my full name. And it's not fraud. Those are my initials." She poked his chest. "And let's get something else straight, cowboy. No matter what you think of me, I don't have affairs."

"Darlin', just because a beautiful woman's integrity is in question, that doesn't keep a man from wanting her."

"I've calmed down," she said suddenly. "You can let me go."

Flint felt the fight go out of her. Loosening his hold, he reluctantly let her slide off the horse.

"I'm flattered you think I'm attractive, McCray." She started toward the house. "But I happen to believe it wouldn't be called lovemaking, if love wasn't supposed to be involved. As far as I'm concerned, one won't happen without the other."

Jenna had just finished running the brush through her recently dried hair when Ryan raced into the room. "Are you going with us? I'll let you hold my puppy."

"But what about supper? Won't Whiskers be upset if we aren't here to eat?"

Ryan's expression brightened. "Oh, Daddy said we'd

get some hamburgers and stuff at Heartburn Heaven before we go to the dog place."

"Where on earth is that?"

"That's what Whiskers calls all the hamburger and taco places. He says if we're boneheaded enough to eat there, we oughtta get sick." The child shook his head. "But we don't. He just says that."

"Don't tell Whiskers," she confided, "but I eat at places like that quite a bit when I'm traveling."

His face eager, Ryan asked, "Does that mean you'll go?"

Jenna hesitated. After their talk on the way back from the creek this afternoon, the prospect of spending an evening with Flint might not be wise. "Does your dad know you were going to ask me?" she stalled.

"Oh, yeah." The child nodded so hard his hair flopped on his forehead. "Daddy said I could. Are you ready to go?"

"I guess so," she said not wanting to disappoint the child. She did need to pick up a few things, and it would save her a trip later.

Ryan grabbed her hand and when they walked into the kitchen, Flint stood by the door, a surprised expression on his face.

Jenna stopped short to look at the child still tugging her along. "I thought your dad knew you were asking me to go."

"He said I could." Ryan turned to Flint. "Didn't you, Daddy?"

Flint searched his memory. Excited about getting a dog, Ryan had chattered from the moment Flint entered the house. He'd even followed Flint upstairs and tried to talk to him while he took his shower. But with the water running, and preoccupied by his conversation with Jenna, he hadn't understood much of what Ryan had been asking and answered with "Fine," "Sure" and "We'll see."

He'd learned a lot about parenting in the few months since Ryan came to live with him, but Flint still had a long way to go. Evidently, paying closer attention when he agreed to something was to be his most recent lesson.

"Of course I told him to ask you," Flint lied. In truth he wished he'd thought of asking her himself.

Jenna looked doubtful. "Maybe I should stay here."

"Please, Jenna," Ryan pleaded, tugging on her sleeve. "I want you to come."

"Go on and have a good time, gal," Whiskers called from the pantry. He limped into the kitchen. "This past week you've been busier than a one-legged man in a butt-kickin' contest. You deserve some time away from the ranch."

"I don't want to impose."

Flint could tell by her wary look that she had her doubts about going anywhere with him after their talk this afternoon. Leaning close, he whispered, "I never figured you for a coward."

He laughed out loud when she brushed past him and headed for his pickup truck.

Several hours later Flint couldn't help feeling dazed as he pulled away from the animal shelter and drove toward home. Whiskers had agreed to having one dog in the house. But what would he do now that Flint had adopted three?

Somewhere along the line, and not exactly sure how, he'd lost control of the situation. But when Ryan couldn't decide which puppy to choose, and Jenna turned pleading eyes to him, he'd caved like an aluminum can in a vise.

He shook his head. He must be getting soft in his old

age. If they'd asked him to, he'd have adopted the whole damned canine population of Texas rather than disappoint either one of them.

"Jenna, will you hold me?" Ryan asked. "Betsy used to hold me when I got sleepy."

She glanced at Flint.

He nodded. "We're on Rocking M land now. There won't be any more traffic."

Jenna released the catch on Ryan's seat belt and took him into her arms.

"I like you a lot, Jenna," Ryan said, snuggling against her breasts. "You're soft."

She treated Flint to a withering glare when she heard his choked laughter. "Watch it, cowboy."

Glancing down at the now-sleeping child, she kissed the top of his small head. "Was Betsy his nanny?"

Flint shook his head.

"Betsy was their maid. She was a decent woman, but she didn't have a lot of time to give Ryan." Jenna noticed all traces of amusement disappear and his grip tighten on the steering wheel. "I doubt Nicole held Ryan more than a dozen times in the four years she had him."

Jenna gazed down at the cherubic face lying against her breasts. "But she was his mother."

Flint cocked a brow. "You've been around ranching enough to know that just because a female gives birth doesn't mean she'll mother her young. I've seen more than one cow reject her calf, no matter what tricks you use to get her to accept it."

"Yes, but people are supposed to be different from cattle."

She watched his expression harden. "If the instinct to nurture isn't present, there isn't much you can do about it."

Jenna swallowed hard. It was something she knew all too well from personal experience. "Then why didn't you—"

"Try to get custody of Ryan before Nicole's death?"

She nodded.

"Until my ex-wife died in that accident, I didn't even know I had a son," he said, his tone bitter.

Jenna looked at Flint, but he stared straight ahead, his face tight with anger. No wonder he had a deep distrust of women. "How could she do that?"

Flint laughed, but the sound held no humor. "If you'd known her, you wouldn't ask that. Nicole had a vengeful streak a mile wide. When we divorced, she tried to hurt me by getting part of the ranch. It didn't sit well when the judge ruled in my favor. The last thing she ever said to me was that one day she'd get even."

"So she kept her pregnancy a secret?"

Flint nodded and steered the truck onto the long drive leading up to the house. "One of the things that came between us was the fact I wanted children and she didn't. Keeping Ryan from me was the ultimate revenge. And the longer she deprived me of time with my son, the sweeter it became." He turned his head to look at her, his eyes reflecting how deeply he'd been hurt by his ex-wife's deception. "I was cheated out of precious years with Ryan I'll never get back."

The thought of anyone using a child in such a callous way made Jenna feel ill. Quiet tears slipped down her cheeks as she touched Ryan's baby-soft cheek. She felt a kinship with the child. Although her own mother hadn't ignored her children before leaving them, she hadn't loved them enough to stay.

Flint parked the truck and came around to take Ryan, but Jenna hugged his son close. When her eyes met his, the anguish in their pearl-gray depths, the shimmering tears, rendered Flint speechless.

He swallowed hard as he wiped a tear from her cheek with the pad of his thumb. He hated to see a woman cry, but Jenna's tears tore at his insides. "What's wrong, Jenna?"

"Ryan will never understand why his mother treated him that way," she said, her voice cracking.

Flint cupped her face with his hands. "How do you know that, darlin'?"

Another tear slipped down her cheek. "When I was nine, my mother walked away and never looked back. She was there to put me to bed one night, and the next morning she was gone." Her voice caught on a sob. "I grew up wondering if I'd done something to make her stop loving me. For a long time I thought that if I'd been different in some way, she might have stayed."

"It wasn't your fault, darlin'."

She nodded. "It took me a long time to realize that I'd done nothing wrong. That it was my mother's way of getting back at my father for traveling the rodeo circuit and not settling down in one place."

Flint helped her from the truck, put his arm around her, and they silently walked to the house. He wanted to take her into his arms, wanted to erase the pain. But when they reached the house, Jenna placed Ryan in his arms.

"What your ex-wife did to you was deplorable, and you have every right to be bitter about it. But what she did to Ryan was worse. She used him as a pawn in her game of revenge." Her hand trembled as she touched Ryan's cheek. "The innocent are always hurt more by vengeance than the intended victim."

Long after he'd put Ryan to bed and settled the puppies down for the night, Flint thought about what Jenna had said. Ryan had been the one to suffer the most in Nicole's quest for revenge.

Why hadn't he seen that? Had he been just as blind when it came to seeing other things as well?

It appeared he had. Otherwise he would have recognized that Jenna never had been, nor would she ever be, anything like his ex-wife.

Chapter 6

Jenna released a contented sigh as she leaned on the fence and watched Black Satin run across the pasture, tail held high, master of his domain. But when a set of muscular arms eased around her midriff from behind, she tensed. She'd been so preoccupied with appreciating the stallion's beauty, she hadn't heard anyone approach.

"You'd better back off," she warned. "I've got a gun in Daisy that can turn you from a stud to a gelding faster than you can blink. And I damned well know how to use it."

"You wouldn't do that to the guy who gave you that gun and taught you what to do with it, would you?" the man whispered close to her ear.

"Cooper!" Jenna turned in his arms. Overjoyed to see her brother, she hugged him close. "Where— How…"

"Slow down, little sister," he said, laughing. "I stopped

by Cal Reynold's place in Houston, and he told me where to find you."

Jenna hugged him again. "I'm so glad to see you. How long can you stay?"

Cooper shrugged as he stared off into the distance. "You know me. Always headed to the next rodeo."

Happy to see her brother for the first time in months, she refused to let anything dampen her spirits. "I don't want to think about that. You're here now. That's all that matters."

When they turned to walk to the house, Cooper asked, "Do you think the foreman of this spread will mind me putting up in the bunkhouse for a couple of days?"

She hesitated. Brad wouldn't have any objections, but the way Flint had been avoiding her since their trip into Amarillo a week ago, it was anybody's guess. "I don't think it will be a problem."

Cooper stopped, his stance rigid. "Has somebody been giving you a hard time?"

"Nothing I can't handle."

"Just say the word, little sister." Cooper playfully chucked her chin. "I'll straighten them out."

Jenna grinned as she stepped back in an exaggerated stagger. Some things never changed. Older brothers the world over had certain rights. They could pick on, tease and even ignore their younger sisters, but let someone else try it and the end results were always the same—a free-for-all.

She heard the door slam and turned to see Flint coming across the yard like a charging bull.

"Is he the one causing you trouble?"

"Well, not exactly—"

His stance ready for battle, Cooper shoved her behind him. "Let me take care of this."

"You got business here?" Flint asked, storming up to them.

"Maybe I do," Cooper drawled. "What's it to you?"

"Around here we don't hit women."

Cooper shrugged. "Where I come from we don't give women a hard time."

Jenna looked from one man to the other. The situation was explosive. Flint was as mad as a grizzly with a tail end full of buckshot, and Cooper had his similar look firmly in place. If she didn't do something soon, all hell would break loose.

"Settle down—"

"Stay out of this," both men ordered at the same time.

Before either man could land a punch, Jenna wedged herself between them. "Stop it! Both of you!"

She placed a hand on each man's chest to keep them apart. "Do either one of you know who you're about to fight? Or why?"

Neither man answered as they stood glaring at each other over the top of her head.

"I didn't think so." She turned to Cooper. "In case you'd like to know, this is my *boss,* Flint McCray." She treated Flint to the same scathing look. "And I'd like you to meet my *brother,* Cooper Adams."

Stepping from between them, Jenna threw her hands in the air. "Now, if you'd like to continue, you can beat each other senseless for all I care."

Both men watched her march to the house like a four-star general on field maneuvers, then eyed each other carefully.

Now that he'd calmed down, Flint could see the resemblance. Though his eyes were blue instead of gray like Jenna's, Cooper Adams had the same dark-blond hair, the same stubborn chin.

"I didn't recognize you," Flint said. "You can't tell much about a man's looks from the seats of an arena, and when I saw you clip her on the chin—"

"Don't worry about it." Cooper grinned. "It's nice to know somebody's looking out for my kid sister when I'm not around."

Smiling, Flint stuck out his hand. "Welcome to the Rocking M."

"Still upset, little sister?" Cooper asked, walking up to the corral to drape his forearms over the top rail.

Jenna finished brushing Satin's ebony coat before turning to face him. "Yes and no."

Cooper gave her a lopsided grin and pushed his tan Resistol back with his thumb. "You're still mad at me. But you forgive me because I'm your brother and I'm as lovable as an old teddy bear. Right?"

"And you're starting to push that."

She led Satin through the gate to the pasture, unsnapped the lead rope, then slapped him on the rump to let him know he had the freedom to run. Walking over to where Cooper leaned on the fence, Jenna eyed her brother. His voice sounded a little too casual, his smile forced.

"Why are you *really* here, Cooper?"

All traces of humor gone, he couldn't quite meet her eyes. "Maybe I just wanted to see my kid sister."

"Yeah, right. Now why don't you put on a tutu, wave a magic wand and tell me a fairy tale."

When Cooper finally looked at her, his blue eyes had turned bleak and his shoulders slumped. She'd only seen her brother this way once before. The morning he had to tell her their mother had left.

"Cooper?"

"Is there somewhere we could go to talk?"

Thirty minutes later Jenna watched Cooper tear off blades of grass, then throw them into the lazy current of the stream while she waited for him to tell her what was troubling him. It had always been this way with them. When life dealt them a blow they found difficult to cope with, they'd always sought out the other's council. But they never pushed, never pressured the other to speak before they were prepared to share their feelings. When Cooper was ready, he would tell her. Until that time, she simply waited.

"Have you ever wondered what you'd do if you couldn't train horses anymore?" Cooper finally asked.

"I haven't really given it a lot of thought," she answered. "But I suppose I'd try to stay involved with horses in some way."

Her hopes rose as she anticipated what he was about to tell her. She'd prayed the day would come when Cooper stopped competing, stopped gambling with fate. He'd been a successful rodeo cowboy for a long time, but the odds were stacking up against him. Fast. Riding the rough stock took its toll, and at the age of thirty, he was considered a seasoned veteran.

He propped his forearm on his bent knee and stared out across the open prairie. "I've never thought much beyond getting to the next rodeo, paying my entry fee and making the eight-second whistle. Riding bulls and saddle broncs has been my life for over twelve years. It's all I know." When he turned to face her, his eyes mirrored his anguish. "I'm going to have to quit, little sister."

Her brother had lived and breathed rodeo all his life. It was a part of him—who he was. To take that from him would remove a vital part of his identity. It had to be devastating.

"How did you come to your decision, Cooper?"

"I've lost my edge." He stared out across the prairie. "I've had a few close calls lately."

"Oh, God!"

Cooper put his arms around her. "It's all right, honey. I shouldn't have said anything. It still bothers you, doesn't it?"

"It always will." She pulled away from him, her eyes anxious. "When do you plan to quit?"

"I'll make my last professional ride next week in Amarillo."

"You're not waiting until the end of the season?"

Cooper shook his head. "I'm too far down in the standings to make the finals this year, and it's getting harder to scrape together the entry fee." When he tried to smile, it looked more like a grimace. "No sense blowing money on a lost cause."

All rodeo cowboys had a competitiveness few other sports matched, and Jenna knew what this confession cost her brother. For years he'd pitted physical strength and mental capabilities against the most rank bulls and wildest horses the stock contractors could deliver. Now to admit he'd lost his edge was like admitting defeat. He had come out the victor in a few battles, but the war was over. The beasts had finally won.

"I think you made the right decision," she agreed. "Only a fool continues to play when he knows the game is over."

"That's what I figure." Cooper plucked another blade of grass and thoughtfully chewed on the end. "Are you going to come watch me take my last ride?"

It was Jenna's turn to stare off into the distance. "You know I can't do that, Cooper."

They remained silent for several minutes before Cooper spoke again. "You can't keep blaming the rodeo for all the things that have gone wrong in your life. Mom left because she always wanted bigger and better. It wouldn't have mattered where we lived or what Dad did for a living. She never would have been satisfied." He threw the blade of grass into the stream. "I think Dad always knew she'd take off one day. He just didn't know when."

"But if it wasn't for rodeo, he and Dan would still be alive," she said, suddenly angry.

Cooper shook his head. "You don't know that. Accidents happen. They could have been hurt crossing the street or falling down a flight of stairs." He captured her chin between his thumb and forefinger, then forced her to meet his eyes. "Fate plays a big part in whether or not your number's up, little sister. If it's meant to happen, it will. And there's not a whole lot you can do about it."

Small puffs of clouds skittered past the sliver of moon hanging low in the inky sky as Flint watched Jenna walk along the oak-lined drive leading away from the house. They hadn't talked since the incident with her brother. In fact, this was the first Flint had seen of her since this afternoon.

And if he had any brains, he'd make himself scarce now. The more he was around her the more he wanted to get to know her and the more he wanted her to get to know him.

But when he moved away from the porch rail, Flint found himself descending the steps and walking straight toward her. He tried to tell himself he only wanted to discuss Black Satin's progress.

Falling into step beside her, he searched for something to say. Damn! Had he forgotten how to make small talk?

He grinned. He wanted to make something with Jenna all right, but small talk wasn't it.

"Did you have something on your mind, McCray?"

Oh, yeah. "No. I just thought I'd explain about—"

"You don't have to. I know you and Cooper couldn't help yourselves." She shrugged. "Jackasses are jackasses. Plain and simple. Dye their coats a different color, weave flowers in their manes, stick a hat on them, it doesn't change a thing. They're still jackasses."

He stopped walking to stare at her a moment before he laughed. "I guess I had that coming."

"Damned right you did," she said, grinning back.

They stood staring at each other. Without warning, the atmosphere suddenly became charged with anticipation, the dark shadows of night breathtakingly intimate, and the warm breeze a whispered voice of sultry promise.

Jenna shivered when she saw the deep hunger in Flint's eyes, his fierce need. "Flint, I don't think—"

"I don't, either," he whispered. "Not when I'm around you." He reached out to pull her to him. "Right now, all I want to do is feel, darlin'." He brushed her lips with his. "You." Again his lips caressed hers. "Me." Yet again. "Together."

Her arms encircled his narrow waist, her hands splaying across his broad back. How was a woman supposed to resist words like that? Flint's mouth moved across hers with such infinite care, she found she didn't want to resist. She wanted to feel his arms around her again, taste the desire on his lips, hear his heart beat in time with her own.

Her body heated as Flint kissed her like she'd never been kissed before. Worshipping her lips, he outlined them with his tongue, nipped at them with his strong white teeth, then soothed them with nibbling little kisses.

"Open for me, darlin'."

With no thought of protesting, Jenna did as he commanded. His gentle stroking sent a frenzied surge of excitement racing to every nerve in her system, and hot, enticing desire settled in the pit of her belly.

For the first time in her life Jenna cast aside her inhibitions and gave herself completely to Flint's kiss. Boldly she allowed her tongue to meet, then dance with his. A heady sense of feminine power came over her when the deep, rumbling groan of his pleasure echoed across her sensitive lips.

The fever of Flint's need burned higher, hotter, brighter than anything he'd ever imagined, when Jenna's inexperienced tongue played a game of advance and retreat with his. His hands traveled the length of her back to grasp her hips and pull her to him, letting her know how she made him want her.

He reveled in her softness warming his arousal, the way her body molded to his. "Feel what you've done to me?"

Her breasts were crushed to his chest, her nipples were branding him with their pebble hardness. He felt a fire building in his soul. He knew that when they finally came together, it would be sheer perfection. Two halves of a whole, unequivocally complete.

As he stood staring down into her passion-glazed eyes, the hairs on the back of his neck prickled. He had the distinct feeling they were being watched.

To hide her from the prying eyes, Flint held her close and glanced around. They had walked well out of sight of the house, so it couldn't be Whiskers or Ryan. Besides, the eyes watching them now were sinister, filled with hatred. He could feel it in his bones.

His first thought was to get Jenna back to the house

and out of danger. Then, and only then, would he come back to seek out the identity of the voyeur.

"Jenna, I could stand here like this all night, but we've got company," he whispered close to her ear. When she tried to jerk from his grasp, Flint held her tight. "I want you to stay right beside me. We're going to walk back to the house like nothing's wrong. But if I give the word, I want you to run like hell and don't look back. You got that?"

She nodded. "Who do you think it is?"

He draped his arm across her shoulders and started toward the house. "I don't know. But he can't be up to any good or he'd make his presence known."

They walked at a steady, seemingly unhurried pace, and when they entered the study, Flint breathed a sigh of relief. He'd felt that same malevolent stare all the way back to the house and knew they'd been followed. Closing the door behind them, he grabbed the phone and alerted Brad, then went to the gun cabinet.

"What do you want me to do?" she asked.

"Nothing." He removed a Winchester with a scope from the rack and shoved cartridges into the magazine. "Just stay here."

"But I could—"

"I said stay put," he ordered. "Brad's going to meet me down at the barn. Whoever it was probably took off once we got back to the house." He pumped the lever on the rifle down, then back up, loading a cartridge into the chamber. Releasing the hammer slowly, he readied the weapon for immediate action and headed for the door. "But I want to see if he left something behind that will tell me who he was and what he's up to."

"Be careful."

Flint turned back to brush her soft lips with his. "Count on it, darlin'. We have unfinished business."

The first fingers of light hadn't cleared the horizon when someone knocked on the study door. Looking up from the breeding register in front of him, Flint called. "Come in."

"You have a minute?" Cooper asked.

"Sure. Have a seat."

After Cooper settled himself in the chair across from Flint's desk, he rested the ankle of one leg on the knee of the other, then hooked his hat on the toe of his boot. "Jenna said you've had some trouble lately."

Flint nodded. "At first it was just some missing cattle. But lately it's started getting nasty."

"So I've heard. Jenna mentioned someone watching you and her last night."

"Brad and I found some tracks, but that was about it," Flint admitted. "Jed was down by the brood mare barn, but he didn't see anyone, either. Whoever it was cleared out pretty fast."

Cooper laughed. "The rules of the game always change when a Winchester gets involved."

Flint watched the man's eyes. He had more on his mind than trespassers. "You got something you'd like to say, Adams? If so, spit it out."

"I like you, McCray. You're a hell of a nice guy."

"But?"

"This thing between you and Jenna has me worried. I don't want to see her hurt." Cooper's gaze clashed with Flint's. "She's already had more than her share."

"I don't see how—"

Cooper held up his hand. "I know she comes across as capable of handling anything. And to a certain extent that's true. But when Jenna gives her heart, she holds nothing back."

Flint didn't quite know what to say. He wasn't about to insult the man's intelligence by denying there was something going on between himself and Jenna. He glanced at the diamond necklace in the dome on the mantel. Thanks to his ex-wife, he wasn't sure he'd ever be ready to acknowledge it.

Before he could comment, Cooper smiled. "I just thought I'd warn you before I leave. Hurt my sister, and I'll be back to do more than just square off for a fight."

Flint nodded. "I'll keep that in mind."

Cooper stood to leave. "Thanks for the hospitality."

"Where are you headed now?"

"New Mexico. But I'll be back next week for the Panhandle Stampede in Amarillo."

Flint grinned. "I'll see if Jenna will let me and Ryan tag along when she goes to see you ride."

Cooper shook his head. "Don't count on that happening."

"Why?" Had Adams warned Jenna away from him?

"She doesn't care much for rodeo." The man squarely met Flint's suspicious gaze. "Jenna blames rodeo for some events in her life that I don't think anyone or anything could have prevented."

"She mentioned what happened with your mother," Flint admitted. "I'm sorry."

Cooper nodded. "That and a couple of other things have her so turned off she won't even watch me ride."

"Your sister can be a little stubborn."

Cooper laughed. "You're not telling me anything I don't already know, McCray." He shook Flint's hand. "If you get the time, go ahead and bring Ryan up to Amarillo. I'll make sure he gets to meet some of the boys."

"Ryan would like that. Thanks."

Flint sat staring at the glass dome long after Cooper left. He could appreciate Cooper's position on protecting Jenna. But the man had it all wrong. Flint had a feeling *he* might be the one left licking his wounds after Jenna moved on.

Chapter 7

Jenna tied Black Satin to a post and placed a blanket on his back. On the outside of the round pen, Flint gripped the top of the fence and braced his booted foot on the bottom rail.

"If you say one word, McCray, it had better be good-bye," she warned. She'd seen him walk up to the fence, but until now he'd shown no signs of interference. Her voice soft and low, she continued to pat the stallion's neck. "I know what I'm doing."

She eased the saddle onto the horse's back to let him experience the weight of it. When Satin snorted and turned his head to see what she was doing, but otherwise stood quietly, she praised him and rubbed his muzzle.

Walking over to where Flint stood, she raised an eyebrow. "Did you need something?"

"I know you don't want a lot of people and noise while you're working with Satin. And I can understand your

logic. But the day you ride him for the first time, I intend to be here."

"It's not necessary—"

"Yes, it is." He nodded at the stallion. "I'll give credit
where it's due. You've made a lot of progress in a short
time. But I've seen the gentlest horse come completely
unglued the first time he feels the weight of a man."

Jenna stood for a moment, her anger escalating like the
mercury of a thermometer in boiling water. She wasn't
a greenhorn. She knew what a horse was capable of the
first time a rider was introduced to him. There wasn't
much she hadn't seen. But she'd learned long ago, if a
horse wasn't given a reason to buck, it didn't have to be
a problem.

She turned back to Black Satin. Arguing with Flint
wasn't getting her job done. "We'll discuss this later."

"You're damned right we will."

She untied the stallion and led him around the corral
for a short time with the saddle cinched to his back. Satisfied with his reaction, she tied him to a post to remove
it. Despite her mood being anything but placid, she spoke
in a low, soothing tone as she placed the saddle on the
top rail of the fence. There wasn't any sense in disturbing
the horse just because she wanted to throttle his owner.

Flint watched Jenna turn Black Satin into the pasture,
take the saddle back to the tack room in the barn, then
zero in on him. Even from across the round pen, he could
see the determination in her eyes. He had to force himself to remain rooted to the spot, when what he wanted
to do was run like hell.

The tongue-lashing she would no doubt deliver on his
interference with Satin's training didn't intimidate him.
He could handle that with little or no trouble. It was the
thought he was getting in too deep, too fast, that had

him scared spitless. He didn't believe Jenna was anything like Nicole, but his past history with women was testament to the fact that he had poor judgment when it came to the fairer sex.

"Listen up, cowboy." Her terse command snapped him out of his unsettling introspection. "If you're going to tell me how to do my job, you can train that horse yourself." She closed the gate behind her, then marched up to stand toe-to-toe with him. "As long as you're quiet and don't interfere while I'm working with Satin, I don't care if you hang upside down from the fence rail. Just let me do my job. Okay?"

He started to tell her there was no way he'd stand back and watch her get hurt, but the words lodged in his throat. He couldn't remember what he was about to say or if he wanted to say anything at all. The phrase, Bull Riders Like It Rough, on her light-blue T-shirt left him speechless. It was the second rodeo shirt he'd seen her wear, and if not for her innocent expression, he'd swear she wore the damned things just to drive him crazy.

"Flint, what's wrong?" Jenna asked, concern marring her brow. "You look as if you've been punched in the stomach."

He grinned as his active imagination kicked into overdrive. He'd promised her last night they had unfinished business. And now was as good a time as any to get it done.

"What the hell," he muttered, hauling her into his arms to crush her lips beneath his. He wanted to prove the attraction between them was mutual.

He slid his hands down to her hips to pull her closer, trying to absorb her into his hard maleness. The smell of her herbal-scented hair, the sweet taste of her lips on his, drove Flint to the brink of insanity. But her soft moan as she settled against him almost sent him into orbit.

Jenna's heart pounded against her ribs. She was angry and she wanted to stay that way. But when Flint's lips melded with hers, her stomach did that wobbly little cartwheel only his kiss evoked. His tongue affected the intimate act of lovemaking, and she tingled with tiny currents of electrified desire.

The sound of approaching footsteps penetrated the sensual fog surrounding her, and she struggled to free herself from Flint's strong arms. "Please, Flint."

"You can run this time, darlin'. But next time we're going to finish what we started."

Her cheeks burning, she stepped away from him. His candid comment caused a heaviness low in her belly, and she gulped at the intense message emanating from his chocolate-brown eyes.

Without a word Jenna turned to walk toward the house. She should terminate the contract and get as far away from Flint McCray as Daisy could take her. But she rejected the thought, even as it materialized. She had never run from anything in her life, and she wasn't about to start now.

"Flint, I think you'd better come take a look at this," Jed called as he jogged over to where Flint stood.

"What's that?" Flint asked, reluctant to turn his attention away from the delightful sight of Jenna's retreating backside.

Jed motioned for Flint to follow, and when they'd entered the barn he pointed to a piece of paper attached to one of the saddles in the tack room. "I found this when I got ready to saddle up. I thought I'd best leave it alone till you checked it out."

Flint stared at the note resting in the center of the leather seat. The words had been crudely pieced together from magazines, but the message couldn't have been more clear.

"It's time to pay for what you've done."

After scanning the paper, Flint went to the phone by the door. "Before we touch anything, I want that note and the saddle dusted for fingerprints."

An hour later Flint and his men watched the county sheriff, Troy Bartlow, brush the saddle with a white powder.

"We have some pretty good prints here," Troy said, once the images became more visible. He took a camera from his pocket, snapped pictures of the prints' location, then covered each one with transparent lifting tape. After transferring them to a special paper, Troy turned to Flint. "We'll run these through the computer and see what we can scare up. If this guy has a record of any kind, we'll find out who he is. Do you know if any of your men have been fingerprinted before?"

"They took mine when I was in the army," Jed spoke up.

When Brad and Tom shook their heads, Sheriff Bartlow removed an ink pad and cards from his investigator's case. "We'd better take your prints to eliminate any confusion." He paused to look at Flint. "Anyone else have access to the tack room?"

"Miss Adams been ridin' that buckskin," Jed offered.

"I'd better get her prints, too," Troy said.

Flint turned to the phone to call the ranch house. He didn't like it, but Jed was right. Jenna had been in the tack room just before the note was found.

Jenna arrived a few minutes later, just as the sheriff finished up with Tom and Brad.

"I can tell you right now my fingerprints will be all over that saddle," she stated bluntly. "It's the one I've been using when I ride the buckskin."

Before Flint left to check the grazing conditions in the northern pastures, Sheriff Bartlow called to say there hadn't been any fingerprints on the note. But Jenna's prints were all over the saddle, just as she'd predicted.

That wasn't conclusive evidence, Flint reasoned, giving his horse its head. He didn't want to believe she was the one at the ranch feeding the rustlers information. But the field of suspects was narrowing. Flint trusted Whiskers implicitly. Jim was unable to get around without crutches and therefore eliminated from any involvement. That only left Jed, Tom and Brad. Flint had known them all for several years and considered all three valued employees. The thought of any one of them being involved in the trouble didn't sit well.

Dried grass crackled like a bowl of rice cereal beneath the bay's hooves, drawing Flint's attention to more pressing matters. He was going to have to move one of the herds to Devil's Gorge. The ground water there was closer to the surface, and the grass more suitable for grazing.

Although it would be a hassle to get the cattle into the gorge, there was an added advantage. Once inside the box canyon, there was no way the rustlers could get to the herd, except on horseback. And that took time thieves couldn't afford.

Flint's gaze scanned the horizon and came to settle on a horse and rider headed for a nearby windmill. When they drew closer, he recognized Jenna as she rode up to the stock tank. She looked in all directions, but evidently couldn't see him for the grove of mesquite between them.

He watched her glance around once more before dismounting. Why was she being so cautious?

Flint's frown turned to a delighted grin. Although the buckskin stood between them, there was no mistaking her purpose. Jenna was removing her clothes.

He stopped his horse to keep her from noticing him, his grin widening as he watched. He should be shot. A gentleman would advise her of his presence.

Shaking his head, he laughed. They'd established right off that he came up lacking in the area of gallantry.

And Flint didn't see any reason to break a perfect record. He headed over to the tank, started to unbuckle his belt and pull it off.

"What do you think you're doing?" Jenna asked, her heart thudding hard against her ribs.

It had been a hard day, and she welcomed the relief from the oppressive heat and gritty dust covering her skin. She'd felt a shadow fall over the water. But when she'd opened her eyes and glanced up, instead of the rain cloud she hoped to see, her eyes had met Flint's and she'd seen the mischievous grin lighting his handsome face. Even though her drawn-up knees hid most of her breasts, there was still a large amount of cleavage exposed that Flint seemed to find fascinating. She sank down to her chin, her eyes wide.

He tugged his shirttail from his jeans and, with one quick jerk, opened all the snaps on the front of his shirt. "It's mighty hot today. I thought it would feel good to cool off in one of my stock tanks before I start back to the house."

"But I'm here!"

"I don't mind." Hanging his shirt on the saddle horn, he unsnapped his jeans and lowered the zipper. "I'll share."

Jenna gulped at the sight of so much skin. Masculine, hair-roughened skin. Flint's skin. When she noticed his jeans gaping open to expose the top part of his white cotton briefs, riding low on his lean flanks, her heart felt as though it stopped completely.

Smiling, he hooked his thumbs in the waistbands of his jeans and briefs. "There's plenty of room." He pushed downward. "You don't have to leave."

She closed her eyes and turned her head when it became apparent Flint wasn't the least bit shy. "I was thinking more along the line—" She heard him step into the water and scrunched her eyes tight. "—of *you* leaving. Not me."

He sat down across from her. "Why would I do that? This feels good."

She swung her head around to glare at him.

His eyes mischievous beneath the wide brim of his hat, he drawled, "You know you shouldn't go swimming without a partner. It could be dangerous."

"The water's only a couple of feet deep."

"Yes, but this tank is ten feet across." He looked thoughtful. "I'll bet if I stretched out and relaxed, my whole body would float."

"Don't you dare." Jenna envisioned Flint, front side up, bobbing around in the water, and her vivid imagination went wild.

His grin faded, and noticing the direction of his rapt gaze, she looked down. In her agitation her body had come out of the water to expose all but the tips of her breasts, and those he could easily see just beneath the surface.

She sank back into the water. "You're a low-down horse's patoot."

"I love it when you talk dirty," he teased. "That was a good one."

"You seem to bring out the best in me," she retorted.

"I'd like to."

Jenna's breath caught. The message in his smoldering eyes left no doubt what he'd like to do. Goose bumps rose on her skin, despite the heat swirling through her body.

"Flint, please—"

"Please what? Please tell you that I don't want to feel you beneath me? Feel myself inside you?" He slowly shook his head, his intense gaze never leaving hers. "I can't do that."

Her cheeks colored with desire at his provocative words. "Flint, we—"

"Not now, darlin'," he interrupted. "But soon." His expression changed, and he allowed her to see the raw hunger in the depths of his eyes. "Real soon."

He hadn't moved from the opposite side of the stock tank, but his eyes held her captive with their seductive message and his husky drawl caused Jenna to feel as if he'd caressed her sensitized skin.

"Now get out of here before I change my mind," he said, his voice low and impassioned. When she hesitated, he raised one dark brow. "Are you extending an invitation?"

"No." She pointed to a spot behind him. "Turn your head."

Flint laughed, the sound deep and rich. "Oh, I've already seen you like this at least a hundred times."

"When?" she asked, appalled.

"Every night in my dreams."

Swallowing hard, Jenna waited until he turned to face the open prairie. She had to get away from him before she gave in to the temptation of staying where she was and finding out if he meant what he said. When she stepped from the water, she made sure the horse stood between herself and Flint's curious eyes long enough for her to pull on her clothes.

"Darlin', where do you get those shirts?"

Jenna looked down at the pale pink shirt she'd just pulled on, Bronc Riders Like It In The Saddle printed across the front. "My brother's warped idea of the perfect gift," she muttered. "He gave me the whole set for my birthday."

Flint winked. "You know, T-shirt slogans are based on fact."

Her cheeks burned, and without a word she mounted the buckskin and headed for the house.

The day had started out with such promise. How could it have fallen apart so fast?

Her session with Black Satin this morning had been very productive, but after that everything had gone to hell in a handbasket. Flint had shown up to place restrictions on her training program, someone was trying to frame her with that threatening note and now her fingerprints were on file with the police. If that hadn't been enough to ruin her day, Flint had caught her skinny-dipping in one of his stock tanks and had taken great delight in joining her. Her body still hummed from the current of unfulfilled desire his presence and candid promises had unleashed.

But as much as her body craved his touch, there was no way she'd give into the attraction between them. Not until he believed completely in her innocence, not until he believed in her.

When Jenna ran her hand along his ebony coat, Black Satin's hide quivered with pleasure. She hadn't intended to work with him this evening, but the temperature had dropped several degrees, making it more comfortable, and there was still plenty of daylight left. Besides, the sooner she finished with the stallion's training, the sooner she could leave the Rocking M and the distraction of its owner. She had plans and they didn't include getting involved with a rough-around-the-edges guy like Flint McCray.

He was a good man. The type of man she'd always hoped to find. Honest and straightforward, Flint worked hard to achieve his goals and didn't believe in playing games. If he wanted something, he went after it.

But six years ago she'd vowed never to let anything stand between her and a home of her own. And that included falling for the owner of the Rocking M. He wasn't offering a long-term relationship, and she wasn't staying around for anything less.

"We missed you at supper."

She glanced up. Flint and Ryan stood by the fence. "I wasn't hungry."

Couldn't the man find something better to do than lean on that cursed fence? It seemed every time she looked up, there he stood, watching her every move, making her more aware of the attraction she felt for him.

"Jenna, when are you gonna ride Black Satin?" Ryan asked, peeping through the rails.

She looked at Flint and Ryan. They'd come to mean so much to her. She'd like nothing more than to be part of their little family. But the longer she stayed, the more of her heart she'd leave behind when she had to go.

She came to an immediate decision. "Right now."

"Now hold it," Flint protested. When she came through the gate to get the saddle from the tack room, he blocked her path. "Why don't you wait—"

"Satin's ready and so am I." She tried to step around him. "There's no reason to put it off."

Flint didn't like the idea of her riding the stallion. Satin still wouldn't accept anyone but Jenna around him. To Flint it signaled an unpredictability he'd rather not gamble on.

"There's plenty of time," he said, stalling, reaching out to stop her. "If he's ready now, he'll be ready tomorrow."

She stared up at him a moment before she pried his fingers loose. "I'm the trainer, remember? I've set up his program, measured his progress and *I* say when he's mentally ready for something new." She shoved at his chest. "Now back off and let me do *my* job."

Flint watched her storm into the barn to get the tack she needed, then enter the round pen. She was upset about something more than his interference with Satin's training. He'd seen the sadness in her eyes, the trembling of her hand as she disengaged herself from him. The woman had no business in the same corral with the stud, let alone trying to work with him.

She patted the stallion, then started that slow, unintelligible crooning he'd come to recognize as her way of reassuring Satin. When she sacked out the horse by swinging a burlap bag around his legs and chest, Flint tensed. But the big animal stood calm.

Standing by while she saddled Satin was the hardest thing Flint had ever done. He knew the horse could blow up at any time. But much to his relief, she finished the task, then led the horse around for several minutes without incident. She continued to croon as she brought Satin to the center of the pen.

Flint held his breath when she slid her boot into the stirrup. He automatically put his own boot on the bottom rail of the fence and gripping the top board, braced himself. If that stallion gave the slightest indication he didn't want to be ridden, Flint was getting her out of there.

Jenna swung up onto Black Satin's back and patted his neck. Instead of the stud tensing as she expected he might, Satin seemed interested in what she was asking of him. Nudging him with her heels, she urged him into a walk, a trot and an easy lope. Confident with his re-action, she praised the horse as they moved around the corral, his gait smooth and comfortable.

Her concentration focused entirely on Satin, she knew immediately that something was wrong. The saddle started to bounce and slip to one side, causing him to shy away from the changing pressure. Then everything happened at once. Jenna and the saddle landed hard in the dirt, while in a blind panic, Black Satin reared and pawed the air.

Jenna saw Flint start over the top rail as she scram-bled to her feet. "Just keep Ryan away from the fence." She walked toward the frantic stallion. "Let me get Satin calmed down."

A combination of fear and adrenaline surged through Flint as he gripped the fence rail. If the horse tried to charge, could he get to Jenna in time? Would he be able to get her out before she fell victim to the animal's slash-ing hooves?

But to Flint's amazement, the stallion stopped his agi-tated movements and twisted his head from side to side, listening to Jenna's murmured reassurances. When she took hold of the bridle, Satin tensed for a moment, then as if he understood what she said, relaxed.

She stroked the stud's neck. "Get another saddle, Flint."

"No." Flint's heart still pounded hard against his ribs

and he didn't think he could survive another episode. "Wait until tomorrow when he's calmed down."

"He has to see there's nothing to fear. Get the saddle."

It went against his better judgment, but Flint retrieved the tack she requested. "You don't have to do this," he said quietly, handing it to her.

"Yes, I do." Their hands touched and they stared at each other for several long seconds. "I'll be all right. I promise."

Flint didn't think he'd ever done anything as difficult as standing back and watching her go through the same routine as before. He held his breath when the stallion pinned his ears back and rolled his eyes as Jenna mounted him. But once Satin realized nothing more was going to happen, he relaxed.

By the time Jenna led the stallion back to the safety of his stall, Flint felt drained. He'd never experienced anything as terrifying as when she took that fall. Nor had he ever felt more helpless. If she'd been unable to get up, he knew he couldn't have gotten to her in time to keep Satin from running her down.

Jenna returned to the corral and without hesitation stepped into his open arms. Flint could tell the incident had shaken her. Her slight body trembled, and she held on to him as if her legs didn't want to support her.

He hugged her close. "You scared me half to death. What happened?"

Before she could tell him, Ryan ran up to them, wide-eyed. "Jenna, are you all right?"

She reached down to touch Ryan's cheek. "I'm fine, honey."

Flint held her in one arm and picked up Ryan with the other. The three remained silent for several long moments while they held each other close.

"Let's go check out that saddle," Flint finally said, setting Ryan on his feet.

"The girth broke," Jenna stated, her voice shaky.

They walked over to where the tack still lay in the dusty corral. Flint scooped it up, placed it on the top rail and examined the girth.

His face grim, he held it out for Jenna's inspection. "This didn't break on its own." He glanced around the area as he once again felt someone watching their every move, could all but smell the hatred. "It was cut."

Chapter 8

Flint sat at his desk, staring at the pieces of the girth. He rubbed the tension at the base of his neck. Under normal conditions when a horse bucked or reared up, the rider could at least try to hold on to the saddle. But in this case, that small amount of security had been eliminated. If Satin had reacted differently...

Flint drew in a deep breath. Whoever cut the girth had anticipated a violent reaction the first time Satin was ridden. One that could have proven fatal.

"Flint?" Jenna stood at his office door. "Whiskers said you wanted to see me."

"We need to talk."

"Okay." She settled herself in the chair across from him. "Is there a problem?"

"I'm going to write you a check for the specified amount stated in the contract plus wages for the ranch work." Flint took a deep breath. His heart wasn't in what he was about to do, but his mind was set. "Then I want you off the Rocking M first thing in the morning."

"What's this all about, Flint?"

He took a check from one of the drawers, filled it out, then pushed it across the desk. "We both know what happened with Satin this evening was no accident. Someone had every intention of seeing you hurt."

"Yes. But—"

Flint shook his head. "As long as it's in my power to prevent it, I can't and won't take the chance on something like this happening again."

Jenna saw the self-reproach in his eyes, the regret. Her heart beat double time at the sacrifice he was willing to make. Flint would jeopardize Black Satin's training program and his goal of a championship, if that's what it took to protect her.

"Thanks." She picked up the check and tore it into tiny pieces. "But I haven't completed the job, and until I do, you're stuck with me. I'm here for the duration."

He reached for another check. "I'm releasing you from the contract with full pay."

"I understand that." She sat back in the chair. "And I appreciate the offer. But I have to decline."

"Like hell you will!" Flint jumped to his feet. "Don't you understand? It's become too dangerous for you to stay. I can't guarantee your safety."

"I'm not asking you to. All I'm asking for is your trust, Flint."

"You've got that, darlin'."

Outwardly calm, Jenna's insides were a mass of quivering nerves. Earlier she might have thought it best to get away from the Rocking M, but now the idea of leaving Flint upset her as little else could. He had big trouble on his hands, and she wasn't about to leave. Besides, it had become a personal matter when the culprit weakened that girth.

"What happened tonight was partly my fault," she admitted. "I should have checked the equipment to make sure it was sound before I saddled Satin."

"There wasn't any reason." He walked around the desk to stand in front of her. "The saddle and the girth were new."

Jenna rose to face him. "Yes, but if I had taken normal precautions and inspected it, the way I should have, I'd have discovered the damage."

Flint took her by the shoulders. "It still doesn't change the fact that someone wanted to see you hurt."

"Then whoever is behind this got a big disappointment."

She took his hands from her shoulders and placed the torn-up check into one of them. Closing his fingers around it, she held his hand in both of hers. "I've never run from anything in my life, Flint, and I'm not about to start now. You'll have your championship horse. I'm going to finish training Satin."

Flint reached for her and crushed her lips beneath his. She opened for him to thrust his tongue into the sweet, hot recesses of her mouth, and a ragged sigh escaped him.

Jenna would jeopardize her own safety in order to help him. He'd never known a woman that self-sacrificing. Nicole certainly hadn't been. His ex-wife's interest in a man never went further than his bank account and how to deplete it. But Jenna wasn't like Nicole. Money wasn't that important to her.

His fist relaxed, and the pieces of the check fluttered unnoticed to the floor. He cupped Jenna's breast, teased the tight nub with his thumb, then gently kneaded the softness surrounding it. Rewarded by her moan of pleasure, Flint shuddered at the molten flow of urgent need racing through him.

How he wanted her. And not just physically. It scared him, but he could no longer deny it. He wanted to possess her body and soul.

"Daddy, is something wrong with Jenna's heart?" Ryan asked, tugging on Flint's shirt.

Unnoticed, Ryan and the puppies had entered the room and stood curiously watching the two adults.

When Jenna started to jerk away, Flint held her tight. "Her heart was beating pretty fast," he said. He removed his hand from her breast. "I was checking to see that she's okay."

"Oh, Lord!" Jenna buried her face in Flint's shoulder. Embarrassment burned her cheeks and a nervous giggle threatened to escape. Couldn't he come up with something better than that?

"I'll bet she's still scared 'cause of falling off Black Satin," Ryan said solemnly.

"I think you're right," Flint agreed, just as serious. "Does Whiskers still have some cookies left from supper?"

"Uh-huh. He told me to come and tell you guys that he's got a snack for us." Clearly puzzled, Ryan gazed up at Jenna. "Your face is awful red. Does your heart still hurt?"

Wishing the floor would open and swallow her, Jenna nodded.

When Ryan patted her arm in sympathy, Flint cleared his throat in an obvious attempt to stifle his laughter. "Ryan, would you tell Whiskers we'll be there in a minute?"

"Okay, Daddy." Ryan trotted to the door, but turned

back. "You'll feel better when you have some milk and cookies, Jenna."

"I think I'll pass on the snack," she said when she found her voice. She escaped Flint's grasp and put some distance between them. "It would probably be best if I go on to bed."

Ryan nodded, then called to Whiskers as he and the dogs ran back down the hall. "Jenna isn't gonna have a snack. She doesn't feel too good, and Daddy had to put his hand on her chest to check her heart. Can my puppies have her cookies?"

Whiskers's hoot of laughter carried all the way to the study.

"Is your heart still racing?" Flint asked, his grin wicked.

Her cheeks flamed anew. "No, it just stopped completely."

Without a word she turned and headed for the door. There wasn't anything she could say that wouldn't make the matter worse. And for the first time in her life, Jenna opted for the coward's way out.

Jenna wiped her brow and walked through the back door. Avoiding Whiskers's twinkling eyes, she went to the refrigerator to get something cold to drink. She wasn't about to comment on last night's embarrassing incident. And if he knew what was good for him, Whiskers wouldn't, either.

"Have you seen Brad?" she asked.

"Flint sent him to town." The old man watched her pour a glass of orange juice and shook his head. "Is that all you're gonna have for breakfast?"

She slumped into a chair. "It's too hot to eat."

"Well, I cain't kick up a fuss with you on that one,"

he said, seating himself across from her. Lowering his voice, he confided, "I wouldn't tell this to jest anybody, but it's days like these make me glad I got old and had to turn to housekeepin'. Stayin' in the air-conditionin' while them young bucks get out and chase beeves don't bother me one bit."

Amused, she asked, "Even if you have to share the house with three dogs?"

"Them hounds are outside where they belong," Whiskers stated flatly. "And they're gonna stay there. They done chewed up the last pair of my boots they're gonna get ahold on. There weren't nothin' left but the soles by the time I found 'em."

Jenna laughed at the disgusted look on the old man's face. She'd seen the boots Whiskers referred to, and he was right. The puppies had even chewed off the heels.

Rising to place her glass in the sink, she asked, "Did Brad leave me a message before he left?"

Whiskers shook his head. "Nope. Flint said you'd be workin' with him today after you got done with Satin."

"Where is he now?"

"That heifer in the birthin' pen dropped her calf last night. He took Ryan down to see it. He's been gone a spell, so I 'spect he'll be back directly." The old man stood and hobbled into the pantry. "He did tell me to have some sandwiches packed, 'cause the two of you won't be back 'fore supper."

Before Jenna could ask if Flint mentioned where they would be working, he and Ryan entered the kitchen.

"Jenna, Daddy gave me a calf," Ryan said, racing past her on his way to the stairs. He turned back suddenly. "Is your heart okay today?"

Her face burning, she nodded. "I'm doing a lot better, Ryan. Thank you for asking."

"Good." The child started up the stairs. "I gotta get my gloves. I'm gonna help Brad with my calf when he gets back."

Flint watched the blush rise on Jenna's cheeks. Her hair spilled onto her shoulders like a dark-gold cloud, reminding him of the feel of his face buried in the silken strands.

His gaze ran the length of her, and he found it hard to breathe. With the sunlight streaming in through the windows behind her, her thin T-shirt might as well have been transparent. The pale-yellow cotton complemented her light tan, but did little to hide the outline of her upper body, the fullness of her breasts. Tucked into her snug jeans, it gave him more than a fair idea of her enticing shape.

The phrase Steer Wrestlers Like It On the Side caused him to gulp. As usual, his imagination and body were off and running at the thought. How the hell was he supposed to work with her all day and keep his hands to himself?

He'd seen the smooth length of her slender legs that first night, and just yesterday he'd caught a glimpse of her luscious breasts beneath the water in the stock tank. His mind filled in the blanks, and his body tightened.

"Flint, are you all right?" Jenna asked. She stepped closer. "You look a little flushed."

Whiskers came out of the pantry to peer at the crimson staining Flint's cheeks. "He'll be okay. I've seen that look before when a man gets a mite too hot." Chuckling, he handed Flint a set of saddlebags, then winked at Jenna. "Throw a little cold water on him. He'll come out of it."

Flint glared at Whiskers, then snatched up the saddlebags and his cellular phones. "Jenna, are you finished with Satin for the day?"

"Yes." She bit back the smile threatening to break through. It felt good to know she wasn't the only one suffering from a heat that had nothing to do with the temperature outside.

"I need you to help me move one of the smaller herds to Devil's Gorge," Flint said, jamming his hat on his head.

"The weatherman says there's a chance of somethin' blowin' through," Whiskers warned. "It starts to lookin' bad, you two find yourselves a hidey-hole. Ya hear?"

Jenna tucked her hair into her hat and followed Flint. "If the need arises, we'll find somewhere to hide," she promised.

When the pair were safely out of earshot, Whiskers chuckled merrily. "That's what I'm countin' on, gal."

As Flint and Jenna rode away from the box canyon, she found she hated to leave. She'd thought it to be one of the prettiest areas on Flint's ranch. The contrast of the lush, green grass against the multicolored strata of the canyon walls they'd had to pass between had been breathtaking. And the spring-fed pool at the far end had reflected the beautiful surroundings, just like in a painting.

"I can understand why they call it Devil's Gorge," Jenna commented when they left the pass and were once again able to ride side by side. "It's hard as the dickens to get to, but it really is gorgeous. Almost like an oasis."

Flint chuckled. "A piece of heaven in the middle of hell?"

"I'd say that pretty much sums it up," she agreed, smiling.

He stared off into the distance a moment before he spoke again. "You won't have to check with Brad anymore to find out where you'll be working."

She glanced at him, but his face revealed nothing. "Why?"

He stopped his horse, then waited for her to do likewise. "From now on you'll be working with me."

"But I'm perfectly capable of taking care of myself."

"This isn't negotiable," Flint said firmly. He reached out to touch her arm. "Yesterday someone on this ranch tried to make sure you got hurt. The only way I can prevent them from succeeding the next time will be to keep you with me."

The feel of his hand on her arm, the protective look in his dark brown eyes, caused her stomach to do a back flip. "All right. But we stay away from stock tanks. Agreed?"

Flint released her arm and shook his head. "I'm making no promises." His grin devilish, he winked and nudged his horse into a walk. "I've just recently discovered what a pleasure it is to own stock tanks."

"A gentleman would forget."

"Darlin', even a gentleman couldn't forget about that."

"Can't or won't?"

"Both."

When the sound of distant thunder rumbled across the land, she pointed to the horizon. "It looks as if we might get some relief from the heat."

Flint watched the bank of dark clouds rapidly rise in the southwestern sky and cursed under his breath. Still several miles from them, the main body of the storm was building momentum as it traveled across the prairie. Jagged columns of lightning streaked down from the low-hanging, greenish-black clouds, and the wind picked up. Fat raindrops began to fall, causing little puffs of dust to rise when they hit the thirsty earth.

He quickly assessed their situation. They were too

far from the canyon to take shelter there, and unless the system changed direction, and damned fast, they were in the direct path of a sizable blow.

"We'll wait it out at the old Circle S line shack," Flint said, making a snap decision. Sheltered on three sides by rolling hills, the sturdy little cabin was only a quarter of a mile away and their best hope for shelter. "Follow me."

He turned his horse and spurred it into a gallop. Jenna kicked the buckskin into a run and fell in behind him. Stinging needles of rain pelted them from all sides, and huge gusts of wind began to whip the grass and mesquite into rolling waves. Arriving at their destination just in time to tie the horses inside the shed, Flint grabbed the saddlebags and hustled Jenna toward the cabin as hail began to beat down.

When they reached the door, he shoved her inside. "All hell's going to break loose!" He slammed the door, caught Jenna in a flying tackle and, protecting her with his body, rolled to the floor. The wind outside built to a deafening roar. "Tornado," he said close to her ear. "Stay down."

Her fingers gripped the front of his chambray shirt, and his muscles flexed in response. He wanted her with every fiber of his being. Wanted to…

And then it was over. As quickly as it began, the storm moved on.

Her legs moved against his, and it took a moment for him to realize she was trying to get to her feet.

"It's okay, darlin'." He rose and brought her up with him. "It's over."

"Thank goodness," Jenna said, her voice shaky.

Flint stared down into her flushed face and felt a flash of white-hot desire. Having her beneath him had been heaven and hell rolled into one. He wanted nothing more than to remove their clothes and take the final step toward ending the torment.

To keep from pulling her to him and doing just that, he forced himself to look around the shack. "I haven't been here for some time, but it looks pretty clean."

"I've seen worse," she agreed.

He walked to the door and peered out. The twister had hit the ridge above them and skipped over, just as he'd hoped. But lightning still flashed, and the driving rain showed no signs of letting up.

He needed his head examined, but he wasn't the least bit sorry they were stuck here. He had reached his limit, and he was man enough to admit it. Biting the inside of his lip to keep from smiling, he tried to think of a way to tactfully break the news he was sure Jenna wouldn't want to hear.

Deciding there was no better way than straight-out, he turned to face her. "We're going to have to spend the night here, darlin'."

"You're joking, right?"

Flint shook his head. "I'm afraid not. Even if the lightning stops right now, there's no way to get back across the wash. Rain like this turns that ravine into a raging torrent."

Jenna didn't doubt Flint's word. She knew a wash could be dry as a bone one minute and a deep, swift river the next. She glanced around the cabin and groaned. There was only one bed.

She looked back at Flint. "No way?"

"None."

Dazed, she watched him make a quick call on the cell phone to let Whiskers know they were safe, then start for the door.

"I'll go tend to the horses."

Incapable of speech, she watched him leave.

Flint entered the cabin a half hour later to find Jenna reading labels on some canned goods. He crossed the room and sat down on the bed. "There were some sandwiches left from lunch."

"Yes, but I thought it would be nice to have something to go with them," she answered without looking up. "Do you think the owner will mind?"

"Nope." He removed his boots and stretched out on the cot. "He's glad there'll be a little variety added to his next meal."

She arched a perfectly shaped brow. "I thought you said this was the Circle S line shack."

"It used to be." He pulled his Resistol down over his eyes, then clasped his hands behind his head. "My dad bought the Circle S about thirty years ago from Jed's father." He saw her eye the can skeptically. "Those should be pretty fresh. The boys use this for a base camp during hunting season."

From beneath the wide brim of his hat, Flint watched her nod, then turn back to the table. She fumbled with the can opener. Her nerves were as frayed as his. They both knew there were no more obstacles—no meddling old men, no talkative little boys, no sinister eyes watching. Tonight nothing would prevent them from exploring the chemistry between them.

When she dropped both the can and the opener, he sailed his hat across the room like a Frisbee, sat up and swung his legs over the side of the bed. His forearms propped on his knees, he watched her struggle with the gadget for a few seconds longer before he rose to his feet, took it from her trembling hands and pulled her into his arms.

"Flint—"

"Hush, darlin'." He ran his hands down her stiff spine and kissed her temple. "I want you. You know that. But I'm not going to jump your bones just because we're alone. I've never taken anything a woman didn't readily give. And I'm not about to start now. When we make love, it will be because you want me as much as I want you."

Jenna drew back to look into his deep-brown eyes. When she'd been younger, she'd convinced herself she wanted Dan. But their few fumbling attempts at making love had resulted in embarrassing shame for both. Now she recognized what she'd felt for Dan had been the pure, innocent love of a young girl. But her feelings for Flint were those of a woman.

She'd never experienced a woman's need, a woman's passion for a man. Not until Flint held her, kissed her.

In that moment she realized she never would again. Not with any other man. Only Flint.

Her mind raced with the complications her actions could cause, but she shoved them aside. The minute Flint had taken her into his arms, the decision had been made.

Mother Nature had placed them here in this desolate, little cabin. And *she* was drawing them together now.

"I do want you," she whispered.

Chapter 9

"Darlin', you don't know what that does to me. I've been on fire since the day we met." Flint's hands stilled and, groaning, he buried his face in her hair. He brought his hands up to capture her face. "Are you sure? If not, say so now. I don't think I'll be able to stop if you change your mind later."

Jenna saw the raw hunger, the deep need in Flint's intense gaze. "You'd better not stop, cowboy. You're the one who made me feel like this. You better do something about it."

He grinned. "I always put out the fires I start."

His lips claimed hers in the most tender, poignant kiss she'd ever experienced. When his tongue swept over her mouth, then darted inside to stroke her, sparks of pleasure raced to every nerve in her body. She savored the taste of him, reveled in his hungry lips moving across her own. Excitement, sultry and provocative, flowed through her.

Flint slid his hands from her shoulders to cup her breasts. He supported the heaviness he'd created there, teased her nipples with his thumbs. Jenna thought she'd go up in flames.

"Does that feel good?" he whispered, his breath feathering her ear. "Or do you want me to stop?"

"Please…"

He raised his thumbs from her shirt. "Please stop?"

"No! If you stop now…I'm not sure I'll survive."

Flint's gaze captured hers and he slowly drew her shirt over her head. Pulling it from her arms, he tossed it at the chair. He smiled and ran his finger along the lace-edged top of her bra, but when he released the clasp and slid the straps down, his smile vanished and his breath caught.

He bent to press a kiss to each breast. "You're perfect. So soft. So sweet."

Tossing her bra on top of her shirt, he took her hands in his and guided them to his shirt. "Your turn, darlin'."

Jenna quickly unsnapped the garment. She'd yearned to touch him like this again, since that first night in the hall. Now as she placed her hands on his firmly muscled chest, the crisp hair tickled her palms. The sensation caused sparks of excitement to skip along every nerve in her body, and passion stronger than she'd ever known rose within her.

A smile curved her lips when the tips of her fingers found the tiny nubs buried beneath the thin curls. Flint's groan of pleasure escaped on a ragged sigh, and it thrilled her to know he was as sensitive to her touch as she was to his.

When he brushed her hands away to crush her to him, the feel of skin against skin, the nestling of her nipples amid his chest hair made her moan. Certain her hunger had reached its peak, she gasped when he cupped her bottom to lift her close. The evidence of his hard arousal, pressed into her lower belly, sent ribbons of desire weaving their way through every part of her.

"Flint—"

The passion in her voice aroused him as little else could. "When you say my name like that it drives me wild."

He kissed her, letting her taste his need, the depth of feelings he no longer wanted to hide. Somehow finding the strength to set her from him, he broke the kiss, quickly shed his shirt, then bent to remove her boots. He swung her up into his arms and ground his teeth to maintain the slender thread of control he had left.

He wanted to go slow, to make their first time together special. But when he carried her to the small bed in the corner and stretched out beside her, he realized just how difficult that would be. The feel of her breasts in his callused palms, her warm heat nestled against him, nearly sent him over the edge.

Gazing down at her, he realized he was hotter than he'd ever been in his life. "Darlin', I can't stand much more of this. I need to feel all of you against me."

When he unbuckled her belt, released the snap of her jeans and slowly lowered the zipper, he watched her grasp the quilt in tight fists. As he eased her jeans and panties from her slender hips, then down her thighs, she moaned his name. He'd never been so turned on by a woman's excitement. But then, he didn't think he'd ever excited a woman this much before.

A satisfied smile turned up the corners of his mouth. Jenna's response to his slightest touch and the unbridled passion he saw clouding her eyes was something that couldn't be faked. She didn't need just any man. She needed *him*.

The knowledge sent a surge of heat straight to his groin. He had to grit his teeth against the sudden rush and, quickly rising, he removed his jeans and briefs.

Jenna's first impulse was to cover herself. But Flint's sharp intake of breath, the hunger darkening his eyes made her feel truly beautiful for the first time in her life. His gaze caressed her, and a heavy coil of need settled in the pit of her stomach. Had a man ever made a woman feel more special?

He pulled off the rest of his clothing, then turned to face her. Her heart pounded against her ribs, and her breath caught. Flint was the perfect specimen of a man in his prime. Broad, heavily muscled shoulders tapered to a flat, rippling stomach and lean, narrow hips. Her gaze drifted lower. Her breathing became shallow, and her pulse began to race. He was heavily built and thoroughly aroused. She lifted her gaze to meet his, and the empty ache inside her tightened unbearably. He was looking at her as if she was the most desired woman in the world.

In a short time she would belong to Flint in every sense of the word. And he would be her man. At least for tonight.

Flint tucked the small packet he'd retrieved from his jeans pocket beneath the pillow and lay back down beside her. When he pulled her to him, he closed his eyes. The shock of his skin finally touching all of her and the thought of no more barriers between them nearly proved to be more than he could take.

He'd never wanted to please a woman as he wanted to please Jenna, but his body throbbed with anticipation, and the tension arcing between them turned his blood into a molten flow of need.

Her curious hands smoothed down his back, and his lungs ceased to function. "Darlin', don't get me wrong. I love the way your hands feel on my body…" Her fingers skimmed the curve of his buttocks, and a strangled sound emerged from deep in his throat. When he regained his voice he finished. "…but if you keep this up, I'm going to embarrass both of us."

He smiled at the blush of passion on her cheeks, the hesitancy of her breathing. Not sure how much longer he could endure the torture of holding her without taking the final step, Flint slid his hand down between them to cup her tawny curls.

Her readiness for him, her startled gasp as he stroked her, inflamed him further. When she arched against him, he knew he couldn't stand much more. "Easy, darlin'."

Reaching for the packet beneath the pillow, he took care of their protection, then nudged her knees apart. He clasped her hands in his and pinned them on either side of her head. "What is it you need, Jenna?"

"You."

She looked a little hesitant. "Are you sure?"

"Yes!"

At her impassioned admission, Flint claimed her with one smooth stroke. But his elation turned to shock at the resistance he felt, the unusual tightness surrounding him and the flash of pain clouding her soft eyes.

He froze. "What the hell—"

She bit her lower lip, and Flint felt her body involuntarily try to resist the foreign invasion of his. He hadn't even considered she might still be a virgin. The woman was twenty-six years old, and these days it was unusual to find a girl of eighteen who hadn't experimented in the back seat of a car. At least once.

"Why didn't you tell me you'd never been with a man?" he demanded, his voice sharpened by the thought of causing her pain.

"What made you think I had?" Her voice was little more than a whisper.

Flint watched a tear slip from the corner of her eye. He felt like a complete ass. He'd hurt her, and now all he could do was complain about it.

Holding the lower part of his body still, he gathered her to him and kissed the droplet away. She had just given him a special part of herself, and the very last thing he wanted to do was make her regret it.

"I'm sorry, Jenna. You didn't deserve that." Buried inside her as he was, his body urged him to complete the act of pleasuring them both. But he knew she needed time to adjust. He took a shuddering breath and fought for control. "I just wish you'd told me. I would have been more careful."

"I'm fine. Really."

Just as he reached the limit of his endurance, he watched her eyes soften and knew the pain was giving way to the ache of unfulfilled desire. "I'm going to love you now, darlin'."

Flint moved slowly, watchful for any sign of her discomfort. His body urged him to unleash the tight rein he held on his control, but he didn't want to hurt her more than he already had. She was new to lovemaking, and he was new to being with a virgin. How long did the pain last? What could he do to lessen it?

She placed her hands on his lower back, then slid them down to his buttocks, and Flint's control snapped. He gave to her as she gave to him, and when he felt her body stiffen, he quickened the pace and drove them both over the edge.

When Jenna cried his name and he felt her pleasure surround him, satisfaction like he'd never known rushed through him. Only then did he give in to his own intense need and, with a final thrust, felt the triumph of his explosion overtake him.

"That was incredible," she said several minutes later.

"Yes, it was." Flint moved to her side and covered them with the quilt. Brushing his lips against her temple, he placed his hand on her lower belly. "Are you all right?"

"I'm fine."

"I wish you'd told me." He gently caressed her, trying to heal any pain he might have caused. "I could have hurt you."

"But you didn't." She nibbled at his shoulder. "Besides, it was my choice."

Her words flowed over him like a silken caress. She'd chosen him to be the first, and a sudden burning in his gut told him he damned well wanted to be the last. The thought of another man touching Jenna, making her come apart in his arms the way she had in Flint's, caused the blaze to intensify and his body to tighten with the need to once again brand her as his.

When her hand slid from his chest down to his flank, fire raced through his veins to burn at his groin, and he abandoned all speculation. He could analyze his emotions later. Right now her timid exploration was driving him wild.

"Don't…be shy, Jenna," he encouraged, his breath coming in harsh gasps. "I promise…I won't break."

She snuggled closer to his side and her innocent touch when she captured him sent Flint to the brink of insanity. He groaned like a man in pain.

Her hand stilled. "Did I do something wrong?"

"Geez, no!" he growled and turned to pin her to the mattress. "You're doing everything just right." He pressed himself to her. "Too right."

Her eyes met his, telling him of her need, pleading with him to end the sweet torture.

When she looked at him like that, Flint felt he might never breathe again. Her moan of pleasure, as he made them one, urged him to give her everything he had. He could tell, as their cries mingled to celebrate the joy of mutual release, she gave him all of herself in return.

The next evening Flint sat at his desk, his gaze riveted on the large brown envelope in his hand. The investigator had completed his report, but Flint wasn't sure he wanted to know what secrets it held.

Two weeks ago he'd wanted Jenna off the ranch at all costs. Now all he could do was think of ways to prolong her stay.

They hadn't talked since arriving back at ranch headquarters earlier in the day. He'd been busy with paperwork, and she'd been occupied with Black Satin's training. But they both knew things had changed between them. She had given him something very precious last night, something she could only give once. And he'd never experienced anything like what they'd shared.

Throughout the night they'd awoken to renewed desire, and each time their passion had been more intense than the last. He'd instructed her in the physical act of loving, but she'd taught him much more. She'd drawn emotions from him that he'd never known existed.

He wanted her to know how very special it had been for him and how it made him feel knowing she'd chosen him to be her first. He'd never been comfortable expressing his emotions with the tender words women wanted to hear. He grinned. But he could damned well show her.

His mind on how he planned to do just that, Flint reached for the metal clasp on the flap of the envelope, removed the papers and scanned the information. His expression turned grim, and he leaned back in his chair to stare at the necklace on the mantel. The glittering stones mocked him with their beauty.

He felt like a fool.

Oh, he'd thought there might be something like an unpaid parking ticket in her background, but he'd never dreamed the information about her would be of this magnitude. Nor had he anticipated the report posing more questions than it answered.

Jenna switched on the barn lights and peered down the long row of stalls. She could have sworn the brood mares sounded restless. Now that the heat wave had let up a bit, humans and animals alike were less edgy, which made the horses' nervous movements even more curious.

Shrugging, she walked over to the first stall. It was probably her imagination, colored by her own turbulent mood, she decided.

A curious chestnut mare poked her head over the stall door, and Jenna absently rubbed its muzzle. She'd gone for a walk in hopes of putting things in perspective. Unfortunately, she still hadn't been able to come up with a solution.

She'd made love with Flint, and nothing could ever make her regret what they'd shared. But when the time came, how would she leave the Rocking M without her heart staying behind?

"What are you doing in here?"

Jenna jumped at the harsh sound of Flint's voice. When he continued to stare at her through the scope of a rifle, she glared at him. "Put that gun down."

His face a stony mask, he lowered the weapon. "I asked you a question."

Shaken by the venom in his voice, she sat down on a bale of hay by the wide, double doors. "I went for a walk. When I passed the barn I thought the mares sounded restless, so I decided to check on them."

"They don't seem nearly as edgy as you."

She wondered if he'd lost his mind. "Wouldn't you be shook up if someone pointed a rifle at you?"

"How was I to know you weren't someone else?"

Remembering the trouble, her indignation cooled. With the problems he'd experienced, it was only natural he would assume the worst when he saw an unexplained light in the barn. "I'm sorry. I should have told someone I was going for a walk."

"Yes, you should have." He leaned the rifle against the barn wall, placed a booted foot beside her on the bale and crossed his forearms on his thigh. "But right now we have other things to discuss besides your evening walk."

"Okay," she said, meeting his icy glare. What could she have done to deserve such an ominous look? "What would you like to talk about? The weather? Cattle prices?"

"Cattle prices might be a good start. It seems several of the ranches you've worked for have had rustling problems."

She stared at him. He thought she was stealing his cattle? "Yes. Several of the places where I've worked have had cattle stolen. But we both know spreads the size of yours are easy targets. Always have been and probably always will be."

"But you were in residence at the time."

Jenna clenched her fists to her sides and struggled for patience. A certified saint would lose it with this man. "Did you have trouble before I arrived?"

"Yes."

"Then doesn't it stand to reason I'm not involved?"

"Things heated up as soon as you arrived."

"So did the weather," she shot back. "Are you going to blame me for that, too?"

"If I were you I wouldn't be so insolent." His eyes narrowed. "We still haven't discussed why you live the life of a transient when you have over a quarter of a million in a bank down in Austin. And another twenty-five grand in Oklahoma City."

She sucked in a sharp breath. "How dare you? That's none of your business."

"I think it is." He pinned her with a piercing gaze. "Explain to me why someone with that much money would live like a nomad when she could well afford a place of her own. Not to mention a decent vehicle to drive."

"As far as I'm concerned, we have nothing to discuss," she retorted, jumping to her feet. She had no intention of explaining her lifestyle to Flint or anyone else. And she refused to listen to any more of his accusations.

"You haven't answered me," he said, catching her arm.

Jenna looked down at the large hand encircling her upper arm. The reaction that always accompanied his touch was there, but she ignored it. He had pried into a part of her life she had no intention of sharing with him or anyone else. And at the moment she despised him for it.

"You had no right sticking your nose into my affairs, McCray." Leveling her furious gaze on him, she jerked from his grasp. "And I'm not going to justify your high-handedness by answering your questions."

"You're working for me now. I make it a point to know all about my employees."

She glared at him. "Our contract states I'm to train your horse, not sell myself into servitude."

Jenna started for the barn door but Flint blocked her

path. "Wouldn't you be suspicious of a top-notch horse trainer who drove a truck that looks like the loser from a demolition derby?"

His accusations hurt, and hot tears stung the backs of her eyes, but she refused to let him see the extent of her misery. "You don't know what you're talking about, McCray. And I'm not going to enlighten you. You have your mind made up. You wouldn't believe me, anyway."

She tried to step around him, but like a vise, Flint's large hands clamped her shoulders. "Why, Jenna? Make me understand."

Suddenly engulfed by years of desolation, she stared past his shoulder into the darkness outside. Her voice devoid of emotion, she whispered, "You couldn't possibly—"

The sudden commotion of agitated horses at the far end of the building caught their attention. Jenna turned to see an eerie glow quickly grow into dancing, orange flames licking at the entire back wall of the barn.

He set her aside and ran toward the fire. "Get the men."

Their confrontation forgotten, Jenna grabbed the rifle and ran through the big, double doors to fire several shots into the quiet night sky. Propping the rifle against a water trough, she ran back into the barn and opened the first stall she came to.

As she led the nervous animals out to one of the exercise pens, Flint's men arrived to uncoil lengths of hose and soak saddle blankets with water. The ranch hands shouted for her to stay back, but she ignored them. The flames were spreading, and the valuable mares were in danger of being lost. She had to evacuate as many as she could.

Sparks swirled everywhere, and the crackle of wood

being consumed by hungry flames deafened her. Tears streamed down her cheeks, and her lungs ached from the thick smoke, but she refused to give up. There was only one stall left.

She opened the enclosure to grab hold of the mare's halter, but the panicked animal proved to be more than she could handle. She found a burlap bag just outside the stall, wrapped it around the mare's eyes and, with dogged determination, guided the horse into the wide aisle. The nervous horse pranced in a circle around her, and Jenna had to summon every ounce of her flagging strength to hold the animal.

The loud crack of an overhead beam caused the terrified mare to lurch to the side, pinning Jenna against the side boards. Pain shot through her, and the air rushed from her lungs.

She searched for Flint among the men battling the blaze, but when she called his name, her voice failed. A sweet lethargy swept over her. His image became fuzzy, and sounds grew distant. As she slipped into the peaceful quiet of an all-consuming black abyss, she welcomed the respite from the oppressive heat and the pain of trying to breathe.

Her last thought was of Flint. She didn't want to leave him. He needed her whether he realized it or not.

Chapter 10

Flint turned to shout orders to his men, but the scene a few feet away caused the words to die in his throat. As if in slow motion, he watched Jenna crumple to the barn floor, her body dangerously close to being trampled by the terrified mare.

He dropped the hose he held, called to Brad and the other men to take control of the blindfolded animal, then scooped Jenna into his arms. Running for the safety of the cooler outside air, he felt fear tear at his insides. Had the horse already stepped on her? Could she have internal injuries?

He gently cradled her limp body to his and sprinted across the ranch yard to enter the house. "Get the first aid kit," he ordered, rushing past Whiskers on his way to the stairs.

Taking the steps two at a time, he passed Jenna's room

and carried her to his. When he placed her on the bed, she moaned.

"Jenna. Darlin', can you hear me?"

Her eyes fluttered, then slowly opened. "Flint—"

"Easy, darlin'. You're safe now." Searching for signs of injury and praying he'd find none, his hands shook as he ran them along her body.

Assured there were no broken bones, he sat down beside her to smooth her hair from her face. He couldn't see any visible signs that she'd been injured, but it was the possible internal injuries that concerned him.

Ryan ran into the room, followed close by Whiskers. "Is she hurt bad?" the old man asked.

"I can't tell." Flint bathed her face with the damp cloth Whiskers pressed into his hand. "Get her some water."

Ryan stood beside Flint, his little chin wobbling. "Daddy, please don't take Jenna to the hospital. I love her. I don't want her to die."

"I'm…" She coughed several times before she could go on. "I'm all right." She took Ryan's hand. "I promise." Glancing at Flint, she asked, "What about the mare?"

"The men got her out."

"I called Mac," Whiskers said, handing Flint a glass. "He oughtta be here in fifteen minutes."

Knowing Ryan felt as helpless as he did, and not wanting to upset the boy any more than he already was, Flint hugged his son. "I need you to do something very important. Could you go to the kitchen and watch for Dr. McEvers?" When Ryan nodded, Flint smiled. "Good. Bring him up here as soon as he arrives. Okay?"

"Okay, Daddy," Ryan said, already halfway to the door.

Flint turned back to support Jenna while she sipped the water. "Just rest, Jenna." He eased her back on the bed. "Doc's ranch is only a few miles away. He'll be here soon."

"It's not necessary," she protested, her voice raspy. "My throat's a little sore, but otherwise I'm fine."

"I want to make sure."

Sheer terror was an unfamiliar emotion, one he hadn't dealt with more than once or twice in his thirty-three years. But in the past few days Flint had come to know the feeling quite well. Icy fingers had gripped his heart until he thought it would burst a couple of nights ago when Jenna had fallen from Black Satin. And then tonight, as he'd watched the panicked mare dance around her helpless body, the feeling had returned full-force.

"Flint?" He turned at the sound of Brad's hoarse voice. "Is Miss Adams going to be okay?" his foreman asked.

Flint nodded. "Whiskers called Mac just to be sure."

Turning his hat in his hand, Brad shifted from one foot to the other. "The brood barn's a complete loss. The best we can do is keep it from spreading to the other buildings and let it burn itself out."

Flint could tell from the look on Brad's face and his agitated actions that the man had more on his mind than the status of the fire. Taking Jenna's hand in his, Flint said, "I'll be back in a little while."

"Go ahead." Her grip weak, she squeezed his hand. "I just had the breath knocked out of me. I'll be fine."

He hated to leave her but, placing her in Whiskers's care, he followed Brad down the hall. "What's up?"

"It looks like whoever we're fighting just took another punch." His face grim, Brad led Flint out of the house toward the barns. "That fire was no accident. It was set."

When they rounded the end of one of the buildings, Brad pointed to a couple of discarded fuel cans. "Jed stumbled across these on his way to fight the fire."

Clear liquid dripped from the opened cans, a small, dark circle spreading where the fluid wet the dusty soil.

Flint squatted down to wipe a droplet from the rim of the can. He sniffed the substance on his fingers. "Kerosene."

Brad nodded. "I checked the shed. Somebody's been into the supply we keep for the heaters in the calving barn."

Flint got to his feet, his anger and frustration increasing tenfold as he felt the malicious eyes once again watching him.

Jenna slowly opened her eyes to the late-afternoon sunlight streaming through the window. For a second or two she wondered where she was, but as events of the past evening returned, she glanced around. She was in Flint's room.

Curious, she sat up to survey her surroundings. Knotty pine paneling provided an excellent foil for the pieces of Native American artwork and heavy, dark mahogany furniture. She noticed several pictures of Flint and Ryan on the dresser along with a ragged looking, one-eyed teddy bear.

She smiled and, throwing back the patchwork quilt, got up for a better look. She touched the frames with gentle reverence, and tears filled her eyes. She loved them both so much. How would she ever be able to leave them?

And after Flint's accusations last night, leaving the Rocking M *was* inevitable, once she finished Satin's training. Saddened by the thought, she made the bed, then went to her own room for a shower and fresh clothes.

Twenty minutes later Jenna descended the stairs to a silent house. She listened for sounds of Whiskers moving around in the kitchen or Ryan's excited chatter. But the house remained strangely quiet. Too quiet.

Just as she reached the bottom step, Flint walked out of the study. They hadn't talked after he'd left her to check on the fire, and as they stared at each other now, an uneasy feeling came over her. He still thought she might be involved in the trouble.

"How are you feeling?" he finally asked, breaking the strained silence. "Mac gave you something to sleep. Are you sure you feel like being up?"

"I'm fine."

"He said you were a little bruised, but otherwise okay."

Jenna nodded. She couldn't stand the tension. It was time to set things straight. "We need to talk."

Flint gazed at her for several long, uncomfortable moments before he stepped back for her to enter the study. Once they were both seated, he watched her twist her hands into a tight knot. A dull ache squeezed at his gut. He wasn't sure he wanted to hear what she had to say.

"Where did you want to start?" he asked.

He watched her take a deep breath. When she raised her eyes, she met his gaze head-on. "First off, other than coincidence, I can't explain why some of the ranches I've worked at have experienced rustling problems. But we both know stealing cattle has always been quite profitable. Depending on the market, a thief can make hundreds of dollars on each animal."

Flint leaned back in his chair. "You've amassed a lot of money in a very short time."

Gray sparks lit her eyes. "Where did you get your information on my financial affairs?"

"I had your background investigated."

"Why?"

Looking back, it seemed pretty lame, but at the time

he'd thought it extremely important. "I wanted out of the contract. You knew that. I was hoping to find something to prove you weren't suitable for the job."

One of her brows rose. "Now you think you've found it?"

He met her gaze, before his eyes sought out the dome on the mantel. "I'm not sure."

Clearly angered, Jenna sat forward. "Then why did you confront me last night as if I'd committed a crime?" When he started to answer, she shook her head. "I know why. You naturally assumed I was guilty of stealing cattle and banking the profits. Didn't you?"

Flint didn't like admitting it, but that was exactly what he'd thought. "Facts and figures don't lie. People *do*."

"Then let me set you straight, McCray." Her eyes sparkled with gray fire. "First off, I wouldn't use that investigator anymore, because evidently the man is incompetent. If he'd done his job, the figures would have added up. We both know my price for training a horse is quite high. If you want the best, you have to pay for it. Plain and simple. I've trained dozens of horses in the past six years. That's why it seems like I have a lot of money stockpiled."

"But—"

"I'm not finished," she snapped. "You inherited this spread, and that's great. I don't begrudge you one inch of it. But I've never had that advantage. I've had to scrape and claw for everything I've ever had. And, believe me, when you earn it the hard way, you learn to hang on tight."

She glared at him. "Did it ever occur to you that I might be saving my money because I'm working toward a goal? Are you so arrogant you think you're the only one with plans? The only one to have a dream?"

"No." Flint felt guilty as hell. Everything she accused him of fell too close to the mark. "But—"

"It was so much easier to assume the worst. Right?"

Before he could answer, she rose to her feet and paced the length of the study. "You've always had a home, Flint. But I've never had that luxury, never had a place where I truly belonged. Believe it or not, a camper on the back of Daisy is the only thing I've ever been able to call home. That's the reason I keep her. I could afford to replace her with a brand-new, top-of-the-line truck and camper. But I won't. She's not just my home, she's the only thing I have left of my father."

She turned to look at him, her eyes defiant. "Don't get me wrong. I'm not ashamed of where I came from or the fact that I've been poor most of my life. But I want something better. I want a permanent home and horses of my own. That's what I'm working for. Why I save every dime I can."

Flint's guilt increased. Jenna had mentioned her lack of roots before, but he assumed she'd exaggerated. His gaze darted around the study. He'd always taken everything he had for granted. He couldn't imagine not having a home or the pride he always felt when he thought of the generations of McCrays who carved a thriving enterprise from the dusty Texas soil.

She was right. He had been an arrogant son of a gun not to consider she might have dreams and goals of her own. He'd been too busy comparing her to his ex-wife. But Jenna was nothing like Nicole, and it was way past time he faced that fact.

"I've never stolen anything in my life, nor have I ever tried to destroy what someone else has," she stated. "All I ask is a chance to work hard and realize my dreams."

The more she explained, the worse he felt. "So why

haven't you bought a place? You have more than enough money."

She shook her head. "No, I don't. When I buy a ranch where I can raise and train horses of my own, there won't be any liens or mortgages. Everything will be paid for, free and clear."

Flint admired her determination, but as a successful rancher, he saw the impracticality in her reasoning. He left his chair, walked up to her and encircled her waist with his arms. "If you deplete your reserves, how would you handle the emergency expenses that arise?" He gazed down at her. "It would be more feasible to make a sizable down payment, take out a loan for the balance and keep the rest in savings for the unexpected."

She shook her head. "Once I have what I want, I don't intend to give anyone the chance to take it from me."

Flint pulled her forward and cradled her to him. He could identify with her tenacity. He'd always felt if something was worth having, it was worth fighting to keep.

His heart told him Jenna was worth fighting for.

"Darlin', I'm sorry. I was out of line." Words didn't even begin to cover how low Flint felt. "Do you think you can find it in your heart to forgive me?"

He tunneled his hands through her glossy hair, the dark-gold strands flowing over his tanned skin like fine, silken threads. He needed to show her what he couldn't put into words.

Jenna's lips tingled at the first brush of Flint's mouth on hers, and her hands came up from where they gripped the belt loops of his jeans to splay across his broad back. His suspicion and distrust had hurt her deeply, but his heartfelt apology, the magic of his touch and the feel of his hungry lips on hers, transformed the hurt into an entirely different emotion.

Restless with the need building inside her, she ran her hands down Flint's spine, then slid them into his hip pockets to squeeze his tight rump. Men thought women had sexy rear ends, but women found a man's to be no less exciting.

And Flint's bottom was perfect. Slightly hollowed on the sides, the firm muscles rounded as they sloped away from his back, then tucked in tight at the tops of his thighs.

"You have a very sexy behind, cowboy."

"Not as sexy as yours."

When his hands slid into the hip pockets of her jeans to pull her forward, Jenna gasped. The electric current from the contact flowed through her to pool with aching heaviness in her lower belly. Her knees tried to buckle.

"Easy, now." He steadied her, then made quick work of removing her shirt.

Not quite sure how it happened, Jenna found herself naked from the waist up. But when he opened the snap on her jeans and started to lower the zipper, she stopped him.

"This isn't fair," she protested.

She reached up to release the snap just below his open collar and kissed the newly exposed skin. She did the same with the next snap and the next, until she came to the waistband of his jeans. Her kiss there caused a growl of pleasure to escape from deep within his big body.

Without warning, he swung her up into his arms and headed for the stairs. "I've had about all this torment I can take."

Her arms circled his neck as she allowed Flint to carry her to his room. When he set her on her feet, Jenna stopped him from turning down the covers.

Reaching out, she unsnapped his jeans, but instead of lowering the zipper, she traced the metal teeth with the tip of her fingernail. He started to pull down the tab, but she shooed his hands away. Her gaze meeting his, she slowly brushed her hand across the straining, faded fabric.

"I have a fantasy," she said huskily. "Do you mind?"

"Not in the least, darlin'." His smile was dazzling. "Go right ahead."

Jenna had never played seductress before, but Flint didn't seem to mind her lack of experience. His gaze had turned smoldering, and his breath came out in short puffs. With every move of her hand across the tight denim, she could see the hunger build in his eyes, feel his need for her grow.

"Woman. You're going to drive me out of my mind."

She toyed with the zipper tab. "Do you want me to stop?"

He shook his head and seemed to have trouble finding his voice. "H-hell, no!"

She smiled and knelt to tug off his boots and socks, then slowly lowered the zipper and removed his jeans. She cast them aside, but when she noticed the way his briefs outlined his heaviness, the magnificence of his erection, her smile faded into one of utter amazement. "Wow."

Her hand trembled as she touched the hard ridge, and her own arousal built. When she heard him swallow, felt his body pulsate at her touch, power and triumph flowed through her. Never had she been more aware of her femininity than at that very moment.

Guiding her hands to the elastic band, his smile made her feel as though she might just melt into a pool at his feet. "Don't stop now. This is just starting to get interesting."

When she lowered his briefs and circled him with her hand, his smile faded and his breath hissed out from between his clenched teeth. He clasped her wrists to stop her exploration.

"This isn't fair. I want to touch you, too."

He tried to pull her to him, but she stepped back. "Not yet, cowboy. This is my fantasy, remember?"

Jenna had never stripped a man. But she enjoyed the feeling of control the experience gave her.

With a seductive glance she turned and bent over to remove her boots and socks. The denim stretched to define each curve and, rewarded by his harsh intake of breath, she smiled and turned to face him. Reaching for her own zipper, she lowered it with painstaking care.

The feral light in Flint's eyes inspired her and, undulating her hips, she placed her hands on her flat stomach to slowly let them glide down beneath her jeans and panties. Her breath caught at the heightened need etched in his handsome face, the fine sheen of perspiration glistening on his bronzed skin. She reveled in the knowledge that she'd caused that look and, inch by slow inch, she revealed herself to him.

By the time her clothes had been tossed on the floor with his, Flint looked like a man in pain and she felt little better.

"Come here," he commanded.

She proudly walked toward him and into his embrace. But when he tried to pull her to him, she shook her head. She had no intention of ending the performance before she'd exhausted every bit of knowledge she'd ever heard or read about seducing a man.

Her voice a sensual purr, she scolded, "Not yet, cowboy. There's more."

Flint's groan of frustrated pleasure delighted her and, remembering something she'd read in a book, she lightly brushed the tips of her breasts against his hair-roughened chest. Never allowing their bodies to touch completely, she wrapped her leg around his and slid her foot along the back of his calf.

When it came to the next step, her courage threatened to desert her. She wasn't sure she could do what the heroine in the book had done, but she'd gone too far to turn back now. Besides, Flint hadn't complained so far.

Swallowing her inhibitions, Jenna bumped the lower part of her body to his, then arched her back to bring them into full contact. The jolt of torrid desire that resulted had them both gasping for air.

"Enough, woman!"

His reaction far exceeded Jenna's expectations, and her confidence blossomed. "Then lie down, cowboy."

Flint had no idea what Jenna intended next, but her wide, gray eyes promised ecstasy, and he found her taking the role of seductress excited the hell out of him. Reclining, he watched her gaze caress his body. She was as turned on as he was, and he knew it would be like nothing he'd ever experienced when they came together.

She straddled him, her body consuming his, slowly, completely, and he felt as if his head would come right off his shoulders. Flint wanted it to last forever, but he was close to the point of no return. He grasped her hips to keep her from moving, in an effort to fight the wave of need that urged him to end the sweet torture.

When he finally felt a degree of restraint, he gazed up at her. "Ride me, darlin'. Ride me like you ride Black Satin."

Filled with him, Jenna's eyes locked with Flint's, and she slowly rocked against him. Her body tightened when the pressure inside her quickly built to a throbbing crescendo and she fought to prolong the feeling even as she raced to end it.

She was suddenly there, and she moaned Flint's name as her muscles contracted around him. But moments later, when his body stiffened, then gave up his essence in great, quaking spasms, Jenna gasped at the pleasure rippling through her a second time. And she responded yet again to the man she loved.

Flint held Jenna close. He felt as if he could move mountains. He'd heard it was possible, but he'd never before incited a woman to such heights of passion. Nor had he ever reached them himself. At least not until today.

He hugged her tight. He wanted to tell her what he was feeling—how much she'd come to mean to him. But she suddenly jerked from his embrace, sat up and grabbed for the sheet.

"What's the matter, darlin'?"

She eluded his grasp, got out of bed and scrambled to pull on her clothes. "Good grief, Flint. We didn't even close the door. What if Ryan or Whiskers had walked by?"

He propped his hands behind his head and regretfully watched her cover her delectable body. "You don't need to worry. They left before dawn. They've gone to visit Whiskers's sister." He left the bed to give her a quick, hard kiss, then pulled on his own clothes. "After the trouble with the saddle and the fire last night, I couldn't be sure Ryan wouldn't be a target."

She pulled her shirt over her head. "I'm going to miss them, but I think you made the right decision."

Before she could tuck the garment into her jeans, Flint stepped behind her and reached around to cup her breasts. Damn, but the woman could even drive him wild putting her clothes *on*.

"I want you in here with me tonight, Jenna," he said, nuzzling the side of her throat.

"Okay. But on one condition."

He nipped at the hollow behind her ear. "What's that?"

She turned, grabbed him by the shirt collar and drew him down for her kiss. "You strip for me tonight, cowboy."

Delighted with her playfulness, Flint lowered his lips to plant tiny kisses at her temple, her eyelids and the tip of her nose. Leaning back, he grinned. "Another fantasy?"

The ringing of the phone interrupted her answer. Irritated, Flint snatched the receiver from the cradle. "Rocking M."

He listened a moment, then covered the mouthpiece and turned to Jenna. "Could you go down to the study and see if I left my truck keys on the desk?"

Waiting until she'd left the room, he asked, "Is he still alive?" Flint listened to the answer, his gut twisting into a tight knot. "We'll be right there."

Flint pulled on his boots, a mixture of fear and dread racing through his veins. Meeting Jenna on her way back up the stairs, he placed his hands on her shoulders. "Darlin', there's been an accident. We have to go to the hospital."

Her face bleached white. "Ryan?"

Flint shook his head. "Cooper was gored in the back by a bull at the rodeo in Amarillo."

"Oh, God, no! Not again."

Her knees buckled, and Flint caught her to him. "He's hurt pretty bad, but he's still alive."

Trembling against him, her tears wet his shirt. "I can't lose him. Not like this. I can't go through this again."

Flint gave her a little shake as he tried to get through to her. "I said he's alive, Jenna. He's in surgery."

He led her out of the house and helped her into his truck. Her reaction bothered him. If there was one thing he'd learned in the past few weeks it was that Jenna wasn't prone to panic. He'd seen her give a good accounting of herself in several emergency situations, and she'd handled each one with calm efficiency. But the way she stared straight ahead without seeing things, the way she stumbled along beside him without seeming to care where he took her, scared him as little else could.

Putting the truck in gear, he formulated a plan. Maybe if he could get her to talk, she'd come out of the disturbing lethargy. "What did you mean you can't go through this again? Are you talking about your father's accident?"

"Yes." Her voice caught. "I lost Dan at the same time."

"Dan?"

She turned to look at him as if she hadn't been aware he was even in the truck with her. "My fiancé."

Flint felt as if he'd taken a sucker punch to the gut. She'd been engaged? She hadn't mentioned it before and neither had the investigator's report.

His hands clenched the steering wheel. "What happened?"

"Bull riders didn't wear flak vests like they do now," she answered, her voice flat. "Daddy was one of the bullfighters that day. He did his best to draw the bull away from Dan. But after the bull injured Daddy, it turned back to Dan. Dan died in the arena."

Flint felt as though he'd taken another punch. No wonder she was in a state of shock. She knew this nightmare all to well.

Reaching over, he unfastened her seat belt, then pulled her into the center of the bench seat. He hugged her close, offering her his strength. "Dan Tyler?"

She nodded. "Did you know him?"

"No. But I remember reading about his death. That was up in Oklahoma City, wasn't it?"

"Yes." She shuddered. "That's why the money is in the Oklahoma bank."

"You were the beneficiary on his insurance policy," Flint stated. He felt lower than dirt. Last night and this morning, he'd all but accused her of acquiring the money from selling his cattle.

She nodded. "But I'll never spend a penny of it."

"Why do you say that?"

"The last thing I wanted was to profit from his death," she said, her voice dull. "I wanted Dan, not the money."

Flint's gut twisted and his guilt increased. He wasn't proud of it by a long shot, but he felt a stab of jealousy at the thought of Dan Tyler holding Jenna, kissing her. But the more Flint thought about it, the more precious he realized the gift of her virginity had been. She'd been engaged to the young man, but she'd chosen Flint to be the first man she made love with.

They rode in silence for a time before Jenna spoke again. "When Cooper came by the ranch, he told me this was his last rodeo." Her voice caught on a sob, and she buried her face in her hands. "Why didn't he quit sooner? And why wasn't he wearing his flak vest?"

"I can't answer that, darlin'," Flint said, tightening his arm around her.

"Do they think he'll make it?" she asked, her voice reflecting her fear.

"They didn't say," Flint hedged.

He wished he could tell Jenna everything would be fine, that Cooper would be okay. But he couldn't. The hospital had informed him the man was in critical condition and they wanted the next of kin notified immediately.

"Thank you for being here with me."

"I wouldn't be anywhere else, darlin'."

He didn't want to leave Jenna. She needed him. And whether it was due to the guilt he felt or the fact that he felt more for her than he had any woman, Flint needed for her to need him.

Chapter 11

If she lost Cooper, she'd have no one. No family left at all, Jenna thought as she paced the length of the empty waiting area, then stopped to stare out the window.

"Would you like some coffee?" Flint asked, coming to stand behind her. He wrapped his arms around her and drew her back against him.

Within the security of Flint's arms, she drew strength and tried to chase away the chilling numbness. She couldn't imagine life without her brother. After their mother left, their father had more or less lost interest in life, and Cooper had taken it upon himself to help her through the difficulties of growing up.

A ghost of a smile touched Jenna's lips. She could remember the time he'd taken her to a discount store, and together they'd tried to pick out her first bra. Neither one of them had any idea what to look for, but they'd done their best. And not once had Cooper teased her about having to stuff the cups. Then, a year later, uncomfortable and blushing furiously, Cooper had done the best a seventeen-year-old boy could to explain how her body was changing, and that it didn't mean she would die just because she'd gotten her first period.

Cooper had been with her the day of her father's and Dan's accidents, too. He'd held her while her world fell apart, then had seen her through the difficult days following Dan's funeral and her father's hospitalization.

Whether real or imaginary, there had been so many times Cooper had helped her over the hurdles of life. And even though she knew he'd been disappointed by her reluctance to watch him ride, he understood why she couldn't.

Dear God, what would she do if something happened to him?

Flint tightened his arms around her. He'd heard the broken sob she tried to hide. "Why don't we sit down, darlin'?" he asked gently. He led her to the couch, settled her beside him, then gathered her into his arms.

Normally he got as far away from a teary female as he could. He never knew quite what to say or do when the waterworks started. But each one of Jenna's quiet sobs tore at his heart, and he felt her pain all the way to his soul.

He held her close and rocked her while her tears wet his shirt and burned his skin beneath. "Jenna, is there anything I can get you?"

"No. Just hold me. Please."

Flint hugged her close and brushed his lips across the top of her head. "Don't worry. I won't let you go, until you tell me to."

* * *

Several hours later a man in surgical blues appeared at the door of the waiting room. "Are you here for Mr. Adams?"

"Is my brother going to be all right?"

Flint tried to judge the doctor's expression, but the man's stoic look gave nothing away. Bracing himself for whatever would come, he took Jenna's hand in his.

"Mr. Adams made it through surgery," the man assured them. He sat down in the chair across from them. "I'm Dr. Langston. I was the surgeon on call this weekend."

"Is my brother going to make it?" Jenna demanded. She gripped Flint's hand as if it were a lifeline.

"I'm not sure," Langston answered honestly. "He's suffered some very serious injuries. We had to remove his spleen because of the puncture wounds, and he had several broken ribs. One of them pierced his left lung and, due to compression on the heart, we had to administer CPR before we got him into surgery."

Jenna gasped and Flint put his arm around her. "How soon will you know?" he asked.

Dr. Langston rested his forearms on his knees and squarely met Flint's gaze. "I'd say if Mr. Adams can make it through the next twenty-four hours, he has a fair chance. He's strong and in good physical condition. That's in his favor. And he seems to have a pigheaded determination to live. Otherwise we'd have never made it to surgery with him."

"When can I see him?" Jenna asked.

"He'll be in postop for a while, then we'll move him to intensive care." Dr. Langston stood up. "I'll make arrangements for you to see him as soon as he comes out of recovery. After that, I'd like to keep the visits to short intervals every few hours. Right now, rest is important. His body needs time to get over the trauma of the accident and start the healing process."

Flint rose to shake hands with the man. "Thanks."

Dr. Langston smiled as he pumped Flint's arm. "I'll have someone show you to the ICU."

"Miss Adams?"

Instantly awake, Jenna jerked from Flint's arms. "Is it Cooper? Is he all right?"

"As far as I know, your brother is still doing fine," the woman said. She smiled, but it wasn't friendly. "My name is Miss Hart. I need to talk with you in the business office."

"Can't it wait?" Flint asked, coming to his feet. "Miss Adams isn't up to dealing with this right now."

Of medium height, the woman managed to look down her nose at the man towering over her. "Are you a relative?"

"Friend of the family."

Jenna noticed Flint's tone matched the same chilling degree as Miss Hart's.

The woman sniffed and turned back to Jenna. "There are papers to be filled out and method of payment to discuss." She waved her hand and walked toward the door. "Follow me."

Entering a small office, the gray-haired woman seated herself behind a desk. She motioned to the only other chair in the office. "Sit down, Miss Adams. Your brother wasn't capable of furnishing any information last night." Miss Hart turned to her computer keyboard and entered Cooper's patient number. "I understand he's a bull rider?"

"That's right," Jenna answered, sitting down.

"And I suppose the only insurance he carries is the

standard policy issued when he became a professional cowboy?" Miss Hart asked.

Jenna nodded. "He rides the rough stock. It's the only insurance he can get."

"I'm well aware insurance companies won't write policies for people in so foolish a profession." Miss Hart keyed in the information. "If he expires there will be the death benefit. Does he have a savings account?"

"That's none of your business," Flint said flatly.

"And *this,* sir, is none of yours," Miss Hart retorted.

Jenna jumped to her feet. "Don't worry about the bill. What insurance doesn't pay for, I will. Show me where to sign."

Miss Hart looked dubious. "Are you employed, young lady?"

"Gainfully!" Jenna pointed to Flint. "If you don't believe me, just ask this man how much I'm charging to train his horse."

When Flint nodded, Jenna grabbed an ink pen, signed her name to the paper the woman shoved across the desk, then slammed it on the polished surface. "You'll get your money, Miss Hart. But I'd better get an itemized statement listing everything that's done for my brother. And I don't want to see the word miscellaneous anywhere on it. If a nurse so much as combs his hair, I'd better see it listed on the bill."

"Now see here—"

"No!" Jenna planted her hands on the desk and leaned forward. "You see here. Cooper is the only living relative I have. He means the world to me, and I'm worried to death that I'll lose him. But his life means little or nothing to you. All you see is a six-foot dollar sign in that bed."

"Well, I never—"

"That's probably what's wrong with you," Flint interjected.

Miss Hart stood up. "Every time a rodeo comes to town, one of your kind gets injured in his quest for eight seconds of glory. Then I'm stuck with working out a payment plan."

Flint didn't normally throw his weight around, but this woman had it coming. And he was more than glad to give it to her. "Have you heard of the Rocking M Ranch, Miss Hart?"

"Of course." The woman's chin rose haughtily. "It's one of the largest ranches in the panhandle, and Mr. Mc-Cray has been quite generous with his donations to our hospital."

Flint stuck out his hand. "I'm very glad to meet you, Miss Hart. The name's McCray…Flint McCray."

Miss Hart peered at him through her glasses, then suddenly looked as if a bee had flown up her skirt. "Oh, dear! I didn't recognize you in—" she pointed to his clothes "—in that attire."

Satisfied he had her attention, Flint smiled. "Appearances can be deceiving." He put an arm around Jenna's shoulders. "Take this lady, for instance. She has enough money to buy and sell *you* several times over. But just because she's wearing jeans and boots, you treat her like a second-class citizen."

"Well…I, uh…you see—"

"I'm afraid I do, Miss Hart," Flint interrupted, his smile turning to a deep frown. "But, just so we have things clear between us, let me spell it out in terms even *you* can understand. Cooper Adams is a rodeo rider, but he's also a personal friend of mine. He'd better receive the very best care this hospital can provide, or the gravy train will dry up. There won't be any more 'generous donations' from me. Is that understood?"

"Yes, but—"

"Good. Because if my contributions to this hospital cease, I can guarantee my old friend, Nate Bolinger, will contact me to find out the reason." Flint steered Jenna to the door. Turning back, he smiled. "And we both know damned good and well I'll be obligated to tell him… Miss Hart."

Jenna stepped out into the hall. "I could buy and sell her? Where did that come from?"

Flint grinned and fell in beside her. "I was on a roll."

"Who is Nate Bolinger?" she asked.

"The hospital administrator," he said, grinning.

Walking along the quiet corridors, Jenna jammed her hands into her jeans pockets. "I shouldn't have lost my temper with Miss Hart, but she really knows how to push a person's buttons."

"Darlin', the only heart that woman has is her last name."

"Miss Adams?" The intensive care nurse coming toward Jenna grinned. "Your brother's awake and asking for you."

Jenna was only vaguely aware Flint followed her when she rushed into the room where Cooper lay hooked up to an IV and monitors. Gently touching his dark-blond hair, she searched every inch of Cooper's face. He had several bruises, and his blue eyes were clouded with pain, but otherwise he looked good for all he'd been through.

"My number wasn't up yet, little sister," Cooper said, his voice weak. "I'll be fine. I promise."

"Oh, Cooper, why didn't you wear your protective vest?"

"Must…have lost it. It wasn't in my riggin' bag."

When he reached up to take her hand, she couldn't keep a tear from rolling down her cheek. "Are you in a lot of pain?"

"Enough." Cooper noticed Flint standing at her shoulder. "Have you two…been here all night?"

Flint smiled. "Couldn't think of anything better to do."

"You couldn't think of a better place…to spend the night with my sister?" Cooper asked, his voice little more than a hoarse croak. "You must not…get out much, Mc-Cray."

Jenna noticed Cooper was having a hard time keeping his eyes open. "Just rest. We'll be here when you wake up."

Cooper shook his head, then looked directly at Flint. "Take care…of her, McCray."

"I will," Flint promised as Cooper lost consciousness.

After scanning the same entry five times without an inkling of what he'd read, Flint shoved the ranch books aside. His thoughts went back to the scene in Miss Hart's office a week ago. He still couldn't get over the way Jenna had signed the paper accepting responsibility for Cooper's medical bills. Without having to think twice, she'd put her own dreams on hold, in order to see her brother taken care of.

She'd do anything for Cooper. Would she do the same for Flint? Would she be willing to base her training business at the Rocking M and stay with him?

When he heard a truck pull up the drive, Flint abandoned his speculation. A smile spread across his face, and his mood lightened. Switching off the desk light, he left the study. Jenna was back from the hospital, and the endless hours he'd spent trying but accomplishing nothing were over.

"Hi, darlin'," he said, opening the door and taking her into his arms. When she snuggled against him, Flint tightened his embrace. "How's Cooper?"

"They moved him out of intensive care today." Jenna smiled up at him. "Dr. Langston said if he keeps improving at this rate, he'll be released in a few days."

"Great." Flint nibbled a path of kisses from her temple down to the hollow of her throat. "He can use Whiskers's room just off the kitchen. That way he won't have stairs to climb."

Jenna drew back to look at him. "Flint, do you mean it? You want Cooper to come here?"

"Of course." Flint gazed down at her, his body tightening at the feel of her in his arms, the herbal scent of her hair. "He'll need somewhere to convalesce. What better place than the Rocking M?" He kissed her until they were both weak. "Besides, you'll be here to take care of him." He kissed her again. "And I'll be here to take care of you."

The hours she'd been gone had stretched out like an eternity, and Flint wondered how he would survive if she left the Rocking M. But Jenna was in his arms now, and the magic of her touch, her response to his kiss, fueled the hunger that had gnawed at him all evening.

Jenna gave a startled squeak when Flint scooped her up and headed for the stairs. She smiled and wrapped her arms around his neck. He had been so wonderful the last few days, so loving. He'd understood her need to be at the hospital, and even though he couldn't always go with her to visit Cooper, there wasn't a night he hadn't waited up for her.

"I bought a new T-shirt today." Nibbling on his earlobe, she asked, "Do you want to know what it said?"

"What?"

"Texans like it hot and spicy," she whispered, allowing her words to feather over his ear.

When his steps faltered and a growl rumbled up from deep in his chest, she laughed. "Does the Texan have a problem?"

"Not for long." Flint shouldered open the door to his room and set her on her feet. "This Texan is about to prove T-shirt sayings are based on fact."

He started to pull her to him, but Jenna side-stepped his grasp. "A few days ago we made a deal."

He looked confused. "We did?"

She nodded and took hold of his shirt to draw his head down to hers. "Your turn, cowboy."

"My turn?" His face lit suddenly. "To do the stripping?"

"Uh-huh."

Flint grinned and bent to take off his boots. He was as excited at the thought of stripping for Jenna as he'd been when she stripped for him.

"Music." He pointed to the bedside table. "If I'm going to do this right, I need music."

Jenna switched on the clock radio and a classic Garth Brooks song filtered into the room. She grinned. "This should be interesting."

By the time he had them undressed, his exaggerated bumps and grinds, his outrageous lip-sync about friends hanging out in low places, had them both collapsing on the bed.

He'd never before thought of laughter and playfulness as arousing, but with Jenna it seemed all things were possible. "Did that meet your expectations, darlin'?"

Jenna laughed. "You should take that show on the road, cowboy. You're quite talented."

He shook his head and gathered her to him. "That was just for you, Jenna. Only you."

The friction of flesh on flesh, male touching female, worked its age-old magic, and their amusement quickly faded.

Flint gazed down at Jenna for endless seconds. He found he wanted to give to her in a way he'd never given to any woman, to take her to heights never before reached. Trailing kisses down the length of her, he pressed his lips to the inside of her thigh.

"Flint…"

Waves of desire shot through her at the first intimate contact of his kiss, and Jenna clutched his hair. Never had pleasure been so keen, so intense that it bordered on pain. Without warning, she was poised on the edge, her body tight with feeling, her mind reeling with wild need. Flint took her beyond the brink, then, with a tenderness that brought tears to her eyes, he slowly rose above her and joined their bodies in one smooth stroke.

Pleasure—exquisite and perfect—raced through her again, and Jenna felt as if her heart had been branded by the power of it. Surprised by the force of her fulfillment, she cried out as Flint took her to a place only lovers go, and moments later she felt his soul touch hers as he gave in to the force of his own climax.

Chapter 12

When Flint got out of the truck and walked across the ranch yard toward her, Jenna smiled. He'd left early that morning to go visit Ryan and Whiskers up in Oklahoma, and she'd found her day interminable without him.

"Did you have a nice trip?"

"Not as nice as if you'd been with me," he said, putting his arms around her.

His warm breath close to her ear sent a streak of longing straight through her. "You know I couldn't leave Cooper here alone. He's only been out of the hospital three days."

The back door slammed, and Flint stopped nibbling on her ear. "Speaking of your brother, we'd better go see if he needs help."

Jenna rushed forward at the sight of Cooper descending the porch steps, while trying to balance his cane and a lawn chair. "Why didn't you ask for help?"

"Dammit, Jenna! I can do a few things for myself. Just back off and stop hovering." Cooper looked at Flint. "Can't you manage to keep her busy, McCray?"

Flint grinned and took the chair. "I'm doing my best."

"Try a little harder," Cooper grumbled. He glared at her. "She makes me nervous."

"You make *me* nervous." She watched her brother limp toward the corral. "You've only been out of the hospital a few days, and Dr. Langston told you to take it easy."

Cooper frowned. "If I take it any easier, moss will start growing on my butt."

"Moss on your backside beats pushing up daisies."

"Look, Sis, if I have to watch one more cap-toothed, game show host give away a year's supply of dog food or laundry detergent, I'm going to go crazy. Now leave me alone." Cooper pointed to an oak tree near the corral. "I'm going to sit over there and watch you work with Satin."

Jenna could understand her brother's restlessness, his need to be out in the fresh air. He'd always been very active, and to be confined for almost two weeks had to be nerve-racking. But he needed to take it easy, and she intended to see he did.

Once Cooper was settled in the chair Flint set up for him, she went to saddle the stallion, and by the time she led Black Satin into the round pen, she had a full-fledged audience. Assisted by Jed and Tom, Jim used his crutches to walk over from the bunkhouse, and the three had joined Flint and Cooper under the oak tree.

"Do you mind putting on a show for the walking wounded?" Jim asked, settling in the chair Jed brought with them.

"Not at all. Satin needs to get used to working in front of an audience."

She mounted the stallion and, starting with a warm-up, moved on to the patterns he would need to execute in competition. Using the reins and leg pressure, she put Satin through a series of spins, loped him in both large and small circles, brought him to a sliding stop, then directed him to back up.

"That stallion don't act like the same horse," Jed commented, his disbelief evident.

"If I didn't know better, I'd swear somebody replaced Satin with a ringer," Tom added.

"I haven't seen a horse yet that my little sister couldn't train," Cooper said, smiling proudly.

Satisfied with Satin's performance, Jenna patted the stud's ebony neck and rode over to the side of the corral where the men sat. "Looks like my job here is almost finished."

A deep scowl lined Flint's features. "Boys, I need to talk to Jenna. Jed, help Jim to the bunkhouse. Tom, you see that Cooper gets back inside."

When the grumbling men were out of earshot, Flint demanded, "How much longer before Satin's training is finished?"

She pulled the saddle from the horse and placed it on the top board of the fence. "A couple of days."

"Where's your next job?"

She brushed Satin with vigorous strokes. "From here I go back to Cal Reynolds's Houston ranch, then Fort Worth. Why?"

"How would you like to train those horses here?"

Jenna searched Flint's face. She'd observed his frown at the mention of her job being completed, and a bubble of hope began to form. "What do you mean?"

"After paying Cooper's hospital bill, it's going to be some time before you have enough for your own place." He took the brush from her hand and pulled her into his arms. "Besides, I don't want you to leave. I want you to stay here with me."

"Why?" *Say it, Flint. Tell me you love me.*

The seconds ticked by as Flint stared down at her. "Because this is where you belong."

"What makes you think that?"

"Because you love me."

"And?"

He hesitated. "I want you. You're the most exciting, passionate woman I've ever met. We're good together."

"That's not enough." She stepped away from him and led Satin to the pasture gate. Releasing the stallion, she turned back to Flint, tears blurring her vision. "You want me to stay, but with no strings attached?"

His hands propped on his hips, Flint shook his head. "I didn't say that."

"What are you saying, Flint?" she asked softly.

"You know I care for you," he hedged.

"But?"

She watched him rub the back of his neck in an obvious effort to relieve the tension. "I still have some things to work through."

Jenna felt a chilling numbness settle over her. "I'm not your ex-wife, Flint. I'm not Nicole."

"I never said you were."

Tears ran unchecked down her pale cheeks. "You didn't have to." Jenna squared her shoulders and took a deep breath. "Cooper and I will be leaving the day after tomorrow, as soon as I finish Satin's training session."

When she turned to walk away, Flint reached out to stop her. "Jenna—"

"No, Flint." She shrugged out of his grasp and started for the house. "There's nothing left to say."

* * *

Jenna shivered against the icy solitude of her bed a moment before she threw back the covers. She couldn't stand another minute lying there while her mind and body warred with her heart.

She loved Flint, ached for his touch. But if he couldn't believe in her, then they had no basis for a relationship and no reason for her to stay on the Rocking M.

She sniffed and padded barefoot down the stairs and into the kitchen. She rarely ever cried. But with her emotions in such turmoil, she couldn't seem to stop. Maybe if she drank some milk it would help her relax enough to sleep for what few hours were left of the night.

"What's wrong, little sister?" Cooper asked, leaning against the door frame.

Whiskers's room was off the kitchen and, afraid she might disturb her brother, she hadn't turned on the overhead light. But from the moonlight streaming through the window, she could tell he'd been up for some time. His dark-blond hair was mussed as if he'd run his hands through it several times, and his face wore a ravaged look.

"Did you have the nightmare again?"

He gave her a tight nod. "Each time I close my eyes."

"The doctor told you it might be a while before you stopped reliving the accident." She opened the refrigerator. "Would you like some milk? It might help you relax."

"No." He walked over to sit down at the table. "And it won't help you, either."

"It might."

Cooper snorted. "Milk never has been, nor will it ever be, a substitute for a man's arms."

Jenna sucked in a sharp breath. "What do you mean?"

"Don't play dumb, little sister. Your room is right

above mine. Tonight's the first night you've been in there since I was released from the hospital."

"Oh, Lord. I...I didn't realize—" She closed the refrigerator door, the milk forgotten.

Cooper shrugged. "It's no big deal. You're an adult. And besides, I know you and McCray are in love."

Without warning, tears began to stream down Jenna's cheeks. "Oh, Cooper, you couldn't be more wrong."

In spite of the soreness from his injuries, Cooper was at her side, folding her into his arms. "What's wrong, sweetheart?"

"Nothing. Everything," she sobbed. "Oh, Cooper, I love him so much."

"So what's the problem?"

She buried her face in his shoulder. "He doesn't love me. If he did, he'd believe in me."

"Now hold it," Cooper said, drawing back to look at her. "I know he cares for you. I've seen that with my own eyes."

Jenna nodded. "But he doesn't trust me."

"Why don't we sit down and you tell me all about this?" Cooper led her to the table. "Then I'll decide whether or not I'm going to have to kick McCray's butt."

"Are you sure you're up to it?"

He grinned. "I may have to wait a month or so before I can do the job right, but rest assured, I'll do it." Taking her hand in his, his expression became serious. "What's wrong, little sister?"

Jenna took a deep breath, and by the time she finished telling him about Flint's ex-wife's greed and how she kept Ryan from him, Cooper was shaking his head.

"No wonder Flint has his doubts about getting involved with another woman. I'd feel the same way if some woman did that to me." Cooper squeezed her cold hand.

"Give Flint some time, little sister. He'll eventually get a handle on things, then nothing will stand in the way of you two working things out."

"But how long will that take?"

"A day, a week, a month. I don't know." Cooper smiled. "But I don't think it will take too long. From what you've said, Flint doesn't want you to leave." His smile turned to a chuckle. "I know if I had it that bad for a woman, I'd move heaven and earth to see she stayed put."

Jenna shrugged. "Maybe you would, but I'm not so sure about Flint."

"I am," Cooper said firmly. "He'll find a way to stop you from leaving."

"But what if—"

"Trust me. He will." He slowly rose to his feet, then pulled her up beside him. "Now go get some sleep, little sister." He winked. "If you don't, you'll look like I feel."

Her smile tremulous she asked, "Are you going to be all right?"

"Sure thing." Cooper started to enter his room, but turned back. "What's Jed's last name?"

"Summers," Jenna answered. "Why?"

Cooper shook his head. "He sure doesn't seem to like me much. He takes off every time I try to talk to him. I know I've seen him somewhere before, but for the life of me, I can't remember where."

"You probably met him when you stopped by a few weeks ago. And don't worry about his being unfriendly. From what I've seen he's a loner."

"I don't think so." He looked thoughtful. "Jim was still in the hospital, and Tom and Jed had the night off. The only one of the guys I met was Brad. By the way, where was Brad tonight?"

"Flint sent him to check out another packing house he

thinks might be accepting the stolen cattle." She yawned. "He should be back sometime tomorrow."

"You'd better get back to bed, little sister."

She kissed his cheek. "Thanks, Cooper."

"Everything will work out. Wait and see." He chuckled and started through the door to his room. "If they have to, big brother and his Smith & Wesson will make sure of it."

By the time Flint finished off his first pot of coffee, his head felt as if it had gone down from the size of a beach ball to that of a basketball. He knew better than to mix inner strife with a bottle of Scotch, but like a fool he'd done it, anyway. And this morning he had to pay the price. Only now he faced it with an unmercifully throbbing head, a stomach that churned like a cement mixer and eyes so bloodshot they could be used for road maps.

The ringing phone made him wince. The sound felt as if it went straight to the center of his brain and just sat there vibrating.

He picked up the receiver before it could ring again and cause more pain. "Rocking M," he said quietly.

"Flint?" Jed sounded excited. "I think you'd better get up here to the Circle S shack as fast as you can."

Instantly alert, Flint straightened. "What's up?"

"I caught a couple of the rustlers."

"Can you hold them?" Flint asked, his headache forgotten.

Jed chuckled. "I reckon so. I've got 'em trussed up like prized pigs."

"I'll be right there." Flint pressed the flash hook, dialed Sheriff Bartlow to report the situation, then took his rifle from the gun rack. On his way to saddle his horse, he met Jenna coming out of the tack room.

"What's up?" she asked, pointing to the rifle.

"Jed called on his cell phone. He caught some of the rustlers up at the old Circle S cabin."

He reached out to trace the dark circles under her eyes. He wanted to tell her how much he'd missed her last night, how even through the liquor-induced fog in his brain he'd craved her touch. But now wasn't the time.

"I need to get up to the cabin," he said, dropping his hand to his side. "We'll talk when I get back."

"Flint, I don't—"

He put his finger to her lips. "When I get back, darlin'."

Resigned, Jenna sighed. "All right."

Flint caught the bay, saddled and mounted it, then rode up beside her. Leaning down he gave her a quick kiss. "We'll work things out."

Watching him ride from the ranch yard, Jenna stood staring in the direction he'd headed long after he disappeared from sight. She loved Flint so much her insides ached with it, but could their problems be solved that easily? By catching the rustlers, any lingering doubts he had about her being involved would be erased. But was that enough for him to trust her?

Shaking her head, she walked toward the house. She just wasn't sure he'd ever be able to put the past behind him and trust again.

"Where did Flint go?" Cooper asked when she entered the kitchen. "He took out of here like a scalded dog."

"He's headed for the Circle S line shack." She started for the stairs. "Jed caught a couple of the rustlers."

Cooper looked thoughtful a moment before swearing a blue streak. "It's a trap."

She whirled around to face him. "What do you mean?"

"I just remembered where I've seen Jed." He grabbed a set of keys from the hooks by the back door and shoved them into her hand. "We've got to stop Flint. He's walking into a trap."

Jenna stopped short. "Slow down, Cooper. You're not making any sense. Now what's this about a trap?"

He took a deep breath and held his side. "When you mentioned the Circle S, I remembered where I've seen Jed." He paused for breath, then continued. "A couple of nights before the accident, I was in a honky-tonk in Amarillo. This guy was tanked up and spouting off about finally getting the Circle S back. I didn't know he worked for Flint or that the ranch he talked about was part of the Rocking M. He just said he'd been pestering the present owner for several months and by the time he got finished with the guy, there wouldn't be enough left to stuff in a paper bag. It was Jed."

"His family did own the Circle S before the McCrays." Jenna felt sick inside. "But he's worked for Flint's family for years. Are you sure?"

"Positive." Cooper motioned toward the door. "Now get your rear end in gear. We've got to stop Flint."

Jenna threw the keys on the counter. "I'll have to go on horseback. The only road leading up there comes in from the north and it's miles out of the way."

As she ran for the corral, Cooper hobbled after her. He stopped to retrieve something from Daisy, and by the time he made it to the barn, she had the buckskin saddled.

He shoved a heavy object into her hands. "Here. You might need this."

She took the hand gun and placed it in one of the saddle bags. "Can you make it back to the house?"

"Hell, yes! Now get up there and stop Flint from walking into a trap."

Jenna mounted the buckskin. "There's a list of numbers by the wall phone in the kitchen. Call the sheriff, then get hold of Tom on his cellular. Tell him what's going on and have him get up to the cabin as soon as he can."

"Did Flint take one?"

She tried to think if Flint had his cell on him. "No. He was in a hurry and I don't guess he thought of it."

"Be careful!" she heard Cooper call as she kicked the horse into a run and headed in the direction of the Circle S.

Flint rode up to the little cabin and dismounted. He looked around the area but found no sign of Jed or the rustlers. He checked inside the lean-to. Jed's horse stood tied to a rail, but the man was nowhere to be found. Something wasn't right.

Removing the rifle from the boot on his saddle, Flint went to the front of the cabin and nudged the door open. He cautiously looked inside, but the interior was deserted. As he walked back out into the sunlight, he felt the hair on the back of his neck prickle. The now familiar hate-filled stare was boring a hole into his back.

"It was you all along," Flint said, turning to face Jed Summers. "I should have known. You were the one who conveniently found the note and the empty kerosene can."

"That's right, McCray." Jed stepped from behind a small thicket of mesquite. He pointed his gun at Flint's chest. "Drop your rifle and kick it over here."

Weighing his options, Flint hesitated.

"Don't even think about it." When Flint placed the rifle on the ground, Jed nodded. "Smart move. I'd hate to kill you before you sign this quitclaim deed and I get my property back."

"That piece of paper won't hold up. My lawyers will tear it apart in court."

"Your lawyers can go to hell." Jed laughed. "And you won't be around to argue with what I tell 'em."

"That's murder."

Shaking his head, Jed slipped on a pair of leather gloves, then bent to pick up Flint's rifle. "Accident."

"Of course."

Jed checked to make sure Flint's gun had a cartridge in the chamber, then handed him a paper. "Sign this, so I can kill you."

"How are you going to set up the accident?" Flint asked, stalling for time.

Jed's eyes flashed. "What do you care?"

Staring at Jed's contorted features, Flint realized he had very few options. The man was insane. But the longer he kept Jed talking, the bigger the chance Sheriff Bartlow would show up. "Morbid curiosity," Flint answered tightly.

"Your horse got spooked and when he piled you, your rifle went off," Jed explained, laughing.

Flint detected movement on the hill behind Jed, and when he realized Jenna was making her way down the side, his heart came up in his throat. He had to keep Jed talking in hopes of distracting the man and keeping her location concealed. Flint refused to consider what might happen if he didn't.

Careful to keep from revealing her position, Flint asked, "How do you intend to explain my signing over the Circle S?"

Jed chuckled. "That's the best part yet. I saved my cut of the profits. Those beeves we got two weeks ago put me over the top. When they find you, you'll have the cash tucked in your pocket." He laughed out loud. "Money made off your own cattle."

"Who were you working with?"

"What do you care? You'll be dead."

"I told you, I'm curious."

"I got a couple of buddies up in Oklahoma with a semi." Jed looked pleased with himself. "And another one who used to work at a packing house. He'd dress them brutes out in a refrigerated trailer and take 'em to another guy with a counterfeit stamp."

Flint made a show of disgust by rolling his eyes in order to let his gaze dart to where Jenna stood. He almost wished he hadn't. She'd managed to slip around to the side of Jed. If the man decided to take a shot at her, there wasn't a damned thing Flint could do to prevent it from happening.

"You won't get away with it," he warned Jed.

"And just who's gonna stop me?" Jed's grin was filled with confidence. "Dead men cain't tell no tales."

"I will," Jenna said, leveling her gun on Jed. She'd never before pointed a firearm at another human being, but she'd do whatever it took to save Flint.

Chapter 13

"What the hell are you doing here?" Jed asked.

"Cooper finally remembered why you looked familiar." She shrugged one shoulder. "When you drink, you get very talkative."

Jed's curse was crude and guttural. "He shoulda died."

Jenna narrowed her eyes. "What do you mean?"

"I saw you two talkin' down by the creek that day he stopped to visit, but you didn't see me. After I spouted off in that bar, I figured I'd better cover my tracks. So I asked around and found out he'd drawn The Shredder for his first ride. The mornin' after the fire, I broke into his truck, stole his vest and messed with his equipment." Jed shook his head. "If that bull rope had turned loose one jump sooner…"

Jenna had heard enough. The bull Jed mentioned was notorious for trying to hook a rider with his sharp horns, and Jed had already said he'd intended for Cooper to die.

"Drop that rifle or I swear to God I'll shoot you."

Jed sneered. "That's a mighty big gun you've got there, missy. It takes a lot of guts to pull the trigger and I don't think a little gal like you—"

Jenna took aim at Jed's hat and fired.

When his hat landed in the dust several feet away, Jed cursed. "Dammit to hell! You pull another stunt like that and I'll kill McCray. This is between me and him."

"Not anymore." Anger coursed through her. "Not after you made me a target by cutting that cinch. Then you went after my brother. I'd say that makes it my business, too."

"I figured you'd tuck tail and run." Jed sneered. "As many times as I set you up, you shoulda got the message."

"I don't scare easy. And I'm not afraid to fire a gun. I've proven that. Now drop the rifle."

Jed waved the gun at Flint. "I'll shoot him first!"

"I haven't signed the deed," Flint reminded him. "Your plan won't work unless I do."

"Sign it," Jed demanded.

Flint shook his head. "No."

Wild-eyed, Jed started to swing the gun toward Jenna. "Sign it or I'll shoot *her*."

Jenna had already redirected her aim to the rifle in Jed's hand and braced herself for the kickback. She didn't want to take a chance on his reflex action causing the rifle to go off, but the second the barrel cleared Flint's chest, she fired again.

As the bullet grazed his hand, Jed let out a yelp, dropped the gun and sank to his knees. Cradling his hand, he looked up at Jenna. "You ruined everything."

"Watch him," Flint said, bending to scoop up the rifles. He placed them well out of Jed's reach, then got his rope from the bay's saddle. When he had Jed tied up, he looked down at the man. "Why, Jed? Why did you do all this?"

His eyes filled with hatred, Jed stared at Flint. "You and your damned family stole what was rightfully mine. I should be ranchin' the Circle S instead of you."

"Your father sold this land over twenty-five years ago," Flint reminded him. "You were listed as a MIA in the army, and he lost heart in trying to hang on when he thought you were dead."

"And you McCrays were standin' by, just waitin' to take advantage of a broken-down old man." Jed's face twisted with disgust. "You didn't have enough of your own land. You bastards had to come after mine."

Flint shook his head. "Your father offered us first chance to buy the Circle S, since it bordered the northern boundary of the Rocking M. We paid fair market value for the property."

Jed laughed hysterically. "By the time I got back to the States, the old man had killed himself by drinkin' up the money, and I was left with nothin'."

"If you felt this way, why did you start working for the McCrays?" Jenna asked. "Surely you can't blame them for something your father did."

Jed's wild gaze turned to Jenna. "I wanted my ranch back."

"But why now?" Flint asked. "Why wait all this time?"

"Every one of you McCrays have done somethin' to make the Rocking M bigger," Jed snapped. "When you found that brat of yours, I couldn't stand by and watch him grow up to take over. I'd a never got my land back."

"Why didn't you try to buy back the land?" Jenna asked.

Flint watched as something inside Jed seemed to snap

and he began to babble incoherently. The man had let years of angry resentment fester into vengeful madness.

Flint ushered Jenna away from Jed. "Let's wait over here."

Her hands shook uncontrollably, and it appeared she might drop the ominous-looking weapon she still held.

"Where did you get this?" He took it from her and put it with the rifles. "It looks like a damned cannon."

"When I started traveling around by myself, Cooper bought it for me and made sure I knew how to use it." Her voice sounded shaky, and Flint could see the strain etched in her beautiful face. "He said I'd probably never have to fire it—that the sight alone would discourage anyone from bothering me."

She shivered and Flint wrapped his arms around her as distant sirens drew closer. Jed had been right. It did take a lot of courage to point a gun at someone and pull the trigger.

"I'm glad you showed up, darlin'." He kissed the top of her head and held her tight. "I was beginning to think I'd seen my last sunrise."

It was well after dark by the time Flint called Whiskers to tell him it was safe to bring Ryan home.

"You say that little gal saved your bacon?" Whiskers chortled. "Didn't I tell you 'bout her?"

Flint smiled. "Yes."

"You're gonna lasso her and brand her, ain't ya?" The old man's voice crackled across the long-distance wire.

Flint glanced at the glass dome on the mantel. "I'm thinking about it."

"You're a damned fool if you don't try." Whiskers's voice sounded suspiciously choked. "I kinda got used to havin' that little gal around."

Long after he hung up the phone, Flint sat staring at the necklace. He'd kept the necklace he'd bought for Nicole to remind him of what women were really after from a man. But Jenna wasn't like Nicole, and it was high time he stopped comparing them. He knew Jenna would never ask him to get rid of the necklace. It just wasn't her style.

He rose from his chair, walked to the fireplace and lifted the glass dome. He stared at the glittering stones in his hand. He would do everything he could to make Jenna happy for the rest of their lives. And tomorrow morning was as good a time as any to start by laying the past to rest. He fully intended to remove the only barrier standing between himself and the woman he loved.

Jenna stood at the corral and watched Black Satin run across the pasture. The day she'd been dreading had arrived. She'd completed the stallion's training, and, an accomplished rider in his own right, Flint could show the horse himself.

Besides, it was obvious Flint wanted her to go. He knew she would finish with Satin today and leave the ranch. But he'd left early this morning and still hadn't returned. He probably wanted to avoid an uncomfortable situation when she and Cooper departed.

She took a deep, shuddering breath and walked back to the house. Six years ago it had taken her a long time to pick up the pieces of her shattered dreams and move forward with her life. But this time she knew for certain she'd never recover from the pain of loving Flint and not having that love returned.

Hearing a truck coming up the long drive, Jenna turned to see Whiskers and Ryan pull into the ranch yard. She'd hoped to be gone by the time they got back. Leaving the Rocking M would be one of the hardest things she ever had to do, and the thought of saying goodbye to them only added to her sorrow.

"Jenna!" Ryan ran across the yard to hurl himself into her outstretched arms. "I missed you. Did you miss me?"

"Of course I did," she answered around the lump rising in her throat. She picked him up and held him close. "I haven't been able to play Go Fish since you left."

"I'm home now." His arms encircling her neck, Ryan hugged her back. "You want me to go get the cards?"

"I, uh…" Jenna couldn't bring herself to tell him she had to leave. When three lively balls of yellow fur came racing around the corner of the house, the dogs' excited yaps put an effective end to Jenna's dilemma of having to tell the little boy goodbye. She hugged him once more, then set him on his feet. "Your puppies missed you, too."

The dogs licked Ryan's cheeks. "I'm glad to see you guys."

As Ryan ran across the yard with the puppies in hot pursuit, Whiskers limped up to Jenna, his toothless grin wide. "It's good to see you, gal."

Jenna smiled. "We all missed you, Whiskers."

The old man apparently saw through her cheerful demeanor. "What's wrong?"

"Nothing," she lied.

Frowning, Whiskers shook his head. "I don't see like I used to, but I ain't blind, gal."

She gazed at the open pasture. "I…I'll be leaving the ranch in a couple of hours."

"Does Flint know 'bout this?"

"No." She swallowed around the lump in her throat. "He's not here."

"Well, where is he?"

"I don't know. He left before I got up this morning."

"Then you just sit tight and don't go nowhere till he gets back," the old man commanded.

She smiled sadly. "I can't do that."

Whiskers jerked off his hat, threw it to the ground and stomped it. "If I live to be three hundred, I don't guess I'll ever see two people as mule-headed as you and Flint. You both been chompin' at the bit for one 'nother ever since the day you met." He picked up his hat, slapped it against his leg and started for the house. "The way you two pussyfoot around one 'nother is enough to make a body sick."

Jenna watched Whiskers slam the door behind him. She realized his anger was fueled by disappointment. He'd made it crystal clear from the minute she came to the Rocking M that he'd like to see her stay.

Tears filled her eyes. There was nothing she wanted more than for the Rocking M to become the home she'd always longed for, to stay on the ranch with the people she loved. But Flint's absence indicated he wanted her gone.

Jenna squared her shoulders. She'd never groveled for anything in her life. And she wasn't going to start now. If Flint decided he could put his distrust and the past behind him, he'd have to come looking for her. She wouldn't embarrass either one of them by being here when he returned. She had more horses to train and a life to put back together.

"Have you tried talkin' to her?" Whiskers asked Cooper.

"Until I'm blue." Cooper stuffed another shirt into his duffel bag. "But once she makes up her mind, bulls will start roosting in trees before she changes it."

Whiskers scratched his head. "Well, ain't there some way we can keep her here 'til Flint gets back?"

Cooper shook his head. "I don't think so. I've already taken three times as long to pack as I should have."

"What about your back?" Whiskers asked. "Ain't it startin' to pain you a mite?"

"I've already tried that, too." Cooper grinned. "She made me take a pain pill."

By the time Jenna got Cooper to leave, it was late afternoon. He had so many excuses for prolonging their departure that she'd finally just thrown his duffel bag in the back and demanded he get in the cab of the truck.

When she pulled away from the ranch yard for the last time, her hands clenched the steering wheel so hard her knuckles turned white. Tears threatened to spill down her cheeks, but she impatiently blinked them away. Flint had failed to show up all day, and the significance of his absence was devastating.

"After we get my truck out of the storage yard in Amarillo, are we going to get a motel room and wait until morning to head out for Houston?" Cooper asked.

"We will if you need to. But Daisy doesn't have air-conditioning, and traveling at night would be cooler."

"It doesn't matter to me," Cooper said, staring out the window. "Stop the truck!"

She hit the brakes. "Why?"

He frowned and got out of the truck. "I heard a hissing sound. We may have a tire going flat."

Jenna opened the driver's door and checked each one of Daisy's tires. "I didn't hear anything. Are you sure?"

"Looks like Flint's back," Cooper said, folding his arms across his chest and leaning against the fender. He looked way too pleased with himself.

She whirled around to watch the truck turn into the long ranch drive. Turning back to Cooper, she blessed him with a string of creative phrases, then accused, "You saw him coming."

"Somebody had to save you from yourself." When she jerked open Daisy's door, he touched her shoulder to stop her. "I think you should at least talk to the man."

Her throat tightened, and unshed tears burned her eyes. "I don't know if I can."

Cooper shrugged as Flint stopped the truck a few feet from where they stood. "What have you got to lose?"

"Pride, dignity, self-respect—"

Flint walked up to them, planted his feet and folded his arms across his chest. "Just where do you think you're going?"

Jenna brought her chin up at his imperious tone. "My job here is finished. It's time I move on."

He shook his head. "We still have a few matters to clear up. I haven't been shown that the work you've done with Satin is to my satisfaction."

"You know it is. You watched me put him through his paces the other night."

"Cooper, can you drive her truck up to the house?" Flint asked, taking her by the arm to lead her to his own truck.

Cooper's grin broke through. "No problem."

"Get in, Jenna," he ordered.

"No."

"If that's the way you want it, darlin', that's the way you'll get it." Flint picked her up and set her on the bench seat, then slid behind the wheel and started toward the house. "We have things to settle. I haven't paid you for the ranch work or the training."

Jenna slid over to the passenger side and hugged the door. "You can mail me a check."

Flint parked the truck next to the house. "I don't do business that way."

"It's about time you started."

When they got out, Flint waited for Cooper to park Daisy. "I need to talk to you, too."

"Cooper, are you just going to stand there and let him order us around?" Jenna demanded.

"Yep." When she glared at him, Cooper grinned and splayed his hands. "I'm not well enough to kick his butt."

"You wouldn't, even if you could."

Cooper glanced at Flint, then his sister. "Nope."

Flint led Jenna into the study. "Stay put while I talk to Cooper."

Closing the door before she could protest, Flint motioned for Cooper to accompany him to the kitchen. "Have you given any thought to what you'll do now that your rodeo days are over?"

Cooper shook his head. "Not really."

"Good." Flint handed Cooper some papers. "I just talked to a friend of mine. He's looking for a commentator-announcer for his rodeo company. Think you'd be interested?"

"Hell, yes!" His grin wide, Cooper shook Flint's hand. "Thanks, McCray."

Flint shrugged. "You'll have to talk to him, but the job is yours if you want it." He paused. "I have something else to ask you. Do you have a problem with me marrying your sister?"

Cooper laughed. "No, but I gotta warn you. She's a handful."

Relieved the man had no objections, Flint grinned back. "It should make life interesting."

Whiskers came out of the pantry, his face glowing.

"It's 'bout time you got back." He pointed a gnarled finger toward the hall. "Now git in there an' lasso that little filly, 'fore she gets away."

Why couldn't he let her leave with at least a modicum of her dignity? Jenna thought as she clenched her fists and paced the floor. She was furious with Flint for forcing the upcoming confrontation.

When she walked by the mantel, she stopped and turned back. Something wasn't right. Something was missing. Before she could figure out what it was, Flint walked into the room.

"Miss Adams, please be seated." Flint walked to the desk and picked up some papers. "We need to discuss the terms of our contract."

Jenna blinked as she sat down in the chair. "Don't you think it's a little late for renegotiations, McCray?"

"No." Flint sat on the edge of the desk in front of her and held up one of the documents. "I find our contract completely unacceptable."

"Now, hold it, cowboy. You agreed—"

"I want a new agreement."

"That contract is legal and binding." She came to her feet. "You can't just suddenly decide after the terms have been met, that you want things changed."

Flint tore the offending document in half. "Yes, I can."

She narrowed her eyes. "Ripping up your copy means nothing. I still have mine."

"I want our arrangement to be completely different."

"How?"

"You merge your training business with my breeding program and train *our* horses exclusively."

"And?"

"I'm giving you Black Satin as payment for the training. You'll live here. The Rocking M will be the home you've always wanted, and we'll share the profits from the merger." Handing her Satin's ownership papers, Flint reached out to take her into his arms. He drew her forward for his kiss. When he lifted his head to stare down at her, he finished, "We'll also share my bed."

The look in his smoldering brown eyes took her breath. "What are you trying—"

It was then she realized what was missing. Her gaze flew to the mantel. The diamond necklace in the glass dome was gone.

Staring at the empty space, Jenna tried to suppress the hope that began to blossom. The necklace's absence could mean everything—or nothing.

She turned to face him, her heart pounding like a jackhammer. "Where's the necklace, Flint?"

"In a safe deposit box at the bank."

"Why?"

"Since it belonged to Nicole, I thought Ryan might want it when he gets older."

Jenna nodded. "I'm sure he will."

"But I don't want to talk about that now," Flint said smiling. "We have more important things to discuss."

"The merger?"

He nodded. "I want this partnership to state in no uncertain terms what will be expected from both of us."

"My contract covered all that."

Flint brushed a strand of hair from her face and placed a kiss on her cheek. "Too many details were left out, darlin'."

The love she saw in his eyes caused her toes to curl inside her boots. "What...details?"

"For one thing, there were no witnesses to the signing of the first contract. When this document is finalized, I intend to have half of Texas bear witness to the terms we agree on."

Her heart came to a screeching halt, afraid to believe what he was telling her. "And what would that be?"

Flint grinned. "It's really quite simple. I'll promise to stay with you for richer or poorer, in sickness and in health, as long as we both shall live."

Tears filled Jenna's eyes as love and happiness filled her heart. "What will I promise?"

His expression rapturous, Flint smiled. "In return, you'll promise to love, honor and o—"

"Don't say it, cowboy."

Flint laughed. "Cherish me?"

Grinning, she nodded. "Do you really mean it?"

He hugged her close. "More than I ever meant anything in my life. Will you marry me, Jenna? Be a mother to Ryan and the children we'll have together?"

But he still hadn't said the words she wanted to hear. "Why, Flint? Why do you want me to marry you?"

"Because I can't live without you." He kissed her. "You've become part of me."

"And?"

"I love you, Jenna. With every breath I take, I love you."

He sat her back down in the chair before removing a small velvet box from his jeans pocket. Dropping to one knee in front of her, he opened the box to reveal a diamond-and-sapphire engagement ring. He placed it on her finger, then cupped her face in his hands. "Now will you say yes?"

"Oh, Flint! Yes!" She threw her arms around his neck. Happiness, complete and pure, engulfed her. "I love you, cowboy."

"And I love you, darlin'."

Epilogue

Jenna reached down to give Black Satin a reassuring pat. This was it. They'd made it through the preliminary rounds of competition with flying colors and gained an automatic berth in the National Reining Horse Association Futurity finals. Only one ride separated them from the championship.

When she heard their names come across the loud speaker, she took a deep breath. "We're playing with the big boys now, Satin. Let's show them what you can do."

Riding against veterans with more than a quarter of a century of experience under their belts, Jenna walked Satin into the brightly lit show ring, his blue-black coat gleaming. The texture of the ground in the arena was excellent, and she knew early on they were in complete control.

The NRHA pattern called for eight spins, then large and small circles in each direction. The stallion executed them flawlessly, and it appeared his hindquarters dropped from beneath him as he came to a sliding stop. The ride was picture-perfect, and as they left the arena, Jenna knew they'd won the prize.

Passing the box seats, her gaze searched out and found Flint among the spectators giving her and Black Satin a standing ovation. Ryan and Cooper stood beside him, but she barely noticed. Flint's smile held her captive. All the pride and happiness for the win were there, but more than that, his expression revealed all his love for her.

Later in the hotel room Flint held Jenna close. He ran his finger along the neckband of her turquoise nightshirt. "Darlin', you know what I like best about your nightshirts?"

"What?" she asked, snuggling against him.

"I love taking them off you." When he started to do just that, Jenna stopped him.

"Did you notice what this one says?"

He kissed the pulse at the base of her throat. "No."

"Maybe you should."

He glanced at the garment. An arrow pointed down to the word Baby Buckaroo.

Jenna reached for his hand to place it on her flat stomach. "You told me one time that T-shirt slogans were based on fact."

He slipped his hand beneath the hem of the shirt. "Do you have something you'd like to tell me, Mrs. McCray?"

"You know that little getaway we had a couple of months ago at the Circle S shack to celebrate our one-year anniversary?"

He nodded.

"You gave me more that weekend than just a wonderful memory. You gave me a baby. In about seven months you're going to be a daddy again, Flint."

Emotion like he'd never known welled up inside. "Ryan is going to be thrilled."

Jenna nodded. "He's been asking me when he's going to get a brother to play with."

"I wouldn't mind if he got a little sister," Flint said, his hand caressing his wife's warm flesh. "A little girl who looks just like her mother."

"Boy or girl, this time you won't be cheated the way you were with Ryan. You'll be there for everything. We'll go to childbirth classes—"

"Now hold it, darlin'. I'm not sure—"

"You hold it, cowboy." She poked his chest with her finger. "This was a joint effort. *We* got me into this, and *we* are going to get me out of it. *Together.*"

Unable to stop grinning, Flint held her gaze and caught her hand in his. "Together, darlin'." He kissed the finger she'd used to make her point. "Always together."

* * * * *

We hope you enjoyed reading
the bonus book

THE ROUGH AND READY RANCHER

by *USA TODAY* bestselling author

KATHIE DeNOSKY

This story was originally from our
Harlequin Desire® series.

*Look for six new romances every month
from Harlequin Desire®!*

HARLEQUIN®
Desire

POWERFUL, PASSIONATE AND PROVOCATIVE.

Available wherever books are sold.

NYTHDKD12

When playboy rancher and entrepreneur Jackson Worth
mixes business and pleasure, he gets more
than he bargained for....

Enjoy a sneak peek from USA TODAY *bestselling author*
Charlene Sands's new Harlequin Desire story,
WORTH THE RISK.

A woman's boots.

They sat on the floor, next to the bed. Seeing them brought a smile to Jackson Worth's lips. Images invaded his mind of how sexy she'd looked wearing those boots.

He couldn't deny that after taking one look at his sister-in-law's best friend, Sammie Gold, approaching him at the hotel bar last night, he'd been thunderstruck with lust.

But Jackson Worth was no fool. There'd be hell to pay for what he'd done. He'd hear it from both his brothers, Clay and Tagg, but the worst of the wrath would come from Tagg's wife, Callie.

The woman beside him on the king-size bed stirred and the scent of jasmine filled the air. She rolled over and her arm flopped onto his chest. She murmured something in her sleep that sounded too much like *boot-scooting boogie.*

He glanced at the top of her pixie cut. She was cute, but not the kind of woman he usually dated. He winced.

He hadn't dated her. He'd slept with her.

Slowly, Sammie lifted her head off the pillow. Disoriented, she peered at him with deep brown eyes. "Jackson?"

"Morning, darlin'."

Her gaze darted around the elegant room. With a gasp, she looked down and grabbed the sheets to her chest.

"Oh, no!" She sent him a questioning stare, blinking rapidly. "We didn't."

It wasn't the usual reaction he received from a woman after a night of great sex. "Apparently, we did."

"Where am I?"

"Paris."

Her voice squeaked. "France?"

This was worse than he thought. "Las Vegas."

She collapsed against the feather-down pillow. "How did this happen?"

"Boots."

Yesterday, she'd gone to the annual shoe convention, hoping to muster some interest in her failing business. No one was interested in infusing capital in her small, very unique boutique.

No one…except Jackson Worth.

Then it dawned on her. "Oh, my goodness, Jackson. We're…*partners.*"

Jackson's mouth quirked with a quizzical smile, then he sighed deeply. "We made a deal *before* the champagne arrived, darlin'. You signed on the dotted line. Boot Barrage is now half mine."

Find out how intimate this partnership gets in
WORTH THE RISK.

Available October 2012 from Harlequin® Desire.

HARLEQUIN® Desire

ALWAYS POWERFUL, PASSIONATE AND PROVOCATIVE.

Save $1.00 on the purchase of

WORTH THE RISK

by **Charlene Sands,**

available October 2, 2012,
or on any other Harlequin Desire® book.

Available wherever books are sold, including most bookstores, supermarkets, drugstores and discount stores.

Save $1.00 **on the purchase of WORTH THE RISK by Charlene Sands,** available October 2, 2012, or on any other Harlequin Desire® book.

Coupon valid until December 31, 2012. Redeemable at participating retail outlets in the U.S. and Canada only. Limit one coupon per customer.

52610543

Canadian Retailers: Harlequin Enterprises Limited will pay the face value of this coupon plus 10.25¢ if submitted by customer for this product only. Any other use constitutes fraud. Coupon is nonassignable. Void if taxed, prohibited or restricted by law. Consumer must pay any government taxes. Void if copied. Nielsen Clearing House ("NCH") customers submit coupons and proof of sales to Harlequin Enterprises Limited, P.O. Box 3000, Saint John, NB E2L 4L3, Canada. Non-NCH retailer—for reimbursement submit coupons and proof of sales directly to Harlequin Enterprises Limited, Retail Marketing Department, 225 Duncan Mill Rd., Don Mills, ON M3B 3K9, Canada.

5 65373 00076 2

(8100)0 11813

U.S. Retailers: Harlequin Enterprises Limited will pay the face value of this coupon plus 8¢ if submitted by customer for this product only. Any other use constitutes fraud. Coupon is nonassignable. Void if taxed, prohibited or restricted by law. Consumer must pay any government taxes. Void if copied. For reimbursement submit coupons and proof of sales directly to Harlequin Enterprises Limited, P.O. Box 880478, El Paso, TX 88588-0478, U.S.A. Cash value 1/100 cents.

® and TM are trademarks owned and used by the trademark owner and/or its licensee.
© 2012 Harlequin Enterprises Limited

NYTCOUP0912

REQUEST YOUR FREE BOOKS!

2 FREE NOVELS
FROM THE ROMANCE COLLECTION
PLUS 2 FREE GIFTS!

YES! Please send me 2 FREE novels from the Romance Collection and my 2 FREE gifts (gifts are worth about $10). After receiving them, if I don't wish to receive any more books, I can return the shipping statement marked "cancel." If I don't cancel, I will receive 4 brand-new novels every month and be billed just $5.99 per book in the U.S. or $6.49 per book in Canada. That's a saving of at least 25% off the cover price. It's quite a bargain! Shipping and handling is just 50¢ per book in the U.S. and 75¢ per book in Canada.* I understand that accepting the 2 free books and gifts places me under no obligation to buy anything. I can always return a shipment and cancel at any time. Even if I never buy another book, the two free books and gifts are mine to keep forever.

194/394 MDN FELQ

Name	(PLEASE PRINT)

Address	Apt. #

City	State/Prov.	Zip/Postal Code

Signature (if under 18, a parent or guardian must sign)

Mail to the **Reader Service:**
IN U.S.A.: P.O. Box 1867, Buffalo, NY 14240-1867
IN CANADA: P.O. Box 609, Fort Erie, Ontario L2A 5X3

Not valid for current subscribers to the Romance Collection
or the Romance/Suspense Collection.

Want to try two free books from another line?
Call 1-800-873-8635 or visit www.ReaderService.com.

* Terms and prices subject to change without notice. Prices do not include applicable taxes. Sales tax applicable in N.Y. Canadian residents will be charged applicable taxes. Offer not valid in Quebec. This offer is limited to one order per household. All orders subject to credit approval. Credit or debit balances in a customer's account(s) may be offset by any other outstanding balance owed by or to the customer. Please allow 4 to 6 weeks for delivery. Offer available while quantities last.

Your Privacy—The Reader Service is committed to protecting your privacy. Our Privacy Policy is available online at www.ReaderService.com or upon request from the Reader Service.

We make a portion of our mailing list available to reputable third parties that offer products we believe may interest you. If you prefer that we not exchange your name with third parties, or if you wish to clarify or modify your communication preferences, please visit us at www.ReaderService.com/consumerchoice or write to us at Reader Service Preference Service, P.O. Box 9062, Buffalo, NY 14269. Include your complete name and address.

SPECIAL EDITION

Life, Love and Family

NEW YORK TIMES BESTSELLING AUTHOR

DIANA PALMER

brings you a brand-new Western romance
featuring characters that readers have come to
love—the Brannt family from Harlequin HQN's
bestselling book *WYOMING TOUGH*.

Cort Brannt, Texas rancher through and through,
is about to unexpectedly get lassoed by love!

THE RANCHER

Available November 13 wherever books are sold!

Also available as a 2-in-1
THE RANCHER & HEART OF STONE

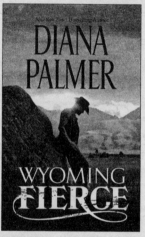